MY Fair Spinster

Also by
Rebecca Connolly

The Arrangements:

An Arrangement of Sorts

Married to the Marquess

Secrets of a Spinster

The Dangers of Doing Good

The Burdens of a Bachelor

A Bride Worth Taking

A Wager Worth Making

A Gerrard Family Christmas

The Spinster Chronicles:

The Merry Lives of Spinsters

The Spinster and I

Spinster and Spice

Coming Soon

God Rest Ye Merry Spinster

MY Fair Spinster

REBECCA CONNOLLY

Phase Publishing, LLC
Seattle

Text copyright © 2019 by Rebecca Connolly
Cover art copyright © 2019 by Rebecca Connolly

Cover art by Tugboat Design
http://www.tugboatdesign.net

Phase Publishing, LLC first paperback edition
October 2019

ISBN 978-1-943048-88-5
Library of Congress Control Number 2019914274

Cataloging-in-Publication Data on file.

Acknowledgements

To Shannon, my beautiful, talented, hilarious, hopeless romantic friend, whose delightful personality brightened my life at just the right time. It was not coincidence we were thrown together, and I'll love you for eternity, coolers full of ice cream, Scottish indulgences, and all. Can't wait to walk the red carpet with you in our future, girl!

And for Julie Andrews, the one true goddess on the earth. May I one day possess such grace, poise, wisdom, and incandescence half as well as you. Can we be best friends? Please?

Want to hear about future releases and upcoming events for Rebecca Connolly?

Sign up for the monthly Wit and Whimsy at:

www.rebeccaconnolly.com

Prologue
London, 1817

"Miss Morledge, it's a crime to have you sitting in the corner at an event like this."

Grace looked up at Georgiana Allen and Isabella Lambert, who now stood before her with friendly expressions. They'd met on several occasions, usually while occupying the same space, though they had never met outside of public events. Still, there was a sort of bond between spinsters, regardless of how or when they met. The two of them were part of the famed Spinster group, whose papers she had come to adore.

"A crime, Miss Allen?" Grace queried with a polite tilt of her head. "In what way? I hope I am not to be faulted."

"No, indeed," Miss Allen said, laughing easily. "I do believe the gentlemen in the room are the criminals, and you the innocent party."

Miss Lambert nodded fervently beside her. "Without a doubt, though I am sure it's only because they do not know you, Miss Morledge. We mustn't fault ignorance."

Miss Allen scoffed. "Well, we mustn't excuse it either. She's not actively avoiding anyone, is she?"

"No, but one might be intimidated by all of her fine qualities."

"Oh, London gentlemen are intimidated by a pretty woman?"

Grace smiled at the easy banter between the cousins, wishing she had similar relationships in her own life. Her older brother was a good sort, but the two of them had never been particularly close. He thought too much of their standing in Society, and she, too little. They had nothing in common but their bloodlines. Her younger brothers were better than James, though they were never at home, and they were closer with each other than they were with Grace. Her older sister, Anne, had been a close friend for her in childhood, but it had been given up as Anne matured and no longer had time for a younger sister. As for her cousins, the only one of sense was Felicity, and she was growing less and less sensible as time went on.

"Do forgive us, Miss Morledge," Miss Lambert suddenly said, smiling shyly. "My cousin and I do tend to go on."

"Not at all," Grace assured her, her smile turning warmer still. "On the contrary, I was only thinking how fortunate it is for the two of you to have each other, and to enjoy such banter."

Miss Allen smiled at her in a mischievous, almost indulgent way. "Well, Miss Morledge, then the conversation we wish to have with you may be a bit more interesting for all of us."

Grace raised a brow, still smiling. "Intriguing. Do go on, then."

Miss Lambert shook her head. "First, I hope you will forgive me, but I must ask you, Miss Morledge. How in the world is a woman like you unmarried?"

Grace's smile never wavered, but the effort behind it did.

How, indeed…

Chapter One
London, 1819

One ought to temper one's judgments of young ladies, no matter their circumstances. Her situation may not be immediately evident, and she is destined to have secrets, as any young woman does. Save your judgments, readers, and give her the benefit of the doubt.

-The Spinster Chronicles, 24 March 1819

Failing. There could be no doubt about it now; she was failing in every respect.

Or so her father's latest letter had so gently assured her.

What other explanation was there?

None that he cared to hear, especially from her lips.

But Lord Trenwick had never cared what his younger daughter had to say about anything at all, and Grace was convinced he wasn't about to start now.

She looked down at the letter in her hand, shaking her head as the fury rose within her again. She'd already been over it four times, but she was determined to commit the scathing words to memory as she had done with the other letters.

Please explain to me how the extensive effort we have put into your training and education, not to mention the necessary accoutrements to make you appealing, have been completely for naught and a waste of such significant funds. Your sister had a husband and three children by your age. How have you failed in every aspect?

Grace's eyes filled with burning tears, and she forced her fingers to avoid crumpling the paper in her fist. Instead, she took a deep breath, calmly folded it, smoothed it, and placed it in the small drawer in her desk with the rest before shutting the drawer softly.

Then, she covered her face and screamed, muffling the sound just enough that, hopefully, it would not attract the attention of her mother.

Hopefully.

"Grace?"

A startled gasp escaped from her as she whirled to face the door, though it was closed still. She wiped at her eyes and pinched her cheeks, desperate to avoid any pressing questions from her mother.

Provided she did not already know.

The door opened with some hesitation, and her mother poked her head around the door with a smile. "Darling, are you all right?"

"Yes!" Grace insisted, forcing a too-bright tone and smile. "Of course! Why wouldn't I be?"

She almost winced at the inanity of the question, and the manner in which it had been delivered. Clearly, one of her many failings was the inability to lie with any conviction.

Her mother glanced at the clock on Grace's mantle, then back at her. "You're going to be late for your Spinsters gathering, if you don't leave now."

The words took a moment to sink in, and then seemed to shoot through her body and into her toes with a painful jolt.

"Oh!" She jumped to her feet and brushed at her dress, not entirely sure what she was wearing at the moment, or whether it would be appropriate.

One did not think about such things when they received a scolding missive from an irate father who did not care enough about her to spend more than three weeks at a time in her company.

"You look lovely, Grace," her mother assured her as she came and adjusted a lock of her hair. "Perfectly suitable. Perfect, as always."

Grace sighed, smiling easily at her mother, who had never seen

4

the slightest fault in her, yet was not blind to any part. "I'm glad you think so."

Her mother's face tightened, and she hugged Grace quickly. "I knew he had sent you another letter. I just knew it. I don't know who is filling his head with ideas about you, but it's not me. And I wish he would write to me instead of you, but alas…"

"Why would he?" Grace muttered, pulling away and smiling at her mother. "Clearly, you are complicit in all of my glaring faults."

"Clearly."

Her mother didn't show it, but Grace knew that the recent attacks from her father ate at her mother and left her feeling uneasy and unsettled. There was very little comfort to give in it, as her father had always, and would ever, act independent of anyone else, regardless of their ties to him. They were all at his mercy, in a sense, and would have to cope with whatever ramifications his actions brought.

Grace sighed once more and rubbed her mother's arms. "I'll be all right. He's in Austria, after all. What can he do from there?" She grinned rather cheekily before moving to her closet and grabbing a pelisse.

"I've already called the carriage for you," her mother told her as she moved towards the door. "Do give my regards to the girls, especially the new Mrs. Morton."

Grace grinned at that and shook her head. "Mrs. Morton. Good gracious, that does sound rather perfect, does it not?"

Izzy Lambert had married the handsome and agreeable Mr. Morton only a month ago, securing one of the only men the Spinsters, as a whole, considered a friend. They were so perfectly suited for each other that it had given them a sweeping sort of romantic whimsy. Some even dared hope that they might secure such a match for themselves.

Well, Elinor Asheley hadn't felt anything of the sort, but she was opposed to matrimony and men at all costs these days. She was not yet twenty, and somehow had become the exact stereotype of a bitter spinster that the entire world seemed to expect.

And she wasn't even a spinster. Without a capital S, at any rate. But she was certainly well on her way.

Then again, Lady Edith Leveson was one of the Spinsters, and she was a widow.

No matter.

Grace made her way down to the carriage quickly and climbed in without any fuss. It was a short drive to Charlotte Wright's home, where they now held their Spinster gatherings, at least weekly. Originally, they'd been held at the Lambert residence, but as there was no longer a Spinster in residence there, it seemed rather impolite to continue to infringe upon their hospitality. Besides, the tea was infinitely better at the Wrights'.

She smiled to herself as she rolled along in the coach. No matter what her father or his letters had to say, the Spinsters would be able to set her to rights. They might not know the whole of the complaints leveled against her, as she had stopped informing them of the letters, but they knew enough to know that her father was less than pleased with her.

If Charlotte had any idea of the number of letters that had arrived, detailing with excessive repetition the absolute displeasure Grace's father felt towards his daughter, she would rage with such an entertaining fury that it was almost tempting to bring it about. But that would also ensure that a great outpouring of sympathy would be directed her way, more from Prue and Izzy than anyone else, and there was often a decent crossover between sympathy and pity.

Sympathy she could endure. Pity she would not.

There was pity enough in being a spinster, without a capital S, from outside the group. Any more from within would be intolerable.

Besides, she was well enough off by comparison. Her fortune was more than respectable, and her family's lineage impeccable. She was respected and admired by a great many people, and, as far as she knew, was not disliked by anyone at all.

The only person who did not approve of her was her father and, apparently, all of the eligible bachelors of London. But her father was the only one vocal about his disapproval, and he was not due to return to England for some time.

The bachelors were simply uninterested. There was very little she could do about that, she supposed. She'd given up trying to understand what they wanted. What her father wanted. What anybody wanted.

The carriage rolled to a stop and the door was opened with a swift efficiency she admired. She smiled at the footman as he helped her down. He bowed, but not before giving her a quick wink.

Impertinent, but she enjoyed it.

They were always doing that when her father was away. Everything was so much more relaxed about the house when he was away, undoubtedly because no one was being critical. James was fussy, it was true, but he was a far cry from their father.

Small mercies.

In no time at all, she was shown into the house, had her pelisse and bonnet taken, and was brought up to the spare parlor where the Spinsters now met.

"I'm so sorry for my tardiness," Grace told them all as she entered, moving to the open chair without any ado. "I lost track of the time, and if my mother hadn't reminded me, I would have forgotten entirely."

Charlotte waved a nonchalant hand, smiling blandly. "Nonsense. As you can see, we are not all assembled. And our last issue of the Chronicles went over so well, I'm feeling rather indulgent."

Grace glanced around the room and saw that, to her surprise, only Edith and Izzy had arrived. She frowned and looked at Charlotte. "Where are Georgie and Prue?"

"No doubt being delayed by those husbands of theirs," Charlotte returned. "Must be dreadful to have a husband."

"It's not," Izzy insisted with a knowing smile. "Believe me, it's quite wonderful."

Charlotte scoffed. "Your husband is practically perfect, Mrs. Morton, and I defy anyone other than you and his sister to find a flaw."

Edith laughed once. "I believe you could find a flaw, dear, if you only put your mind to it."

"Please don't," Izzy protested, echoing the laugh. "I rather like everybody's high opinion of him."

"I am not a finder of faults for my own amusement," Charlotte insisted, gaping at the others, though her eyes twinkled.

"Since when?" Georgie asked from the door as she and Elinor

entered.

Charlotte grinned up at them. "Can I help it if faults and flaws seem to appear before me?"

"Yes," Elinor told her at once, moving to the open sofa and reaching for the tea nearby. "I, for one, would appreciate some discretion in that regard from you."

"Perhaps if your faults and flaws were better hidden, I would not find them so easily," Charlotte shot back.

Grace rolled her eyes and looked at Izzy and Edith in exasperation. They echoed her expression.

"How is Sebastian, Izzy?" Grace asked as the others continued to banter about Charlotte's abilities. "Are you accustomed to having him always underfoot yet?"

Izzy beamed in a splendid manner; her entire face alight. "Oh, he's wonderful, Grace. So thoughtful and loving, and he has begun to tease me quite mercilessly."

Edith coughed discreetly, listening in. "And do you enjoy it?"

"I love it," Izzy said with great emphasis. "He never used to tease, you know, he was quite serious. But now, he has this lightness about him that I love so very much. I know it's early in our marriage, and the glow is destined to fade, but I truly think I have married my best friend."

"What a lovely thought," Edith murmured as she seemed to stare off at nothing. "Would that all were so fortunate."

Grace nodded in silent agreement.

At this rate, she would be fortunate to marry at all, let alone marry someone she could consider a friend. She'd given up the idea of love ages ago, but could friendship be possible?

"And as to him being underfoot," Izzy went on, smoothly riding over Edith's melancholy comment, "I would have to say yes." She giggled to herself and sipped her tea. "We've been hard at work on our collection of stories, you see, and yet there is still so much work to be done."

"How is all that going, Izzy?" Georgie asked as she finally settled onto the divan. "Miranda talks of nothing else."

Izzy rolled her eyes at the mention of Georgie's mother-in-law. "Miranda as patroness of our project is generous to a fault and takes a great interest. It's getting to the point where Sebastian suggested we give her one of the bedchambers."

"God forbid," Charlotte muttered, crossing herself quickly.

"I always thought Miranda Sterling was a more polite version of you, dear," Edith pointed out with a raised brow. "Surely you can see the similarities."

"I can only hope to grow into such a woman," Charlotte sighed, drumming her fingers. "And I did not say that I did not like Miranda. I adore her. I just cannot see Miranda living with Sebastian and Izzy is all. The poor man might break out into a rash of sorts, and then where would we be?"

Izzy shook her head in Charlotte's direction. "Sebastian will be so pleased that you have such concern for his welfare."

Charlotte cocked her head, pursing her lips. "Why don't you sound as though you mean that, I wonder?"

The room laughed easily, then greeted Prudence Vale with warmth as she entered at last. She began to apologize for her tardiness when Charlotte interrupted her.

"Let me guess, your husband delayed you?"

Prue gave her a hard look. "No, in fact, although Cam d-did ask me to tell you that he is claiming a d-dance with you at the Pipers' on F-Friday, as you have been too much in demand to d-dance with him of l-late."

Grace looked at Edith and Izzy quickly before returning her focus to Prue. "Prue, are you all right?"

"Yes, why the stammer, lamb?" Charlotte asked, her tone infinitely gentler than before. "What's happened?"

Always uncomfortable with so much attention, Prue's cheeks flamed in a way they had not in some months. Not since her wedding, come to think.

The other Spinsters in the room glanced around at each other in concern.

Prue moved to sit beside Georgie on the divan and sighed. "My m-mother has returned to London."

"Oh lord," Elinor breathed, eyes going wide.

"She's not staying with you, is she?" Charlotte asked, recoiling in alarm.

Prue shook her head and swallowed when Georgie covered her hand. "No, she n-never even asked, for which we are grateful. But she called on m-me today, and..." She exhaled roughly and raised a trembling hand to demonstrate the effect the encounter had had on her.

Grace could say what she would about her father and his domineering ways, but even he was nothing compared to Marjorie Westfall and the horrors she had subjected her daughter to. Prue's gentle, shy nature had not been helped in any way being raised by such a woman. But Camden Vale had done a nearly heroic thing in the months since his marriage to Prue, and everyone could see the change it had brought about. No one would ever call Prue bold or independent in any way, but she'd found a new level of comfort and ease that was enviable to anyone privileged enough to witness it.

They could not let her go back to the way she had been now that her mother was back.

Cam certainly would not.

"How long is she staying?" Georgie asked.

Prue exhaled, some of the tension leaving her diminutive frame. "Not long, thank heavens. A few weeks, at most. She very much enjoys her house in Somerset. Apparently, she and my aunt are quite the s-set in their little s-society. And she was kinder today than she has been in the last five y-years."

"Which says nothing," Charlotte chortled with some derision. "I think she is only kind to you because she knows now what a viper Lizard Liza is and what her lies cost you. So she cannot dote on her adored niece any longer without bringing criticism upon herself."

"Or she could be terrified of Cam," Izzy pointed out. "She is entirely at his mercy now."

"Oh, who could be terrified of Cam?" Charlotte smiled indulgently. "He's so delightful, and you may tell him that I will gladly dance with him on Friday, and at any time, if he will just press past the rest. I will never be too occupied for him."

Elinor gave Charlotte a bewildered look. "Who is terrified of him? Would you like a list?"

Charlotte shushed her quickly then returned her attention to Prue. "Marjorie didn't find fault with you, did she, Prue? Surely, she

10

cannot."

"She could, and she did," Prue told her. She smiled thinly. "Thankfully, Cam was with me and ensured it stayed civil. She only c-criticized my dress, as I surely have enough status and funds to find something flattering now instead of something the c-color of a dead c-cat's tongue."

Edith raised one brow with alacrity. "And how would your esteemed mother have any idea what a dead cat's tongue looks like, eh?"

Prue shrugged and leaned forward to make herself some tea. "I d-didn't care to ask."

"Speaking of parents disapproving of their children…"

Grace's cheeks flamed at Charlotte's comment, and she met her friend's dark eyes knowingly, but waited to respond.

"Charlotte…" Georgie warned as she removed her hand from Prue's.

Charlotte ignored her, as usual. "Has your father given up on his ridiculous tirade? Or is Terrible Trenwick going to cause us problems?"

Grace smiled ruefully at the title her friend had bestowed. "Are you going to create unflattering entitlements for everyone of whom you do not approve?"

"Quite possibly," came the quick reply, "and that will undoubtedly be as popular as my latest Society Dabbler about this Season's best bachelors. But the question remains, Grace."

There was no way to avoid it; not with Charlotte. She was like a dog with a bone when she set her mind to something. Putting it off would only make her all the more determined.

"No, he has not given up," Grace admitted. "In fact, he's getting worse. Since you are so skilled at finding flaws and faults, or having them appear before you, perhaps you ought to set your attention on me, so that I might have something to tell him as to why I am a complete and utter failure."

"He said that?" Izzy gasped, covering her mouth.

Grace nodded once. "More or less. He tends to be a bit more loquacious about the whole thing, but I had the general idea two lines in."

Edith grumbled something under her breath in what Grace suspected was Gaelic, and it sounded less than flattering, so she thought it best not to ask for a translation.

"No," Charlotte quipped in a falsely bright tone, her eyes cold.

"No?"

Charlotte shook her head very firmly. "No. I will not try to find a fault in you. Truth be told, I did that ages ago when *I* wondered why you were a spinster. Couldn't find a single reason. No one can. That's why Lady Hetty doesn't trust you, you know. She can't find a reason either, and that unnerves her."

"Yes, I'm apparently perfect," Grace muttered, putting a hand to her brow. "Because that is so helpful."

"I didn't say you were perfect," Charlotte replied easily, drumming her fingers once more.

Grace looked at her, dropping her hand. "No? What a relief."

"Ignore your f-father, Grace," Prue insisted with a rare intensity. "Don't give it another thought."

Sweet Prue, thinking Grace could actually stop thinking about her father or his letters or his statements, but she nodded all the same.

She didn't need to know that a prickle of worry and doubt had begun to eat away at Grace in a painfully gnawing manner. None of them needed to know.

Not yet.

"In much brighter news," Elinor chimed in, smiling without a care, "Hugh Sterling is *still* gone from London, and if my sources are to be believed, he will be gone the remainder of the Season!"

Georgie shook her head at the younger woman in disbelief. "Elinor, I could have told you that myself. He is *my* husband's cousin. And you need not be so gleeful, I can assure you he is still suffering for what Alice endured."

"And why should he not? His own sister to be so besmirched by his friend…"

"She's not besmirched!"

Grace exhaled slowly, grateful the conversation had shifted away from her. Anything was better than the discussion of her and her father, even if it was about unfortunate Alice Sterling and the absence of her more troublesome brother.

There had been no indication that Grace's father would take any action one way or the other, but along with the prickle of worry had come a strange tingling of anticipation.

There was no telling what that could mean, but she would not feel easy until it was gone.

Chapter Two

A gentleman's club is no business of any woman, or so we are led to believe. But really, what could they have to talk about over billiards, cards, and drinks?

-The Spinster Chronicles, 9 October 1818

"A letter for you, my lord."

"During breakfast? Can't it wait?"

"That is not for me to say, sir."

Aubrey Flint, Lord Ingram, sighed heavily as he set his silverware down and reached for the folded paper on a platter before him.

"Thank you, Locke."

His butler bowed, the bald spot at the back of his head glinting briefly in the morning light, then he left the room.

Aubrey grinned to himself as he watched the retreating back of his trusted butler. Locke had known him from childhood and had served his father to perfection. With his passing and Aubrey's ascension to the title, Locke had done the same for him. Despite Aubrey's proper training and upbringing, he rather thought Locke would have been more equipped to take on the title and responsibilities than Aubrey.

Locke would never have said so, but surely, he must have thought it once or twice.

Over the course of any given week.

Particularly now with Aubrey being in London for longer than a few weeks.

But Locke would have to adjust his thinking, were he truly thinking such thoughts, because Aubrey had no intention of leaving London for the time being, no matter how appealing the thoughts of Breyerly and Derbyshire might be.

Considering Aubrey was currently dealing with correspondence during his breakfast after a rather poor night's sleep, Breyerly was actually becoming quite an appealing prospect.

More's the pity.

Derbyshire, with all its rolling hills and glorious peaks, its beauties and wonders, would not catch sight nor sound of him before autumn. There was too much to tend to before he could return to the solitude of the Peak District. He had responsibilities that required his continued presence, and his presence was requested in the House of Lords for more than just a dutiful visit or three.

Duty. Responsibility. Work.

Someone should have told him that adulthood was really quite a drudgery, and having a title made it all the more unpleasant.

He broke the seal on the letter and skimmed it, smirking to himself at the contents. Tony Sterling was as good a man as he had ever found, and though Aubrey had been in London for several weeks now, Tony was still taking pains to invite him for dinners and the club. They'd known each other for ages, since their days at Eton and Cambridge, and Tony had been just the same then, adopting Aubrey as though he were a lost and wandering puppy in need of a proper home and attention.

Of course, it was probably true, but what else did one expect to happen when Aubrey had been raised by parents who had no regard for each other and without a single sibling for company? He'd been the most lost little boy to ever set foot at Eton, and Tony Sterling had taken him under his wing.

Which was astonishing, as they were in the same year.

But that was Tony's way, and it had seen them both through their educations. It was a pity that Aubrey hadn't kept in contact once he'd left Cambridge, but the moment Tony had heard Aubrey was in London, the friendship had been resumed.

Now, apparently, he was requested to meet one of his very few friends at the club shortly. A rather early venture, but he suspected Tony had his reasons.

The man usually did.

All told, Aubrey hadn't been particularly prolific with social engagements upon his return to London, which would have disappointed his father to no end. His mother had always preferred the quiet solitude of Breyerly, or so she had told him, and so she would have approved to the same extreme.

He'd always taken after her, no matter how he might look like his father.

But he had done everything as pertaining to his duties, he could say that without reservation. Parties had been attended, dinners had been eaten, balls had been danced at, and he'd even ventured to the theater twice. He had been unusually present in the House of Lords, drawing curious attention from those who expected him to be less than involved in his duties there.

Strangely enough, doing so had brought about more invitations for Aubrey, which would enable him to attend more events, and be more social, and meet more people, which would give him more amusement and less time to revel in his solitude.

He hadn't decided what to do about that. He rather liked his solitude. But solitude wouldn't help him if he wanted to avoid being labeled a recluse. He wasn't; he simply did not find socialization particularly enjoyable. As a matter of fact, the only socializing he had ever been fond of had been with Tony and their other friends at school. And with the Morledges, he supposed.

He exhaled as he refolded the partially-read letter, wincing to himself.

There, he supposed, was one duty he had not fulfilled. After spending his entire childhood as neighbor to the Morledges, and spending time with the children romping through the lands on one or both estates, he surely owed the family a visit, and yet he had not done so. Lord Trenwick was abroad, as per usual, but Lady Trenwick was in London, as were two of her children, and though none of them were children now, there was that closeness in their youth that ought to be respected.

He'd seen Grace at various events, of course, and he had engaged in polite conversation with her, but only in passing. She'd grown prettier than he'd imagined she would, though she had always been a pretty girl. Certainly prettier than her sister, though Anne had been fair enough. But Grace... Grace had always been different from Anne. Calmer, sweeter, wittier, and in every respect a step above, aside from wildness, which Anne had mastered into an art form.

Which made her continued unmarried state all the more puzzling, but he could not have said that he ever knew her all that well, and certainly not as well as he had known Anne. It was entirely possible that there was a glaringly obvious reason for her spinsterhood upon closer acquaintance, but out of loyalty to the family, he would never permit himself to see whatever it was.

Her brother, James, on the other hand, had only grown more ridiculous in the intervening years, but that was a bit more expected. James had not inherited a single iota of sense from his mother, nor the judgment of his father, and as such, was destined to ruin the family in some respect once he came into the title. The younger brothers could not be vouched for, given their absence, but he suspected that they would be a credit to the rest by comparison.

Really, good manners did dictate that he should pay a call upon Lady Trenwick, if not Mr. and Miss Morledge themselves, and should have done so by now. He hadn't seen any of them in years, now that they had all but given up Withrow Park. His mother would have been appalled that he had let the connection lapse, given her friendship with Lady Trenwick.

But he had not called upon them as yet. And he didn't know if his manners were that good. There was no reason to avoid it, he supposed, though he was reluctant to do so. Something about the awkwardness of calling upon a family he once knew, without having anything particular to talk about, made him wish to flee to the nearest doorway, no matter his current situation.

If Anne had been present, it would have made everything a bit easier, but she and her husband remained in Shropshire with their children, and he did not have a high enough opinion of Mr. Taylor to permit himself to venture there for his own sake.

Aubrey blinked, collected himself, and returned his attention to his rapidly cooling breakfast. He made a quick face as he took another bite of ham, forgetting that his cook served the meats already cold at breakfast, and downed his disappointment with a bit of tea, though it did little to rid of him of the taste.

Lord above, he missed Breyerly. Mrs. Tomkins knew exactly how Aubrey liked his breakfast, and always served it the same, down to the amount of preserves for his rolls. Adams, here at his London residence, had yet to learn the way of the thing.

Then again, Aubrey hadn't told him.

Details.

He finished his breakfast quickly, if for no other reason than to get it over with, and called for his carriage, which was shortly brought about. He glanced down at what he was wearing, shrugging mentally at his valet's choices. Had Sundrey known that Aubrey was going out to associate with other gentlemen, he might have had more refined choices laid out for him. Not that there was anything lacking, but Sundrey tended to care a great deal more about what Aubrey wore when he would be mixing with members of Society as opposed to dealing with matters of business.

This would undoubtedly be one of many times when Aubrey would not tell Sundrey of the change in his plans, for his valet's sake. It wasn't as though he were going to White's or Brooks', for heaven's sake. No one of any great importance would be there, and he would only be seeing his friends.

All two of them.

He had several acquaintances, but friends had ever been in short supply. There had been a pack of five of them at school, but only Tony had remained in contact. Aubrey was fairly certain one of them had died in a duel a few years ago, which spoke to the quality of his efforts in educational matters, no doubt.

Poor Simms.

At least, he thought it was Simms. He had been the least intelligent of the group, and he thought it more than likely he would have been so unfortunate. Though Brickner hadn't been the brightest, particularly with his temper.

Still, Tony and his friend Lieutenant Henshaw were far and away better than any of the other men Aubrey could have associated with in London, if he had to be in London at all.

18

Aubrey covered his face with a groan as the carriage rolled to a stop. He sounded like an unsociable curmudgeon, even in his thoughts. He might have been nearing seventy years in age rather than thirty, and for all his love of the country, the seclusion there had only added to such things. Which was why he was in London.

Sort of.

He exited the carriage and made his way up the surprisingly grand stairs into the club, taking care not to touch anything gilded for fear of staining it with his country manners or clothing. Even the wood paneling seemed overly intricate, given the club was not one of the more prominent ones, but Aubrey supposed there was room for compensation in anything to be found lacking by comparison.

He nodded at the few gentlemen he recognized as he entered and made his way over to a table where Tony, Henshaw, and another gentleman sat.

Oh good. Introductions.

He forced a smile as he approached. "Sterling. Henshaw. Glad to see you both."

Tony grinned and rose, as did Henshaw. Both reached out to shake his hand firmly in succession.

"Ingram, this is my cousin, Lord Sterling. Francis, my great friend Aubrey, Lord Ingram," Tony introduced, gesturing to the man opposite Henshaw. "We were at school together."

"A pleasure and my apologies, my lord," Lord Sterling offered as he reached out a hand. "You must have suffered a great deal."

Aubrey grinned, liking this particular Sterling cousin immensely. "Nothing that left me with lasting torment, but I managed well enough besides."

Lord Sterling returned his grin, and the likeness between him and his cousin when he did so was striking. They resembled each other, certainly, but the smiles were identical. Even Tony's brother didn't look so like him as this.

"I meant to introduce the pair of you at Allandale's some weeks back," Tony explained as they all sat. "The evening rather got away from us, I'm afraid. Francis has only just returned to town, so I thought introductions should be made."

Aubrey sobered and considered the man in a new light. "I hope your sister is recovering, my lord. I can assure you, I only am aware of it due to Tony's explanation of the events. There has been no gossip, as far as I can tell, surrounding her."

Lord Sterling gave him a thin smile. "Thank you, and please, call me Francis. Alice is doing well, and the weeks at Crestley Ridge have done wonders for her, which is why we have returned to London now. My brother, on the other hand..."

Henshaw hissed, shaking his head. "Poor lad. I may not care for him all that much, but to be in some part to blame for a sister's injury is to suffer the torment of the damned."

Francis nodded in agreement while Tony and Aubrey merely shared a sympathetic look. "Where is he?" Aubrey asked with all politeness.

"We're not entirely sure," Francis admitted, though he didn't seem especially concerned about it. "He's sworn off drinking, gambling, and all social activities for the time being, and we received word from a cousin in Norfolk that he had stayed there for a time." He shrugged a shoulder and sat back. "He writes to Alice regularly, but I don't press her about it."

"Probably for the best," Tony murmured with a smile for his cousin. "Alice nearly bit my head off the last time I treated her with sympathy. She's an independent one, that is for certain."

Francis groaned at that. "God help me..."

"That may not help," Henshaw reminded him with a wry grin. "I've prayed for years and years for help with my sisters, and nothing changes but the effects of their antics."

Aubrey raised a brow at him. "Remind me, how many sisters do you have?"

Henshaw met his gaze squarely. "Seven."

"Good lord," Aubrey coughed. "I'd forgotten."

Tony chuckled. "Yes, Aubrey has no siblings whatsoever, so we all seem rather crowded to him."

"Some of us more than others," Henshaw claimed, toasting Aubrey with his glass.

"Trust me, I've had my share of family antics," Aubrey protested, waving a finger. "My neighbors in Derbyshire had many children, and they were quite an active bunch. I used to run around with the lot of them and pretend to be one of the pack."

Francis grinned ruefully across the table at Tony. "Sounds like our family gatherings, eh, Tony?"

Tony shook his head. "There were always too many Sterlings running around. One got quite lost amidst the rest."

"Who were your neighbors?" Henshaw asked Aubrey. "Anyone we know?"

Aubrey smirked just a little. "I believe you would. Lord Trenwick and his family."

Francis snorted under his breath. "I trust Lord Trenwick wasn't the one running amok?"

The jab made Aubrey laugh out loud, drawing some attention from the more reserved club members about them. "Lord, no. He was almost never there. But I got very well acquainted with the children, and with Lady Trenwick, as well."

"Trenwick," Henshaw mused thoughtfully. "Isn't that...?"

"Grace Morledge," Tony finished with a nod. He grinned at Aubrey mischievously. "You know my wife is great friends with her, don't you?"

Aubrey only shrugged. He knew, but he wasn't sure why that mattered so very much.

"Georgie's friends are all great in her mind," Francis scoffed, though he smiled with genuine warmth. "Everyone that falls into that category could be her best friend."

"Why do you say that as though it were a bad thing?" Tony asked. "Are you upset Georgie treats Janet as a sister?"

Francis glared at him. "Of course not. I object that it brings you into my life more often than is convenient."

Henshaw let out a guffaw and cuffed Tony on the shoulder. "Are you going to take that?"

"Why not?" Tony replied easily. "He's been trying to get rid of me our entire lives. But back to Grace Morledge..." He eyed Aubrey with some speculation.

Aubrey returned his look. "What about her?" he eventually asked.

"Ignore him," Francis muttered, leaning over to Aubrey. "Ever since he married Georgie, he's been obsessed with pairing off

21

everyone else."

"So, telling him I'm not looking for a wife would be…?"

"Pointless," Francis finished with a nod.

Aubrey returned his nod, then looked Tony in the eye. "I am not looking for a wife."

Tony only smirked. "Pointless."

"I often tend to do pointless things."

The others laughed, but Tony focused on Aubrey. "Trying for Grace wouldn't be pointless."

Henshaw sputtered a cough. "Sterling, leave the poor man alone. All he said was that he knows Grace, not that he was in love with her."

"But he *could* be in love with her if he tried." Tony leaned forward. "I adore Grace, and I think she deserves to be happy."

Aubrey stared at his friend without expression for a long moment. "Forgive me, but did you somehow infer from anything that I have said that I feel opposite to that sentiment? Or that I have a particular interest in her? For God's sake, Tony, I haven't spoken more than a dozen words to her at any time since she was ten years old." He narrowed his eyes. "Is this Georgie talking? Is she trying to marry off her friends?"

"No…" Tony protested without any conviction at all.

Francis barked a laugh. "Georgie is marrying off the Spinsters? Don't tell Janet, she'd jump into the fray with her. So would Miranda. They'd plot for the whole lot of them."

Henshaw crossed himself and bowed his head. "Lord, let me be left alone in the forthcoming madness. Spare me from any feminine machinations that I may not be bound against my will…"

Aubrey grinned at that. "Pray for me, too, Henshaw."

Henshaw cracked open an eye. "Every man for himself, Ingram."

"Rude."

"Georgie is *not* marrying off the Spinsters," Tony insisted. "Not officially, at any rate. Izzy and Prue are married, it's true, but can you see her having any success with Charlotte or Elinor?"

Henshaw and Francis winced, shaking their heads.

Aubrey, living in his ignorance, had no such reaction. "I'm sorry, who are we talking about?"

The others looked at him in utter bewilderment. "Have you been living under a hedge?" Henshaw asked with real concern.

"Not lately."

"You sure?" Francis inquired as he aimlessly spun his glass against the wood of the table. "You've never heard of the Spinster Chronicles?"

Now it was Aubrey who scoffed aloud. "Of course, I have. And I've read them, too. Surprisingly witty and astute for a column allegedly written by spinsters. If they included anything regarding Parliament or world affairs, there would be no need for any other newssheets."

Tony glanced at the others with a surprisingly smug expression, then sat back in his chair. "You don't know, do you?"

The question was likely not meant to be rhetorical, but Aubrey took it as such and only met Tony's gaze in the same polite manner as before. Then he gestured with one hand that he should get on with it, which was undoubtedly less polite.

Francis and Henshaw chuckled to themselves, but Tony maintained his previous façade. "Georgie's one of the writers of the Spinster Chronicles."

Aubrey didn't bother hiding his surprise. "Are you serious?"

"Believe me," Francis said with a laugh, "Tony is quite proud of it. He was nearly adopted by the Spinsters. That's their name, you know. Spinsters, with a capital S."

"Duly noted," Aubrey murmured, now considering Tony's wife from an entirely different angle. "So, she's... a writer?"

Tony nodded proudly. "And a matchmaker, a defender, a fashion expert, and whatever else the situation calls for. Everybody knows this. I'm surprised you don't."

"Why should I know it?" Aubrey asked. "I don't gossip, don't listen to gossip, and I'm never in London, if I can help it. How would I know it?"

"Have you a working set of ears?" Henshaw inquired mildly, seeming particularly amused by something.

Aubrey quelled him with a look, then returned to Tony. "That's impressive, I must say."

"That's not all," Francis mused in a voice laced with humor. "Tell him the rest, Tony. Don't hold it back."

Tony's dark eyes flicked to his cousin, then returned to Aubrey. "Grace Morledge is a Spinster too. With a capital S."

Aubrey blinked once, then blinked again. "She can't be."

"I think you'll find that she can," Henshaw assured him, still finding the whole thing hilarious.

Aubrey looked over at him in derision. "I know her family well, Henshaw. There is no way on earth her father would ever let her subject herself to the category of spinster, let alone wear it so proudly, and certainly would not let her write something so public under such a title."

"Who can confirm it?" Tony shot back with a defensive edge. "There are no names to the Chronicles. No authors. Only suspicions."

"He would *still* object."

Francis grunted and looked over at him. "Then perhaps he doesn't know."

Aubrey turned to look at him as the idea settled rather coolly over him. "You think she would do this without consulting him?"

Francis shrugged. "Trenwick is never in England, from what I know of him, and takes no pains to observe his children himself. Lady Trenwick is amenable and indulgent without being careless. Perhaps it was she who gave consent, and Trenwick himself is ignorant."

There was a thought. He'd always been quite fond of Lady Trenwick and her generosity, and she was certainly giving, as Francis had said, without being in any way flippant or ridiculous. She would be considerate of the effect such an association would have upon her daughter, and yet be open to Grace's opinions on the subject.

The question was what would happen if Trenwick were to find out.

And what fresh hell that would unleash.

"Or perhaps a woman of twenty-six does not need her parents' permission to do such a thing," Henshaw suggested.

That made Aubrey smile. Clearly Henshaw had never met Lord Trenwick.

Grace Morledge was not only a spinster, but unofficially

proclaiming that status, and writing for one of the most popular columns in London. Making herself a Spinster, with a capital S.

How peculiar.

He couldn't dwell on that for the moment, not in the company of these men, one of whom wanted to make a match for him, so he forced any thoughts of Grace, Trenwick, or spinsters out of his mind, and turned to Tony.

"Did you bring me here to make a case for a wife, or...?" he asked.

Tony laughed and shook his head. "No, not at all. My wife is growing closer to her confinement, and as you have no friends, I wanted to give you some before I left with her."

"Marvelous," Henshaw said, clapping his hands and rubbing them together. "Forced friendships are my very favorite kind."

"Huzzah," Aubrey replied in the most lackluster tone he knew, smiling blandly for effect.

Francis raised a brow. "Is it too early for a real drink, gentlemen?"

"No," the others responded as one.

Chapter Three

⸻ ❦ ⸻

Timing is everything in this life. In fact, it could be all that we have.

-*The Spinster Chronicles, 17 April 1817*

Grace couldn't wait to tell her mother about the meeting the Spinsters had just had.

She tended to enjoy hearing about the antics of each girl, the topics of conversation, and what they had planned for the next issue of the Chronicles. It was fortunate indeed that Grace had been blessed with a mother who indulged her, no matter how her father disparaged. He didn't know about the Spinsters, which meant she and her mother could take pleasure in its developments at their leisure. After nearly every meeting, her mother would set out tea and cakes, eager for her report on the proceedings.

Today's meeting had provided no shortage of entertainment. Charlotte was determined to keep up her popular Best Bachelors segment in the Society Dabbler, and she had Elinor running ragged to compile all the best and most current information about each of the candidates. Prue had decided to take up a controversial Fashion Forum topic in the form of stockings, apparently with some encouragement from her husband, which had delighted the entire room. Edith was writing the main article about running a house, which was destined to amuse them all, as she had the smallest household of any of them, and the others divided up the remainder of the articles eagerly, trying desperately to keep up with the rest.

Grace had opted to tackle the Quirks and Quotes for the next issue, and her mother would be of great help there. She tended to hear a great many things, and only repeated them to Grace if they were suitable for publication.

It was a glorious day, and the ride back to Trenwick House had proven to be just as glorious, though she had not opted to take the open carriage. The sun was shining high in the sky and the temperature was perfectly mild, ensuring that many people would venture out of doors and be walking the parks. Perhaps she could convince her mother to walk Hyde Park with her later, if for no other reason than to enjoy the day.

There had not been another letter from her father since his last and most disagreeable one, which made it all the easier to put him from her mind, and any day would seem brighter with such a pleasure in its folds. She knew the bliss could not last forever, so she would endeavor to make the most of it while she could.

Sighing to herself, she allowed the footman to help her down from the coach, then tipped her head back to feel the sun just a moment longer.

"Miss Morledge?" the footman asked with some hesitation.

"Just a moment, Peter," she replied, reveling in the warmth upon her skin. "I used to lay upon the grass of Withrow on fine days, just to feel the sun. If I focus on this feeling long enough, I might think I'm there again."

Just then, a particularly loud phaeton rushed by, its wheels clattering against the street, and its occupants cheering loudly at the pace.

Grace sighed again, this time in disappointment, and opened her eyes, looking at the young footman. "So much for that idea."

He fought a smile and bowed. "Yes, Miss Morledge."

She looked up at the house, which looked nothing like Withrow, but she supposed it would have to do. She proceeded up the stairs and through the door, nodding warmly at Bennett as he greeted her.

"Miss Morledge," Bennett murmured, his tone strained somehow.

Grace smiled at him. "Bennett, are you well?"

"Yes, Miss Morledge," he replied, though it didn't feel very convincing.

She was not about to pry, so she nodded again. "I presume my mother is in the parlor waiting for me?"

Bennett shuffled slightly. "Yes, Miss Morledge, but..."

Grace was already moving in that direction. "Not to worry, Bennett. Mrs. Clarke already told me there would be no cakes today. I will survive the deprivation, I assure you."

She hurried down the corridor, already giggling in anticipation of sharing her Spinster report with her mother. She'd have to take care to get the best quotes of the meeting just right. There was no substitution for the wit and banter the girls could unleash with each other.

"Mama," she called as she neared the parlor, "you will never guess what Charlotte said today."

She rounded into the parlor, all smiles for her mother, then she jerked to a stop.

Her mother was in the room, though not at her usual place with a waiting tea tray. She stood by the tall window facing Grace, her fingers knitting together, the edges of them turning white. She smiled tremulously at her now, and Grace could see the apology in her eyes.

And no wonder, for standing before the fireplace, his attention on the weak and flickering flames within, was her father.

He straightened and turned to face Grace; his dark eyes narrowed, though his expression wasn't particularly displeased. Still, there was no warmth in him either. He looked over Grace as though she were a painting in a gallery that he did not quite comprehend.

He quirked a brow in surprise at her silence, and Grace hastily curtseyed.

"Father," she greeted even as her stomach seemed to sink to her knees. "I did not expect to see you. I had not heard you would be returning to England."

"No, I had not told anyone," he informed her as he clasped his hands behind his back. "Not even your mother. Who is Charlotte, Grace?"

Grace's palms began to perspire, which usually occurred when her father directly questioned her in that tone. "Charlotte Wright, Father. I visit with her often. We've grown close in the last two years."

Her father grunted to himself, then turned to glance at his wife. "Is that Miss Wright the heiress? Daughter of John Wright?"

"Yes, Trenwick," she replied, smiling in the same fashion as before. "She and Grace are very good friends, and the Wrights think very highly of Grace."

"Good." Her father returned his attention to his daughter. "Excellent, Grace. It is important to maintain beneficial connections, and to gain the good favor of those with influence. I am very pleased to hear it."

Because that was why she had formed a bond with Charlotte. To forge beneficial connections and to please her father.

Grace forced a tight smile and inclined her head. "Thank you, Father."

He stared at her again for a long moment, his eyes on her face.

He looked older than she recalled, his hair sprinkled with more grey and white than before. He was tanned, and his face was just as it had been, no additional lines or creases had formed, except for a pair of them at his mouth. No doubt due to frowning too frequently about his younger daughter's failures. In all other respects, he was just as she remembered. The same stature and stance, the same style of dress, and the same domineering intensity in his gaze, all perfectly her father and all as she recalled.

But why was he here?

She glanced at her mother, who held absolutely no answers in her expression or manner, and barely avoided biting her lip. Any sight of behavior or habits less than ideal would be cause for comment, and she did not need a discussion on childish behaviors at the present.

"Come and sit down, Grace," her father suggested, though his tone was rather commanding. He gestured to the sofa nearest him, ironically where Grace usually sat for tea with her mother.

Knowing she had little choice, Grace did as her father bid and moved to take a seat. "How was your journey from Austria, Father?" she managed, stammering slightly.

He noticed the stammer and a furrow formed between his brows for a brief moment. "Tolerable, thank you."

When he said nothing else, Grace made herself smile. "Do you plan to stay long with us in London? It has been such an age."

29

"That all depends."

"On what?" she asked, though she was sure it was unnecessary.

"On you, my dear girl."

Of course, it did. She should have guessed.

Her mother sat on the settee opposite her, her eyes flicking between Grace and her father with a startling frequency. Grace wanted one moment, just one, with her mother alone. Something to give her an ounce of comfort with this sudden development, anything at all to hint at what her father's plans were, to prepare her for whatever was coming.

There was no moment. And there was no preparation.

Grace forced herself to meet her father's gaze as he stood before her. "Why do your plans depend on me? What have I done?"

"Nothing, nothing," her father assured her, his tone surprisingly gentle, given the tone of his letters. "Believe me, I've had my solicitor look into every eventuality. Discreetly, of course. He tells me your reputation is excellent, and that you are a well-respected young woman."

She heard the compliments in his words, but something else caught her attention. "Your solicitor? Mr. Bryant?"

Her father raised a brow at her tone. "No, another one I secured to see to other matters while I am abroad. Recently, when certain questions and concerns were raised…"

"About me," Grace added, forcing her tone to be as mild as possible while being impertinent to her father.

"Yes, about you." He gave her a severe look, and Grace dropped her gaze to the floor. "Can you blame me?"

Grace shook her head, her eyes burning. "No, sir."

Her father sighed and sat down near her. "I am concerned, Grace, about your situation. You are set up well enough that you will never be an unfortunate spinster without means, like so many other women."

Women that she was friends with, no doubt.

"But I refused to believe that the situation was as bewildering as I saw it," he went on. "Surely, there had to be a reason for all of this."

Yes, surely there must be a reason that none of the men in London wanted her. Clearly, the fault was hers and not theirs.

"But," her father continued, not requiring any response from her, "no reason has presented itself."

Of course, it hadn't.

Wait… It hadn't?

She looked up at her father in confusion. "Father?"

His expression was sympathetic, which was one of his lesser utilized looks, and he shook his head. "I don't know where your faults lie either, Grace. From what I can tell, you are everything a father could wish for in a daughter. I could not be more pleased."

Grace blinked uncertainly, an odd warmth filling her chest. "Thank you, Father."

"Except, of course, for your being a spinster. It's shameful. Just shameful."

It was all Grace could do to avoid throwing up her hands and rolling her eyes. Charlotte certainly would have done so under these circumstances, but Mr. Wright was hardly the same man as her father and would not be surprised by such a thing. If Grace gave in to these impulses, her father would consider it a fault and do something about that.

"We are all blinded in some way, Grace," her father said with another sigh. "We are confounded by your unmarried state, which is why we must look elsewhere for answers."

"Elsewhere?" Grace cried suddenly. "Surely, you're not sending me away, Father! I could not bear going abroad for a suitor, not when I adore England so."

Her father gave her a look, a mixture of surprise and disgruntlement. "No, Grace, I am not sending you abroad. I want you to remain in England, disappointing though it has been for you."

She heaved a sigh of relief, then glanced up at her father quickly, wondering if he would consider that inappropriate. But he had no reaction, his gaze upon her remained steady.

Grace looked at her mother, who still had no answers.

Did she even know what her father was talking about? Had he shared any details with her before Grace had arrived? It had never truly occurred to her to wonder about the nature of her parents' marriage, about their relationship with each other, but it seemed that her father tended to act without consideration for anyone else, including his wife. Was she simply expected to acquiesce to his commands and wishes with no opinions of her own at all?

Was that any way to manage a marriage?

Not that she had any experience with such things. After all, she was, shockingly, a spinster.

Oh, the horror.

"I had something else in mind for you, Grace," her father went on with a slight clearing of his throat. "Something that will undoubtedly be more beneficial to us both."

Grace's skin began to tingle warily. "Oh?" she managed to ask as her fingers played at the embroidery along her skirts.

Her father nodded, smiling at last, which was always a suspicious sight. "Yes, although the details still need to be worked out." He straightened in his seat and lifted his chin. "As we are all blind to where your faults lie, it only follows that in order for us to discover what we can improve in you to bring about suitors and marriage, we must bring in a new set of eyes. One not at all limited where you are concerned."

A new set of... *what?*

Grace blinked once. "And do what?"

"Why, find your faults, of course."

Her mouth dropped open, and she stared at her father for a number of heartbeats, waiting for him to crack a smile or even laugh. Surely, he had to do so; it was a ludicrous idea.

But there was no hint of a smile, nothing at all resembling amusement.

Grace's eyes flicked to her mother, who stared at her husband in absolute horror.

"Trenwick," her mother said at last, placing a hand on his arm, "you don't mean..."

He shook her hand off, turning to her. "Of course, I mean it. We must bring someone in and have them examine her, Leonora. They must spend time with her, truly get to know her, and find whatever it is that we are missing."

"What... what would they do?" Grace whispered, her fingers numb against her skirts.

He returned his attention to Grace. "Observe you. Your manner, your accomplishments, your comportment, your speech… Anything they can think of. Their task will be to study you, to even be critical, if it comes down to it, but only in the most respectful way. After all, we are all trying to find the things that are keeping you from being married."

Grace's brow furrowed in thought. Her father's tone was not nearly as severe as his letters had been, and in fact held far more warmth. But the words were much the same. There was something wrong with her, in his mind, and bringing some stranger in and paying them to perform a sort of analysis on her as though she were an experiment was the only way to discover what it was.

Someone would be tasked with observing her specifically to find her faults. It would be worse than being back in the schoolroom with a governess, for even her governesses, stern though some of them were, had never been cruel.

Her father let the silence stretch on, then leaned forward, his expression now eager and earnest. "You must see why this is necessary, Grace."

Why it was necessary? For someone to examine her for no other reason than to discover what was wrong?

No. No, she did not.

Still, she found herself dipping her chin, not quite a nod. "Who?"

"I beg your pardon?"

Grace cleared her throat. "Who would be the one coming to assess me? Have you selected someone as yet?"

Her father shook his head, seeming pleased by the question. "I knew you would come around, Grace, and that you would do your duty."

Duty. Was that what she was doing?

"But to answer your question," he went on, "no. I have not selected someone as yet. I am leaving the task of finding candidates to my new solicitor, Mr. Hayes. He will find suitable, respectable people who are knowledgeable in the ways of Society and who are not familiar enough with you to be blinded as the rest of us are."

Grace nodded to herself, her thoughts whirling with possibilities. None of them good, but possibilities nonetheless, and she knew that no amount of crying or arguing on her part would change her father's mind. Everything had already been set in motion, even if nothing had been officially set. This *was* happening. Someone *would* come and find whatever insurmountable faults kept her from attracting a man. And she *would* spend the extent of whatever length of time it took living in a cloud of doubt and discouragement.

Because she couldn't get a husband for herself. No, she had to have someone come in and find everything that was wrong with her so she could be mended, and *then* she would be able to get a husband for herself.

That was all that mattered. All she was good for. Just marriage. Except she needed help to accomplish that, and an official faultfinder.

How pleasant.

"Might I offer suggestions for potential candidates?" she heard herself ask, though she hadn't the faintest idea whom she would suggest. Everyone she knew well enough to ask had expressed the same confusion about her spinster status and apparent faults as she now felt.

"If you have any ideas, yes, of course," her father said with a nod. "I welcome any assistance you can give us in this. After all, it is your future we are hoping to change."

He smiled with more warmth than he had given her in at least fifteen years, then rose and left the room, leaving Grace alone with her mother.

Silence prevailed in the parlor, which it almost never did, and Grace focused her efforts on regaining warmth and feeling in her fingertips. Various bits and pieces of her had flickered between freezing and flaming, between a tingling sensation and no sensation at all.

She heard herself inhale and exhale, one, twice, three times, before she forced a hard blink and made herself look over at her mother.

There was hardly any color in her mother's cheeks, and she seemed to be staring at her crocheted fingerless gloves as though they held some answers for her.

Grace wet her lips. "Mama?"

That brought her mother's eyes up and she heaved a sigh. "I am so sorry, Grace. He sent no word he was coming, and he certainly

34

never mentioned finding someone to examine you."

"I know, Mama," Grace assured her. She laughed once without humor. "It was written all over your face. He shocked you as much as he did me."

Her mother smiled and put a hand to her brow, leaning back against the settee. "I do wish he had consulted with me first. This plan of his can only bring more trouble, mark my words."

Grace shook her head. "Mama, not only is that going to be mortifying for me, but surely it is not at all respectable. A stranger taking stock of areas in which I lack? All to improve the chances of my getting married off? You might as well hang a bell around my neck and have me eat from a trough."

"It will not be so bad as that," her mother protested, albeit weakly.

Grace gave her a look. "Yes, it will. Someone will likely be paid by my father, either monetarily or in some other way, just to compile a list for him of everything that they can find that is wrong with me. By the end of the sessions, no doubt I will have learned to moo on command. That should improve the price of this particular cow, yes?"

"Oh, Grace," her mother laughed, though there was compassion in her expression. "It will be all right."

"Will it?" Her voice cracked in the question, and she averted her eyes, clearing her throat.

Her mother rose and came to sit beside her, taking her hand. "I don't know how, darling, but I do know that somehow this will be all right. We will get through this, and then your father will leave you alone. Or go back to the Continent."

Grace looked at her mother dubiously. "You do realize that wishing your husband away from you does not provide the most encouraging example for marital bliss…"

"Oh, we are looking for bliss?" her mother asked, her mouth curving in a lopsided smile. "That changes everything, absolutely everything."

Grace giggled and slouched inelegantly against the sofa. She shook her head and drummed her fingers against her stomach. "I know very well I am not perfect, Mama, and I know very well that I have flaws."

35

"As do I, Grace," came the soft reply. "And so does your father. We know you are not perfect, despite your father's claims that we expect you to be."

"So why is it so hard for anyone to find a reason that I am unwanted in the marriage mart?" Grace asked, gesturing slightly with her hands. "I'm not extraordinary in any aspect, especially since Father did not want me to be a spectacle for either praise or criticism. I am the same sort of girl that fills every dance hall and ballroom in London."

Her mother tutted softly. "You're better, dear. Infinitely better."

Grace frowned at her. "Which is mother-speak for 'I cannot agree with that statement by virtue of having birthed you,' yes?"

"Something like that." Her mother fluttered her eyelashes, smiling blandly.

"Lovely." Grace groaned and stared up at the too-ornate ceiling above her. "He doesn't know about the Spinsters, does he? That would be…"

"Oh lord, no. I would never tell him that. No, that secret is safe, unless his solicitor knows."

Grace shook her head slowly. "I have to tell them about all this. The Spinsters. Charlotte will be beside herself. And she just might volunteer to find the faults."

"Your father might let her."

"Don't tell her that. She'd either be delighted or offended, and I'm not sure which would be worse."

Chapter Four

⌒∽⌒

𝒫aying calls can be a tiresome excursion no matter how we feel about those we are calling upon. And sometimes receiving calls can be even more tiresome.

-*The Spinster Chronicles, 13 March 1816*

"I'm doing my duty, I'm doing my duty, I'm doing my duty…"

Aubrey shook his head as the carriage rolled up to Trenwick House in Mayfair, wishing the statement actually gave him some encouragement or strength. But alas, it provided neither comfort nor motivation. Worst of all, it did nothing to keep him from this visit.

He didn't have anything against the Morledge family, nothing at all. He simply hated paying calls. It was a forced formality which led to an unnecessary awkwardness that he despised. Even with families and people he knew well and liked, the engagement became unbearable and stilted. He was really much better in the more casual situations of life.

Unfortunately, very few of those happened when in London among Society.

He looked up at the façade of Trenwick House, wishing one could enjoy a foreshadowing of one's forthcoming experience by examining its location beforehand. Preparation would be so much the better if such a thing were possible.

But sitting out here wouldn't solve anything, nor would it make this experience any more pleasant.

He groaned and stepped out of the carriage, setting his hat firmly atop his head. Surely this wouldn't be so bad as other calls he'd had to make. He had once known the Morledges better than he'd known his own parents, and he'd been invited to more impromptu meals at their table than he could now recall.

Ages ago. When they had been neighbors and friends. They were practically strangers now.

He trudged up the stairs and bit back a sigh as he rang the bell, looking up at the underside of the window ledge above him.

"Lord, if I've ever done a good thing in my life, let this visit be painless. And be sure to inform my mother that I'm doing it, even though I hate paying calls."

The Lord did not write a message for him on the window ledge, but Aubrey would go with the assumption that the message had been received. He might not have been on the most familiar terms with anything remotely resembling deity, but he was not about to risk denying it.

The overly-carved door opened, and a tall, sallow-faced butler answered, raising a furry brow at him.

Aubrey smiled, unsure if it was in amusement or anxiety. "Good day. Lord Ingram to see Lady Trenwick and her children."

The butler's expression immediately shifted into one of deference bordering on delight. "Of course, my lord. Please, do come in." He stepped back and smiled.

For some reason he'd never understand, Aubrey had always been fascinated by servants, and by butlers in particular. He thought this one might rank up there with Locke. He was perfectly composed and respectful, but something about him made Aubrey want to ask impertinent questions and use the wrong fork, just to see his reaction. He inclined his head as he stepped into the house, removing his hat and tugging off his gloves.

"Is the family expecting you, my lord?" the butler asked with all politeness as he took the hat and gloves.

Aubrey shook his head and handed the butler his card. "No, they are not. But it's long past time for me to pay a call upon them, so I hope they will forgive the lack of advanced warning."

The butler smiled and nodded at him. "I am sure they will, my lord. If you will follow me, I will have you wait in the parlor until I secure permission…"

"Ingram!"

Aubrey turned with a forced smile to James, wishing that anyone else from the family had found him rather than this peacock. "James. How fortuitous, I have come to call upon you all, if you will permit the intrusion."

James approached with a lazy smile that spoke of too much indolence and not enough sense. "I believe that Mother would permit you making off with one of my sisters with a polite smile and a gracious hand of friendship, Ingram. Even after all this time. Come, I'll take you up. Thank you, Bennett." He smirked at the butler and moved down the corridor.

Aubrey watched him go for a moment, then looked at the butler. "Is he always like that?" he murmured quietly.

"Unfortunately, my lord," Bennett replied with a hint of distaste. He bowed, then disappeared.

Aubrey grumbled under his breath and followed James, sending up another prayer to the Almighty, though this one was far less polite.

He'd risk being struck by lightning. He'd find it preferable at the moment, come to think of it.

Please let Grace be sensible, please let Grace be sensible, please…

"Mother, Grace, look who has come to call on us at last."

Well, he could have done without *that* particular introduction.

Aubrey fixed his most polite smile on his lips and strolled into the room, attempting to pretend that he wasn't holding his breath.

Lady Trenwick looked almost identical to the woman he recalled, though perhaps with a few more faint lines, though her hair was still the same color of aged-gold from his childhood. To his surprise, she was smiling at him, also identical to the manner he remembered, which proved she was a much kinder soul than he expected.

Or remembered, as it were.

"Lord Ingram!" she greeted with sincere delight. "What a wonderful surprise!"

He bowed, his smile far more effortless than before. "Lady Trenwick, you are remarkably unchanged from when I last was graced with your presence."

She chuckled and held out a hand to him. "Aubrey, dear, you haven't lost your charm."

He came to her and took her hand, kissing it fondly. "Of course not, my lady. I simply save it for select people and occasions."

Lady Trenwick wrinkled up her nose with a laugh and touched his cheek. "So grown up, Aubrey. And handsome! Your mother would be so pleased."

Aubrey straightened and found himself sobering. "Mother would no doubt wish me to be more of a gentleman than I am, but there is time for redemption, I trust."

"Of course, there is." She squeezed his hand and turned. "You remember my daughter, don't you, Lord Ingram?"

Aubrey turned to consider Grace, standing nearby, watching his exchange with her mother with steady eyes, and a hint of a smile. But only a hint. "Of course. Miss Morledge, you are looking remarkably well today."

Remarkably well was a blatant lie and a sin against humanity and all the arts. Grace Morledge was one of the most beautiful women he had ever seen, and somehow her impact was all the more potent for not being surrounded by other young women in all their finery. Here in this well-furnished drawing room, in her simple day dress of pale green, she bore the air and appearance of a goddess.

Which would explain the sudden dryness in his throat as her perfectly full lips curved into a smile.

Goddesses. Such trouble.

"As well as I did last week at the Johnstons' ball?" Grace asked as her smile turned coy. "You didn't say so then."

"Grace," her mother scolded half-heartedly. "Leave poor Aubrey alone. He could hardly pay such attentions to you in public, particularly at the Johnstons'. Mrs. Johnston alone would have..."

Grace wrinkled her nose. "Yes, she would have told Miranda Sterling, Mama, but Mrs. Johnston is only half the busybody Miranda is, so she would have forgotten the details." Grace returned her attention to Aubrey, smiling again. "But please forgive the impertinence anyway, Lord Ingram. I should be better behaved than that."

Aubrey chuckled and waved a dismissive hand. "Not at all, Miss

Morledge. And I'm afraid that I am more reserved than my usual nature in such a public spectacle as a ball. I've never been particularly comfortable standing on ceremony."

The goddess tilted her chin, appearing amused. "And you're so comfortable in a more informal setting?"

He shrugged. "Perhaps. At the moment, I am feeling quite thoroughly examined, Miss Morledge, and I don't find that at all comfortable."

She grinned outright, and his lungs forgot the manner of inhalation.

"Oh, for God's sake, Grace, leave him alone," James blustered with a simpering sort of laugh. "Sit down, Ingram, and let me pour you a drink."

Grace looked at her brother in disgust. "It is eleven in the morning, James."

"It's none of your concern when I choose to begin my imbibing, princess," James returned with a surprising amount of spite as he moved to the sideboard. "And certainly not when Ingram does."

Aubrey turned to James. "Actually, Morledge, I will forgo a drink for the present, but thank you." He looked back at the ladies, smiling further. "One never knows what will come out of my mouth when under the influence of a decent vintage."

"Sound judgment," Grace murmured as she sat, her cheeks coloring slightly. "Would that all men had it."

This comment was lost on her brother, who continued to fill his own glass.

Lady Trenwick also sat, and silently gestured for Aubrey to do the same. "Aubrey, dear, how is Breyerly? Such a lovely place; I do remember it so fondly."

A genuine warmth filled him at the mention of his beloved estate. "It is in need of some small repairs, my lady, but only for upkeep. We've expanded the gardens since I saw you last, and we've included a new fountain in honor of my mother. And you remember the large oak by the hill on the west side?"

"Yes, of course!" Lady Trenwick replied, clapping her hands in delight. "Such a fine old tree, with such character."

"Even I remember that tree," James blustered as he came to sit down. "The boys and I spent a great many hours climbing up into it, and I believe you were with us, Ingram."

Aubrey managed a chuckle. "Yes, so the scar on my left knee reminds me."

"I used to just walk around that tree," Grace murmured, smiling wistfully at nothing. "Looking up into the leaves, trying to find a ray of sunlight through them…"

James scoffed loudly. "So fanciful, Grace. I thought you were more sensible than that."

Grace glared at her brother, shaking her head, her jaw tightening.

Aubrey would have given a considerable fortune to know what she was thinking at this moment. But instead, he went on. "Unfortunately, the tree was struck by lightning and had to come down."

Lady Trenwick's face fell a little. "Oh, how terribly sad. Such a loss for the grounds."

"It's only a tree, Mother," James blustered pompously. "Dry your eyes."

Well, that was unnecessary, but Aubrey was hardly in a position to shut him up.

"But what of Withrow?" Aubrey asked, shifting the subject at once. "It's been an age since I've had the pleasure of seeing any of you there. The rose bushes have fully bloomed, and I can see them from my study. Such glorious colors, Lady Trenwick."

James sniffed in the most dismissive manner possible, settling back into his chair. "Oh, we're not going back to Withrow. Such an eyesore of a place, and a drain on all our finances."

Grace looked at her brother, expression hurt. "James…"

"He's right."

They all turned to the new voice, and Aubrey was stunned to see Lord Trenwick standing there, more aged and tanned than he recalled, but in every other regard the same.

Aubrey rose quickly and bowed. "Lord Trenwick. My apologies, sir, I had no idea you were in residence."

He eyed Aubrey in an oddly paternal manner for a man so formal, and nodded in greeting. "Ingram, my lad, you've grown into a fine man. Your reputation precedes you. Quite respectable."

"Does it?" Aubrey asked, suddenly feeling the urge to stand up straighter and answer with all politeness. "And I had hoped to keep myself as particularly unobtrusive as possible while here in London."

A soft laugh was muffled behind him, and Aubrey fought the temptation to glance at Grace, suspecting it had come from her. But there was no diverting one's attention from Lord Trenwick when he was engaged in conversation with you. It simply was not done.

Aubrey cleared his throat quickly, seeing Trenwick's gaze flick to his daughter. "So, Withrow is not prospering?"

"Not at all," Trenwick replied gruffly, returning his attention to Aubrey. "I'd get rid of it altogether if any reasonable offer was made on the place."

A strange mixture of surprise and the reverse filled Aubrey at the thought. It would be entirely in the nature of Trenwick to hold no sentimentality for an estate in his care, and yet as far as he knew it was the only estate Trenwick had, which meant it was his only source of viable income in England. Oh, he surely had investitures elsewhere, and possibly an estate on the Continent, but here in England, it was only Withrow.

And he would give it up?

Curious.

"Ingram, perhaps we might speak in private?" Trenwick suggested as he gestured faintly for the corridor. "There is much I would discuss with you."

Damnation. He had very much hoped to avoid such an interview, but Trenwick had always treated Aubrey as though he were a son, despite never showing true parental measures. In his youth, Aubrey had grown used to receiving the same lectures on responsibility and duty from him that his father had given, all to be delivered in much the same tone, although without the same level of intoxication.

Aubrey's father had been more like James Morledge than Lord Trenwick, but without all the frills.

Small mercies.

"Of course," Aubrey replied in a smooth tone, his cheeks beginning to ache from forcing his smile. He turned to the ladies and James, nodding to each in turn.

"Shall I come too, Father?" James asked, sitting forward in his chair.

Lord Trenwick looked at his son in mild derision. "Whatever for?"

James blinked in surprise.

Trenwick gestured again for Aubrey, who moved to the door without another word to anyone else. Trenwick turned down the corridor and headed to a room at the end of it, not speaking at all.

Not that Aubrey minded the silence. On the contrary, it gave him ample time to rearrange his mind, which was sorely needed, now that he was expected to converse on topics destined to be tedious and business-related. Two of his least favorite things.

All with one of the sternest men he'd ever met.

This was another reason he hated to pay calls, and actively avoided doing so. If only he'd paid more attention to the less honorable part of his inclination and had stayed at home. This all might have been avoided.

More's the pity.

They entered Trenwick's study and Aubrey waited as Trenwick situated himself behind the desk. Then he sat in perfect time with the older man, lacing his fingers together loosely in his lap.

Trenwick exhaled audibly, then gave Aubrey a grimacing smile. "I am pleased to see you here today, Ingram. It's been far too long since we've had an opportunity to speak."

Aubrey let his polite smile return. "Well, I have been at Breyerly, sir, or at school, as the case might have been, and, as I understand it, you have been on the Continent much of the time."

"It's true, I have been," Trenwick admitted freely, his fingers tenting. "I found far better opportunities in Europe than could be had here. My children had their mother for supervision, and there was little enough to tempt me into the House of Lords, especially considering the services I rendered in all the years preceding it."

"You don't have to defend yourself to me, my lord," Aubrey insisted, waving a hand. "I have always found that a man is best suited where he feels most comfortable."

Trenwick made a face. "I disagree. Respectfully."

Of course he did.

"It's not about comfort," Trenwick continued, completely unaware of Aubrey's impending disgruntlement. "A man must go where he can be productive and make the most of his skills, his time, and his resources. I had run the course on what I was capable of accomplishing in England, so it was no longer feasible to remain here. At least for any length of time, you understand."

Aubrey didn't understand, not in the least, but he nodded as if he did.

"My children do not require a father's supervision or intervention, now that they are matured," Trenwick went on. "James is a waste of a man, but he will inherit, and there is nothing I can do about that but protect the assets from his extravagance. The other boys will make up where he lacks."

From what Aubrey had seen, that should not be too hard. The younger Morledge sons were certainly better than their elder brother, but he wasn't sure how much that was saying.

"In fact, if I could only get Withrow off my hands, I would have no real reason to return to England at all," Trenwick mused hopefully, apparently willing to continue his somehow-productive, one-sided conversation without any intervention. Then, Trenwick's face suddenly turned into a scowl. "That and Grace."

Aubrey looked at Trenwick in shock. "Grace? I mean, Miss Morledge? What could she have to do with anything, my lord?"

Trenwick's brow furrowed, then cleared. "Ah, I forget that you have not been in London much at all, so you might not be fully aware. Grace is a spinster, Ingram."

Was he expecting Aubrey to gasp in shock at that pronouncement? Grace was clearly living in their home, was clearly unmarried, and unless Trenwick anticipated Aubrey to be incapable of counting, she was clearly of an age where it was atypical to be either of those things. But must such a statement be made as though she were on the brink of certain death? Surely there were worse things.

He settled for a bland disappointment. "That is most unfortunate."

"It's worse than unfortunate, I can assure you." Trenwick shook his head and leaned on his desk in utter defeat. "Can you imagine what others must be saying about a man who cannot secure a match for his eligible daughter? Her fortune is enough, her accomplishments are enough, her looks are enough. She ought to be more than enough for any gentleman to wish for in a wife."

Aubrey nodded sagely, as what was being said was true, however little he cared about it.

"If only I could find a suitable man who would not care about something as sentimental as romance or the like. It would be a very simple and straightforward business venture, and nothing more. I would welcome any such sensible man."

Aubrey's stomach clenched in sudden apprehension and the perspiration of dread prickled at the back of his neck. Surely Trenwick wasn't about to suggest...

"But alas," Trenwick sighed, "none have come forward." He shook his head again and looked at Aubrey. "Which is why I cannot go back to Europe, much as I should like to."

"And Lady Trenwick?" Aubrey asked before he could stop himself. "What does she think?"

Trenwick smiled tightly. "Lady Trenwick and I mutually benefit from my remaining on the Continent. She agrees with me."

With that tone, Aubrey wouldn't have been at all surprised if Lady Trenwick had no choice but to agree with him. She likely hadn't been given an opportunity for any opinion on the subject whatsoever. In which case, it was entirely probable that she *did* agree with him by this point, ironically enough.

How did any couple in the world endure matrimony at all? Between his parents and the Trenwicks, Aubrey had been raised with a particularly poor impression of the state, and nothing at all to recommend it.

Not that thoughts of matrimony had any place in his mind at the present. In this room. In this house. With an eligible woman living within. A deuced attractive one, but that was neither here nor there.

It really wasn't.

"What can I do to assist you, my lord?" Aubrey asked in the most polite, most bland tone possible. "I have no recommendations to give you for potential suitors for Miss Morledge, I know little of London Society. And as for Withrow..."

"Oh, I don't expect you to know what to do for my daughter,

Ingram," Trenwick interrupted with a scoff. "I doubt anyone can truly help me there, but I have set some plans in motion to correct the situation, if all goes according to my wishes."

If all... What? How could he possibly have plans for Grace if he just admitted to not having any gentlemen willing to take her off his hands?

Trenwick cleared his throat, and his expression eased into an almost comfortable expression. "But Withrow is another matter entirely."

Aubrey raised a brow. "Indeed? In what respect? Surely you don't think me in need of two estates in the same county and in such proximity."

"Of course not, of course not." Trenwick tapped his fingers against the smooth wood of his little-used desk. "But you've spent a deal of time at Breyerly. Much of your time, I expect."

"You are correct," Aubrey acknowledged with a nod. "As you may recall, my father was not particularly adept when it came to managing our estate, though he managed to keep from losing the bulk of our fortune."

Trenwick winced. "I did warn him, you know. Poor man."

Aubrey smirked at that. "I doubt he listened to a word, but I appreciate the attempt. At any rate, the last several years have been spent working tirelessly with my steward and the estate manager to rebuild the estate's prosperity and increase her holdings, if possible. We've certainly managed to do that, and Breyerly is flourishing. Truth be told, my lord, I do not know quite how to behave in London, I have spent so long in the country laboring for my tenants."

"That speaks well of your character, Ingram," Trenwick said with an approving nod. "It's good to have the trust and respect of your tenants. It engenders loyalty among them, which ensures they will work hard for you for many years. You must be fair but firm with them, or you will find yourself in the same poor straits as your father."

It would take a good deal more than being too friendly with his tenants to sink him that far, but Aubrey would leave that bit of insight unsaid. How could Trenwick offer him such advice on estate matters, when he, himself, had abandoned his estate and tenants without so much as a fare-thee-well, or any explanation at all?

Aubrey knew all too well how the tenants felt about Trenwick; they had come to him and his estate manager often. Unfortunately, there was no land to spare on Breyerly for the poor farmers begging to become his tenants, though it was not for want of trying.

And he most certainly did not need two estates to manage, now that he'd finally salvaged one.

"So, from one landowner to another, what can I do to make Withrow more appealing for prospective buyers? I haven't set foot there in years, but my estate manager has been taking care of upkeep, so the house should be well enough off."

Trenwick needed a new estate manager. The house was in shambles, gaping holes in the roof, and anything that could find its way within to inhabit the place had done so. It was an eyesore and the land had turned wild but for the farms that were still carefully kept by those who had not found other options for themselves.

He wanted improvements? The only improvement Aubrey could think of would be to raze the house entirely and sell the land. Yet he couldn't tell him that. Mad as it was, Aubrey still had an attachment to Withrow, and all the memories there.

So, he smiled at the older man and drummed his fingers restlessly against each other. "Have you considered the younger gentlemen, sir? Those without appealing prospects for a young woman might benefit from such an opportunity. And if you play your cards right, if you'll permit the phrase, you might find you kill two birds with one stone."

Trenwick's eyes lit up and his mouth curved. "Indeed, Lord Ingram? Well, that is a thought I certainly hadn't considered before. Intriguing notion…"

Chapter Five

———— ⌘ ————

There are ideas and there are good ideas. And then there are ridiculous, foolhardy, utterly moronic ideas that do absolutely nothing to credit the intelligence of the one unfortunate enough to speak it. Listeners must try not to berate such a person, for surely they are in need of some assistance and education to prevent such an expression.

-*The Spinster Chronicles, 16 September 1818*

"I'm sorry, your father wants you to do *what?*"

"Shh!" Grace insisted, looking around at the various guests as she and Charlotte strode arm in arm into the ballroom of the Campbells, their hosts for the evening. "The last thing I need is to draw attention to myself, especially given… you know."

Charlotte tugged her closer, fixing her usual public smile on her face and nodding at the few people smiling at her in greeting.

"You mean to tell me," Charlotte continued through gritted teeth, her tone far less pleasant than her smile, "that your father is literally having you inspected… for faults."

"Yes." There really was nothing more to say on the subject, as that summed the mess up quite nicely.

Grace felt Charlotte stiffen beside her, and glanced over to see her friend glowering darkly, no longer playing at politeness for her usual audience. And people were staring.

"Charlotte…" Grace murmured.

Charlotte exhaled roughly through her nose. "Some people need to spend quality time at the receiving end of an aggressive and especially thick tree branch applied to particularly sensitive areas." Charlotte flicked her eyes to Grace, smiling very tightly. "Even if he is your father."

Grace bit her lip to keep from laughing and shook her head. "This is why I love you."

"I thought you hated my impertinence and vocal contempt for convention."

"It's a complicated relationship. At the moment, I quite adore it." Grace grinned and pulled at Charlotte's arm. "Now, stop glowering where everybody can see."

Charlotte's face instantly transformed, but her eyes held the same coolness. "It's astounding how much more difficult this expression is when I feel quite the reverse. It actually pains me."

"How you must suffer."

They moved around the edges of the ballroom towards Lady Hetty, who was their usual marker for a gathering place at such events, noticing Prue and Izzy already seated there. Their husbands were nowhere to be seen, which was a blessing. Not that Camden Vale and Sebastian Morton were a trial to endure, but Grace did not need them to hear what she had to share with the others. She really did not need their opinions on the subject.

She was already worried about what the rest of the Spinsters would say.

Or Lady Hetty.

The ladies saw them approach and smiled in welcome. Then Izzy frowned. "Oh dear. What is the trouble?"

"How do you know there is trouble?" Grace asked with a nod to Lady Hetty, who only grunted at her.

Izzy gave her a knowing look. "You look strained. You are smiling, but it's quite forced." She patted the seat next to her, and Grace took it, releasing Charlotte's arm as her friend came to stand before them.

Charlotte let her expression fall again and sighed, rubbing at her cheeks. "Ouch."

"Why so f-forced?" Prue inquired, looking a trifle anxious.

Charlotte shook her head quickly. "Don't make her say it yet.

Wait for the others so she won't need to repeat it."

"Repeat what?" Georgie asked as she approached on Tony's arm.

Grace looked at her with a weak smile. "My father has a plan."

Georgie's eyes widened, and she looked at her husband. "Go elsewhere, please."

Tony snorted and bowed to the Spinsters. "I trust someone will inform me of the situation when it is necessary for me to be made aware."

"You hope, you mean," Charlotte muttered good-naturedly, waving him off.

Tony gave her a playful glower and walked away, shaking his head.

Charlotte grinned at the rest. "I love doing that to him."

"I'll be sure to inform him," Georgie replied with a soft snort, sitting beside Grace and looking at her fondly.

Grace tried to return the smile, but it faltered.

"Oh dear," Georgie murmured, reaching out to cover Grace's hand with her own. "Should we wait for Elinor or...?"

"Heavens no," Charlotte protested as her hands formed fists at her side. "The child will make a scene. Get this out of the way, Grace, and then we can tell Elinor and Edith at our next meeting."

Grace nodded, swallowing with some difficulty. "My father is in London."

"What?"

"What?"

"Since when?"

"That's unfortunate."

Grace coughed a laugh, as the last interjection had been from Lady Hetty. Traditionally, Lady Hetty did not like Grace as much as she liked the rest, allegedly because she could not pinpoint why it was that Grace was a spinster like the others. In her mind, there must have been some treachery of sorts.

It wasn't; it was simply the unfortunate truth of things.

"My mother and your father are in London at the same time?" Prue said without a hint of stammer. She scoffed quietly. "That's unheard of."

Charlotte looked green. "I feel the overwhelming desire to pray at this moment." She swallowed and waved a hand at Grace. "Tell them the rest. It gets much worse."

"Worse?" Lady Hetty remarked in a wry tone. "How can that be?"

Strangely enough, Grace took the comment as an improvement of her relationship with Lady Hetty, and she met the older woman's gaze squarely. "My father has decided that the only solution to finding out what is wrong with me and get me married off is to have someone come into our home and study me thoroughly over the course of several days or weeks."

Lady Hetty's brow furrowed. "To what point and purpose?"

Grace smiled weakly. "To find my faults."

Her brow cleared, and her eyes widened. "You cannot be serious."

Grace nodded once. "Entirely, I'm afraid. He's having his solicitor bring suitable candidates for the position in for interviews with him to find someone that will suit his needs."

Georgie's hold on Grace's hand clenched hard and Grace looked at her friend. Georgie's jaw was taut and her eyes blazing. "He wouldn't dare."

"He would," Charlotte and Grace said at the same time. They shared the same wan smile.

"F-find your f-faults?" Prue repeated, stammering slightly, showing how distressed she truly was. "And h-have someone make a s-study of you?"

Izzy put her hand over Prue's, though her expression was just as troubled. "When would he expect this to start?"

Grace lifted a shoulder. "As soon as he finds someone acceptable for the position, I expect."

"It's like finding a ruddy governess," Charlotte muttered as she fidgeted with a ringlet near her ear.

"How would you know?" Izzy asked with a laugh that almost sounded natural.

Charlotte gave her a look. "I went through many, many governesses. By the end, Papa had me sitting in for the interviews and asking the questions. Believe me, I am more than familiar with the process of application there."

Grace tried to smile, but found her eyes prickling with tears instead, as well as a faint tremor she could not seem to rid herself of. Sharing this secret with her friends had somehow brought the painful truth from a purely theoretical situation into reality. The shame of having to be analyzed and continually criticized by someone who likely didn't know her just to prove a point to her father was more than she could bear. It hadn't even begun yet, and she already felt humiliated. How much worse would things get when she was actually in the process of being critiqued?

Izzy noticed and squeezed Grace's hand gently. "Don't worry, dear. We'll find a way to take care of this."

"How?" Grace asked. "My father is determined that this is the only way. He will bring in some sanctimonious miser who will waste no time criticizing the shape of my nose, and all of my self-respect will be brought to dust blow by blow."

"Then we provide him with a more sympathetic option in an assessor!" Georgie insisted firmly. She immediately glanced about the room. "Someone that your father would be unable to disapprove of."

Grace sniffed without humor. "That is such a short list, I don't even know who is on it."

"There's a list?" Charlotte asked with surprise. "Astounding. I didn't think he approved of anyone."

"Again, rather like my mother," Prue mused with a smile. "Except she approves of Charlotte."

Charlotte gave her a cold look. "What have I told you about curses, Prudence Vale? I don't deserve such an iniquitous accusation."

Grace smiled but said nothing. She believed in Georgie's sincerity in helping her, and believed she truly thought this would work, but she knew better.

Nothing would work. No one would work.

"Oh, Lord Ingram!"

Good lord, she wouldn't...

But of course she would. She was Georgie.

Aubrey came over to their group, smiling with genuine warmth at Georgie. "Mrs. Sterling, what a delight to see you! And you are looking so well. Such loveliness."

Georgie smirked in a knowing way. "I do hope you remember that when you hear what I'm about to suggest."

Aubrey raised a brow, still only looking at Georgie. "Oh?"

Please say no… Please say no…

"You must help us discover why Grace is a spinster."

Aubrey was quite sure he hadn't heard the deranged woman correctly. He flicked his gaze to Grace quickly, who looked as horrified as he felt.

That was something, at least. Clearly this wasn't her idea.

"I beg your pardon?" he asked as he returned his focus to Georgie.

Her mouth curved in a wry smile. "I do believe you heard me correctly, my lord."

"I was afraid you were going to say that," he muttered, wishing he were anywhere else at the moment. He looked at the other ladies and smiled. "Apologies, ladies. Mrs. Sterling, if you would…"

Georgie rolled her eyes and quickly made the introductions, though Aubrey certainly knew who each of them were. A delay was all he really needed just now. Something to allow him to collect his thoughts and create an appropriate rebuttal.

"And Grace Morledge I believe you know," Georgie finished simply, smiling at her friend.

Grace did not return her smile, and stared without shame, a faint wrinkle appearing between her brows.

"I do, yes," Aubrey admitted. He bowed to Grace slightly. "How are you, Miss Morledge?"

"Fine," she replied in a very faint voice, finally looking at him. "Thank you."

Charlotte Wright huffed loudly. "No, she is most certainly *not* fine, Lord Ingram. Not with the episodic torture that awaits her."

"Really, Charlotte," Mrs. Morton scolded with a surprising degree of impatience.

"You have a better name for it?"

Lady Hetty made a sharp hmph of a sound. "I thought it was perfectly apt."

"D-don't encourage her," Mrs. Vale pleaded.

Aubrey would dearly love to escape this ridiculous exchange between spinsters and former spinsters and flee to another corner of the room. Even marriage hungry mamas would be preferable to this.

"Don't you agree, Lord Ingram, that a father should take care of his daughter and not expose her to gossip and ridicule?" Miss Wright asked rather pointedly.

Aubrey swallowed. "Yes... I suppose..."

"And don't you agree that if the father has plans for his daughter that would subject her to those things, something should be done to circumvent those plans?"

"I..."

Aubrey suddenly found himself without words, without any proper thought, let alone one he could relate aloud. He was being trapped; he could feel it. The world was closing in around him in the form of spinsters, and he would never be able to escape from their clutches.

His chest actually began to ache and quiver in panic.

"Georgiana, do kindly explain the situation for Lord Ingram," Lady Hetty said with a wave of her hand. "Without the dramatics and hypothetical scenarios Charlotte seems so keen on, if you please."

Miss Wright made a soft sound of offense, though Aubrey sensed there was none taken.

"Please don't," Grace whispered, her cheeks flaming.

Oddly enough, no one seemed to hear her but him. And he had heard her quite clearly.

What could possibly be so horrible as to warrant these antics from her friends and such a reaction from her?

Georgie nodded and smiled a very thin, not-quite-polite smile. "It seems, my lord, that Lord Trenwick has decided that the best course of action for Grace and her inexplicable unmarried state is to bring in a veritable stranger to assess her for faults, errors, and flaws."

Aubrey blinked at her, then pointedly looked at Grace. "Tell me she is lying."

Grace's slender throat worked on a harsh swallow. Then she shook her head, averting her eyes at once.

Various curses in several languages passed through his mind at a rapid pace. He hadn't thought Trenwick this idiotic. He knew the man was a bit stiff in his views and expectations, and certainly eccentric in the manner with which he handled situations, or his own life, but never this.

An overwhelming sense of pity filled him as he continued to look at Grace. Perfect goddess or not, she did not deserve this.

No one did.

He opened his mouth to offer his condolences when Georgie spoke again.

"So, in an effort to prevent poor Grace from being a spectacle for analysis by some curmudgeon with outdated ideals and expectations, we want to find someone that might be more suited to our needs." She smiled at Aubrey in encouragement. "Hence, I have called upon you."

Aubrey stared at Georgie for another long moment. "Wouldn't having someone more suited to your needs defeat Trenwick's purpose? He'd be bound to find out."

"That's a fair point," Mrs. Morton conceded, her tone laced with worry.

Lady Hetty coughed. "It would not defeat anything if the person actually looked for flaws."

Aubrey turned to the older woman almost wildly. "So, this person would still do the task assigned them? How does that help Miss Morledge at all?" He glanced at Grace quickly. "Pardon the harsh tone, Miss Morledge, this has nothing to do with you personally."

Grace gave him a mixture of a nod and a shake of her head, which he took to be encouraging.

"It helps Grace," Miss Wright insisted with a particularly sharp tone, "because this person will not be so severe about the task as to crush her spirits and break her soul, does *that* satisfy you?"

Aubrey gave her a careful look. She was terrifying, outspoken, and disrespectful of position, rank, or influence.

He liked her immensely.

"Mildly," he replied. He returned his attention to Grace, noting anything of interest. The color in her cheeks, the faint tremor to her frame, the slight pulling at her full lips, the roundness of her eyes…

She hadn't appeared so when he had called upon them the other day, though he was quite sure she had known about this ridiculous plan before he called. Which meant that this reaction was entirely because of him.

She didn't want him to do this.

For some reason, that was significant. He hadn't wanted to take on this madness as it was, but the fact that Grace was so clearly against it settled the fact.

But he could not admit that. These women were likely to pounce on such a statement and take it as a confession of love that he had noticed such a thing, which would only torment he and Grace further, and then he would *have* to agree to find fault with her purely to avoid the abuse.

He made himself sigh and shake his head. "I am terribly sorry, ladies, but I am a gentleman. I cannot in good conscience intentionally seek out the faults of any woman, let alone one of such quality. I won't."

He saw Grace's shoulders move on an exhale and knew his suspicions had been correct. Well, that made two of them that were relieved at the moment.

Georgie, however, looked speculative. "This will not be the last you hear of this, Ingram."

"But it will be the only answer you will hear, madam," he informed her. Then he scowled. "And don't get your husband to pester me about it. You have no idea how annoying that is."

An odd hum came from Miss Wright, and he turned to her briefly.

"I like you, Ingram," she said, her lips curving in satisfaction. "Disappointing though your answer is, I like you."

He bowed. "I will take that as a great compliment, Miss Wright."

"I w-wouldn't," Mrs. Vale offered in a voice so soft he almost missed it.

Miss Wright glared at her friend. "Excuse me, Prudence? Now is not the time for you to miraculously turn candid."

Sensing there was no need for him to remain among the group for the present, he bowed to them all in general. Then he locked eyes with Grace, fought the urge to offer a consoling smile, and nodded.

She swallowed, then dipped her chin in a nod.

Which, coming from a goddess, nearly made his knees do unspeakable things.

Damned traitorous things, knees.

Aubrey wrenched himself away before the sudden knee-betrayal became evident to anyone, and quickly moved on to dancing with a wallflower inhabiting the wall opposite of the Spinsters. Mindless dancing would be just the thing to keep him away from the schemes of Georgie Sterling and her cohorts. He would simply stay occupied for as long as he must remain at the Campbells', and then make his exit as soon as it was polite to do so.

Or he could go to the card room. Plenty of gentlemen did that, and it would be an easy enough occupation. He'd never been particularly adept at cards, but he was not precisely abysmal at them, either.

Dancing or cards, cards or dancing…

Or he could socialize.

He nearly laughed aloud at himself. He hadn't properly socialized in his entire adult life, and he most certainly was not going to start at an event like this.

But he probably should converse with the young woman he was dancing with. She didn't need to suspect that he was only dancing with her to avoid being cornered again. It wasn't her fault that she'd been conveniently located for his needs.

So, he attempted to converse.

As it happened, there was a reason she was a wallflower.

Which suited him just as well. Every now and then, he would say something, and she would respond, and then they would enjoy dancing in silence. They both seemed to be enjoying dancing in silence.

Well. Perhaps he should marry this rather intelligent, sensible woman.

He looked at her and forced himself to focus. She was certainly attractive enough to avoid being labeled as plain, but not attractive enough to be a diamond of the first water. Rather agreeable for a potential wife. She danced well, did not giggle, and had a pleasing smile. Her voice was mellow in tone, her figure was better than average, and she dressed sensibly while still adhering to current fashions for such an event.

Yes, he could very well marry this girl.

If he could remember her name.

That should probably have been his focus from the start.

Ah, well. He would not be rushing off to get the banns read, after all.

The dance came to a close, and he bowed, escorted his partner to the wall he had plucked her from, then started towards the card room. With any luck, he would find a table of players more abysmal than himself and win a little pocket money.

"Ingram!"

Lord, have mercy on his soul...

He turned with a polite smile to see Tony and Francis approaching, Tony wearing an expression of speculation, Francis looking more resigned. "Gentlemen, would you care to join me for a game of cards?"

"Why not?" Francis replied, smiling a little.

"Why were you dancing with Emma Young?" Tony demanded as he fell in next to Aubrey.

Aubrey gave his friend a look. "Because she was there. And thank you for the reminder of her name, I had quite forgotten."

Francis barked a laugh, which he covered quickly.

Tony was less amused. "What do you mean, she was there?"

"Just as I said. She was there and I had the desire to dance."

"Leave him alone, Tony," Francis urged in delight. "He can dance with someone without an impending proposal."

Tony scowled at his cousin. "Fine. Fair enough." He looked at Aubrey with the same resignation Francis had worn moments ago. "Apologies. But why dance with someone just on a whim? You hate dancing, unless your opinions have changed there."

"I do hate dancing, for the most part," Aubrey confirmed as they entered the card room. He dropped his voice to avoid being overheard. "I had to dance because your wife was going to

59

commandeer every ounce of dignity and self-respect I have in a foolhardy scheme."

Tony smirked. "That sounds like Georgie."

"Certainly does," Francis agreed. "What was the scheme?"

Aubrey hesitated, debating over the matter in his mind. It wasn't his story to tell, and it had the potential to seriously upset Grace if it were made known, even if she trusted Tony and Francis enough. He couldn't hurt her, couldn't spread her situation about like gossip. Though he would admit to never being particularly close with Grace, he had too much respect for her and her family to make light of any of this. Even if her friends with good intentions might.

She would have to be the one to tell them.

He would not.

"It doesn't bear repeating," he said at last. "Now, whist or loo, gentlemen?"

Chapter Six

Sometimes what we most fear comes to pass, and there is nothing to be done about it.

-The Spinster Chronicles, 14 December 1816

"Sir, you have a missive."

Aubrey looked up from his breakfast yet again to stare at his butler with the utmost disgruntlement. "Locke, can you not see that I am eating? Or rather *trying* to eat, as I have yet to manage one single bite?"

"I can see, sir. But the missive remains."

Locke was very carefully avoiding looking at Aubrey directly, and his expression was completely impassive.

Wise man.

"Fine," Aubrey snapped, taking the missive from the tray and setting it on the table. "But I am not reading it until I've eaten something."

Locke inclined his head. "As you wish, sir. It matters not to me when you read it, only to see it delivered in a timely manner."

The almost impertinent response made Aubrey sit back in his chair and eye his butler curiously. "Timely would have been after I had eaten, would it not?"

"No, sir."

"You sure?"

"Quite sure, sir."

"Absolutely certain?"

"Completely, sir."

Incredible. The man did not flinch in the face of needling provocation.

Aubrey grinned up at him. "Thank you, Locke. You may go."

Locke nodded, then turned towards the door.

"A moment, Locke. Who is this from, do you know?"

"Lord Trenwick, sir."

Aubrey turned his attention to the missive, his eyes wide and staring as though the paper was about to burst into flames and start speaking to him.

Where Trenwick was concerned, that sort of thing might just occur.

Whatever contents lay within that folded missive would surely curdle his stomach in some direction or another. But Trenwick was also the sort to send repeated messages if his first was not precipitously responded to.

So, he had to read it and respond.

Aubrey groaned and shoveled some of his breakfast into his mouth before his appetite could flee completely, as it was threatening to do. Sure enough, a few bites in and he could not stomach another morsel.

Cursed Trenwick.

He sighed and reached for the missive, scowling darkly. He broke the seal, though it took two attempts, and scanned the very brief contents.

It would be much appreciated if you would call upon me today at your earliest convenience.

Trenwick

Aubrey blinked at the single line, then turned the paper over to check for any additional information.

There was none.

He heaved another sigh, this one accompanied by a groan, and slouched inelegantly in his chair, making a face. He did *not* want to call upon Trenwick, he did *not* want to know what this was all about, and he most certainly did *not* want to risk seeing Grace after that uncomfortable evening at the Campbells'. In fact, he had been strictly avoiding any opportunity that could even remotely risk him seeing Grace.

Venturing into her house would certainly increase that risk exponentially.

His eyes widened, and a choking sensation gripped him.

Oh *lord*. What if that was what Trenwick wanted to discuss? What if he wanted to seek Aubrey's counsel on the matter, or worse, include him in it?

Had Georgie gotten to Trenwick and planted the idea in his head? No, that was ridiculous. The Spinsters, as a group, despised Trenwick, and Georgie would certainly never venture so far as to tell Trenwick what to do, especially concerning Grace.

Still, he felt remarkably uneasy. He could not honestly refuse to call on Trenwick, as there was always a chance the exchange might have nothing at all to do with his plans for Grace, but he found himself wishing most fervently that he would suddenly be struck with a malicious fever. Or perhaps even the pox.

But not in any visible places. No need to mar his appearance for the sake of avoidance.

He looked down at himself and threw his hands up. He'd not thought he'd be going anywhere today, so he'd had Sundrey dress him comfortably. The sort of look that was typical for his life at Breyerly.

This would never do for Trenwick, unless he wished to receive a fatherly scolding for improper dress for a lord.

Which, of course, he did not.

He pushed out of his chair and moved out of the room. "Sundrey! Sundrey, I need to change!"

Minutes later, Aubrey was in the carriage and rolling on towards Trenwick House.

"Sorry, my lord, I cannot oblige you," he recited as he fidgeted with his gloves.

Trenwick would never accept that.

Aubrey shook his head. "My lord, I wish I could help, but…"

No, that was a lie, and there was no point pretending otherwise. "No."

There. That ought to be simple enough.

Well, hope was eternal, at least.

He stepped out of the carriage just as it pulled up to Trenwick House, not waiting for it to completely stop. Once this was over with, whatever it was, he could get on with his day and his life. He only needed to stand his ground, if what he suspected was about to be, and resist the urge to tell the old man what a stupid mistake he was making.

Surely, he could manage all of that.

Bennett had clearly been instructed to expect Aubrey, for his arrival was met without any surprise or additional attentions. He was immediately escorted to Trenwick's study, though Aubrey could easily remember the way from his visit the other day. But butlers were always so intent on doing the tasks that fell within their stewardship, so he would just let Bennett fulfill that role.

Trenwick was seated at his desk and looked up at their entry. He rose with surprising swiftness. "Ingram. Good, good, you got my message."

Aubrey smiled thinly. "Yes, my lord. Though there was little enough to go on within its contents."

"That was intentional." Trenwick nodded at Bennett. "Thank you, Bennett, you may go."

Bennett shuffled out the door, shutting it behind him.

Suddenly, Aubrey was filled with the oddest notion that he was trapped.

He cleared his throat. "Intentional, sir? For what purpose, may I ask?"

Trenwick exhaled and gestured for Aubrey to sit. "Something quite sensitive, Ingram. My daughter, Grace."

Hellfire and damnation...

"I have settled it," Trenwick continued, oblivious to Aubrey's current state of death, "that in order for Grace to marry and cease with her troubling spinsterhood, the only true course is for a thorough examination to be completed."

Good lord, he truly believed this.

"Of?" Aubrey managed.

Trenwick gave him a markedly sardonic look. "Of Grace, of

course."

There was no "of course" about it. Nothing about examining a young woman as though she were a horse at Tattersall's was even close to an obvious course of action, particularly from a father.

"Is that truly the best course?" Aubrey asked, taking great care that his tone should remain mild. "Surely..."

"Give me one reason why my daughter is a spinster, Ingram."

Aubrey's mouth dropped, and it took a moment for him to close it. Frantically, his mind searched for any reason, anything at all that he could say.

But there was nothing. Everything about Grace from the surface was nothing short of perfection. Even he could admit that, though he had no personal stake in it.

"I'm afraid I do not know Miss Morledge well enough to give you an answer, Trenwick," he admitted, grateful that his deferral was actually accurate truth.

Unfortunately, Trenwick smiled. "Exactly. That is why you must be the one to examine her."

There were not enough profanities in any language to adequately curse that statement.

"Assess your daughter for flaws, sir?" Aubrey shook his head very firmly. "I cannot. It goes against everything a respectable gentleman stands for."

Trenwick slammed his fist on his desk. "Dammit, man, don't you think I know that? But I have no other option! The longer we prolong it, the more of a pariah she will become. I cannot face my peers or Society without the shame of my daughter following me. I cannot be ashamed of my own daughter, Ingram. We *must* discover what is wrong with her so that it can be mended! She needs to secure a favorable match for our future to be equally secure."

Aubrey blinked at the sudden passion and felt queasy that Trenwick considered his daughter's unmarried state to be a stain upon the entire family. That somehow her securing a match would relieve him of whatever bleak future he saw for the family as a whole. The man had three sons, for pity's sake, and daughter already married.

Why should Grace bear the burden of all this?

Aubrey pressed his tongue to the roof of his mouth in thought.

"I cannot see how I am an appropriate choice for this endeavor, sir. I am not many years beyond the age of Miss Morledge, and my experience in the accomplishments and behaviors of Society ladies is singularly lacking."

"I don't need Grace to be compared to other young ladies of the day," Trenwick insisted. "I know full well she is more accomplished than the vast majority of them. Trust me, we spared no expense in her education in that regard, and her instructors sent me regular and detailed reports. I need her *flaws* to be discovered. You have an eye for detail, Ingram, you are impeccable in your business affairs, you are honest in your dealings, and with your tenants."

Yes, he was, but…

"And you are not close enough to Grace to be overly sympathetic to her plight."

Also, technically true, but…

"You must see that you are the obvious choice."

Yes, he supposed he must, but…

Wait, what?

"Obvious choice?" Aubrey repeated slowly. "I cannot see why."

Trenwick raised his brows. "I've just explained it."

Not adequately. Not convincingly. Not enough.

"My reputation would be destroyed if anyone knew that I was intentionally looking for faults in your daughter, sir," Aubrey told him, letting a sharp note enter his voice. "I have to consider that above all else. And my calling upon your daughter would lead to speculation about us, and I cannot have that hanging over me, no matter how I respect you or your daughter."

Something flashed in Trenwick's eyes and a light of victory appeared, though Aubrey had not given him any sort of favorable answer. "We can come up with a feasible explanation, Ingram. No one will need to know what the true purpose is here."

Aubrey shook his head, the trapped feeling increasing and causing panic to swell. "My lord, surely there are others…"

A paper was slid across the desk, as though this was anticipated. "You are the best choice. But my solicitor has given me a few other names, should we fail with you."

With all the reluctance in the world, Aubrey reached for the paper and read over the list.

Then he swallowed and folded the paper, meeting Trenwick's eyes. "When would you like me to start, sir?"

"Why didn't anyone tell me this?"

Charlotte gave Elinor a disparaging look. "Because we knew you would react like this. Sit down, you're making me nervous with all your flailing and pacing."

Elinor looked at Charlotte, then turned to the rest in bewilderment. "How are you all so calm about this?"

"Because we've had a week to process and adjust to the idea," Izzy reminded her in her eternally calming voice.

It didn't calm Elinor. She jabbed a finger in Edith's direction. "Edith only just found out. She hasn't had time to process and adjust either!"

"And yet, she is not raging as you are," Charlotte mused mockingly.

Elinor's brow furrowed, and she whirled to face Edith. "Why are you not as upset as I am?"

Edith took a careful sip of her tea before answering. "Because I am more concerned about Grace than the fact that she is currently being subjected to an indignity by her father. I know something of that myself," she added in an undertone.

The room of Spinsters stared at her in stunned silence.

Grace couldn't believe her ears. Edith had shared very little with them about her past or her situation, let alone her family. Her father had treated her poorly, as well?

Edith looked at Grace with sympathy and understanding, smiling slightly. "No matter what happens, lass, we will be here for you."

Unbidden, tears sprang to Grace's eyes. "Thank you."

"Oh, don't make us cry!" Prue begged, dabbing at the corners of her eyes.

"Seconded," Georgie offered from the sofa. "I despise crying. It makes me look a mess."

They all laughed at that, even Elinor, and she moved back to her seat, plucking a biscuit from the tea tray before she did so. "Well, I say shame on your father."

A weak smile flickered on Grace's face. "My one comfort is that he has not found a suitable candidate yet."

"Thank God for that," Izzy murmured.

Charlotte scowled. "I still think Georgie had it right. Lord Ingram would have done quite well and could have been turned to our side."

"That wasn't why I asked him," Georgie insisted.

Grace's cheeks flamed as her friends continued to banter over the idea of Lord Ingram as her designated faultfinder. She had never been more grateful than when Aubrey had refused to do as Georgie bid. It was one thing to have someone examine her for faults. It was quite another to have *him* do it.

He, whom she had followed around like a puppy in childhood. He, who had taught her the proper way to climb trees. He, who had been her very first dance partner when her brothers refused.

He, who had captured her childish heart.

Oh, the thought of him being the one to do her father's bidding was beyond anything. It was worse than the idea of her being examined at all.

Not that she knew him now. She hadn't had a real conversation with him in perhaps ten years, and she knew full well there had been nothing praiseworthy in that conversation on either side. He had always been closer with her sister, as they were of an age, and Anne and Grace had never particularly gotten on. Lord only knew how Aubrey had tolerated Grace following him around as she had done. But he had never said anything on the subject, for which she was grateful now.

It made no difference, she supposed. Aubrey had refused Georgie, so there was nothing to be done about it. Aubrey would continue to be polite in public, and Grace would do likewise. He might call on occasion, as their families were friends, and that would be the extent of it.

Perfectly polite, and no fault-finding.

"Well, we shall see," Georgie finally said, smirking suspiciously.

Grace frowned at her friend, wishing she had followed the conversation. Were they still talking about Aubrey? Had they moved on to another topic? Were they going back to talk of the Chronicles again? They'd already settled who would write which article, and there couldn't be more to discuss.

She glanced at the clock, then exhaled, rising. "I fear I must return home, my dears. Mama will want a full report, and we have a very small window of opportunity, what with Father lurking about."

Charlotte grinned without hesitation. "He doesn't know you're a Spinster?"

Grace smiled back. "He doesn't even know about the Spinsters. Bennett has been taking care to provide him with alternate newssheets on the days the Chronicles come out. He hasn't noticed yet, and he never goes out in Society, so he won't hear of it easily."

"But he will eventually," Prue reminded her, her eyes wide with meaning. "They always find out our secrets."

"I know," Grace admitted. "But until he does, I will enjoy every moment of his ignorance."

She nodded to them all, then swept out of the drawing room and down to her carriage. Then, she was off towards home, praying her father would continue to be shut up in his study as he had been doing since his return. Any time he was at home, he was in his study. If he was out, he was with his solicitors or investigating certain business investments.

The family never particularly missed having him about.

Well, James did tend to complain about it, but he imagined himself his father's apprentice, and the neglect was wearing on him.

However, it was perfect for Grace. Especially when she wished to have her regular tea and conversation with her mother. One where there were no limits on the topics of discussion, and they could laugh at whatever volume they pleased.

Not that they had accomplished that as yet, but she could hope.

The house was surprisingly quiet as she entered. Even Bennett was somewhat subdued as he took her things, and he left before she could ask where her mother was.

Odd. Bennett had taken to being particularly kind to her since her father's arrival, sometimes straying into familiarity, which her father would have despised.

She shrugged and moved towards the parlor, hoping her mother would already be waiting for her there. They needed to discuss these teas of theirs and see if there was another location within the house where they might be able to meet as before without disturbing her father.

A door opened as she passed by, and a few footsteps were heard. "Grace?"

Blast.

She turned to face her father with the almost smile she saved for him alone. "Father."

"I am pleased you've returned," he told her, clasping his hands behind his back.

"I wasn't aware that my return came with an announcement of it," she replied, turning her smile cheeky to avoid being scolded.

He missed the humor and the impertinence. "I had Bennett inform me of your arrival."

Grace lost her false humor and any politeness. "I didn't realize that you'd been waiting for me, sir, or I would have been more expeditious in my return."

Her father shook his head slowly. "No, no, my dear girl, I have no desire to interfere with your social agenda. It is good for a young woman, or one not so young, to engage with other women."

Well, she could have done without *that* specific addition.

Wait... he'd never called her his dear girl in her life.

"With whom were you visiting today?" he asked, still smiling very politely. "Someone of influence and importance, I hope."

Grace nodded in familiar obedience. "Yes, Father. I was at the home of Charlotte Wright again."

He nodded in satisfaction. "Ah, yes. I am so pleased you are associating with her, Grace. It is most satisfactory to your reputation."

Yes, her reputation. Clearly the most important part of her.

"She is one of my dearest friends, Father," she admitted with a real honesty she did not usually employ with her father.

He bowed slightly to lean closer. "Even better."

Charlotte would most certainly *not* be pleased to hear how

approved of she was by her father. Grace might keep that secret for some time.

"You were waiting for me," Grace reminded her father. "Do you need something?"

Her father straightened and nodded repeatedly. "Ah, yes, yes, thank you for bringing me back to topic. You will recall, I hope, the discussion we had not long ago about a plan I was implementing to assist us in your search for a husband."

Grace swallowed, her hands turning cold. "I do recall, yes."

"My solicitor has been very dedicated in his research to find someone suitable for the position. After all, we must have someone respectable, knowledgeable, and discreet." He smiled in what was undoubtedly supposed to be an encouraging manner. "We don't want word of this getting out and about in Society, now do we?"

Was she supposed to answer that question? Of course, she didn't want word of this getting out! She didn't even want to do this! If word got out that she was being examined, it would ruin her reputation and actually devastate her chances of marrying at all.

Ever.

"Unfortunately," her father sighed, "I was unable to agree with any of those candidates. Poor Mr. Hayes was so disappointed."

Hope burst into flame within her, and she clamped her hands together to prevent herself from showing her delight. "So... we will not be going forward, then?"

Her father smiled a satisfied smile that doused her hope in one swift stroke. "No, my dear, we are moving forward. You see, I have found someone far more perfect for the task than any of the options Hayes brought me."

Grace's stomach clenched and dropped at the same time. "You have."

A nod. "I have." He turned slightly, exposing the door of his study.

She held her breath. Waited. Hoped. Dreaded.

A man exited the study, his hands behind his back, a hesitant, almost apologetic smile on his handsome face.

Aubrey Flint, Lord Ingram.

If only it were ladylike to spit.

Chapter Seven

———

If one has a particular position on a certain topic, one must stand by it, and express it with all of the fervency and passion that one feels. Within polite constraints, of course. We must not turn wild for the sake of our positions, after all.

-The Spinster Chronicles, 11 November 1817

"What are you doing? Just what exactly do you think you are doing?"

"Saving you?"

"Wrong!"

"Is it?" Aubrey queried. "Is it really?"

"Don't make light of this!" Grace snapped. "I have never been more humiliated in my entire life!"

"That this is happening, or that it is me?"

"Both!" she shrieked.

Aubrey shushed her, looking out of the drawing room towards the study. "Don't make this worse than it already is!" he whispered fiercely.

She matched his tone. "I don't see what can be worse than having a man who said it would be against his gentlemanly nature to find fault in a young woman to then change his mind and take up the idiotic venture." She glanced out the door, then back at him. "It smacks of hypocrisy!"

A sudden snarl lit his features. "Do you think I actually want to do this? That I *want* to spend my time in London evaluating you to make your father feel better?"

"Well, I don't know, considering you accepted the position and are here now for that express purpose!"

Aubrey moved closer, almost threatening in his approach. "Would you prefer some aged stickler for propriety who thinks you smell too seductive for polite society? Because I've seen the list of other candidates, Grace, and I can promise you..."

"Compared to you," Grace interrupted, hissing coldly, "yes, I think I would! And what does my smell have to do with anything?"

"Not a thing, it was just an example! And I promise you that anyone else would take great pleasure in finding your no doubt numerous faults."

Grace quirked a brow. "But you won't?"

Aubrey's expression shifted so quickly it startled her. Now he was cold, calculating, and almost haughty.

"Is that what you think of me?" he asked in an even lower voice.

She refused to feel guilty for what she'd said, not when he had committed the far greater sin. "I don't know you from Adam, Ingram. I knew you as a child, and there is nothing here to suggest that boy lives anywhere inside you."

He blinked, then seemed taken aback by what she said. Heartbeats passed, then a bland smile slid into place on his features.

"All right, I deserved that." He sobered quickly. "But I promise you that nothing about finding faults in you, or in anyone else, will give me pleasure."

Grace shook her head in disbelief. "Then why in the world would you do this?"

"Because if you saw the names on the list, you would choose me, too."

She scoffed and folded her arms. "I highly doubt that."

He matched her pose. "You would."

Grace stared at him, grinding her teeth. "Is it going to be like this the entire time?"

"Probably."

She tilted her head in consideration. "Perhaps you should go back to my father and refuse."

73

Aubrey uncrossed his arms and slid them into his trouser pockets, a surprisingly casual stance given his position and his being a guest in her home.

"Oh, I don't know," he drawled, "it's been a long time since I've argued with someone, and I find I'm quite enjoying it."

Somehow, in some way, some small part of her found that amusing, and her mouth twitched against a smile.

Aubrey noticed, and actually smiled.

Maddening, arrogant, infuriating, handsome man…

She couldn't help it; she laughed. Tears of mirth welled up, and she had to turn away to wipe at her eyes.

It was so ridiculous. She had just spent the last few minutes arguing with Aubrey, Lord Ingram, over going along with her father's scheme, all because she was embarrassed that it would be him. In reality, he was likely right. Someone else would have been worse. Aubrey wasn't cruel, unless he had changed in the years that had passed, and it was inevitable that *someone* would be assessing her.

It might as well be him.

She turned back to face him and caught the incredibly attractive crooked smile he was sending in her direction.

Oh lord, not this again…

Grace smiled and gestured faintly for the couches. "Shall we sit?"

He shrugged and did so without waiting for her to sit.

For some reason, that amused her as well.

"So," she said as she returned to the couches and sat. She was unable to keep from perfect posture, but she did her best to keep her expression relaxed, at least. "When does my father want you to begin assessing me?"

"He's leaving that decision entirely up to me." Aubrey exhaled shortly, shaking his head. He rolled his eyes and gave Grace an exasperated look. "You wouldn't believe how determined he is."

Grace hummed in disgruntled amusement. "Believe me, I know exactly how determined he is."

Something in her tone must have said too much. Aubrey suddenly looked at her with more concern and more gentleness than he'd done in her entire life. "How can I do this in a way that will be as painless as possible for you?"

74

She looked at him sharply. "Are you seriously asking me that?"

"I am." He leaned forward, resting his elbows on his knees, his expression earnest. "I don't want to hurt you, Grace. Believe it or not, that isn't in my nature."

"Oh, I believe that," she told him, smiling fondly. "You always were quite nice."

Aubrey wrinkled his nose up at that. "That's a dreadful word. Nice."

Grace laughed once. "My friend Izzy would agree with you there."

"Mrs. Morton? I've heard excellent things about her."

"All true, I can assure you." Grace stared at Aubrey for a long moment, then clasped her hands before her. "How can you make this relatively painless for me? Be kind about it. Tell me what you find before tell my father. Be my…" She bit her lip, unable to finish.

Aubrey knew, though. "Be your friend?" he suggested.

Still biting her lip, Grace nodded, looking away.

A warm hand covered her own, and her eyes moved back to Aubrey of their own accord. He was smiling again, this time surprisingly genuine. "I believe I can manage that."

Her heart began a strange fluttering dance, and she had to catch her breath at the sensation before covering any visible evidence of such a thing with a sardonic look. "You think you can. You have no idea what being my friend entails, or what it will do to you. Poor Ingram."

He snorted and slid his hand back, easing further into the couch. "First of all, if we are friends, you are entitled to call me Aubrey. Secondly, it cannot be *that* much of a trial, or your poor Spinsters wouldn't come anywhere near you."

"Shh!" Grace glanced towards the door, then back at him. "My father has no idea about the Spinsters, and I'd much prefer to keep it that way."

Aubrey grinned a devious grin. "I knew it!"

"Aubrey!"

"I won't tell, I won't tell," he insisted raising his hands in surrender. "I read the latest issue, and I loved every line in it. I have no desire to see that disrupted." He cocked his head slightly. "How can you be called the Spinsters when half of you are married?"

Grace smirked. "Less than half, if you count Elinor, which most do. And Spinsters is with a capital S, as in the writers of the Chronicles. Marital status notwithstanding, we are all Spinsters with a capital S."

"And who decided the marital status rule?" Aubrey prodded, though she suspected he already knew.

"Georgie, of course."

"Of course." He suddenly chuckled and dropped his head back on the couch. "What would you wager that she's the one who got to your father?"

Grace slumped against her corner of the couch finally, suddenly out of breath at the thoughts. "I'd say it's more than likely."

"What would you wager, Grace?"

She rolled her head to look at him. "I am not wagering on my friends or on my father. Wagering would be a fault."

He groaned and covered his eyes with one hand. "Spoilsport. That would explain everything, though. Why would he even think of me for this? It had to be a suggestion. Which would mean that list wasn't truly a list of candidates, but a ploy to get me to accept. It's far more devious than I would have thought Trenwick capable of."

Grace frowned at him. "My father is never devious. He is perfectly straightforward about everything."

Aubrey lifted his hand and stared at Grace. "Hence, Georgie."

It did sound rather like her, and given her behavior only earlier today...

It would be best for Georgie to enter her confinement very, very soon. In the country. Out of London.

Grace exhaled in irritation, then sat up once more. "Tell me who was on the list."

"Why?" Aubrey asked rather bluntly. "It's a moot point now, and if our hypothesis is correct, they were not truly feasible."

"But you didn't know that at the time," Grace reminded him. "I want to know who could possibly be horrifying enough that you would agree to find faults in me."

Aubrey pushed himself up on the couch, grinning outright. "Well, I don't anticipate finding many faults in you, so it should be fairly easy on my part, which I approve of entirely."

"You're too generous," she muttered with a smile.

He inclined his head in all sincerity. "But if you truly want to know who the alternatives were…"

"I do."

"Try not to scream."

"I never scream."

His grin turned a peculiar shade of evil that she didn't trust at all. "You will, Miss Morledge. You will." He tossed a pillow at her, barely avoiding a collision with her face. "Here's this for when you do."

"Oh, really, Aubrey," she moaned, taking the pillow and putting it in her lap. "I associate with Lady Hetty, I hardly think anyone could be much scarier than her."

"She was the very first name on the list."

Grace went wide-eyed, swallowed, then brought the pillow to her face and screamed into its depths.

"So, what will you tell people?"

Aubrey glanced over at Grace as he walked with her in the garden of Trenwick House, keeping his hands behind his back. "About?"

She gave him a brief, dark look. "*This*, Aubrey. People gossip, and I highly doubt you are going to want the rumor going around that you are courting me."

"Well, I would only be so fortunate," he replied pompously, bowing very deeply.

Grace scoffed. "Please, be honest."

Aubrey straightened and exhaled. "Honestly? I haven't the foggiest. Your father says we'll figure something out, but I'm afraid of what that means."

"As am I." Her brow furrowed, and she twirled the handle of her parasol in her hands. "Could you be calling upon James? Renewing an old friendship?"

A powerful shudder coursed through him, and he made a face. "That would require me to be seen with him in public, would it not?"

Grace smirked, her dark eyes flashing with a hint of mischief he found quite becoming. "Undoubtedly."

Aubrey shook his head firmly. "Pass. No offense, Grace, but James is as useful as shaving soap for an infant. Surely we can come up with something better."

She bit back a laugh, which made Aubrey grin. For all his memories of Grace as a child, he couldn't ever recall her being so warm and charming and... real. There were absolutely no airs about her, and she was well aware how ridiculous certain members of her family were, as well as the oddity of her situation. Yet never once had he detected any pity for herself or bitterness about any of it.

Which made his task even more bizarre, and her unmarried state bewildering to the extreme.

"Then you must resign yourself to being my father's apprentice," Grace told him with a shrug of her dainty shoulders. "No one would believe anything else."

Given the choice between two evils of equal measure, how was one to proceed?

Perhaps a faux courtship wouldn't be so bad...

No, no, that was impossible. Tony Sterling alone would be intolerable, and it would not be fair to Grace to pretend at such a thing to save them both and then to have it dissolve when his task was finished. Gossips were notoriously brutal, and she was far too good for that.

"Would anyone have to *see* me with your father?" he asked with a wince.

"Of course not. Father never goes out into Society."

Aubrey exhaled in a rush of relief. "Then I will allow it."

Grace gave him a sidelong look, which he caught and returned warily. "What?" he asked.

She bit her lip very briefly. "I'm wondering if I should tell you something that might make *you* scream."

"I never scream," Aubrey insisted with a firm shake of his head. "I retain control of my emotions and reactions at all times."

Grace raised a brow. "My father once had aspirations for you as a son-in-law."

Aubrey yelped before he could help himself, then cleared his

78

throat quickly as Grace laughed in a rather throaty manner. "That was not a scream."

"No, indeed," she laughed. "It was a yelp. Rather like my aunt's lapdog used to emit. Or a child being surprised."

"I never promised not to yelp," he grumbled, running a hand over his hair. "How the devil do you know he wanted me in the family?"

Grace waved a hand. "Oh, he used to discuss it at dinner when I was a child."

Aubrey blinked. "He was trying to pair you with me when you were a child?"

"Not me, silly. Anne."

Now Aubrey was floored. "Why was he discussing matchmaking for Anne at the dinner table when we were all children?"

Grace twirled her parasol again, looking ahead in a thoughtful manner. "He used to discuss everything he wished for any of us at the dinner table. Michael's profession, James's studies, Mama's social agenda…"

This was too impossible to believe. Trenwick might have been many things, but Aubrey would hardly consider him a tyrant. Yet he could not consider Grace a liar. It must have been simply a misconstrued memory of a child, as was so easily done.

He pursed his lips. "But Anne and I?"

Grace looked at him in surprise. "It's not that impossible to imagine. Even I thought there would be something between the two of you, and Father's plans had nothing to do with it."

"Did you?" Aubrey thought on that, surprised by the idea. Well, perhaps not surprised as much as caught off-guard. Then again, he and Anne were of an age, and they had spent a great deal of their childhood time together.

Why shouldn't that have been a thought?

"Was it really so unlikely?" Grace asked, her voice careful.

Aubrey shook his head. "No, I suppose not. Perhaps there was a time I wondered about more than friendship, but I never seriously considered it, and as far as I know, neither did she."

Again, the parasol spun. Did she realize she was doing that? Particularly when she was thinking?

"But she wrote to you," Grace reminded him, "and you to her."

Her statement made Aubrey chuckle as memories flooded back. "Yes, we wrote to each other, but there was nothing romantic about it." He looked at Grace with a crooked smile. "I believe we fought in our letters more than anything else. You know how combative Anne can be."

She returned his smile with a blinding one of her own, and it seemed his eyes had trouble adjusting to its brilliance. Thankfully, it faded quickly, and his eyesight was restored.

"Oh, yes," she replied in a softer tone. "I do know."

Aubrey stepped closer in an obvious motion. "Please tell me you are about to divulge some long-hidden stories about your sister and your childhood."

She pushed him away halfheartedly. "There's really very little to tell!" she protested with her own laugh. "You were there for most of the instances."

"Was I really?"

"Surely you aren't so unobservant."

"Boys of a certain age have very selective memories." He shrugged helplessly. "I could more likely tell you the outcome of a game of soldiers and what I had for supper following such a game than I could about fights between neighboring girls."

Grace looked bemused for a moment. "Even the time when you helped her tie me to a tree?"

Aubrey put a hand to his chest and coughed in shock. "I beg your pardon! I would most certainly remember doing such a thing, if I had participated in such antics. And I do not remember anything of the sort."

Grace rolled her eyes and twirled her parasol. "Right..."

"I don't!" Aubrey insisted, turning serious. "Did I really do that?"

She nodded once. "You did. You even told Anne how to improve her knots so that I had even less chance of escaping."

He shook his head repeatedly. "No, now I know that you are having me on. I am abysmal with knots of any kind, and I am quite sure your sister could do better."

"She did, and you were furious."

80

Aubrey laughed and shoved his hands into his trouser pockets. "I would be if Anne bested me in any way. I still don't recall being so horrid to you."

"You weren't," Grace murmured, her voice dipping. "Anne was horrid. She wanted to leave me overnight and was quite serious about doing so. You insisted I was too young to be left there all night. The pair of you had a rousing fight, and she took off running. You chased her for a bit, then came back and cut my bindings with some kitchen shears you'd swiped from the cook." She smiled over at him in an almost tender fashion. "It really was quite dashing to a girl of six."

Whatever power he thought her blinding smile had, it could not hold a candle to this one.

Where were his lungs, exactly? He'd had them a moment ago, and they had seemed to be functioning properly…

"A dashing boy of, what, ten?" he managed without his lungs participating in any way.

Grace lifted a shoulder in a shrug, looking away. "Roughly, I suppose."

Freed from her smile, his lungs reappeared in their proper place, and he took a moment to appreciate the glories of inhalation and exhalation. "What a pleasant thought," he said, trying for a carefree tone. "A gentleman even then."

"A gentleman who is now going to find my faults," Grace quipped as she closed her parasol and tipped her head back to lift her face to the sun. "And don't you dare call this a fault, Aubrey Flint."

He wasn't about to. He couldn't have done so.

Damnation, he would need to start eating a heartier breakfast before venturing to Trenwick House. He was starting to hallucinate Grace as a fairy of sorts, and it was most disconcerting.

"It's Lord Ingram now, remember?" he told her in a shockingly weak voice.

She shook her head, eyes closed, still sunbathing her face. "Your father will always be Lord Ingram to me. You are simply Aubrey Flint, and likely always will be."

He wasn't sure why, but he liked that.

He liked it very much.

He cleared his throat and moved to the nearby bush, kicking at its roots lightly. "I promise not to find fault until our next meeting. I'm not even sure where to begin, honestly."

Grace cracked open an eye. "That wasn't spelled out extensively for you upon your acceptance of the assignment?"

Aubrey snorted once. "No, and there were no preparation materials, either."

"What a shame." She closed her eye and sighed into the sunshine. "It's as if he had no idea what to do and is looking for you to figure it out all on your own. Poor Aubrey."

"Oh, stop," he protested dryly. "I don't need pity or sympathy, or anything mocking those things either."

Her chin dipped in an almost nod. "Duly noted, sir."

"And don't call me sir."

"As you wish, my lord."

"Grace…"

She opened her eyes and brought her face down from its sun worship, looking fairly smug. "Aubrey, don't throw a barb if you cannot take one."

He bit back a laugh and looked at her with newfound appreciation. "Miss Morledge, are you the sort of woman who engages in provoking behavior and bantering for sport?"

Grace tilted her head in impertinence, clasping her hands behind her back. "Would that be considered a flaw?"

"Not today."

She raised her brows at that, but he only grinned in response. "Is it going to be like this the entire time?" she asked in a far different tone than when she had asked it earlier.

"Absolutely," Aubrey replied with more confidence and certainty than he'd ever admitted anything in his life.

"Good." Grace stepped forward and held her hand out as if to shake his. "Then I think we have discovered a painless way to find my faults, Lord Ingram."

Cheeky creature, she was quite a wonder.

But she was not about to have the upper hand, in this or in anything else. Aubrey took her hand, shook, then raised it to his lips for a quick kiss. "Indeed, Miss Morledge. Indeed."

As if to prove her perfection, she rolled her eyes and tugged her hand away, turning for the house. "You are impossible."

He jogged to catch up with her. "I am, I freely admit it."

"I have no idea why anyone sees a creature of sense in you."

"I never said they did."

Grace stopped and looked at him, eyes narrowed. "What makes you qualified to find my faults, then?"

"Not a thing," he shot back.

Her lips curled into a smirk of a smile. "Perfect. You'll do." And with that proclamation, she strode into the house, apparently not caring if he followed.

But he did follow, and he did so without hesitation.

He was dying to see what else Grace would do that might surprise him.

Which was surprising in and of itself.

Chapter Eight

When in doubt of a particular course of action, it is sometimes advisable to consult with others and take the consensus thereof into consideration. Provided, of course, that a consensus can be found, and that those questioned are creatures of sense. There is nothing worse than poorly given advice from those who know nothing at all.

-*The Spinster Chronicles, 15 April 1816*

"And then we will remain at Hazelwood for the duration of the Season, and likely into the fall."

"So long?"

Georgie looked at Elinor in wry amusement. "I am having a baby, Elinor. I don't think it very likely that I shall be travelling, or even have the desire to do so, for quite some time. But you are all welcome to Hazelwood after the baby is born."

Grace smirked at that. "Tony won't mind?"

"Who cares if Tony minds?" Charlotte asked as she jotted something onto her paper. "He would only be so fortunate to have us come to tend on Georgie and his child. He might manage to go for a ride or hunt or some other manly pursuits."

Izzy shook her head and gave them all a long-suffering look. "What are you writing, Charlotte?"

"Yes, Izzy is the writer, so what are you doing?" Edith queried with a raised brow.

Charlotte glanced up at the Scottish beauty with a scowl. "I'm anticipating the number of issues of the Chronicles we will be down a writer and trying to figure out who can make up the difference." She turned her attention to Izzy. "Would Kitty be available to come and write again? Or would that set off a marital spat between you and Sebastian?"

Georgie coughed weakly. "Charlotte!"

Izzy, however, was not perturbed. "It would be perfectly fine, and I think Kitty would adore the opportunity, but is it necessary?"

Edith frowned, her brow wrinkling. "I haven't written a full article for the Chronicles yet. I can certainly manage to do so for the duration of Georgie's confinement."

"Yes, why not do that?" Prue looked at Charlotte hopefully. "Then Kitty will not have to be troubled. And we do manage to submit articles even when we are away from London, you know."

"But it delays our publication!" Charlotte cried. "And the number of issues lessen!"

Grace sighed heavily. "Which tends to make sense when people are out of London. Fewer people in town mean fewer who will read it. Why are you so suddenly working with a head for business, hmm?"

Charlotte went slightly slack-jawed, then returned to her scribbling, muttering incoherently under her breath.

Grace looked at the others, and they all shared the same look, except for Elinor, who appeared just as concerned as Charlotte. There was just no explaining either of them, and it never failed to amuse her.

She eyed Georgie as she sat in her chair, looking more than a trifle uncomfortable in her growing state. It was good they would be departing London soon, but only if she would truly rest when they got to Hazelwood. Tony would have to mind her carefully there. Or perhaps recruit Miranda to come in and see to Georgie.

That was a cheering thought. Miranda would drive Georgie to her wits end, but there would be no arguing with her about anything at all. She would have Hazelwood reworked to her satisfaction in the course of one afternoon, and it would no doubt be more efficient for her correction. Tony would certainly need to escape the house for rides or hunting then, but there would be no escape for Georgie at all.

She would deserve it.

After her discussion with Aubrey the other day, she was growing more and more convinced that Georgie had something to do with the situation they now found themselves in. With her determination to see Aubrey involved, and her perseverance in anything she set her mind to, there was no possibility that she would let Aubrey's answer stand. She *had* to have done something.

And in a few moments, she fully intended to prove it.

"What's that smug look for, lass?" Edith asked beside her with a slight nudge.

Grace immediately cleared her features. "You'll see soon enough."

Edith laughed a faint giggle. "That sounds ominous."

"It just might be."

She glanced at the clock, then cleared her throat. "Everyone, I have an announcement to make."

Every voice in the room silenced, and all attention was on her.

Elinor's eyes were round, and her mouth worked awkwardly. "Please tell me you aren't getting married," she managed.

Grace looked at her in utter bewilderment. "Why would you even consider that a possibility?"

The girl shrugged. "I'm used to announcements being that sort of thing, and well… you're you."

As if that meant anything.

"Ignore her," Charlotte insisted, clasping her hands before her. "We of mature years know that there is more to life than being married, or not being so. Please, continue."

Returning her attention to the group as a whole, despite Elinor's squawk of protest, Grace put a smile on her face. "I have invited someone to join us today. On a matter of personal necessity."

Every one of her friends looked confused, and she couldn't blame them. Nor could she help grinning at the sight of their confusion.

"Who is it?" Izzy asked.

"Whose personal necessity, exactly?" Charlotte demanded.

"How will we be able to help?" Prue wondered.

"When are they coming?" Georgie inquired.

Footsteps could then be heard in the corridor and Grace gestured at the sound.

The Wright family butler, Robbins, appeared in the doorway and bowed. "Lord Ingram, Miss Wright."

"*What?*" Charlotte exclaimed, torn between delight and disbelief.

Grace snickered softly. "Surprise."

Aubrey appeared in the door then, his face fixed in an apologetic smile, hands raised in the air. "I come in peace…? If that helps? I would have brought a white flag, but those are shockingly difficult to come by."

Grace snorted into her hand and rose, as did the rest, and they curtseyed as Aubrey bowed.

"Why do you look so terrified, Ingram?" Georgie asked with a laugh.

"Because I have a quite legitimate fear of appearing as a feature in your Society Dabbler."

Charlotte looked as though someone had just brought her a tray of pastries. "Ah, you read the Chronicles."

He nodded once. "Most thoroughly. And might I suggest the topic of cravats for your next Fashion Forum? They are really getting to be lavish in the extreme."

"Yours is fine," Grace pointed out.

He shrugged. "I'm peculiarly simple in my style of dress. My valet cries about it every morning."

Charlotte grinned outright. "Oh, do come in, Ingram. Do you know Miss Asheley?"

He looked at Elinor with polite fondness. "Only by name." He bowed for her alone. "Pleasure to meet you."

Elinor beamed at his politeness. "Please, call me Elinor."

Grace blinked. The girl's tone was awkwardly breathless. Aubrey wasn't *that* attractive, was he? Enough to make Elinor forget that she hated men?

"I couldn't possibly," Aubrey protested, again with too much politeness, though he somehow avoided making it seem at all stiff.

"You could," Charlotte corrected. "We are entirely without formality here, Ingram. Believe me, no slanderous tales of ungentlemanly behavior by way of informality will escape these walls."

Aubrey looked at Charlotte, then turned his attention to Grace. "She says it so helpfully."

"She does that," Grace acknowledged with a dip of her chin. "You get used to it."

He nodded as if instructed, then clasped his hands behind his back, returning to look at Charlotte.

"And I don't believe you will have met Lady Edith Leveson," Charlotte continued as she gestured to Edith.

Aubrey smiled with real warmth at Edith, which did something strange and sharp to Grace's stomach. "No, but the name is quite familiar."

Edith smirked wryly. "No doubt you would have heard of my late husband, Sir Archibald."

"Ah, yes, I recollect now. I'd offer my condolences, but I hear they are unnecessary," Aubrey stated, the corner of his smile ticking with his usual mischief.

"That is correct, my lord," Edith replied with a regal incline of her head.

Aubrey nodded himself, then asked, "Is it true you were only married for five minutes?"

"Aubrey!" Grace scolded, though she knew it was commonplace for people to ask such things where Edith was concerned.

True to her good nature, Edith's mouth curved, and she lifted a shoulder. "Something like that."

Aubrey grinned and bowed to her. "Fair enough." He glanced at Grace with a superior look, and she rolled her eyes in response.

Charlotte gestured to a nearby chair, which Aubrey accepted, and they all sat. "So, Ingram, what brings you to our little Spinster gathering?"

"Flaming curiosity to gain insight into the inner workings of such a dominant force," he recited with a sincere intensity, his smile turning markedly mischievous.

Grace flopped back against the chair she was seated in. "Oh lord, Aubrey…"

They ignored her.

Charlotte turned to Elinor, then snapped her fingers. "Elinor.

Snap back into yourself and inform us of the details regarding Lord Ingram."

As if on command, Elinor jerked out of her lovesick daze and turned to the stack of materials beside her. She rummaged through a few pages, and then reported, "Lord Ingram. Bachelor, rumored to be near on thirty years of age, unconfirmed. No military record. Exemplary marks in school. No outstanding gambling debts. No courtships, jiltings, or scandals. Suspected fortune of... fifteen thousand a year, unconfirmed. No family living, riding abilities unknown, and a country estate in Derbyshire. Breyerly. Rumored to be the finest sight in Derbyshire."

Grace bit her lip, restraining a laugh at Aubrey's thunderstruck expression.

Charlotte nodded and turned to him. "Any questions, Ingram?"

Aubrey blinked once, then again, then swallowed. "I'm feeling rather exposed and intimidated at this moment."

"Don't worry about it, Lord Ingram," Elinor soothed, though it didn't sound at all soothing. "By this report, you are practically perfect."

Grace snorted without reserve. "Lies."

Aubrey glared at her. "Hush."

Georgie howled in delight at that. "Oh, I cannot bear it, the two of you are so delightfully spiteful!"

It was the perfect opening, and Aubrey's suddenly satisfied look told Grace he knew it, too.

"It's interesting that you would think so, Georgie," Grace mused in a slow tone, giving her friend a speculative look. "Would you care to hazard a guess as to why Aubrey is here with us today? And why he and I are so 'delightfully spiteful', as you say?"

Georgie's innocent look was really very good, but it did not fool Grace in the slightest. "Why would I know what brings Ingram into our circle, or to speculate as to the spiteful nature of your relationship?"

Aubrey crossed his legs over each other. "Because you objected to my objection of being involved in the fault-finding of Grace, Georgie. You even told me that it was not the last that I would hear of it."

"And you said your response was the only answer I would receive," she shot back. "Has something changed?"

Grace looked at Aubrey, and he returned it, then gestured with his hand.

He was letting her lead.

Surprisingly respectful of him.

She smiled a brief thanks, then turned to Georgie once more. "My father has decided that Aubrey is the only candidate that will do for his fault-finding expedition."

"Say exhibition, by all means," Aubrey added. "It is a bit of a farce and a show."

That was much less respectful. She sent him a quelling look, then turned back to Georgie, who did not seem as surprised as she ought to have.

"Are you really going to, Ingram?" Charlotte asked eagerly.

Aubrey nodded without the same enthusiasm. "I had very little choice in the matter. The other candidates would have torn several holes in Grace, and it was made very clear to me that one of them would be the next choice if I continued to refuse." He smiled tightly at Grace. "I couldn't do that, much as I don't want to do this."

She returned his smile in the same vein. United in their dislike for their situation and what was before them.

What an odd partnership.

"You are going to attempt to find fault in Grace?" Elinor repeated in disbelief.

"Attempt is an appropriate word choice for the situation," Aubrey replied with a nod.

"I would prefer," Grace broke in, looking at her married friends, "if your husbands would not be made aware of this as yet. I know they will hear of the fault-finding, if they don't know already, and I know that Aubrey's involvement must come out to them eventually, but at this moment…"

All of them nodded obediently. Prue smiled broadly. "Camden would be livid. He's quite protective of us, you know."

"And we adore him for it," Charlotte assured her. She turned to Grace, frowning. "Why would Georgie have anything to do with this?"

Grace looked at Georgie again. "Because my father would never think of Aubrey for a candidate on his own. Aubrey knew that my father was concerned about my being a spinster and had plans to amend it. What's more, my father specifically told him that he did not think Aubrey would know what to do about me, nor did he expect him to." She cocked her head to one side, smiling at her friend. "Yet, now, he's hired him to assess me. An odd shift in his perspective, is it not?"

The others began to look at Georgie in speculation, but Georgie kept her eyes dancing between Grace and Aubrey. "I did not write to Trenwick about Aubrey as a candidate, Grace, if that is what you are insinuating. And I did not speak to him, either. I hope to never speak to him again, truth be told."

"Brava!" Charlotte praised.

Aubrey heaved a sigh. "Then, truly I don't know what possessed him to do it. Grace?"

Grace still stared at Georgie. Clearly this wasn't all there was to the story. "Then what *did* you do, Georgie? I know you, and I know how driven you can be. What did you do after Aubrey refused that night at Campbells'?"

Georgie stared back at Grace, her lips curved into a smile, and then suddenly broadening with mischief. "I may have written to Miranda."

"Oh, saints preserve us," Edith breathed, crossing herself twice.

"Why would you do that?" Prue asked with a hiccup, eyes wide.

Georgie smirked proudly. "Because I happened to recollect that Miranda knows Lord Trenwick personally. Knowing her tenacity for anything and everything that strikes her fancy, I thought it was worth the effort."

"Good lord, Georgie," Aubrey said with a look of sheer horror. "You told Miranda Sterling that I had refused?"

She nodded, this time looking very smug. "And what the entire situation was. I have no idea what she said in her missive to Trenwick, I only know how she responded to my own letter."

Grace swallowed hard. "Which was?"

"She said, 'I will handle it'."

There could be no more ominous words from Miranda Sterling.

Grace looked over at Aubrey, and he looked at her. They swallowed at the same moment, then Grace exhaled roughly.

Aubrey's exhale came with a muttered curse.

She would have echoed it if it would not be marked as a flaw.

"Don't worry," Georgie said with a laugh. "It's only Miranda, it will be fine!"

"Says the woman shortly entering her confinement," Aubrey commented, "away from London and Miranda." He returned his attention to Grace, shaking his head. "What hold over your father could Miranda have?"

"I haven't the faintest idea, and I'm not at all certain that I want to."

Various nods around the room echoed her thoughts.

Aubrey couldn't believe what he was hearing. It *had* been Georgie that had interfered with Trenwick's plans via Miranda. She had orchestrated this horrid demise of his and given her friend fresh cause for embarrassment in the process.

Not that it would change his mind back to his original inclination. He would stand by his promise and see it through, mostly out of fear of the other candidates. Only now he would also have to fear the wrath of Miranda Sterling.

Which was infinitely worse.

"Was that all that you came for, Lord Ingram?" Mrs. Morton asked politely. "To inform us of your... assignment?"

He shook his head firmly. "Sadly, Mrs. Morton..."

"Izzy, please," Grace interrupted.

Gads, but this was awkwardly informal for him. Still, better to follow their preferences and gain their trust and assistance rather than remain at a formal distance.

He inclined his head with respect. "Izzy, then. I have also come because I am in need of assistance."

"Ah," Charlotte interjected with her version of a sage nod. "The matter of personal necessity."

Grace gave her friend a sardonic look. "Yes, Charlotte, it is. For me and for him."

That seemed to intrigue Charlotte. "Indeed?"

"Indeed." Aubrey cleared his throat. "I am designated to repeatedly attempt to find faults in Grace, and I have absolutely no idea in what direction I had best move. What categories ought to be evaluated, what potential faults to look for, how to proceed..." He exhaled, slumping his shoulders. "You know Grace better than anyone. I don't know where else to turn."

Grace smiled a mixture of apology and comfort, which he very much appreciated. For someone he would soon be evaluating for flaws, she was a remarkably supportive woman.

Why? Why wasn't she fighting him tooth and nail? He knew she could fight well, their few spats of late were proof enough. So why not fight him? Make this task impossible?

Resist more?

Take the victory, old man, his mind hissed, clapping him soundly on the back of the head.

It was true enough. If his task were impossible as it was, at least he would not be miserable in the interim.

"Well, well," Charlotte said, rubbing her hands together. "This, I believe, we can help you with."

"I am afraid," Grace announced to no one in particular, making Aubrey chuckle.

Charlotte speared her with a look. "You, Miss Morledge, need to leave the room."

"What?" Grace cried. "Why?"

"Because it will be deuced uncomfortable to assist him in finding fault in you if you're here to experience the plotting of it all." Charlotte nudged her head towards the door. "Out you go. The music room isn't far, you should play while we plot."

Grace rose, blinked, then looked at Aubrey. "She says it so helpfully."

He grinned. "She does that."

With a disgruntled sigh, Grace left the room, and with her, some of the light.

Strange phenomenon.

"Right," Charlotte began, sitting forward in her chair. "What have you come up with? Anything at all?"

"Not a thing."

"I thought not." Charlotte turned to Elinor. "Tell him some of the categories we use for young ladies. Or better yet, make a list for him, but say them out loud. He's going to need all this spelled out specifically so as to remember with clarity."

Aubrey frowned and looked at Edith. "Should I be offended by her inference of my ineptitude?"

Edith shook her head at once. "Not a bit. Never let Charlotte offend you, try as she might. She thinks she's being helpful." She rolled her eyes for effect, and Aubrey smiled at it.

Make that three Spinsters he liked immensely.

Four, if he counted Grace.

He really should.

"Fortune, fashion, reputation," Elinor recited, her quill dancing across the page before her, "musical accomplishment, artistic ability, riding, languages, dancing." She looked up meaningfully. "And it really must be said that one should be able to satisfactorily dance a waltz, quadrille, jig, and country dance. Very separate abilities there."

"Noted," he muttered.

"But Grace d-dances so very w-well," Mrs. Vale protested, seeming rather worried about this whole thing.

Izzy sighed and put her hand over her friend's. "Yes, dear, but that won't help Ingram to find his way through all of this."

Mrs. Vale bit her lip hesitantly. "I s-suppose." She looked at Aubrey quite directly for so shy a person. "Be sure to c-consider how she treats others, both of her s-station and beneath it. Such a thing can be q-quite telling."

So was her suggestion of it. Aubrey nodded at her. "An excellent point, Mrs. Vale, and I quite agree."

A smile flickered. "You can c-call me Prue, if you like."

He returned it easily. "If it would make you comfortable, I shall. If the reverse, I shall not."

Now her smile spread. "I would like it if you would call me Prue, Lord Ingram."

Why did such a simple thing feel so momentous? He held his

smile in her direction. "Then I shall. And anyone may call me Aubrey, if they prefer. Ingram is a reminder of my responsibilities, which I do not need in this moment."

A light round of chuckling lit the room almost musically.

"Right," he said with a clap of his hands. "What else?"

"Comportment," Charlotte said with some firmness. "How she walks and moves, the manner in which she holds herself."

"Which Grace excels at," Edith added quietly.

"Conversation," Izzy suggested. "Especially with the male sex, as it relates to her present state."

"Tea?" Elinor wrinkled up her nose in indecision. "Face and figure?"

"All of which Grace excels at," Edith added again.

Charlotte huffed and looked at her in exasperation. "We know that Grace excels in everything, Edith, but there is nothing we can do about that when her father is subjecting her to an evaluation. Helping Aubrey is not betraying Grace."

Edith did not look remotely convinced, but she wasn't exactly looking sour either.

He quite liked her defensive streak where Grace was concerned. She deserved someone like Edith in her life.

"Her writing," Izzy said, clearly trying to smooth over the moment. "Composition of a letter, for example."

"Or an article," Elinor added with repeated nods.

Charlotte gasped. "Are you suggesting we inform Aubrey as to which articles Grace writes? Betray our anonymity?"

Edith rolled her eyes, laughing. She looked at Aubrey with remnants of the laughter. "I don't know which part of this I am sorrier for, Ingram. Your forced involvement with us or your task of finding faults in Grace. I can only apologize for all of it as a whole."

Aubrey grinned, then sobered in mock solemnity. "Thank you, Lady Edith. I shall do my utmost to endure with a good, Christian charity about me."

Georgie scoffed across the room. "If only I believed that."

"Speaking of," Elinor broke in, looking around, "do we evaluate her religious devotion?"

Charlotte made a face. "Only if we run out of other things and her father wants a God-fearing daughter. I wasn't aware he had any religion at all but what he thinks of himself."

"Charlotte Wright!" Prue protested, her cheeks coloring, though she smiled at it.

"He's about as Christian as your mother, Prudence," Charlotte shot back with a devious smile. "Which tells me your father named you Prudence, for your mother wouldn't be at all familiar with the word or the virtue."

Prue covered her face in laughter, though Aubrey could see her cheeks flaming beneath her hands.

Edith leaned over to him. "You wouldn't believe what a remarkable sight that is, Ingram. To see her laughing about something anyone said about her mother. 'Tis a glorious thing."

Aubrey nodded in understanding. He hadn't experienced Prue's crippling shyness from before, though he had certainly heard about it. He wasn't sure how anything about her mother related, or why it should be so humorous, but that was neither here nor there.

"Her tastes in reading ought to be evaluated," Charlotte went on, ignoring Prue's muffled laughter. "One does not wish to be a bluestocking, but one must be well-informed, and certainly have read current novels of taste."

Georgie made a face. "Her father might find that a flaw. Novels are sometimes controversial."

Charlotte waved a hand at that. "A little controversy is good for a body."

Aubrey snorted to himself, but Edith heard him.

"I hope she writes a guidebook for young ladies one of these days," Edith murmured, reaching for the tea set and pouring herself some. She looked at Aubrey. "Would you care for a cup?"

He nodded absently. "Please. However you take it is fine."

Edith winked, and poured him some, then handed the cup and saucer to him.

"Oh, what about games?" Georgie suggested. "Lawn bowls and pall mall and cards and the like."

"Excellent thought," Charlotte praised, whirling to Elinor. "Have you been getting all of this down?"

Elinor turned the page over and kept scribbling. "Yes, yes, I've got it."

"Oh, good," Aubrey replied weakly. "I was ever so worried we would miss one."

Georgie grinned at him. "Are you overwhelmed, Ingram?"

He gave her an equally weak smile. "Wouldn't you be?"

"Well, it shouldn't be easy to find flaws in someone like Grace," she replied without concern.

Charlotte nodded her approval. "And it *won't* be easy, Aubrey. Not in the least."

Prue winced as she looked at him. "It is really going to be a struggle, I am s-sorry to say."

"You're going to get very frustrated," Elinor said bluntly.

"And we really won't be of very much help," Izzy added with some sympathy. "We adore her too much."

Edith reached over and patted his hand. "You'll likely regret ever agreeing to this."

Aubrey looked around the room, feeling suddenly incredibly small and quite disheartened. He scowled. "You're all being very helpful. Really. So encouraging."

Charlotte grinned rather swiftly. "You're all on your own, Aubrey. We're hoping you find nothing so that her father will finally shut up about the whole thing."

Finally? What did she mean by that? He was going to demand an explanation when the sounds of the pianoforte flowed into the room, a beautiful concerto that seemed filled with every emotion one had the ability to contain. Faintly, a clear voice could be heard singing with it, though the words were lost.

It was a stirring, almost heavenly experience, so different from the recent flurry of their conversation that it ought to have been a jarring shift.

Except it wasn't.

It was absolute perfection.

Blinking was suddenly difficult, and the tension in his chest was remarkably uncomfortable. Music was something he was occasionally sensitive to, but not like this. He sipped at his tea, not quite tasting it, waiting for someone to say something.

Anything, really.

"That, Ingram," Georgie said at last, pointing towards the music room. "That is what you have to find fault in."

He smiled grimly and swallowed his tea.

This was going to be hell.

Chapter Nine

───────⟨∞∞⟩───────

One should never intentionally find fault in a young lady. Never. One should let the faults appear naturally, and then ignore them as politely as possible.

-*The Spinster Chronicles, 9 August 1817*

"Breathe. Just breathe. You can do this. It will be fine."

"Indeed, sir."

Aubrey glared at Locke, who stood in the doorway of his bedchamber. "How long have you been standing there?"

"Long enough to hear your speech twice, my lord."

Aubrey frowned and looked at his valet, currently finishing his cravat. "Sundrey, you knew about this?"

Sundrey didn't even look up. "I am so fixated on my task, my lord, that I pay no mind to who or what is at the door."

"Liar."

Sundrey met his eye then. "It's not my business to report on Locke's position or movements, sir."

Aubrey frowned at his servants in turn. "Remind me to check the silver when I return tonight. There is no telling how Locke behaves if no one checks him."

"I shall lay it out for your inspection, sir," Locke recited with a half bow.

Aubrey nodded, then glanced at the butler again. "How much silver do we have, anyway?"

Locke's lips quirked, but he did not smile. "I will leave the numbers out for you as well, sir."

Damnation, he was so close to getting the man to break, but he had clearly underestimated the strength of his butler's composure.

"What is it, Locke?" Aubrey finally asked with a laugh. "Do you have something for me?"

"Sir, you have received a message from Miss Morledge of Trenwick House."

Aubrey's brows shot up, and he started to turn towards the butler, only to have Sundrey yank him back rather forcibly to finish his task.

"Steady on, Sundrey," Aubrey muttered. "Kindly remember who employs you."

"Sorry, sir," Sundrey replied without any hint of apology. "Kindly remember who dresses you."

Fair point.

"What does Grace want?" Aubrey asked, tilting his head towards Locke as much as he could without being punished again.

"I did not open the missive, sir," came the prompt reply

"Kindly do so," Aubrey ordered with a sigh. "As you can see, I am presently detained."

The sound of a seal breaking and paper unfolding filled the room. Aubrey had the sudden urge to tap his toes against the floor, but he resisted.

His knees, however, began an odd bouncing where he stood. That one he let go.

"She begs to inform your lordship," Locke began, "that she is waiting upon your arrival with some anxiety, as she wishes to begin, and also begs to inform you that her father will be occupied with business the whole course of the day, and thus you will not be encumbered with his presence."

Aubrey frowned and turned even more to face Locke. "All right. How did *she* say it, Locke?"

Sundrey tugged him back to center as he pinned the cravat.

Locke grunted softly. "She said, and I quote, 'I am already anxious and nervous, so get here soon so we can get this over with. Also, Father won't be a problem today. He's meeting with solicitors all day, for which we can both give thanks.'"

Aubrey grinned and chuckled at Locke's almost disgusted tone. "That sounds more like Grace. I am sure she would appreciate your making it all sound so much more polite."

"Thank you, sir."

"You should meet her, Locke," Aubrey suggested as Sundrey finally stepped away to fetch his coat. "She is rumored to be the most perfect woman."

Locke did not look convinced. "The tone of this missive would suggest otherwise, sir."

Was his stodgy butler expressing his own opinion? Would wonders never cease?

Aubrey slid his arms into the coat that Sundrey held out for him. "Oh, she's only like that with me, Locke. She spars with words better than most men with fists. Again, only with me. As far as I can tell, at any rate."

Locke gave another half bow. "Then, I have no reason to doubt rumors of her perfection, my lord." He turned and removed himself from the doorway, leaving Aubrey and Sundrey gaping in the bedchamber.

"Did he just…?" Aubrey began, unable to complete the thought.

"He did, sir," Sundrey confirmed, no less at a loss.

Aubrey shook his head, then looked at his valet rather blandly. "I'd dismiss him, but I'm almost perishing with curiosity."

Sundrey gave an approving nod. "Indeed, sir. As am I."

Nodding to his valet, and tugging briefly at his cuffs, Aubrey strode out of the room and down to his waiting carriage.

Despite Locke's slightly mocking statement, Aubrey continued to encourage himself to breathe and to remember that this was not a battle. It might feel as though he were going into treacherous territory, and possibly would risk life or limb doing so, but he was simply calling upon Grace Morledge. And beginning the process of finding faults in her.

Her. A very nearly perfect woman.

No pressure.

He swallowed and tugged a little at his cravat, taking care not to disrupt Sundrey's meticulous work. He knew better than that.

Somehow Sundrey always knew when he did something, and his scolding look was rather like the ones he had received in childhood.

It would be fine. It would all be fine. It was just Grace.

A ridiculous bubble of mirth welled up, and he laughed rather heartily at himself.

Just Grace.

There was no such thing.

Far too soon, he was at Trenwick House, and Bennett was letting him in, surprisingly cool towards him. None of the warmth or wit of late, and it was almost as if he refused to meet Aubrey's eyes.

One butler teasing him, the other ignoring him. Clearly there was some butler conspiracy against him to turn him more than slightly mad. Provided this venture didn't do that first.

He was silently shown into the drawing room they had met in before, and then Bennett was gone.

Aubrey stared after him, then turned towards Grace, who was standing by the window as though she had been posed for a portrait.

"Is he angry with me?" Aubrey asked, gesturing behind him.

Grace smiled, though it didn't seem to reach her eyes. "He is, yes. He doesn't like the idea of someone finding fault with me."

"I'm not particularly keen on the idea, either," Aubrey protested, "but I didn't really have a say in the matter. Does he know that?"

She shrugged a shoulder. "I've tried to tell him, but he is really quite resistant to hearing anything about it."

Aubrey shook his head. "How peculiar."

"That's not the only thing."

No, it was not.

It was then that he properly looked at Grace. Her fingers were clenched tightly together, her posture was perfectly straight, shoulders high, and her face, while perfectly composed, held all the signs of strain. And then there were her eyes: dark, wide, and utterly terrified.

"Heavens…" Aubrey shook his head. "You really are afraid."

She nodded jerkily, exhaling a brief sigh. "I really am."

For some reason, that made his own nerves ease. "It's just me, Grace. We agreed this would be as painless as possible."

"For you," she corrected, her voice wavering. "I am the one

being examined. Everything I say or do, or don't say or don't do, is now being evaluated for any little mistake. I don't know that there is a painless way to do it."

Aubrey stared at her for a long moment, then sighed. "I know. I was more nervous on the drive over this morning than I'd ever thought possible."

"You were? Why?"

He let his mouth curve into a crooked smile. "Because I'm supposed to be analyzing you for faults, which is something that will not be easy for me and will cause pain to you."

Grace swallowed with some difficulty. "You don't seem nervous now."

"I'm not," he admitted easily, and surprisingly truthfully.

"Why? How?"

He smiled further still. "I came here, I saw you, and I was reminded that we are friends, which means we can make this experience whatever we want it to be. There are no rules, and there are no expectations. It's just us."

Grace stared at him for a long moment, then her shoulders relaxed, as did her face. "You're right. Of course, you're right."

"Of course, I am."

She glared. "Don't take that as a statement of consistency on previous behaviors. I only mean this time."

He nodded sagely, folding his arms. "Naturally."

"I'm serious, Aubrey."

"So I see."

"You're impossible."

"So we have established. That, I believe, will be a consistency. I'm quite certain about it." He nodded again, pressing his lips together.

Finally, Grace smiled, lighting the room quite effectively. "Right. Shall we begin, then?"

Aubrey nodded, delighted to have the Grace he liked best returned to him. This was an uncomfortable situation, and if they were not at the very least comfortable with each other, it would only get worse. He needed to be comfortable with Grace. He needed her to be comfortable with him.

Why, he couldn't say. He refused to dwell on it. He only knew he needed it.

Grace came closer and stood before him. "What will we be focusing on today?"

Aubrey had been thinking about this, and he knew how to begin. He might not know how to proceed after that, but he knew how to begin.

"Actually, before we get started, I have to ask: why do *you* think you're a spinster?"

The question earned him a blink and a blank stare. "Seriously?"

"Seriously."

She scoffed softly. "If I knew that, there would be no need to do this."

"Humor me," he said with the utmost patience.

Grace gave him an odd look, then looked away, her brow furrowing in thought. "I don't know," she eventually murmured.

Aubrey tsked with a hint of a scold. "Grace…"

Her eyes met his, utterly serious. "I don't know why I'm a spinster. I've always been this way, and it's never been enough to attract a suitor."

Wait, *never?* How could she never have had a suitor?

She shook her head slowly. "I don't know how to be anything else. I can only presume I'm not enough as I am, as all the evidence of my past proves. So, I carry on, on my own. What seems to come easily to me is just as painful now as it was the very first day I bore it. Only my acting has improved." She smiled sadly, but there was still no hint of pity in it.

Aubrey stared at her, in awe and in disbelief. "I don't know that I have ever met a spinster quite like you."

Her smile turned far less sad. "Well, there is quite a variety to the spinster status. We're not all cut from the same cloth, you know."

"As the meeting the other day proved."

She laughed, and very faint lines creased at the corners of her eyes, which was strangely adorable. "Yes, there is variety even within the Spinsters with a capital S. But here's the thing about spinsters, Aubrey, not all of us have similar situations. Not all of us are upset about our status, and not all of us find satisfaction in it. Charlotte is an heiress, and she has no need to marry if she does not wish to. Lady Hetty was the same way. In the lower classes, a woman who is unmarried can find employment and fulfillment. But for the rest of us, it is a sea of murky waters and no sure way to navigate them." She wrinkled up her nose and leaned forward as if to convey a secret. "And we don't really like to be called spinsters. It's not very flattering."

Aubrey smiled at that. "I will remember that. I have no desire to say anything unflattering."

Grace's eyes narrowed at him. "I'm not entirely sure I believe you."

"Hmm," he mused, his brows knitting together. "Disparaging a gentleman. Quite possibly a flaw."

She made a face. "I didn't disparage a gentleman. I disparaged you."

"That you did."

They smiled at each other, and something seemed to shift around Aubrey. It wasn't obvious, it wasn't monumental, and he wasn't even sure what it was, but something moved. Or morphed.

Grew.

He could have smiled at Grace for a good long while without ever getting tired of it.

Shocking thought. He didn't even like smiling, particularly as a pastime. It took entirely too much effort.

But not with Grace.

Perhaps that was a flaw. She changed his opinion on smiling against his will.

Heartless captor.

He stepped back with a gruff sound and folded his arms, trying to look speculative. "First and foremost, Miss Morledge, tell me how your finances are arranged. I know it's a distasteful topic for polite society, but in the interest of this assignment, it must be considered adequately."

Grace clamped her lips together and giggled.

"This is quite serious, madam," Aubrey insisted with as much stiffness as humanly possible.

"I'm sure it is," she laughed. Then she sobered, though there were laugh lines ticking at the corners of her full lips. "My dowry is thirty thousand pounds, and I have discretionary pin money of a generous nature, much of which I keep stowed away in an undisclosed location, as my dowry is of no concern to me but is to my husband. Poor man."

Aubrey snorted a laugh. "Not that poor. Thirty thousand is a right pleasant sum. That should encourage several gentlemen to venture to your door, once I let word of *that* spread about."

"Rude, Aubrey!"

Well, this was going better than she'd thought it would.

Surely she could hope in that, right?

Aubrey was making this all so easy, taking care to make her comfortable and keep her smiling, and turned impossible the moment she exhibited the slightest bit of tension. Miraculously, it never failed to bring her out of her anxieties and make her laugh. And then he would turn less impossible and they were able to continue on.

Not that they had made an especially significant amount of progress.

Aubrey had no idea what he was doing, and he made that perfectly clear.

Grace didn't mind. In fact, she was taking great pleasure in seeing him confused and at times flustered. He never became angry or frustrated, but he couldn't seem to decide on a course, and his indecision was oddly charming. There was a very specific furrow that appeared between his brows when he was thinking. For some unfathomable reason, she enjoyed seeing that. It suited him, in a way. Enhanced his too-tan complexion that spoke of days in the sun working with his tenants.

Which suited his dark hair, and his perfectly portioned brows, and his impeccable physique, and...

She straightened up in her chair, craning her neck. Yes, Aubrey was an attractive man, and at times remarkably so, but there was absolutely no sense in dwelling on that fact. He was impossible. He was grating. He was…

Smiling. At her. In a way that made her toes curl in her slippers.

Oh, no. Not happening.

"What else?" Grace asked quickly, praying he wouldn't notice.

With her luck, he would notice it. He tended to notice everything.

Her favorite furrow appeared, and he pulled a piece of paper from his waistcoat pocket, reading it over.

"You have a list?" she asked with a laugh.

Aubrey looked over it at her. "Yes, I do. Provided by Elinor and the you-know-whats." He returned his attention to the list, twisting his lips.

Grace exhaled. "Of course. Let me see it."

Again, he looked over. "No."

"Come on," she scolded, giving him a look. "You're going to be going through the whole thing anyway, so I am going to find out."

He shook his head firmly. "I am not having you privy to this information in advance, thus giving you time to prepare for each examination and avoid potential flaw detection. No, Miss Morledge. Give me a minute."

Shaking her head, she held up her hands in surrender, then bit down on her lip to avoid laughing. Then, she quickly stopped, just in case he would consider that a flaw.

"Ah ha!" Aubrey exclaimed, folding the paper and tucking it back in. "I know what to do."

"Oh, good," Grace muttered, raising a brow. "What is it?"

He smirked at her. "Writing composition, Grace. More specifically, I want to see a letter you have written, and an article for the Chronicles you have done."

She blinked unsteadily. "You want to invade my privacy and that of a recipient of one of my letters?"

"I mean no offense, but you don't exactly have privacy with me anymore." He made an apologetic face that she almost believed. "If you don't have a letter you will allow me to read, then we'll have you write one."

Grace stared at him in disbelief. "You're serious."

His mouth pressed into a thin line. "I am."

She exhaled roughly, her mind whirling. How in the world could he expect her to show him one of her letters, let alone reveal which articles she had written for the Chronicles?

Then again, Aubrey wasn't asking. Technically, her father was.

She groaned and forced herself out of her chair. "Wait here."

He gave her a querying look. "As opposed to coming up to your bedchamber?"

There was no point in addressing that, but she simply *had* to glare at him. "The one room in this house that you blessedly have no reason to enter, and the only bit of privacy I will be allowed."

Aubrey pursed his lips. "Why would I have reason to enter your father's bedchamber? Or your brother's? Certainly, I wouldn't need to go into your mother's…"

Grace restrained a shriek and strode from the room, marching down the corridor and up the stairs to her bedchamber.

"Of all the irritating, aggravating, infuriating people on this earth," she snarled as she stomped, "it *had* to be that one."

A door opened upstairs. "Grace?"

Blast. Her mother.

She quickly transformed her expression into a pleasant one as her mother appeared, coming from her rooms. "Mama. I'm only going to fetch a letter."

"For what purpose?" she asked, clearly waiting for Grace.

Grace moved past her and reached out to squeeze her hand. "Aubrey is evaluating my writing as part of the scheme. We're working into the assessment with innocent things to make it easier."

Her mother accompanied her, her expression too knowing. "I heard you on the stairs, my love. I know how you're really feeling."

Of course, she did. Grace let her face relax. "It's not so bad as all that, I promise. Aubrey simply knows how to provoke me with some exactness. I'm unused to it. Everyone treads around me with such care, and he simply barges on through."

A soft chuckle beside her brought Grace around, and she was astonished to see her mother smiling a little.

"What," Grace asked rather pointedly, "could possibly amuse you about that?"

Her mother's smile spread as she looked back at her. "This is the liveliest I've seen you in years, even with your friends. Perhaps this will be good for you."

"The fault-finding?" Grace cried, hurt, defensive, and a thousand other things.

"No, my dear. Aubrey." Her mother gave her a pointed look, then turned back to her private sitting room.

Grace stared after her, agape. That was... there wasn't...

No. Utterly and absolutely no.

She hurried into her room and grabbed a letter she had just finished that morning, then raced back down the stairs so as to avoid letting her mind spin on the ridiculousness her mother had just spouted.

Aubrey still sat where she had left him, as nonplussed as any man had ever been. He turned his head in her direction as she entered and smiled with faux pleasantry. "Ah, you found a letter."

She nodded briskly. "I finished it only this morning. It is for my cousin Felicity, who lives near Brighton."

"Fortunate girl," Aubrey grunted, reaching for the letter.

Grace bit back a response to that and sat, very perfectly, back in her chair, fixing a cold look at the man currently perusing her private correspondence.

He was nodding to himself, his face finally free of pretense. "Excellent sentence structure, not overly descriptive. Familiar without being simpering. Warm without being sentimental."

"Are you going to do that the whole time?" she asked without the bite she'd intended.

Aubrey chewed on his lip as he read. "Possibly..." He looked up at her then. "Why are you warning her about her mother?"

It was on the tip of her tongue to tell him to mind his own business, that he might be privy to her life, but not Felicity's, but she found she didn't have the heart for it. She scowled. "Because her mother is determined to see her married off and isn't particular as to whom, so long as he is wealthy enough to bring Felicity status."

"That isn't uncommon in Society, you know," he murmured, his tone all gentleness.

Grace nodded once. "I know. But my aunt would sell Felicity if it would do the job, and that is not an exaggeration. She's not unfeeling towards her; in fact, she overly praises her, if anything. She is simply obsessed with the idea that Felicity avoid becoming... me."

Aubrey's face hardened at once, and he looked down at the letter once more. "And how old is Felicity?" he asked in a strained voice.

"Seventeen," Grace replied, smiling at him for his response.

The letter seemed to crackle in his hand as his hold tightened briefly. "She's just a child."

"Yes, and a very innocent one." Grace sighed and folded her hands together. "Hence my warning."

"I'll write to your cousin and warn her myself, if I must," Aubrey replied, folding it neatly and rising to give it back to her.

Grace took it, smiling up at him. "Any flaws in it?"

"There's a distinct lack of obscenities for such a warning," he commented, "but you have better taste than I." He returned her smile. "No flaws. Not even a spelling error."

She nodded her thanks and tucked the letter into the chair beside her. "And as for an article, I have none for you to read at present." She glanced towards the door, then leaned forward a touch. "We've taken to not keeping any copies at the house while Father is in residence," she whispered.

Aubrey bent closer to her, his eyes dancing. "Then tell me which article you wrote in the most recent issue. I can assure you; it's still fresh in my mind."

His whispered encouragement made her grin. "The main article. The one about the risk of naïveté in young women."

Aubrey's eyes widened, and he straightened. "Good lord. That was you?"

Grace nodded without hesitation, smirking proudly. "That was me."

His jaw dropped for a moment, and then he beamed rather brilliantly. "Extraordinary doesn't begin to describe that article. It was bloody brilliant, Grace!"

She giggled at the compliment. "Thank you. I was particularly proud of that one. It was certainly an improvement over the Fashion Forum I wrote before that. There's only so much one can say about embroidered stockings."

Aubrey still stared at her, then he relaxed his stance, leaning back on the table behind him. "Grace, I am impressed beyond words. You'll pardon my asking, but how did you learn to write like that?"

Her cheeks colored in delight. "Well, I don't believe I *did* learn it, truth be told. My earlier articles were not so impressive, nor were they so well-constructed."

"Drop the modesty," he begged.

"I'm not being modest," she told him with real honesty. "The more I write for the Chronicles, the better I get. The better we all get. Izzy is still the best of us, and Charlotte is the most shocking, but we are improving. And this time, I decided to address a topic I felt particularly strongly about." She lifted a shoulder. "It's one of the main reasons they started the Chronicles in the first place."

Aubrey leaned forward, resting his arms on his knees and clasping his hands. "They?"

"I was a late addition to the group." She gnawed the inside of her cheek for a moment. "I don't know why they approached me, actually. There were several other spinsters in London they could have asked to join the group."

"They were smart to include you."

Grace jerked slightly to look at him again. "What?"

He nodded fervently. "I mean it. Georgie is no fool, Grace, and I have no doubt she made a study of the other unmarried women in Society. You are the best of the lot. It was only natural they should choose you."

Her heart leapt for joy and seemed to be burning within her. "You don't know the rest of the lot, Aubrey."

"Don't have to," he quipped. "I know you."

Oh, but the look in his eyes made her feel like a lovesick girl of twelve again, and it was all she could do to keep from smiling an accompanying lovesick smile that would have been entirely too obvious.

Not that she *was* lovesick. She was simply touched. And embarrassed. And perhaps a bit feverish.

That was all.

Aubrey blinked and the look was gone. He slapped his thighs and rose fluidly, running a hand through his hair and disheveling it in a way that reminded her of the boy she had known in Derbyshire, and her heart lurched.

"Well, I suppose that's enough for today," he rambled, his words not quite as crisp as normal. "I will see you tomorrow at the Sterlings', and I will assess your interaction with various people at that point."

Grace slowly rose, watching Aubrey curiously. "Very well. Miranda will be there, you know. We could confront her."

"Yes, yes, excellent thought," he replied absently. "I'll bring my suit of armor for whatever she tosses in retaliation."

Grace laughed at the image that brought, and Aubrey seemed to shudder at it.

"Right," he said, turning to her and bowing. "Good day, Grace." "Good day, Aubrey."

He left before she finished, and she stared after him, still curious. What in the world?

Then her mother crossed the corridor, casting another knowing look at Grace. All curiosity and delight evaporated swiftly, and Grace snapped back into discontent, moving quickly towards the music room.

He was *not* good for her.

He couldn't be.

Chapter Ten

Confrontation can be a terrible idea.

-*The Spinster Chronicles, 10 December 1818*

"What is he assessing this evening?"

Grace hid a wince, looking at her mother with a strained expression. "My interaction with others. Conversation, politeness, and no doubt flirtation, as well." She exhaled roughly and shook her head. "It's maddening to be on such display."

Her mother patted her hand gently, then squeezed. "I am so sorry that you are being subjected to this. But perhaps Aubrey lessens the sting?"

"Perhaps," Grace replied evasively, unwilling to admit anything. She wasn't at all sure that he did lessen the sting. It was undoubtedly better than another person might have done, she could admit that freely, but there was a sting to being with Aubrey that wouldn't have belonged with anyone else.

She cared what he thought. Specifically.

What would the discovery of faults do to his estimation of her?

It was a selfish, foolish question, but one she could not ignore. And could not elaborate on.

They entered Georgie and Tony's drawing room, which had been expertly turned into a ballroom this evening, to find most of the guests had already arrived. Dancing had commenced, and Charlotte was already being entertained by four or five men near her, with

Michael Sandford hovering at the edges of her circle, as he usually did.

Grace's mother sighed at seeing him. "Poor Mr. Sandford. I know he's not as timid as his behavior would have us believe, so why does he not try for Charlotte? He might actually have a chance."

"He won't," Grace assured her. "Michael and Charlotte have a longstanding history of friendship and nothing more. He's more a protector than a would-be lover, Mama."

"Such a pity."

They approached Georgie and Tony then, all smiles, and Grace received fond kisses from each of them. Her mother was warmly embraced by Georgie, though the embrace was awkward, given her current size, and Tony kissed her hand.

Grace turned to smile at her brother behind her, although he wasn't there, to her surprise. Gathering her anger into a strained smile, she turned back to their hosts, who seemed to already know what she was thinking.

"I don't know where James has gotten to," Grace said by way of apology and explanation.

Her mother's face flushed, and her hands fidgeted. "I am so sorry, Captain Sterling, Georgie. Please..."

"It's fine, Lady Trenwick," Tony insisted gently, smiling for effect. "He's ventured off to the card room, I saw him go. And neither Georgie nor I take any offense towards you by anything *he* does."

He could not have said anything more perfect, and Grace beamed at him, as did her mother.

"You are too kind," her mother gushed in relief.

Tony chuckled. "Trust me, my lady, I am never too good."

"It's true," Georgie confirmed. "He's only ever good enough." She rubbed Tony's arm, and looked at Grace. "Ingram was looking for you. Not sure why."

Grace made a face. "Wonderful."

"Something to share, Grace?" Tony asked, his tone laced with mischief and suggestion.

She gave him a sardonic look. "Only if you have a spear that I might use presently."

"Grace!" her mother scolded, though the other two laughed.

Grace only smiled and moved on, scanning the gathering for Aubrey or any of her friends. She caught sight of Izzy, Prue, and Elinor, and moved in their direction, sighing with relief when she reached them.

"I have to socialize tonight," she announced without any sort of greeting.

Elinor looked at her in confusion. "I'm... sorry?"

She ignored her. "Aubrey is going to be paying marked attention to my behavior this evening, as an example of a public setting, and I am to converse freely."

Izzy's brow furrowed. "But... no one converses with us. Ever."

"Exactly," she replied with a firm nod, "which means I must seek it out."

"I don't envy you that," Prue murmured, her pale eyes wide.

"Envy who what?" her husband asked as he strode up to them, setting his hand on his wife's shoulder.

Grace grinned at Cam, who always seemed the slightest bit irreverent no matter what he was doing. "Your wife does not envy me, Cam."

"And nor should she," Cam blustered, "for my wife is perfection."

Prue looked up at him wryly. "And Grace is not?"

Cam winced and looked at Grace. "I'm stuck. Help."

Grace giggled and waved a hand. "No matter, Cam. It is only right you should think your wife is perfection. To be honest, I grow so weary of people calling me perfect, as if that is supposed to make me feel better. It actually makes me feel worse."

"Does it really?" came a new voice from behind her, and Grace barely avoided rolling her eyes at it.

She turned, fixing a tight smile on her face. "Aubrey. Good evening."

He bowed in his pristine evening wear, then looked her over quickly. "Dare I risk making you feel worse by saying you look like perfection this evening, Grace?"

"Nicely put," Cam praised with all sincerity.

Grace scowled, which made Aubrey grin, and she turned back to

Cam. "Cam, may I present Aubrey, Lord Ingram? Aubrey, this is Camden Vale."

Aubrey bowed, as did Cam, and then they shook hands. "You must be the fortunate man married to Prue, then."

Cam nodded. "I am the most blessed of all men."

"Oh lord," Prue muttered, her cheeks flaming.

Cam smiled and brushed a finger along her cheek tenderly, still looking at Aubrey. "She hates it when I say anything of the sort."

Aubrey shrugged. "It only shows the quality of her good character. True modesty in all sincerity is quite rare, and all the more exquisite when found."

"I cannot breathe for all the hot air at the moment," Grace commented offhandedly. "Weren't you just telling me the other day to drop my modesty?"

Aubrey slid a sidelong look at her. "You don't have Prue's good sense and sweetness. It doesn't suit."

"Easy," Cam chuckled as he, too, looked at Grace. "She's going to strike you."

"Repeatedly," Grace confirmed with a nod.

Cam smiled swiftly. "And how do the pair of you know each other?"

Aubrey sobered and clasped his hands behind his back. "I was fortunate enough to be neighbors with the Morledge family in Derbyshire in my youth. The children and I used to run around together and make all manner of mischief."

"Aubrey has only recently come to London," Grace told Cam. "And with our renewed acquaintance has also come a continuation of our childish behavior."

"It's rather becoming on you," he replied, shocking Grace and setting her thoughts askew. "What brought you to London in the middle of the Season, Ingram? Looking for a wife?"

God forbid, Grace thought, but couldn't bring herself to say it.

Aubrey shook his head. "No, sir, only to partake in Society at last. I've been much occupied with salvaging my business affairs. And with Grace's father having recently come to London, I've taken it upon myself to seek out his advice and set out to assist both of our estates, now that I have inherited."

"I don't envy you that," Cam sighed, squeezing Prue's shoulder gently. "We've only just gotten repairs to our own estate completed and haven't yet had the time or ability to see to the land itself."

"Well, I am happy to offer any assistance you might require," Aubrey said, sounding the most like himself Grace had heard this evening. "I have some experience now and would be glad to look things over if you have a need."

"I might take you up on that."

"Business talk at a ball? No, no, we cannot have that."

The entire group seemed to both groan and grin at the sound of Miranda Sterling's voice, and they turned to face her.

She was as resplendent as ever in a silver gown, her arm gracefully draped through Tony's. Her blue eyes sparkled like the jewels around her throat, and her smile surpassed them all. Say what you will about Miranda, no person alive could find fault with her style. Never in the extremes, and only ever perfection.

It was thrilling to see her, particularly when Grace needed desperately to ask her what she had done to her father to bring this whole farce to fruition, but there was absolutely no way she was doing that in front of the others. Especially not with Cam about.

She glanced at Aubrey, and saw him doing the same to her, and he lowered his eyes ever so slightly.

How had he known what she was thinking?

No matter.

Miranda greeted them all in turn, then her face changed to utter delight when she saw Aubrey.

"Aubrey, darling!" she cried, extending a gloved hand out to him.

He took it, kissing the back fondly. "Miranda, lovely as always. Where have you been? I have been in London for weeks now, and this is the first I am seeing you."

"Gallivanting, my dear boy, gallivanting," Miranda told him. "Particularly out to Mawbry for a time. You really must come see it again. The shooting is beyond anything."

"I should, I know I should," Aubrey agreed with several nods. "But gallivanting, Miranda? In the middle of the Season? That's unlike you."

Miranda tossed her still-dark hair, which danced in its intricate style. "Well, I always say that fresh air and exercise have kept me youthful, so I must ever indulge."

Tony looked at her in bewilderment. "When have you ever said that?"

"Hush, Tony." She smiled dotingly at Aubrey. "I insist on a dance, dear Aubrey, before you are swarmed with partners for the evening. Will you object to dancing with an old woman?"

Aubrey bowed. "If I happen to see an old woman, I would take it into consideration. As it is, I will gladly dance with you."

Grace *did* roll her eyes at that, but bit back a retort.

She couldn't risk Miranda's reaction.

Aubrey leaned close as he passed. "Come find us after. Let's get this over with."

Grace reared back, looking at him in surprise, but he was already gone with Miranda. She watched them move out to the dance floor, her mind spinning.

Was he flattering Miranda in an attempt to soften the accusations they would bring against her later?

Devious man.

She prayed it would work.

"I like him," Cam said to no one in particular.

Grace glowered at him, which he thankfully did not see. She did not need everyone approving of Aubrey while he was gathering information about her. Which reminded her that she had a task to do, and she needed to get to it.

She exhaled slowly, forcing her very best smile on her face. "Excuse me," she told the group as she moved away and towards a group of people she knew well enough to converse with, however out of practice she was at the exercise.

Where the devil was Grace?

He had been finished dancing with Miranda for almost an hour, and he had absolutely no reason to keep her near him just to wait for Grace. And there was absolutely no way he was going to do this by himself.

He was just that much of a coward where Miranda Sterling was concerned.

Aubrey skirted the edges of the room with a carefully surveying look, eyes scanning about for any sign of the maddening goddess. It ought to have been easy enough to find her. There was no one else to compare with her this evening.

From first sight of her, before he'd ever expressed a greeting, he'd had the unfortunate sensation of being choked by his own tongue. She was arrayed in lavender silks that could not have flowed more flawlessly from her perfectly proportioned figure. Her golden hair was plaited, pinned, and curled with a degree of elegance he had never seen, and the combs within those tresses engendered an unholy temptation in his fingertips.

And all this from seeing her from behind.

There was no telling what she could do to him when they were brought face to face. He'd only known such fear but once in his life, and that had been falling from a particularly tall tree.

This felt more dangerous.

Thankfully, he'd heard what she'd said about perfection, and he'd been able to answer in a way he knew would irk her.

Her scowl when she faced him certainly dampened the effect of her beauty, but it did not rid him of it. Rather than his knees evaporating or his head swimming, he'd only felt a few fluttering twitches in his chest, which could easily be explained away by recent exertion in his home from moving his bureau.

At any rate, he was much recovered, even in memory, and now desperately needed to find Grace to proceed with the confrontation. He grew more anxious about it the longer they waited, and the further away from his shameless charming of Miranda they got. She would not be delighted with him forever, so time was of the essence.

Then, he caught sight of Grace in the midst of a group of young men, and a few young ladies, listening intently to what was being said, but also attracting a good many looks from those within the circle.

Surely, she had to know that. She had to see how they looked. How they stared.

Even watching this, he frowned. If she attracted such attention, why should she be unmarried and without any sort of courtship?

Clearly, some people were without any sense or intelligence at all.

She saw him watching and raised a brow.

Odd how that motion seemed to set off a reaction in his gut. He swallowed and dipped his chin, hoping she would understand the signal.

Her second brow matched the other, and she lowered her lashes briefly.

Aubrey watched in fascination as she excused herself and came towards him, noting how every single eye from the group was upon her. They watched her with more intensity than he had been doing.

Well, well. He would certainly keep *that* in mind in his investigation of her.

Grace approached him, widening her eyes meaningfully. "At last. I've been stuck in that group for ages, and nothing of any substance or consequence was being said."

He chuckled, strangely relieved to hear it. There were some very handsome dandies in that group, some of them clearly puppies, but others quite respectable. All would be acceptable marriage candidates, should an offer be made.

Yet, she was pleased to be away.

"You couldn't escape before?" he asked with a crooked grin.

She scoffed and quirked a smile at him. "I'm not as talented at evasive maneuvers as you are. It's not in the nature of a young woman, nor in our education. Not a flaw."

"No, indeed," he agreed. "In fact, I may have to teach you some proper escape mechanisms for the future."

"A worthy endeavor, I am sure." She wrinkled up her nose in distaste. "Shall we get on with it, then? I can see Miranda, and she is currently unencumbered by conversation."

Get on with what?

Oh, right. Miranda.

Aubrey cleared his throat and gestured for Grace to lead the way. "Ladies first."

Grace gave him a look as she passed him. "Such a gentleman."

"Well, I do try."

"It shows."

Her dry tone made him grin, and he had to hide it quickly before any following eyes caught sight of it. Imagine someone thinking he was smiling that way at Grace for personal reasons.

The horror.

Miranda saw them coming and immediately turned to face them, her eyes narrowing. "Tell me the pair of you have not come to ask me to assist you in an elopement."

"What?" they cried together, Grace rearing back while Aubrey merely gaped.

How could she even think such a thing? Cold bursts of shock ricocheted off various parts of him, and it would seem his heart was currently attempting to dance the jig with the guests at this event and was rather painfully failing.

"Such a pity," Miranda said with a light click of her tongue, ambivalent to their distress. "I was so hopeful." She heaved a sigh and straightened up. "What can I do for you dears, then?"

Grace looked at Aubrey, but he shook his head.

This was her battle. He was simply fighting it with her.

Her eyes flashed briefly, then she turned back to Miranda. "We know that you are aware of the situation between us."

"Am I?" Miranda replied with all the expertise of a covert operative.

"And we also know that Georgie wrote to you and explained my particular situation," Grace went on, miraculously not sounding in any way attacking.

Miranda's face softened. "Yes, I will admit to that, my dear. I am so sorry, what a horrid mess of things."

Aubrey's eyes darted to Grace, knowing too much sympathy would make it all too easy for her to break down and cry. But she was entirely composed and smiling with real warmth. "Thank you," she replied. "It is a trial, to be sure."

"I can only imagine." Miranda nodded with even more sympathy.

Too much.

Perhaps she *was* a covert operative, for this was a skillful attempt at misdirection. Would Grace catch it, or would he need to intervene?

"But what astonishes me," Grace continued, her mouth curving, "is how Aubrey could have gotten so wrapped up in this when he refused Georgie's suggestion."

Clever girl.

Aubrey smirked and looked at Miranda expectantly.

She flicked her eyes to him. "Perhaps Aubrey has a taste for distasteful ventures."

"Oh, really, Miranda," he chortled. "You of all people know I despise distasteful things. We know that you wrote to Trenwick, and something you said convinced him that I ought to be Grace's examiner. So come on, out with it."

Grace made a soft sound of amusement beside him, but clamped down on her lips hard, tilting her head at Miranda.

Miranda shifted her gaze between them both, then rolled her eyes. "Oh, very well. Yes, I wrote to Trenwick. We were in the same circles for a time, though he is quite a bit older."

It took all of Aubrey's strength not to laugh at that.

"At any rate," she said quickly, "I happen to know of a particular item in his past that would be remarkably embarrassing should it become public knowledge. I simply wrote him a message that it had come to my attention that he was looking for someone to find fault in his daughter on purpose, and that the only course was to have Aubrey be the person for the task. If he refused, I would reveal what he would like most to be kept secret."

Blackmail. Plain and simple blackmail had been the sole motivator for Aubrey's being involved in this whole affair. Trenwick feared Miranda and her threat so much that he convinced Aubrey he was the best choice for this madness.

He couldn't believe his ears. "But why?" he asked before he could stop himself. "Why me?"

Miranda seemed surprised by the question. "Why not you, dear boy? If anybody was going to be tasked with this, why shouldn't it be you?"

"Shall I compile a list for you?" he snapped.

"Aubrey," Grace murmured, putting a hand on his arm.

He seethed silently, but the pressure of her hand kept him steady. A soothing warmth spread from it that did not take away his irritation completely, yet it softened it enough that he could contain it.

"I won't apologize for this, Aubrey," Miranda said with her usual bluntness. "Grace was going to be analyzed by someone, like it or not, and it had every possibility of breaking her. Georgie could see that, and she refused to let it happen. I could see it from her account, and I refused to allow it to happen. Selecting you was in no way meant to make either of you uncomfortable, but to make this ridiculous, idiotic, inane venture more bearable for Grace. Because *you* will not break her, Aubrey. You could not. And that is why I am not sorry, nor should you two be."

She scolded them both quite soundly with a look before striding away, her dress sweeping the floor with an audible hiss as she moved.

Aubrey stood there without moving, his eyes staring where Miranda had been, his heart no longer dancing, but somehow completely removed from his person and in hiding.

You will not break her.

No, of course he wouldn't. How could he? How could anyone? Grace was too strong, too perfect, too powerful to be broken, wasn't she?

But he had seen flashes of shocking vulnerability. The slightest glimpses of insecurity. The hints of rawness that she rarely revealed. She was not invincible, which meant she *could* be broken.

There was more to Grace than met the eye, as astonishing as that was to believe, and pushing through the walls of education, accomplishment, and nature of such a woman could very well break her if care was not taken.

No, he would not break her. He could not.

He exhaled slowly and turned to Grace, who swallowed hard, her eyes glistening.

"Grace…"

She shook her head quickly, her lower lip puckering. "Give me a moment, Aubrey. It is only the shock."

She was lying and they both knew it, but he would not press the matter. There would be enough of that to come. In this moment, he had no idea what she needed, but he was willing to provide it.

Whatever it was.

Grace sniffed once, then turned to him, nearly entirely

recovered. She smiled playfully, though it did not quite reach her eyes. "That went well, did it not?"

He snorted softly. "Probably as well as we should have expected of Miranda. And it would seem we have our marching orders."

"Indeed." She exhaled, and then realized her hand was still on his arm. She jerked it away, her cheeks coloring as her smile turned almost sheepish. "So, have you worked anything out this evening as yet?"

Aubrey returned her smile, surprised at how easy it was to do so genuinely. "Some things, but more research is required. I'll be attentive to your various conversations at as discreet a distance as possible to avoid obvious detection, or to make you uneasy, and we will see how much more I observe."

"Uneasy," Grace repeated. "You expect me to not be uneasy this evening? No matter where I stand or what I say, I'll know that you see and hear me, and will judge. That should be comfortable for me?"

He shrugged with as much mischief as he could manage. "That would be the task, my dear. You must get used to observation, by me or by others."

She frowned, though it appeared to be teasing. "It is not the others I am worried about."

Aubrey let his mischief fade a little. "Grace, you know that Miranda was right, don't you?"

"About what?"

He took one step closer, needing her to understand this. "I will not break you."

Her eyes widened, and her breathing seemed to falter. Then, miraculously, a gentle, beautiful smile appeared. "I know that, Aubrey. I might not know much else, but I do know that."

She touched his hand, then moved on past him to find another group to mingle with.

At least, he thought she touched his hand. Or what used to be his hand. Or rather where it used to be.

Everything seemed to be on fire at the moment, and he could not be entirely sure.

He turned to watch her go, saw her join Henshaw and Francis with a few others, and wondered if he was brave enough to venture the same.

Something possessed him to turn back and find Charlotte Wright to check one suddenly nagging thought.

Ah, there he was. Michael Sandford, right where he had been before. Hovering at the edge, never quite brave enough to go all the way.

Suddenly, Aubrey could relate perfectly.

Chapter Eleven

———⚜———

It would behoove a sensible being to accomplish their tasks as quickly as possible while still maintaining the quality of one's work. One must be thorough, but never prolong matters needlessly. There is nothing worse than needless prolonging of anything, but most especially when there is expectation in the results. Simply intolerable.

-*The Spinster Chronicles, 2 January 1817*

"Heavens above, *why* are you here at this time of morning?"

"I thought to begin our task early today."

Grace glowered at him as she sat down to her breakfast. "I'll not be ruled by you as by an overbearing tutor, Aubrey. I dislike being roused from my bed and subjected to an examination before I have eaten a single thing."

Aubrey returned her glower with a bright grin. "By all means, eat something. It would be good to keep up your strength. As for the earliness of the hour, I suppose you must grow accustomed to it."

"Why?" Grace asked as she took a bite of potato. "What could possibly require me to rise early in the future?"

"The duties of a wife, I expect."

The duties of *what?*

Grace set her fork and knife on her plate with a faint clatter. "I beg your pardon?"

Aubrey's smile turned hesitant and apologetic, his fingers anxiously fiddling with his cravat. "Umm... I take it back?"

"Do you?"

"I do, with all my heart."

Grace scoffed and picked up her utensils once more. "Half-heartedly, more like." She gestured to the chair across from her. "You might as well sit and judge my eating habits and table manners. Do you want anything?"

Aubrey shook his head and sat, leaning back against the chair. "Why so violent against even the word wife? Don't you want to marry?"

"Of course, I do," Grace replied, swallowing a bite. "It's only the reminder that I have yet to become one that tends to make me irritable. As if I could not be a complete person without a man to tell me I am so."

"That's not what I..."

She waved him off. "I know, I know. You were only teasing, but I'm a trifle testy this morning, what with everything else. Yes, I want to be a wife. Very much. But I am at the point now where I refuse to marry just for the sake of it. I know what it is to be without a husband, as it's all I have known, and, short of distressing my father, I think I've managed to do very well."

Aubrey smiled and nodded in consideration. "I concur, you certainly have."

Grace allowed his comment with an accepting dip of her chin. "So, *if* I marry in the future, it must be to a man I can actually tolerate, sustain conversation with, and one who does not see my worth and value as limited to the dowry that he will gain upon joining with me. I refuse to be bartered with."

"Too right."

She glanced up at him and saw, to her surprise, a smug smile and warm eyes. It was entirely too becoming on him, and somehow seemed perfectly natural.

"You agree?" she asked him. "Why? It's not a popular opinion."

"No, but I have always been in favor of unpopular opinion. People, in general, are idiots." He grinned cheekily, then sobered. "In truth, I actually agree. Despite what your father thinks, I find no need for you to rush into matrimony for the sake of it. Popular opinion or not, matrimony should be more than a financially beneficial contract if it is to be of any pleasant yield to either party. I think we can both say as much from experience." He widened his eyes, close to laughter.

Grace groaned and nodded, taking another bite of her breakfast. "Among others, to be sure. I could never marry a man who did not know how I prefer my porridge."

Aubrey looked down at her plate pointedly, then raised his cloudy blue eyes to hers. "You aren't eating porridge."

She shrugged as she chewed. "Then you'll be no help to any potential prospects, will you?" She swallowed and tilted her head at him, a strange mischievous streak lighting within her. "And if we are to speak of matrimony over breakfast, we may as well turn to your own prospects."

As she suspected, he blanched in horror. "Good heavens, why?"

"Why not?" she shot back, sitting forward and setting her hands in her lap. "You're of an age, and your situation has improved now that Breyerly is restored."

"Stop. Just stop."

Grace twisted her lips on a laugh. "You should put your mind to it, Aubrey. You need a wife."

He quirked his brows, mouth curving to one side. "I thought I was practically perfect. Elinor said so."

"Elinor is an infant," Grace said at once. "And besides, practically is not completely. A wife would improve you."

Aubrey snorted once. "What if I don't want to be improved?"

What did that have to do with anything? Grace did not want to be improved either, and yet here she was, being evaluated for faults so that she *could* improve.

But that wasn't Aubrey's fault, and she would not pretend it was.

"A wife would humanize you," she added, resuming her eating.

Aubrey released a loud laugh. "How would you know? You've never been one."

Grace paused, raising a brow at him. "I've never been an idiot, either. Yet, I know one when I see one."

His mouth popped open as he coughed another laugh, then grabbed at his chest in mock-pain. "Oh, the agony..."

"I'm sure you'll survive." She smirked and continued to eat her breakfast. "Now, since you're here, amuse me while I finish."

"If my lady doth command," he responded, somehow bowing from a seated position without technically doing so. "What would best amuse you presently?"

Grace glanced out of the breakfast room door, then back to him, letting her excitement show. "Tell me everything about Breyerly and Withrow. Absolutely everything."

Thankfully, Aubrey needed no prodding on that topic, and for the next few minutes, he regaled her with every single detail, not minding her constantly interrupting him for specifics. If they never agreed on anything else, this would be enough. They shared a passion for their home estates, the lands, and the memories had among both. Unlike her father or brother, Grace longed for Withrow and Derbyshire, and would happily spend the rest of her life there, married or not.

As it was unlikely she would ever be able to, she would soak up every image Aubrey painted in her mind and every description he gave.

It just might be her last.

When he'd finished, Grace sat back, sated both mentally and physically, and sighing in a mixture of satisfaction and regret.

"Such a sad sound," Aubrey murmured. "Withrow?"

She nodded and smiled wistfully. "It is unlikely we will ever go back, and no one seems to feel the loss as I do. No one seems to remember it as fondly as I do, though Mama tries. I know Father and James complain that it's not producing enough, but I have seen no evidence of anyone actually trying to salvage it. London will never be home for me; that will only and ever be Withrow. And they want to be rid of it."

Aubrey made a soft, unintelligible sound. "I had no idea you felt that way about it. I thought... well, I thought you would feel the same as all the rest of your family. Your mother aside."

"I am not my family," she told him with all the firmness she could muster.

His smile was swift and sure. "I'm beginning to see that." He eyed her plate again. "Are you finished?"

Grace sat up and nodded primly. "I am. Did you find any fault in my table manners?"

Aubrey chuckled and smoothed down his cravat. "Not a one. You used all the right utensils, kept a proper distance from the table, and maintained equal and appropriately proportioned bites throughout. Most satisfactory."

"You noticed all that?" she asked as she rose from her seat. "Even while you were talking?"

He gave her a look as he, too, rose. "I am capable of doing more than one thing at a time, you know."

"Will wonders never cease?" she mused as she made her way out of the breakfast room.

"Just for that, you get to be judged on comportment today. More specifically, the way you walk and move. Starting now."

Grace whirled around to face him. "What?"

He spun his finger in a circle, indicating she turn. "Walking. Forward. Now."

She glowered and grabbed her blue gingham skirts, and spun back around with a swish of them, snarling through gritted teeth. He wanted to see her walk and try to find a fault? Three years with Miss Godson had stripped her of any flaws in this regard, even if she stomped away in a temper.

She tossed her head, eliciting a snicker from behind her, then strode gracefully towards the drawing room at the end of the corridor.

Aubrey followed silently.

Once in the room, she turned to face him. "Well?"

He sat in a chair and crossed his legs. "Keep going."

Grace frowned at him. "Are you serious? You want me to walk about the room while you watch?"

He reached into his waistcoat and pulled out the list Elinor had made him. "It says so right here. 'Comportment. How she walks and moves.'" He held it out for her. "See for yourself."

She exhaled through her nose and shook her head. "I believe you, I suppose. Very well, I shall continue walking."

It was beyond stupid, but there was nothing to be done about that. They both had to play the game if they ever wanted it to end. And for all she knew, she might have developed a hitch in her step over the years.

Doubtful, but possible.

Over and over again she walked, crossing the room back and forth, tracing the edges of the room. Just walking. It felt awkward and ridiculous. She sent many long-suffering looks in Aubrey's direction, hoping he'd allow her to stop.

He never let her desist. On the contrary, he sat in his chair, one hand near his mouth, and a small smile on his face. Just watching. It was clear the blackguard was enjoying himself at her expense, and she was done with it.

She stopped and turned to him, hands on her hips. "Aubrey, enough! I feel like a horse being carted out for observation. Honestly, haven't you found a flaw yet?"

Aubrey cleared his throat and lowered his hand. "No, Grace, I haven't. So, if you wouldn't mind…" He gestured for her to continue, smiling more fully.

Grace felt her cheeks flush, and she shook her head. "No. No, I do mind! I'm just wandering around pretending that I am not being studied, which is terribly difficult to manage as if all were normal, and that is…"

"I think you would find," Aubrey interrupted, sitting up and giving her a serious look, "that a great many people, men and women, are watching you move. Watching you walk. Dance. Glide. I have seen them do so, and I cannot blame them. Because it's very nearly a thing of art, Grace, and I won't apologize for taking pleasure in its observation."

Her heart stuttered within her chest, then seemed to pound terribly in her ears, drowning out any other sound for a moment or two. She managed a rough swallow.

"Oh."

He smiled at her gently, taking pity on her. "But as you are especially uncomfortable, I think we may stop."

She exhaled in a rush of relief and sat down in a nearby chair, taking care to do so very properly. "Thank you. Any flaws?"

Aubrey smirked at her. "That is for me alone to know. I will not always tell you what I find as I find it."

"You promised!" she protested in outrage.

That earned her a scolding look. "I promised to tell you what I found, but I did not promise it would be immediately. I *will* tell you what I find before I tell your father, but it would be best if we did not exchange findings at every single meeting. I'd rather proceed more naturally and reveal all once we reach the end. Do you consent to that?"

Naturally? His examination of her? It did not seem likely, but she supposed if she began to view things less as an evaluation and more of a meeting with a friend...

A friend? Aubrey?

She looked at him, saw the warmth in his eyes, the comfort in his smile, and the relaxed nature of his countenance. Even in their sparring, she found herself liking him and enjoying herself. Even when he was impossible, he could make her smile, against her will at times.

Yes, she supposed they were friends. And she would much rather be natural with her friends.

"Very well," she finally replied. "I do consent."

Aubrey left Trenwick House with a broad smile and laughter on nearly every breath.

He couldn't help it; it could have been pouring sheets of rain outside, and he would have thought it sunny.

That had been the best session of fault-finding he'd had with Grace yet, and he hadn't found a single fault in any aspect.

After having her parade around the drawing room, which really had been sheer perfection, they shifted to analyzing her language abilities. German, French, Italian, and, surprisingly enough, Latin.

She was fluent in all of them and happened to be just as witty in those languages as she was in English.

Of course.

His own Italian was a little weak, so it was entirely possible that she had neglected a thing or two in her conversation there, but nothing glaringly obvious.

He'd thought about asking her to dance a jig with him after all that, but he'd been so entertained by their multilingual conversation that it wouldn't have been any sort of evaluation. It would likely dissolve into ridiculous bouts of laughter, stumbling, and treading on toes.

And there was no telling how Grace would have acted.

He was sane enough to know that her laughter was too musical, and in close proximity, that laughter could be dangerous.

But it would not keep him from smiling and laughing now as he left.

That last burst of wit she had spouted in German had really...

"Ingram, what a pleasant surprise!"

He turned quickly to see Henshaw and Francis approaching him, and he smiled at them both. "Good day, gentlemen."

Francis eyed him with interest, smirking. "The hat generally goes on the head, Ingram. Not in the hands."

Aubrey barely avoided scowling and replied, "Does it really? What an ingenious notion." He popped it on his head, tapped it down, then gave Francis a look. "Satisfied?"

"Inestimably." Francis grinned, looking rather like his cousin when he did so. "This isn't your side of town, what are you about?"

"Paying calls," Aubrey retorted defensively. "The mark of a gentleman, is it not?"

"Debatable," Henshaw remarked in his offhand way, eying the houses around them.

Aubrey watched him, curious as to his reasoning. "Lost, Henshaw?"

The man looked at him with a sudden, swift grin. "No, but you might be. Why were you calling on Grace Morledge?"

"Who says I was calling on Grace?" Aubrey asked as they began to walk in the direction he had begun. "I've been advising with her father, Lord Trenwick, of late."

"No one meeting with Trenwick would exit the house with a grin like the one you were just wearing." Henshaw's look turned inquiring, though Aubrey suspected he would have turned all out interrogating if the need arose.

Francis made a careful sound of consideration, then looked at Aubrey. "And it is rather early for business arrangements. Or social calls, for that matter."

"That didn't stop the two of you from being out and about at this time of day," he shot back, fighting the urge to shove his hands in his trouser pockets and ambling along as he would have done in the country. London required a stiffer, stuffier approach to his style and manner, and it was beginning to grate on him.

Henshaw and Francis shared a look. "Evasion," they said together.

Aubrey clicked his tongue in mock appreciation. "That was adorably coordinated."

"I surmise," Henshaw announced, ignoring Aubrey's comment, "that you, for whatever reason, were calling upon Grace Morledge at a time when many ladies of her station are still abed, and from the smile I saw on your face, you enjoyed every moment of it."

Laughter erupted from Aubrey, forced and hard, but it came all the same, and he was relieved at its timing. He had to maintain the precedence of their story, even if things appeared to be otherwise, and these two were an easy link back to Tony, who would *not* find his calling upon Grace to be a thing to let go of easily. There would be suspicion and suggestion, and neither Aubrey nor Grace needed anything of the sort.

"Are you quite finished?" Francis queried in a remarkably mild tone.

Aubrey held up a hand, then fisted it over his mouth in a show of hilarity. "Nearly."

"Good," Francis replied. "Because that was a terrible imitation of laughter, which only solidifies Henshaw's point. Any further denials on your part will lead to suspicions of a romantic attachment, if not a secret engagement."

He couldn't be serious. All because Aubrey refused to admit what was going on, they would assume that...?

But of course, they would. He was seen leaving a young lady's house at an hour that was earlier than social norms dictated and had been grinning like a fool. Anyone would have made the same assumption. He could not risk their threat of rumors.

He glowered moodily at them both. "Fine, you gossiping harpies." He looked around quickly, then lowered his voice. "I *was* calling upon Grace, but not for any reasons that you might think."

"Really?" Henshaw asked with a suggestive edge to his tone. "Are you sure?"

Aubrey would have punched him if they were not in public, but snarling seemed an apt alternative. "Positive, and you will agree when I tell you why."

He quickly related the details of the situation and was moderately satisfied to see disgruntled expressions on the other men's faces. They looked at each other but didn't seem to have words for what he'd just told them.

Aubrey shrugged lightly. "Sorry to disappoint, but there it is. And you are now both sworn to secrecy. I don't need all of London knowing that I'm finding fault in an unmarried woman on purpose."

"I don't think anyone needs to know that anyone does that," Henshaw replied with a disgusted look. "And for her own father to arrange it? Just because his daughter is a spinster? Ridiculous and cruel."

Francis was shaking his head and gave Aubrey a bewildered look. "Why did you agree?"

"Sometimes, I don't know myself," Aubrey sighed. "But other times, I'm reminded that there are several worse options than me, and ones that could make Grace's life a living hell."

"I'd say her father is already doing that," Henshaw muttered.

Aubrey nodded at that. "It's going well enough. It's actually getting to be enjoyable, in a way."

"Fault-finding is enjoyable?" Francis asked wryly. "I doubt that."

Aubrey smirked to himself. No, fault-finding was not enjoyable. Being with Grace was.

They continued on silently, mulling over everything, and Aubrey let his mind go back to the way Grace had looked as she'd walked in the drawing room. When she'd stopped being annoyed with him for making her do something so menial, she'd begun to smile a little, and he'd been captivated by it. Such a small thing for her lips to do, and yet it did so much for her features.

Not that they needed any improving or alteration, but that small smile turned her from incomparable to transcendent. And it was absolutely impossible to avoid smiling in return at the sight of it, even if the smile was not aimed in a particular direction. There was simply something transfixing about it, made all the more enchanting by the perfectly formed lips that bordered it.

He'd spent far too much time analyzing her smile and her lips more than he had her walking, but surely that was neither here nor there.

He was tasked with analyzing everything about her, was he not?

"Do your meetings with Grace always go on this early?" Henshaw asked him, his dark brow furrowing. "It's bound to create gossip."

Aubrey snapped back to present, looking at his friends. "No, this was the earliest. I'm trying to vary the schedule a bit. The story should be that I am meeting with her father, unfortunately."

Francis groaned sympathetically. "That is unfortunate. Well, could we have you two find fault in a different location?"

"Unaccompanied?" Aubrey snorted softly. "Highly doubtful."

Henshaw twisted his lips in thought, then turned to Francis. "You have an estate just outside of London. Is there acreage enough for a good ride?"

"Well, it's my wife's family's estate, but yes, and that's an excellent thought." Francis grinned at Aubrey and clapped him on the back. "You and Grace must come out to Darefield, if you haven't already analyzed her riding abilities. We could provide a picnic, and perhaps some lawn games, as well. Tony and Georgie are gone to Hazelwood, and Janet would love to spend a day away from London. It would almost be like you were out in the country, wouldn't it?"

Aubrey stared at him in a brief spell of disbelief. Being in the country with Grace? Riding together and laughing freely while he pretended to analyze what he already knew would be a perfect riding form? It would be as close to being back at Breyerly or Withrow as they would get, yet they were both adults now, not children.

How different would this be?

"That sounds brilliant," he confessed in a surprisingly breathless tone. He cleared his throat and frowned. "How would either of us get to Darefield without comment? I cannot possibly bring her in a carriage unaccompanied, no matter how her father understands the scenario."

"Simple enough," Francis said with an offhand lift of one

shoulder. "Come separately. I'll have Janet send an invitation to Grace, and you just come when you like. We'll see Grace home, and no one will be any the wiser."

Henshaw nodded next to them, clasping his hands behind his back. "Excellent, yes. But are your credentials enough to warrant Lord Trenwick being eager for his daughter to attend? No offense, Sterling, but it sounds to me like he is getting quite restrictive with his adult daughter."

Francis smiled tightly. "No offense taken, I'm simply a minor peer in the scheme of things. My wife, however, is a Demaris, and if that does not tempt Trenwick, nothing else will." Francis turned to Aubrey again, grinning now. "Let's say Wednesday, shall we?"

Wednesday. Three days from now. A foray into the countryside with Grace.

What could be better?

"Wednesday it is." He laughed and looked up into the sky. "If the day is as fine as this one, it will be a glorious thing indeed."

"Oh lord," Henshaw groaned, thumping Aubrey hard. "He comes out of her house near whistling a jaunty tune, and now he's near to tears of joy over a future ride by her side. Fault-finding or not, Ingram, you're soon going to find yourself in a massive fault of your own, tripping over your own shoes to hand the lady a wildflower."

Aubrey squawked in distress as Francis hooted a laugh and spent the rest of their stroll denying every ridiculous allegation Henshaw or Francis could throw at him. Thankfully, he did so with more success than he had done earlier, but they would not be satisfied for long.

If Aubrey could not get his mind to regain its former sense, and his expression to control itself, very many people would be suspecting very many things all too soon.

And he might begin to suspect things himself.

Horror of horrors.

Chapter Twelve

F *resh air and exercise may do a body a world of good. The extent of the good may depend on the company one keeps throughout the excursion.*

-The Spinster Chronicles, 8 July 1816

In all the time she'd ever spent in London, Grace could only recall visiting Darefield twice, and both of those times had been in the company of several others. She had never been invited alone. In fact, she had never even been invited to Sterling House alone.

She truly liked the Sterlings, and Janet, Lady Sterling, was especially a favorite of hers. They were not close, but she was a friend and ally to all the Spinsters. Their conversations had always been pleasant, and occasionally rather lively. She would love the opportunity to know Janet better, and to call her a friend in truth.

Today would likely not be the day to do that, but she would certainly be grateful that she and Lord Sterling were assisting her in today's excursion.

Well, her and Aubrey.

She hadn't believed it when he had sent a note to her the other day with this plan. How could they possibly go off to a friend's estate by themselves and ride by themselves and then picnic by themselves?

Was he *trying* to compromise them in the eyes of Society?

The official invitation from Janet had come as a relief, and finally, Grace began to imagine how this plan might actually work. Of course, there were several other things that had to work perfectly in order to have this be truly successful, but she was willing to put forth a little tentative optimism.

But only a little.

Still, she was out on an excursion away from the house and away from London, and with her father's full permission and excitement, no less. Janet came from a predominant family, and her marriage to Francis was considered a lowering of her station, impossible as that seemed, but the connection was still one her father encouraged.

Clearly Aubrey, or Francis, had known that much.

Conniving, brilliant men.

She sat back against the cushions of the coach, exhaling and smiling to herself. She hadn't been riding in ages, not the way she longed to, and she was desperate to do so today. Her plum-colored riding habit still looked as good as new, though it was a few years old, and she hoped to put the whole ensemble through its paces today.

Especially beating Aubrey in a race.

He might have thought himself an accomplished sportsman, living in the country as he did, but Grace could safely say that she was surprisingly accomplished in all things equestrian. Not even her father knew that, and he would surely have disapproved if he did.

Which, naturally, made her want to improve all the more.

Her one great reservation about trouncing him soundly was that she had no idea what else he had planned on this excursion of theirs, and he was the sort to take his vengeance wherever he could. There was no telling what her penance would be with him as the dictator and enforcer of it.

She might have to tread carefully. Or make the victory seem close, at least.

She nodded to herself as the carriage pulled up to Darefield. Surely losing a close race was no cause for her to receive punishment. She could soundly trounce him some other time when there was less at risk.

The thought caught her off-guard. Some other time? Was she planning on having the opportunity to race against him again? To spend more time with him even after this whole ridiculous circus was over? When had that become something she should want to do, let alone subconsciously consider?

The coach stopped and she swallowed harshly, forcing her expression to clear. Imagine if remnants of her thoughts had stayed there for all to see. Aubrey would have been insufferable with his curiosity.

She disembarked from the coach with some assistance from the footman, which was sorely needed, as the skirts of her habit were surprisingly voluminous, and she had no confidence in her foot placement. She smiled and nodded her thanks to the him. He politely nodded, and then winked, of all things. Grace shook her head, then headed towards the doors of Darefield, exhaling slowly.

Janet came out to meet her before she even reached the steps. She looked quite comfortable in her elegant day dress of blue, her dark hair pulled back in a simple chignon, her eyes sparkling with a very Sterling sort of light.

Grace gave her a bemused look as she curtseyed. "Janet."

Her hostess smiled fondly. "Grace. Welcome." The smile turned into a mischievous smirk. "He's already here. He's at the stables, Tom will show you where they are. Ride as long as you like, and we'll picnic after." She flashed a very tiny wink and turned for the house.

The aforementioned Tom, a tall man with the rough style of workman's clothing, bowed to Grace, then indicated she should follow him around to the side of the house. He began a clearly well-rehearsed speech regarding the stables and horses of the state, his tone deep and warm, though Grace had absolutely no interest in anything he was saying. Years of practice allowed her to respond to him at various points appropriately without actually listening to a single word.

"And here, Miss Morledge," Tom finally said, slowing as they reached the stables, "is everything I have just described in great detail without your hearing a bit of it."

Grace looked up at him in surprise, then smiled in embarrassment at his own smile. "Apologies, Tom. I am... quite distracted."

"Understood, miss." He winked, then gestured for her to go on into the large and well-lit structure.

Aubrey was within, of course, murmuring to the large, black stallion nuzzling him. He turned at the sound of her entrance and grinned at her. "At last. Bernard and I were just wondering if we should ride out and let you find us whenever you showed up."

Grace rolled her eyes, ignoring Tom's chuckle behind her. "I am perfectly on time. You are abysmally early. Poor Janet must have sent you straight out here to avoid enduring your company."

"No doubt." Aubrey patted Bernard on the nose, then waved her over to a beautiful chestnut mare. "Miss Morledge, might I introduce Mulberry? Mulberry, this is Miss Morledge. You are to take excellent care of her and be perfectly respectful at all times. Understood?"

The horse dipped her head repeatedly in a decent showing of a nod, and Grace gasped, then grinned. "How did you get her to do that?" she demanded.

Aubrey tossed a derogatory look in her direction. "I will have you know that Mulberry is the most intelligent horse you will ever meet. I have been markedly impressed."

"That does not surprise me," Grace retorted as she moved to scratch Mulberry gently. "I have no doubt she is more intelligent than you, aren't you, love?"

The horse nickered in response, and Grace turned to give Aubrey an utterly superior look.

He glared at the mare. "Traitor." Then he held a hand out for Grace and led her to the side of the horse, preparing to help her mount.

"Wait," Grace said quickly, her foot already in a stirrup.

Aubrey, stooping already to assist, sighed and gave her a long-suffering look. "Yes?"

She smirked down at him. "Any fault in my riding habit?"

She saw him fight a laugh, then he shook his head, losing the battle with his smile. "Not from this angle. No faults at all."

Considering his vantage point, that wasn't particularly polite, and she blushed, returning her attention to Mulberry. "Ready."

With a quick boost, she was up and settled, and Aubrey moved to his horse and mounted with a smoothness that any red-blooded woman, equestrian prone or not, would have appreciated.

There was no need for that; he should be appreciating her, if anything. He was her examiner, nothing more.

Grace turned Mulberry out of the stables, and Tom dared to wink again, chuckling to himself as Aubrey followed her out. They trotted out of the stable yard, and once out of earshot, Grace turned to Aubrey with a frown.

He reared back at its sight. "Good heavens, what? We've only just started."

"Why does everybody seem to be winking at me today? What did you say?"

He lifted a brow. "Why does the sun make us smile? Why do birds sing? Why does the breeze feel so perfect on a warm day? Because God ordained it should be so."

Grace gaped in derision for a moment, then closed her mouth on a rueful smile. "God decreed that all should wink at me?"

Aubrey shrugged. "It would not surprise me in the least, groveling and pleading for favors from your person being a bit obvious."

"Oh lord," Grace moaned, looking up at the few clouds dotting the sky.

"Aubrey will do," he quipped. "Now ride, woman." He whacked Bernard with his crop and raced off.

Not to be outdone, Mulberry took little prodding from Grace to take off herself, but then she galloped with extraordinary length and stride, keeping pace with Bernard easily before closing on him. The landscape was perfect for such racing with its wide-open expanses and gentle hills, all green and fresh even in these days of summer. With no rain of late, the horses' hooves pounded furiously against the ground, kicking up dust and bits of grass in their wake.

The ride was exhilarating, and Grace breathed in the fragrances of the experience, the cool air filling her lungs with a rare sort of refreshment. Mulberry was the perfect mount, smooth in her motions and steady as any creature, and despite her almost sleepy manner, in truth she was anything but.

"Good girl," Grace praised, forgoing proper riding posture to lean closer to her. "Let's see if you jump as brilliantly as you ride."

Mulberry took the encouragement and pushed further, driving hard against the terrain, and Grace could hear Aubrey's voice calling out to her, but the words were lost on her. A creek ahead would be perfect, and the breadth of it was decent enough, though not so far as to be dangerous, in her mind. A part of her wished it would be dangerous. The number of times she had succeeded with dangerous jumps at Withrow...

"Grace!" Aubrey called, his voice suddenly clear.

Too late.

Mulberry needed no urging and sprang deftly over the creek, giving Grace a momentary feeling of breathlessness, then landed cleanly on the other side.

Grace pulled her to a stop, laughing wildly and patting the horse's neck. She turned around to face Aubrey, who was wide-eyed atop Bernard on the other side. Grace laughed even harder at his expression.

"Bloody hell, woman!" Aubrey finally managed, his face regaining a bit of its color at last.

"Did I frighten you?" she asked, still giggling as Mulberry snorted and panted beneath her.

Aubrey led Bernard over to the edge of the creek, shaking his head. "Out of my wits. Damnation, Grace." He laughed once and shook his head once more. "You are a magnificent, bold, terrifying rider, and certainly the best female rider I know. I have never been more stunned in my entire life, and I freely admit it."

Grace beamed, moving Mulberry to the creek bed. "What do you think I did all those days at Withrow when I had become accomplished and had no company to assess me?"

He ran a hand over his face, laughing more easily. "Did you ever jump the great fallen tree on Breyerly? You must have done. Attempted, at least."

"Attempted," Grace admitted with a dip of her chin, "and succeeded. Often."

Aubrey's broad grin could have been made of pure sunshine. "Of course, you did. Well, well, Grace Morledge, this changes the game almost entirely."

She tilted her head, feeling a bemused smile cross her lips. "How so, sir?"

He bit his lip for the faintest moment, and something tugged in her heart as he did so, then it passed. "Because now I can raise the stakes without being ungentlemanly."

"What, and best me in a race?" She tossed her head back and laughed. "Don't you dare tell me you were being gentlemanly then. I saw your efforts."

"No, no," he allowed, patting Bernard as the horse shuffled uneasily. "I was not. But you are not the only one who spent a lot of time riding across the Derbyshire countryside, let alone our two estates. I will ask you one question. Can you ride astride?"

Grace's lips parted in surprise, then curved to one side as her cheeks heated a touch. "The current fashions render such things markedly uncomfortable. Markedly."

Aubrey's gaze remained steady, his expression unchanging. "Yes, I'd imagine so, but can you?"

"Yes," she said simply.

"Prove it."

The challenge was no surprise, but Grace wasn't an idiot. "Will that be counted a flaw? You are considered polite company, after all."

He scoffed at that. "Fault-finding be damned; I want to see what you can do."

Well, in *that* case...

Maintaining eye contact with Aubrey, Grace shifted her right leg beneath her extensive habit skirts, sliding it from its position at the pommel across to drape tightly on the other side. Pressing herself up from the horse, she rearranged her skirts as best as she could, and, with only her ankles being exposed, settled herself back into the saddle. Then, she nudged Mulberry across the creek, which the horse did with no trouble whatsoever.

Once she reached Aubrey, Grace tilted her head in invitation. "Satisfied?"

He looked her over thoroughly, his eyes gleaming when they finally reached hers again. "Perfectly so. You have the loveliest ankles I've ever seen."

"And how many pairs *have* you seen?" she queried with a snort.

One shoulder lifted casually. "Enough. There is a particularly lovely gazebo at the north end of the estate, I am told. Shall we race there?"

Grace nodded once. "Yes. Let's." With a quick whack of her

crop, Mulberry shot off. Aubrey and Bernard were just behind them, hooves pounding the ground once again.

It was better than he could ever have imagined. If he closed his eyes, he could have been back at Breyerly, and he and Grace would have been riding in a companionable manner there. The racing done, they'd begun meandering the grounds of Darefield on horseback, chatting as any old friends might have done and laughing uproariously about this thing or that.

Except he and Grace had never been old friends. Yet the comfort, enjoyment, and ease were the same.

Unless he looked her in the eye, of course, and then his mind became shrouded in fog and babbled within him like the brook at Breyerly. So long as he avoided that, he was safe.

Marginally.

She was a vision in her riding habit, which he had never considered to be a particularly fetching ensemble on most women, but on Grace it was so. Very much so. Least of all, because she was such a marvelous rider, and he had spent far too long having his vision hindered, or improved, by the sight of her ahead of him.

For the present, he was himself, and he would have been perfectly content to do nothing more than talk with Grace for hours on end. He actually felt himself disappointed when he saw that they were back at Darefield itself, and that Janet and Francis waited for them on the terrace.

He couldn't tell Grace that, however.

He cleared his throat and tried for his usual grin. "Our chaperones await us. Do you think we'll be scolded?"

Grace looked where he indicated, and he saw her deflate a little in the saddle. "Oh. I forgot all about them. I was too wrapped up in enjoying our riding and conversation to recall our true purpose." She smiled at him without any hint of teasing or humor. "Fancy that."

Aubrey couldn't breathe for a number of heartbeats, his eyes raking over her features, taking in every single blessed aspect of such a smile in his direction.

She felt it, too.

"Fancy that," he echoed softly, his lips barely moving.

Her eyes widened slightly, and the smile froze, perfect lips still in their perfect position. The sun came out from behind a cloud then and seemed to beam solely on the person of Grace Morledge, no doubt one of its favorite targets. She glowed with it, and one blink of her long lashes sent a wash of sensation over him.

If he were only closer...

"The picnic is not quite ready," Janet called out to them, breaking the moment, "but what would you say to a bit of dancing while we wait? No doubt that was on the list?"

Aubrey jerked to look at the Sterlings, his mind working backwards. Dancing? Did he dance? Was he supposed to dance?

"I'm happy to partner with Grace myself," Francis broke in, giving Aubrey a slight smile, "if that would make things easier."

Easier? Oh, *hell* no.

"And have my subject return home to her father with bruised and broken toes?" he retorted, coming to himself. "I think not. You will stand safely by the piano with your wife, sir."

Francis laughed to himself, glancing at Grace, which forced Aubrey to do the same.

She had recovered entirely from whatever moment that had been between them and was grinning with good humor at him.

"You want me to dance in my riding habit?" she asked, feigning disbelief. "Do you see this rig?"

He did, and he saw the bits of her leg exposed as she sat astride, which delighted him to no end. "Surely a bit of fabric will not hinder you."

She glowered, despite her smile. "Let me put a bit of fabric in your mouth or around your neck and see how hindered you are."

Aubrey tugged lightly at his cravat. "There *is* a bit of fabric around my neck. Sundrey insisted."

Grace pursed her lips and shook her head as she pulled Mulberry to a stop. Two stable hands immediately came to them.

Aubrey dismounted quickly, not entirely sure what his purpose was until he found himself rounding Bernard and standing right before Grace, who was sliding her right leg back over the saddle. Her face was creased with irritation and focus as she tried to maneuver the thing without being indecent.

She saw him standing there and stuck out her tongue. "I blame you entirely for this."

He chuckled and held out his hands. "I'll take it, and I'll have you know, it was well worth it."

She paused, then gave a small, but distinctly proud smile. "It was, wasn't it?"

She had no idea.

When she'd finally brought her leg around, she reached for his hands. He surprised her, and himself, however, by stepping forward and taking her waist in his hands and pulling her down. She came flush with him on a surprised rush of air, her hands flying to his shoulders and gripping for steadiness. Her eyes were luminous at this proximity, and her lips fuller than he had thought only scant moments ago. He could feel each breath that passed through her, every brush of her buttons against his chest, and the shockingly natural size of her waist. Yes, she was wearing stays, but the tension there…

He swallowed and saw her do the same, then stepped back, bowed, and exhaled while his face was lowered. "My lady, might I have whatever dance Janet will force us to endure?"

Grace hesitated for just a hair longer than he was comfortable with, then put her hand in his. He could feel the faint tremor in it, but chose to ignore it, as he was quite certain he had tremors in various places himself.

"Oh, why not?" Grace eventually quipped.

Aubrey rose to his full stature, made a show of leading her up the terrace steps, and then into the house. They said nothing as they moved, for which he was grateful. He needed time to collect himself, to put on his more playful self, and to forget that the woman beside him was growing more and more attractive, more admired, and more important with every moment in her company.

The fact that her fingers were in his hand and curling around his own in what was likely an involuntary manner, and that it made portions of his toes tingle, did not help matters.

But he was willing to sacrifice that much.

Francis and Janet were chattering on about something, but Aubrey could not spare the use of his ears at the present. Not when he had to prepare to dance with Grace Morledge, of all people, and pretend that he needed to find a fault in it. As if he was in a mindset to find faults at all.

As if there were any faults to find.

They entered a large room with a harp and pianoforte and plenty of space for a small group to dance, given that the furniture had all been shifted to one side.

Aubrey eyed the arrangement and gave Francis an amused look. "Interesting seating arrangement. Are you all so keen on unplanned dancing occurring that you actually plan for it ahead of time?"

Francis returned that look with false irritation. "Well, I must practice, mustn't I? If you consider me such a danger to dance partners."

"Having never partnered with you, sir, I cannot say one way or the other," Aubrey replied politely, drawing soft giggles from Grace.

Janet shook her head and sat at the piano, looking at Grace with sympathy. "I'd offer you a third gentleman for a partner, if only I had one."

Grace nodded in acknowledgement. "I shall endeavor to endure this as best I can."

Aubrey grinned and turned to face Grace, releasing her hand at last. "You'll enjoy this," he promised.

She quirked a brow. "That's what you think."

Janet struck up a jaunty tune, and Aubrey took Grace's hands, proceeding to move with her in a large circle as though joined by other couples. He released her hands to wave Francis over so that he might stand in where and as needed, then linked arms with him to shift right then left before releasing him and moving around Grace. She returned the motion by having Francis portray a fellow female, repeating the same pattern they had done. Then she and Aubrey joined hands and promenaded around the circle, skipping, as the dance required, and pausing to spin each other about once, twice, three times.

"Very lively, Miss Morledge," Aubrey declared as he turned himself about before her. "Spritely, even."

She pursed her lips on a laugh. "And you as well, Lord Ingram," she replied as she turned herself about. "I may have to dance with you again when there are an appropriate number of other dancers."

"I beg your pardon," Francis protested jovially as he tapped his foot, waiting for his part once more.

Grace laughed in earnest then, dropping her head back as Aubrey took her hands and began the whole pattern once more, her feet taking on an even livelier step this time around. And though Aubrey was not the keenest dancer, he found himself laughing more often the longer they danced, and he was desperate to make Grace laugh more. He and Francis made a great show of their parts, which she echoed in her own as best as she could, and around and around all of them went as Janet played, laughing from her corner.

On the last circuit, as Aubrey and Grace turned each other around, laughter rampant on both their faces, Aubrey felt his heart and stomach shift in opposite directions, his eyes fixed on Grace. Her color was high, and her hair was losing its hold even further beyond what the riding had done. Her grip on his hands was firm and sure, and every giggle she emitted took on a tone more musical than anything Janet was playing.

Had any dance ever felt like this? As though he could have danced with her, and only her, for the rest of his life?

To see her like this… There wasn't a more stirring sight.

The jig was followed by a country dance, which, again, required Francis as a stand-in for other couples, which he attempted to do with great comedic effect. Aubrey found it harder to laugh this time around, but had no trouble smiling just as much, if not more. He couldn't help it; he *had* to smile at Grace. Dancing with Grace. Being with Grace.

Every touch of their hands sent warmth into his chest, and every time she passed him, his breath caught. Every promenade felt significant; every turn made him miss her. Every time she partnered with Francis made him want to snarl, and every time she returned to him, his knees shook. He was no longer sure what his feet were doing, as he could only feel the heat of his hands and the pounding of his heart.

And he was supposed to waltz with her eventually? He would

burn alive!

Finally, Janet had mercy on him by ending the song, laughing merrily at the lot of them, and Aubrey forced himself to laugh with the rest. In truth, however, he was scared out of his mind, down to his very core. The goddess had become a tangible, significant being in his life and affections, her effects no less potent, but carrying far more meaning for him.

Mere mortal that he was, it was only natural, he supposed. Suddenly, he understood every story from the Romans and Greeks regarding the relations between the mortal and the divine, and he found new terror in the usually disastrous endings. But as he looked at Grace, leaning against the tall windows near them, a hand wrapping about her waist as she tried to catch her breath, still laughing, he found his fear fading in slow waves.

It could only be right. All of this, any of this, could only be right. Whatever suffering his dealings with this goddess brought him, it would all be worth it.

And suddenly he was smiling again.

"Well," he boomed as he patted his own chest, "I do think that is enough exercise for one day. I'll likely be considered a sportsman if I continue on."

"God forbid you wear that label," Grace returned with a tired smile. "Whatever would people say?"

"I'd like to avoid even the hypotheticals," he insisted. He looked at Janet with a sheepish expression. "Might our picnic be ready, my lady? I am quite famished."

Janet laughed and rose from the chair. "I'm sure it is. Come on, we'll have it brought outside, as the day is so fine. And if you can bear it, we thought we'd play some lawn games after we've eaten."

"And rested," Francis added with a wipe of his non-perspiring brow.

Aubrey put his hands on his hips. "What say you, Grace? Shall we take up arms against the Sterlings in a battle of lawn games?"

Grace sauntered towards them, hands behind her back, wearing the same expression she'd worn when she'd switched from sidesaddle to astride, which sank his stomach most shakily into his thighs. "I'll warn you, I'm not very good at those."

"The way you're not very good at other things?" he asked with all dubiousness. "I see."

Her lips quirked. "No, I mean I am really not very good."

Aubrey gave her an exasperated look. "What have I told you about modesty, Grace? Now, let us commence with the feasting, and then the games. I am determined to find no fault in your playing, so long as we win."

Grace smiled rather cryptically and shrugged, then followed Janet and Francis out to the terrace to begin things.

As it happened, they lost. Grace had been right; she really was not very good.

Strangely, he hadn't minded in the least.

Chapter Thirteen

Involvement of friends and family into one's personal business can tend to grate on a person after a while. Depending on precisely who is involved, that is. And how involved they are.

-The Spinster Chronicles, 2 November 1815

He was whistling again. He really didn't have a reason to, exactly, as he was choosing to walk from his house to Grace's, which was really quite a ridiculous idea. He'd never been much of a walker, and yet he was traipsing the distance without a single complaint of either his feet or his patience.

And whistling.

All because he was going to see Grace.

Technically, he was going to assess her for flaws and faults, though he could not say with any certainty what exactly he would be evaluating today, but that was neither here nor there. Something brilliant and scheming would come to him, he was sure. There was a list, after all, and he had taken care to never venture into the battlefield of Trenwick House without having it at hand.

Although, if he was correct, and he was positive he was, the list was growing shorter and shorter, which meant it could be time to call upon the Spinsters again.

What a horrifying thought.

Surely, he didn't need their interference again, helpful though it had been the first time. He knew Grace far better now, and he would be able to find areas of potential improvement on his own. After all, he'd already assessed eating, dancing, languages, walking...

He chuckled to himself at the memory of that one. Grace's irritated expression as she wandered back and forth across the room, having no idea how flawless she was when she did so.

She had no idea how she appeared when she did anything. Or how impressive she was. Or how lovely. She really had no proper perception of herself at all. She'd spent far too long having to answer for errors in herself that did not exist and being trained up in the ways of perfection without knowing if she'd ever gotten close. She hated being called perfect. But he wondered if she realized just how close to perfect she truly was.

Still, he had been tasked with finding her faults, limited though they might be, and he had to make a good showing of it, if for no other reason than because her father would become insufferable without some sort of result. Perhaps he could convince Grace to pretend to practice on something they might have discovered in one of their sessions, something her father could use as proof of work and improvement...

"Oh my, there is a quite determined face."

Hellfire and damnation...

Aubrey turned with the politest smile he could drum up under the circumstances, cursing himself for indulging in a whim as stupid as walking about London during the Season. "Miranda, what a charming surprise!"

Miranda Sterling strode towards him, her beloved bloodhound on a leash trotting along sleepily beside her. "You always say that, Aubrey, and I'm beginning to wonder."

"What?" he cried, sweeping into a dramatic bow. "How could you doubt me?"

Miranda was not impressed. "Far too easily."

Her dog wore exactly the same expression.

Aubrey straightened with a shrug. "Ah, well. I fear I cannot please everyone."

The dog seemed to harrumph at that, earning him a sardonic look from Aubrey.

Miranda, however, chuckled warmly. "Rufus does not hide his

opinions as well as he ought, I'm afraid."

"That makes two of us," Aubrey muttered with a scowl at the animal. He returned his attention to Miranda with a smile, though he was straining to be away. If there was one thing he knew about Miranda Sterling, it was that she was far too intuitive for her own good, or *his* own good for that matter.

She would sniff out a story better than Rufus if he was not careful.

Sure enough, her mouth curved in a bemused, knowing smile. "Where are you off to, Aubrey, dear?"

Honesty, he must use honesty. Just not full disclosure of said honesty.

"Trenwick House," he replied easily, "as I am sure you suspected."

Miranda fluttered her lashes in a way that resembled a shrug. "I might have done, but one does appreciate confirmation of suspicions all the same. What takes you there today?"

Aubrey sighed and looked up the street for a moment, then stepped closer to her. "Another fault-finding session, I'm afraid."

She immediately sobered, and her lips puckered in an almost sour fashion. "I don't approve of that."

"Nor do I, but we both know who's to blame for this."

Miranda's brow furrowed. "If you're about to blame me again, Aubrey Flint..."

He laughed softly, shaking his head. "No, my dear Miranda, I mean Trenwick himself. I cannot avoid these sessions, but I can be grateful that he is not present for any of them. This way, I can look for whatever indiscernible faults I'm supposed to find, and Grace won't feel so exposed by the experience."

"Aww," Miranda purred, patting Aubrey's cheek fondly. "I knew you would be good for her in this farce."

Aubrey heaved a sigh and took Miranda's hand from his face. "One can only hope. I fear I'm running out of things to pretend to examine, and I may grow tiresome to Grace in all this."

Miranda offered a sympathetic look, while Rufus licked his jowls loudly beside her. "I doubt you could ever be tiresome, Aubrey."

He cocked his head at her and sank to his haunches, reaching out a hand to Rufus, who began to sniff it casually. "And I thought you knew me well, Miranda. I'm a rather tiresome fellow quite often."

She hummed a moment, then turned it to a laugh. "So, don't be so tiresome, my lad. Have you been serious with her?"

Rufus, deciding Aubrey was safe enough, moved to him and flopped his backside down, nuzzling against his hand in a blatant suggestion of scratching his head. Aubrey complied with his wishes, smiling to himself. "I have, actually. Once or twice. It went over well enough, but my natural reaction is to turn to comedic joviality and sharp wit. So much safer there."

He scratched the dog absently, some of his tension easing in this strange confessional to Miranda. Or perhaps he was confessing to Rufus, he couldn't be quite sure. But he found comfort and clarity in confiding, strangely enough, and there was no way he could do so with Francis or Henshaw. He was sure they would sympathize, but that was an exercise in trust and vulnerability he wasn't prepared for.

"Safer for whom?" Miranda mused almost to herself.

Aubrey glanced up at her, squinting.

Whatever he had just thought about confiding, he took it all back. Confiding was highly overrated.

He looked back to Rufus and met the dog's doleful, dark eyes. "I feel for you, old chap. God be with you."

"Oh, please," Miranda huffed with a merry laugh as Aubrey rose. "Go on to Grace, then, and enjoy your challenge. Try her at music. That should be safe enough." She clicked her tongue at Rufus, who immediately got to his feet and resumed his place at her side. She nodded at Aubrey with a wink and continued on her way.

Aubrey watched her go, unable to keep from smiling with a genuine fondness. There was just something about Miranda, and he could not deny it.

But Miranda was not his object for the day. Grace was.

Well, nothing for it then.

He turned to continue down the street towards Trenwick House, arriving only a few minutes later.

Bennett seemed only slightly more pleased to see him than any other time he'd arrived, but he showed him in without a word, unless one counted a disgruntled huff as a word.

"How's the day going, Bennett?" Aubrey thought to ask as they proceeded to the usual drawing room he and Grace used.

To his amazement, Bennett gave him a direct look. "Not particularly well, my lord."

Aubrey blinked at that. "No?"

Bennett shook his head gravely. "Miss Morledge had a visitor that left only moments ago, and I fear it has left her in a less than optimal temper."

Swearing under his breath, Aubrey glanced towards the room, then back to the normally stodgy butler quickly. "Who was it?"

"Her aunt, my lord. Lady Trenwick's sister. My lady just led her out, but Miss Morledge..." He looked towards the drawing room, his expression rife with concern.

Aubrey felt the urge to pat the older man on the arm, which would have broken at least seventy-two items of the code of butlers, so he chose instead to nod as he moved towards the room himself. There was no telling what he would encounter with Grace, but he couldn't exactly leave her to her misery, whatever the cause. Especially not when his own temper was bordering on the indignant without any context.

Entering the room, he scanned quickly for Grace, only to find her pacing with her fists tight by her sides, her face equally tight with emotion.

He closed the door tightly behind him, keeping his back to it. "Grace..."

She didn't even look in his direction, her long legs pushing the skirts of her grey striped day dress out again and again in a rapid pattern. He watched her, seeing how her thumbs ran over her clenched fingers, and, when he looked closely enough, how her jaw trembled despite being as taut as the rest of her. Her color was high, and for whatever reason, her hair seemed bound more loosely than normal, giving her a less composed appearance than what he was used to.

It was quite possibly the most beautiful he had ever seen her.

But this was not the time for that either, so he forced his reactions back as he stepped more fully into the room. "Grace."

She held out a warning hand, her eyes finally moving in his

direction. "Aubrey, I can't…"

"Tell me," he said simply, sliding his hands into his trouser pockets. "Whatever is burning you up, let it out."

Grace stopped her frantic pacing then, swallowed twice, then turned to him with military precision. "My cousin is getting married."

Aubrey blinked, wondering what in the world that had to do with anything. Then he recollected their session with the letters, and comprehension dawned belatedly. "The cousin you wrote to warn off?"

Grace nodded once, sniffing, though he couldn't see a trace of tears. "Felicity. She decided to give in to her mother's bullying. The man proposed purely from my aunt's meddling, and Felicity accepted him. She doesn't even know him, Aubrey. They've met on five occasions. Five. This is exactly what the Spinster Chronicles is supposed to alleviate, and now, within my own family…" She stopped and smiled without any sort of warmth. "And do you know why she accepted, Aubrey? Why she gave in?"

He didn't dare hazard a guess, so he dipped his chin in encouragement.

"Because she was actually afraid of becoming me. Despite what I said, despite our closeness, she actually feared turning out like me." Grace exhaled a humorless laugh. "I was her reason, Aubrey. Me."

There was no air in his lungs, nothing resembling a heart anywhere in his chest, and his jaw went slack. How in *hell* could anyone think…?

Grace nodded repeatedly at his obvious disbelief. "She did. And my aunt, who came to London immediately to procure a trousseau, since the banns have already been read once in Leighton, stopped by today to share the good news and invite us to the fastest wedding without a special license in the history of the institution. And do you know what that condescending shrew said to me as we sat at tea with my mother?"

He didn't want to know. Didn't want to hear. Couldn't see or hear clearly for the seething rage burning within him.

"She said what a pity it was to be so flawed as to not be suitable for marriage to any man of any state at all."

The floor fell out beneath him, and he felt completely suspended in the air, though he keenly felt a massive weight pulling at him.

Not his Grace. Not *his* Grace.

"Flawed," she repeated. Her throat worked once, and her jaw quivered. "Flawed is it, for a woman to not be married? Trust me, there is nothing anyone can say or find that will rival what we already say and think and feel about ourselves. You think we don't feel flawed? And ugly, unworthy, and a hundred other things not worth mentioning? We feel it every single day, moment after moment. But we cannot speak of such things because we must also be patient, demure, and enduring, pain or no pain. So perhaps Felicity has it right. Why turn into someone who must endure all of this when an alternative is before you? Why risk being so very flawed in the eyes of everyone who knows you?"

He couldn't bear this, couldn't take it for one moment more. Her vitriol wasn't even directed at him, and he felt defensive, felt the need to shut her up, to fight her on this. Except he needed to defend *her.* To fight her for herself. To stop herself before she viewed herself as something worse than damaged based on the abuse of one unforgivable relation.

This was beyond words for the present.

Aubrey marched over to her and hauled her against his chest, wrapping his arms tightly around her and pressing her against his shoulder. She struggled against him, fury whipping at every point of contact, but he held firm.

"Grace," he said firmly, one hand clamping the back of her head. "Grace…"

She inhaled sharply, then exhaled in a loud rush that nearly knocked him over. Her arms snaked around him and loosely clung to his jacket, the tremors in her ebbing away with every breath. He touched his head to hers, leaning against her ever so slightly, his heart thudding with a wide blend of emotions, and impossibly, his own tension began to fade the longer he held her.

Blessed goddess.

When she was still, Aubrey wet his lips and shifted his mouth to her ear. "Grace, listen to me."

He felt her nod against him, and he smiled, pulling back just far enough to take her face in his hands. "Grace, I don't find you flawed.

Or ugly. Or unwanted. Or anything else in any way lacking. I'm so sorry for the pain you feel, and even more sorry if I have ever added anything to it. You amaze me, Grace. Beyond words. Any time you want to express how you feel, unseemly or shocking or whatever else, please do so with me. I don't find any flaw in that, and you deserve to be free in that regard. Understand?"

She exhaled, which he felt as much as he heard, and nodded against his hands.

Inevitably, helplessly, his gaze was drawn to her lips. Full and parted and tempting him beyond all unholy temptations. He wanted to trace them, to pull at them, to taste them...

Grace's breath caught, and he felt a surge of satisfaction at his attention being noticed. His eyes darted to hers, only to find her gaze locked on his lips, and a strange keening sensation gnawed at the base of his spine and down his legs. A silent howl of heated agony began to brew somewhere behind his heart, and he swayed towards her.

Then, he jerked and swayed away, clearing the blockage in his throat, moving his hands to her arms. He rubbed a bit as he swallowed weakly. "Good. Glad we cleared that up." He cleared his throat again, not at all obviously, and patted her arms once. "Now, shall we see how you do in a duet? I have it on good authority that I must test your musical abilities."

If Grace noticed his blatantly awkward recovery, she gave no indication. She raised a curious brow at him, those blasted perfect lips tilting to one side. "You don't play."

A delightful smugness filled the remaining sensibilities he possessed, and he grinned as he led her to the piano. "You don't know everything. Sit down."

"Gads, this is a dull event. I don't know why we've even come."

Grace bit the inside of her lip, trying not to show her despair of her brother, currently leading her into the drawing room of the Perry family, wondering just how the idiot could have deduced the dullness of an event they had only just arrived at. Then again, James had never been a creature of any great sense or taste, so it did not follow that his pronouncement was much of a surprise.

"Well, take yourself off to billiards with the other bored fellows, then," she said, removing her hand from his arm. "I'll find my own way about."

Needing no further encouragement, James released her arm and strode towards the room to one side where other gentlemen his age were headed.

She watched him go, shaking her head. He had spent the entire ride over complaining about their father not taking him into his confidence and instructing him in the finer business affairs of the family, which Grace did not care about in the least. She thought it best not to inform him that she quite agreed with their father's avoidance of involving James at all, as it would have been a perfectly useless experience.

Freed from him at last, she sighed and let herself smile, taking a moment to appreciate some of the finest rooms in a private London home she had ever seen. The Perrys were a fine and well-respected family, not the least because they did not flaunt any of their refinery. Miraculously, the Perry children were intelligent, respectful, remarkably kind individuals, which was quite the aberration in society these days.

Amelia saw her first and changed direction to come to her, beaming with all of her usual sincerity. "Miss Morledge! I am so pleased you've come. I hope you don't mind our informality in not greeting everyone as they come in. We wanted our guests to feel as warm and cozy as possible."

Grace lifted a bemused brow. "With fifty people in attendance?"

"Well, we can try, at any rate," Amelia replied with a wink. "Mr. Andrews seems to think it a ridiculous idea, but you know how he can be."

No, actually, Grace didn't know, but she certainly liked Mr. Andrews and would trust his judgment. Nothing about that statement was surprising in the least.

Amelia gasped suddenly, seizing her hands. "You'll never guess! Lady Edith came!"

Now *that* took Grace by surprise, and her jaw dropped. "She did?" She immediately began scanning the room for her. "Are you sure?"

"Quite!" Amelia quipped, directing her towards some card tables to one side. "She's partnering with Mrs. Morton at the present. Mr. Morton is around here somewhere with Kitty, but can you believe it? I am so pleased!"

So was Grace, and she couldn't deny it. Edith had become somehow even more of a recluse of late, only going out for Spinster meetings or evenings at their homes. To venture out to the Perrys was monumental, even with Amelia being a friend to them all.

"Oh! The Vales are here! Excuse me, won't you?" Amelia squeezed her arm quickly before vanishing off.

Grace moved to the card tables, her smile spreading with each step as she approached the dark-haired Scottish beauty. Edith said something that made Izzy and the others at the table laugh, as Edith was more than capable of doing, when she was of a mind to.

Tonight, she apparently was.

Edith looked at Grace when she reached them and smiled, her cheeks tinged with a healthy color, her emerald eyes dancing. "Good evening, Grace. Fancy a round of cards?"

"You seem to be in the middle of one, dear," Grace told her with a laugh. She nodded at two of the Wilton sisters, also sitting at the table with Edith and Izzy. "Who's winning?"

Jane Wilton laughed once. "Lady Edith and Izzy are, of course!"

"Oh, don't tell me Edith is proficient at cards," the voice of Camden Vale moaned somewhere nearby. "I'd be honor bound to test that claim, and she'd never forgive me for beating her."

Edith took on the most superior look possible in human expression. "You're welcome to try, Cam, if you dinna think it would be too much for your sensibilities."

Prue snickered as she and Cam drew up beside them. Cam grinned at Edith proudly, and with not a little mischief. "I don't have any sensibilities and you know it."

"I can vouch for that," Prue broke in, patting her husband's chest gently.

Cam coughed as the rest of them howled with laughter. "You, my love, were supposed to adamantly deny such a claim and defend me!"

Prue smiled up at him, her adoration clear. "Was I? I can never remember when to deny you and when to accept you."

He winked, his expression turning to something that seemed too intimate for their current setting. "Always accept me, love. Always."

"And now would be an excellent time for the Vales to recollect their surroundings!" Charlotte chortled, striding up to the group. "I could choke on the amorous air."

"One could only be so fortunate," Cam said on an exhale, turning to her.

Charlotte made a face, then smiled broadly at Jane. "Jane, dear, I've just seen Mr. Greensley come in, and he's already looking for you."

Jane colored and quickly excused herself from the table.

Mary Wilton watched her sister go, then quirked her brows at Charlotte. "And with Jane occupied, I have less competition for Captain Gracie. Many thanks." She grinned and dashed out of her chair, as well.

Edith, left without competition, put her cards down and smiled placidly at Izzy. "I take it we've won."

Izzy snickered and laid out her cards for all to see. "Between the pair of us, I think we'd have won anyway."

"The Wiltons were never particularly skilled card players," Elinor informed them staunchly as she arrived, flopping herself into a vacated chair.

Charlotte looked at her in disbelief. "As if you would know such a thing, child. I swear, you only learned cards yourself the day before yesterday."

"Give it a rest, Charlotte," Sebastian Morton groaned as he and his sister came to them. "Surely we can avoid a fight at the Perrys."

Charlotte gaped, and no wonder, for Sebastian Morton had never teased her for half a second of her life. But Charlotte, being Charlotte, recovered at once and smirked at the man. "I wouldn't fight, Mr. Morton. I am far too collected for such childish things."

Elinor snorted loudly, then covered her mouth.

Sebastian grinned and kissed the top of Izzy's head as he passed, his sister choosing to lean against the pillar nearest her, smiling with

162

her residual shyness. "Naturally," Sebastian mused. "My mistake."

"Indeed," Charlotte sniffed. She winked at Kitty, who giggled. "Good evening, Kitty. You look lovely. Lavender is the perfect color for you."

Kitty blushed, her porcelain skin transforming with the color, her pale blue eyes lowering even as she smiled still. "Thank you. And only you could wear that shade of yellow and look so majestic."

"Kitty," Edith moaned in mock agony. "Don't say such things to her, you know it only encourages her."

Grace found herself smiling at the banter surrounding her, loving the fun in it, the genuine fondness within the group, and the ease she felt among them all. Whatever she might have felt, or not felt, from various members of her family in her life, this was more of a family to her than most of them. Her mother was the exception, of course, and even she adored hearing about the antics of the Spinsters and their husbands, as they were now being collectively referred.

She found herself looking at the vacancy beside her, and a strange, sad twang pulled at her heart. Aubrey would have fit right into this delightful madness, tossing out quips and wit with the fluency of a man skilled in such arts. Playful, engaging, and amusing to a fault, he would have thrived among them all and added to them all so perfectly.

Perfectly.

She swallowed hard as she realized how his absence affected her. She missed him, though she had just seen him the day before. And it seemed weak to call it something so simplistic as missing him. As if she only missed him. This was different, something deeper and perhaps something there wasn't a word for. She felt that he was missing. She wished that he were here, and desperately so. She couldn't imagine the evening being as enjoyable without him, and possibly could be dull by comparison.

When had Aubrey become such a fixture to her that anything without him seemed somehow lacking?

She could see his wry smirk in her mind's eye, the almost wicked glint in his eye when he was up to something, the warmth and genuine beauty in the moments where all of that faded away… That moment they'd shared after her visit from her aunt, when she had raged, and he had held her, when he had told her she was not ugly, unworthy, or flawed…

The breathless comfort of being in his arms…

Even the recollection of it made her sigh.

"That's a sound that cries for explanation," Edith murmured, thankfully low enough for the others to miss.

Grace looked at her friend with wide eyes. "Shh!"

One side of Edith's mouth curved up. "I'll keep your secret, lass, but I know very well in which direction it leads. Take care, lest you find yourself in over your head."

She swallowed with some difficulty, a slow burn starting somewhere behind her ears.

"Grace," Charlotte suddenly bustled, spearing her with a look, "where is our resident surveyor of Spinsters this evening? Was he not invited?"

"Charlotte!" Prue hissed, her eyes going wide.

Grace closed her eyes, exhaling painfully.

"Who?" Sebastian asked in a curious tone, a hint of something hard in it.

"Who's surveying the Spinsters?" Cam demanded, not bothering with Sebastian's politeness.

Grace opened her eyes and cleared her throat. The time for secrets was over. "He's not surveying Spinsters," she told them. "He's surveying me. Well, assessing me, I suppose. For flaws and faults. Trying to decipher the reason behind my spinsterhood."

Cam's dark brow furrowed further still. "Who is?"

"Aubrey. Lord Ingram."

There was a moment of silence. "I'll kill him."

"I'll help," Sebastian added in a shockingly dark voice for such a polite man.

Grace felt a surge of fondness for both of them but had to laugh at what Aubrey's face would have looked like had he heard them. "Oh, don't get mad at him, Cam! He is doing me a great favor."

That didn't seem to comfort him in the slightest. "By finding your imagined flaws?"

She gave him a pointed look. "By doing the task himself instead of leaving it to some finicky codger or crony that might consider my very existence a flaw."

Cam seemed to consider that, exchanging a glance with Sebastian, who shrugged. "I suppose that could be true, but why are we engaging in this insanity at all?"

Now Grace offered a flat smile and fluttered her lashes. "My father insists there must be something wrong with me and demanded an outside source perform an analysis, after which we will take the findings and make improvements, at which time I should, by all accounts, be able to find myself a suitable husband and end the great disappointment of being unmarried at my age."

Again, silence reigned. Cam had drawn himself up, seeming to hold his breath, his expression unreadable. Sebastian was perfectly composed as he usually was, though a distinct tension resided in him,

Cam swallowed, exhaled softly, then tilted his head in a show of polite deference. "Miss Morledge, may I perform an analysis on your father? With my fists, some odd bits of furniture, and possibly a rusted saber?"

A surprised burst of giggles escaped from Grace, and the rest of the group chuckled along with her.

"I am quite serious," Cam informed her, beginning to smile now. "Even Morton would help, and you know how he feels about physical altercation."

Sebastian shrugged, smiling himself. "I would."

Grace shook her head. "Tempting, but no. Believe me, Aubrey makes the process painless, if it has to be done. I didn't think it would be so at first, but…"

Cam's smile turned almost as mischievous as Aubrey's might have done. "He's surprising you, is he?"

She opened her mouth to deny it, refute it, protest the teasing, but found she couldn't deny it. Or refute it. She had no desire to.

Not in the least.

"Yes," she admitted, lifting her chin despite the increasing heat swirling in her neck and cheeks. "Yes, as a matter of fact, he is."

Chapter Fourteen

There is some debate as to all things inevitable. Are they meant to happen, or do they belong to the category of spontaneity? Can we escape such things, or are we doomed to our fate? A definitive response from the scholars of the world would be most welcome. Nothing terrifies a parent like inevitability in their children, and this author would know.

-The Spinster Chronicles, 11 December 1817

"What will Aubrey be analyzing today?"

Grace looked up from her reading to stare at her mother in surprise. By unspoken agreement, the observations that went on during her sessions with Aubrey were never discussed. Grace had no desire to become a topic for discussion over supper, especially not with her father and brother about. There was no telling what they might say, or what suggestions they might have to offer on any particular subject.

What would she do if they scrutinized the analysis together as a family?

She shuddered and focused on her mother. "Mama?"

Her mother gave her a sympathetic look. "I don't mean to pry, darling, I only wonder if Aubrey might consider staying for tea today. Your father will be gone the entire day, and your brother, too, and I do feel most inhospitable when I think he only comes here to attend to such a vile, tedious task for your father. Surely, he must wish for a reprieve."

Grace blinked, unsettled that she hadn't considered such a thought herself. She supposed Aubrey just might enjoy a moment free of analysis, but she had never thought to ask him so. They had always been more concerned with completing the task and getting it over with than doing the polite thing. And at the moment, she wasn't entirely sure she wanted to share her time with Aubrey with her mother.

Her cheeks flamed in response, and she brought her book up in an attempt to cover it. "I think he would enjoy that, Mama. I don't know what he'll focus on today, he tends to surprise me with the subject. Gives me less time to prepare, or some such nonsense."

"Hmm."

There was something very suspicious about her mother's tone, and Grace slowly raised her eyes to hers. Her mother watched her with a small, bemused smile, and it was clear that she had caught every hint of a blush Grace had felt. Nor had she believed Grace's offhand remarks. And this woman wanted Aubrey to take tea with them.

Oh dear.

Grace swallowed once. "Yes, Mama?"

"Oh, nothing," her mother said with a dismissive wave that did nothing to hide her desire to interfere. "It's just all working out quite splendidly, isn't it? What would we have done if someone less sensitive would have accepted your father's proposition?" She shook her head and turned from the room. "When Aubrey comes, bring him to our drawing room. I'll have a tea service ready."

Grace watched her go, dropping her book back into her lap.

Sensitive? Aubrey? She laughed to herself and leaned her head back against the top of the wingback chair she was in. Sensitive. She would have to tell Aubrey that one.

Her smile faded as she thought about Aubrey, as she recalled missing him so fiercely the other night, and how that feeling hadn't left her since. It rather felt as though her heart were being plucked like the strings of a harp, only there was no music to accompany the sensation. Every moment they had together was filled with laughter and fun, or with comfort and calm. They could banter back and forth for ages, and yet he had a way of helping her see through whatever fog or problems had arisen.

He *was* sensitive. He was sensitive to her and her needs. He made her smile with ease and held her when she raged. He kept this whole embarrassing spectacle free of genuine humiliation and had even gone so far as to make the experience an enjoyable one. She actually enjoyed having him there to analyze her, to come up with something ridiculous for her to do that would prove nothing, to be with him however the circumstances arose.

Aubrey was sensitive. And kind. And witty, cheerful, irreverent, warm, handsome…

The man was so many things, her head began to spin with the lot of it.

Handsome. The word was suddenly emblazoned across her mind. He was dreadfully handsome, with his dark hair and grey-blue eyes, and a jaw that begged to be recreated in stone. His height over her did not intimidate, given her own taller than the average stature, and it was, in fact, rather a delightful distance.

Not that she had a reason to consider it delightful. She did not. No reason whatsoever. It was simply a statement of fact. She had always preferred men who were taller than her, whenever she had found a man to her liking.

Aubrey had always been taller than her.

Grace screeched to herself and flung her hands up to her eyes, as though they were the culprits in this cycle of betrayal. She could *not* face him today with thoughts of how handsome and kind and gentle he was, and how grateful she was that he had accepted her father's proposition.

Grateful! After the noise and fuss she had made over it? He would double over in hysterics for three hours on her floor, at least.

"Who are we hiding from and how far have you counted?"

Damnation.

The unladylike, silent curse shocked her, but she couldn't even be grateful it had remained a thought, considering Aubrey was the one who had interrupted her personal disciplinary action.

She dropped her hands and glared at him, which was the safest course when he was leaning so inelegantly against the door frame and grinning at her in a way that made her toes curl. He would never suspect she was susceptible to him if she glared.

"Blast, I was hoping to hide from you, but it seems I have failed."

He shrugged unapologetically. "I cannot deny that you have, as I am here, and I see you." He tilted his head almost fondly at her. "And what a lovely gown you wear, that shade of blue does compliment you so."

Grace snorted, her brow furrowing in suspicion. "What has you in such a fine, polite mood?"

"I understand I am to be in the company of your mother today." He pushed off the wall, straightening and adjusting his cravat. "I am preparing my very best behavior."

"Ah," Grace replied with a nod as she rose. "Playing a part today, are we? Excellent, I will be a dutiful daughter, and you a gentleman."

On cue, he extended an arm out to her. "Very well. Shall we?"

She smiled playfully at him as she set her hand atop his, tempted beyond reason to lace their fingers, though she refrained. "Lead on, sir."

Aubrey inclined his head, then led her grandly to the drawing room where her mother sat with a fine tea service, ready to receive them. She beamed at their entry and nodded warmly in response to Aubrey's perfect bow of greeting.

"Oh please," she protested with a gesture. "No formality. Come, sit, if you will."

"Thank you, Lady Trenwick." Aubrey played the perfect gentleman, assisting Grace with her chair before seeing to his own, and then sat, giving the spread an assessing look. "I do believe this is the most perfect tea service I have ever seen, madam."

That earned him a crumpet on a plate, and her mother's laughter. "Aubrey, dear, there is no need for flattery. I thought you might appreciate something more than just assessing Grace for Lord Trenwick today."

Aubrey sobered just enough to make Grace curious. "I do not find my time spent with Miss Morledge to be a trial, my lady. Only the reason behind it." He blinked, and then smiled more like his manner. "And you must know, she has not made the task an easy one."

"Indeed not," Grace scoffed softly as she reached for the tea. "Why should I?"

He glanced at her, wry smile in place. "To pity me my hardships?"

She paused in her preparations to pour the tea and raised a brow. "*Your* hardship? Poor man."

"That will do well enough."

"Grace," her mother murmured, smiling in amusement at the two of them, "do pour Aubrey some tea, won't you?"

"Excellent thought," Aubrey agreed, turning his body more fully to Grace. "Now I might assess your abilities with all things tea without creating a fuss about it. Proceed naturally, if you will."

Grace's lips quirked, and she shook her head, fighting a laugh. "You're an idiot," she whispered.

He leaned forward, and her breath caught at the change in proximity. "I know," he replied, leaning back and folding his arms.

Dutifully, Grace poured his tea, then her own, offered him cream and sugar, which he accepted with minimal amounts of both, and stirred the cup in a brisk but not disorderly manner. She handed him the spotless teacup and saucer, unable to keep from smiling a bit proudly at managing the whole thing so perfectly.

Aubrey surveyed her with unreadable eyes, his lips only slightly curved, one hand dangling near his chin. He rubbed his fingers together absently before reaching out to take his cup, the edges of his smile widening just a touch. "Perfect, thank you," he murmured.

Perfect. The word sent a warm burst of delight into her midsection at the same time a faint shiver of cold hit her spine. She hated that word, and had for so long, and yet from him it was a sonnet.

Both sensations were doused as logic set in. The man could very well have been saying she made his tea perfectly, or that the china was perfectly spotless, or that the teacake he had eaten while she made his tea was perfect. There was no reason at all for her to presume that he was referring to her.

Her cheeks flushed in telltale embarrassment, and Aubrey caught it as he sipped the tea, his eyes fixed on her. "And the tea is perfect, too," he whispered as her mother busied herself with fixing her own tea.

Grace felt her eyes widen, and she wrenched her gaze from his, focusing on stirring her tea vigorously. Her cheeks needed to cool, and so did the back of her neck, her ears, and anything else currently feeling quite overheated at the moment.

"What was that, dear?" her mother chimed in, somehow so unobservant at the present as to miss the recent incendiary reaction of her daughter at the hands of the man beside her.

"The tea is perfect," Aubrey told her, his tone returned to normal, though one look at him proved his eyes had stayed on Grace, the same mysterious look in them.

Grace sipped her tea quietly, grateful when her mother began rattling on about tea and the new cook's method of making the cakes and whatever else that seemed to fascinate Aubrey so. He was as engaging as ever, proving once again how sensitive he was, even to her mother. There was enough respect between them that Grace knew he was not simply playing a part in all of this.

Oh, she knew he likely had no real interest in baking or china, or even cake, though the latter might have actually intrigued him. What man in his right mind would truly enjoy sitting in a drawing room with a woman he could consider a mother with such tedious topics for discussion? Even Grace did not care for them, and she was supposed to be the sort to take part.

Normally, she would have begged her mother to find something else to discuss, to leave Aubrey's ears alone, or simply broke in and changed the subject herself. At this moment, however, the only thing she really wanted was to find herself cooled, and then get on with the fault-finding session with Aubrey. To have him to herself. To get back to the feelings she was used to with him.

Sitting in front of her mother while questioning, speculating, and outright burning for no apparent reason was not the most comfortable way she had ever taken her tea, and the fact that she had forgotten to add cream or sugar was a most unfortunate reminder with every sip that she was not at all herself.

To escape or to endure… Neither option would truly set her to rights, but escape, at least, would get her alone with her friend, Aubrey, who could tease her out of this flurry of confusion. Provided, of course, that he wouldn't make things infinitely worse.

She chanced another glance at him, watched as he sipped his tea again, his throat moving on a swallow that made her do likewise in response. And then, of all rotten things, the man winked at her.

So. Burning it was to be, then. Lovely.

Grace sighed silently and sipped her horrid tea once more.

Aubrey had always known he was an idiot, but he'd never thought he was *actually* an idiot in the truest sense of the word.

And yet, the proof was before him in his absolutely inane suggestion that the fault-finding session today focus on Grace's fashion.

Fashion, of all things.

Grace, who was exquisite in every aspect and from every angle, was parading in and out of the room in a wide variety of gowns, and she never looked less than perfect in any of them. To his surprise, constant perfection was beginning to grow less and less striking, and become more of a continual state of admiration that did not wax nor wane.

What an unfortunate curse for a goddess to bear.

That wasn't to say, naturally, that Aubrey wasn't enjoying himself. He was. Quite a lot, actually. But it was the sort of enjoyment one got from a gallery filled with impeccable works of art. A pleasant and constant wave of appreciation, with a pause every now and again to take a more in-depth look, but nothing that made one breathless or soaring with the experience.

Nothing to find fault in. Nothing lacking.

Constant beauty.

What fault had he expected to find in her manner of dress? Or in her while she displayed each item? She was clearly enjoying herself, coming into the room with each gown and showing it off as though she were modeling gowns in a modiste, albeit with more gusto and flare than he suspected ladies normally employed under such errands. He reacted with all good manners, praising her with the same dramatics she herself was making use of, though without much by way of actual flattery.

Not that she wasn't deserving of such. She deserved all the praise able to be uttered by the human tongue, but after spending a painfully long time with her and her mother at tea, transfixed by every quirk of her full lips as they touched the cup, he was already at the end of his wits.

Lord, to see her blushing and averting her eyes away from him! He could have swept her away from the drawing room at that moment, though what that would have accomplished hadn't formed in his mind. He'd just known he had to.

And then hadn't.

Now, her perfect figure in a plethora of shades and styles came and went before his eyes.

Idiot. Blathering, mad, inconceivable idiot.

"You looked so bored with all the day dresses and evening dresses you've already seen on me, I thought I might try something new. I hope you didn't mind the wait, I had to find a maid to help me with it."

"Ah, we are to be fancy now, are we?" he teased, looking towards the door, prepared to admire freely.

Whatever else he might have added to his precluding commentary dissolved without a thought. He lost all feeling in his lower extremities, and every one of the muscles in his face and jaw went slack.

Grace stood before him, smiling as she had been doing, but with a hint of hesitation, which would have unmanned him had he not already been so thoroughly unmanned. The gown was pristine, evidence of a fresh purchase, and somehow it was the exact color of the blush she had just worn at tea. Her figure was enhanced to an artist's perfection, perfectly encased in swaths of rosy pink. Her bodice and skirts draped with the same sheer white overlay that was dotted with lace bits and something that shimmered in the light of the day. Tight around her, just under the bodice, was a wide ribbon the same shade of pink, and his eyes stayed on it for a breath longer than they should have.

The details of it were all but lost on him, though he was positive he would be able to recall every one of them later. It was a gown designed by the hand of God to enhance that tempting shade her cheeks took on, begging anyone seeing it to do all within their power to see her bloom further. She was glowing in the dress, and her fair curls had been swept up but for a few tendrils dancing alluringly against the exposed skin above her bodice.

And suddenly, Aubrey felt like singing hymns of praise and confessing every one of his currently sinning thoughts at the same time.

"Thorough examination," Grace remarked, putting her hands on her hips, which immediately drew his attention to their perfect proportions. "See a flaw?"

Yes, he did see a flaw. In that he was not currently kneeling before this goddess and begging her for favors and mercy. In that she was not captured in paintings and sculptures, or sung about in operas. In that, as far as he knew, not one single pair of eyes had wept at such beauty.

But in the gown? None at all.

In her? Impossible and bordering on the sacrilegious.

He swallowed at least three times before actually succeeding in the supposedly natural action. "It's lovely, absolutely, and even lovelier on you."

What a weak, unimpressive, nearly offensive statement.

If Grace noticed how flat it was compared to what it ought to have been, or how hoarse he sounded in bleating it, she gave no indication. Her hesitant smile flickered with more confidence, though never quite made it there.

Merciful heavens, that was a fetching sight.

She curtseyed playfully, then moved to a nearby chair and leaned upon the armrest. "I had no idea how much exertion went into the repeated changing of many dresses. I'm quite fatigued."

So was he, but not for the same reason.

He smiled with all the weakness of his current state. "Thank you for humoring me."

She raised a teasing brow in his direction. "Did you find anything of substance for your notes?"

Had he ever. He couldn't bear to look at her further, not with the sun coming through the windows and lighting her so exquisitely from behind, so he looked down at his hand currently trying to clench his thigh.

"I believe so."

"Will you tell me?"

"Of course not."

She sighed, and the sound rippled across his skin. "Ah, well. It was worth a try."

They were both silent for a moment, and Aubrey felt himself growing more and more uneasy. He could feel every inch of the distance between them, each hair standing on end as though at any moment she would come towards him.

His stomach clenched in anticipation.

"So," he said rather brusquely, his eyes lifting helplessly to her again, "are you going to show off anything else?"

She bit her lip in thought, and his already clenched gut squeezed further, drawing a very faint grunt from him. "I don't think so. You've seen most of the evening dresses but for the ones still being altered, and you've seen enough day dresses to blind yourself with. And, of course, you've seen the riding habit. I only have the one, but don't tell Society that."

He remembered her riding habit vividly, and when the subject was Grace Morledge, the one riding habit was all that was needed.

"Your secret is safe with me," he replied, trying for his usual carefree air. "And I agree, I've seen enough. I don't want to rid you of the opportunity to surprise me with more grand garments in the future."

Grace tossed him a wry grin and began toying with one of her dangling curls. "I doubt there is anything so very surprising about a lady's evening dresses, Aubrey."

She had no idea.

He tried for a smile in response, then looked at the window behind Grace rather than at her. It was safer, but only just. He had to collect himself, find the joviality that usually existed in their sessions. She was undoubtedly counting on him to bring more laughter into things, and today, he was failing miserably.

"Did it ever occur to you that it could very well be my face or my figure?" Grace suddenly suggested, shifting in her position against the chair. "As the reason for my being a spinster, I mean."

His mind went blank. "No," he said, keeping his eyes on the

window, not seeing anything.

"Why not? It's one of the only things we haven't discussed."

Aubrey's hands gripped his legs tightly, his teeth grinding together. "I am not analyzing your figure, Grace."

"Oh, come now," she teased as one of her legs began to swing just a little. "I would think this would be a perfect opportunity for your less-than-gentlemanly nature to officially act freely in whatever way I suspect it does all on its own anyway."

She had no idea what his less than gentlemanly nature had been doing of late, and what every side of him was trying to avoid doing now.

He forced his teeth to separate and flicked his gaze to her. "It would be impossible in the current styles of the day, and inappropriate without the current styles of the day, and I'm having enough trouble as it is not imagining what that figure looks like at any given point in time on any given day without trying to find a bloody fault in it, all right?"

Grace's eyes widened, and that deuced attractive blush began to spread across every inch of her exposed skin, which made everything infinitely harder to resist. She wet her lips with hesitation, then asked, "But what about my face?"

How many ways could one man dance along the edge of damnation in a single sitting? Aubrey closed his eyes, shaking his head. "Please, Grace..."

"You haven't said," she half-whispered.

He opened his eyes and gave her a raw, frank look. "Are you going to make me confess all my secrets?"

Grace looked small and terrified, her color still high, her breathing uneven. "Would that count as a flaw?"

Aubrey stared at Grace for a long moment, then slowly pushed himself to his feet. "Your face is the closest thing to perfection I have ever seen," he told her, moving towards her in a manner that he would freely admit was far more predatory than leisurely.

Her eyes widened further, and she stilled on her perch.

"Your hair is the color of sunshine and glows twice as bright," he continued, still coming towards her. "Your skin rivals porcelain, except for when you blush, and then it eclipses any sunrise."

He took her hand as he reached her and gently pulled her up, his skin burning where he had touched her, the heat coursing in his blood. "The only possible imperfection anyone could ever find in it is that freckle there." He touched the spot just above the curve of her lip, taunting him with its very existence. "And I adore that freckle most of all because of it."

Grace exhaled shakily, her eyes darker than he'd thought them possible. "Because it makes me imperfect?"

Aubrey's finger began tracing her lips, dragging against the plump skin, his eyes following the pattern. "Because it makes me stare. And smile. And want…"

A faint pant brushed over his finger, and he was completely undone.

He leaned down and touched his lips to hers, a tentative inquiry against the rising tide of passion. Her lips parted beneath his, and he moaned in abject relief, his free hand moving to cup her face and bring her closer. She was curious and timid, her lips moving with inexperience, though there was no denying her ardency. Her fingers flailed against his chest before gripping his waistcoat and pulling him closer.

He kissed her slowly, giving and taking in gradually increasing measures, as much as she would allow without pressing his advantage. He poured every ounce of his simmering desire and adoration into the kiss, sealing his lips over hers again and again. Nipping, grazing, drinking against her lips and mouth, brushing his lips around the edges of hers, enjoying how ragged her breathing grew when he did so.

"Oh, *hell*," he breathed after she had innocently pulled at his lower lip and sent his pulse skittering.

Grace exhaled against him. "What?" she asked. "What is it?

His thumb stroked against her cheek while the other hand slid back into her hair. "You even kiss perfectly." He pressed his lips to hers again, tilting her head back to more fully taste her.

"I hate perfect," Grace replied breathlessly, her lips dusting across his with the words.

Aubrey grinned, nuzzling against her a little. "God help me, I love it," he murmured as he kissed her again, smiling mid-kiss as her hands slid up to his neck, lacing themselves there.

"Lucky you," she whispered, rising to her toes.

"Quite so," he said as he helplessly, inevitably, kissed her again.

Chapter Fifteen

———— ❧ ⚓ ❧ ————

Sometimes it is our reaction to the thing rather than the thing itself that tells the greater story.

-The Spinster Chronicles, 5 February 1819

She needed to spend eleven days in her room, alternating between screaming into her pillow and staring dreamily out of her window. It was possible that there would be long expanses of time of questioning, doubting, and chastising herself, more than likely including the occasional exercise of sprawling out on her bed and reliving every moment.

And this was a full two days after Aubrey had kissed her.

Had *thoroughly* kissed her.

And Grace had kissed him back.

She hadn't even known what she was doing, and she had done it. Instinctively, and purely in response to the gloriousness he was showering on her. She had never been more aware of the beating of her heart until that moment when it had completely drowned out hearing and thought, adding a fervent cadence to the breathless experience. She could swear now that she had felt that throbbing pulse in the bottoms of her feet even before she had risen on her toes to get closer.

Closer. All she had wanted was to be closer. She couldn't understand it, even now, as she had been so close to him already, but it hadn't been close enough. She'd wanted more, wanted to cling, wanted to crawl inside the moment, and that kiss.

Oh, that kiss!

Her face flamed with a sigh of remembrance, and she fanned herself rapidly as the carriage pulled up to the Vale residence. She could *not* go into a meeting of the Spinsters with a flaming face and wistful smile. She could not sigh, swoon, make any sort of sound that would indicate anything particularly romantic had taken place, or drift away from the conversation at any given time. Any hesitation or moment's delay in response could give her up entirely, and the interrogation would commence.

She would not endure that. She could not.

Exhaling slowly, she nodded to herself and stepped out of the carriage, grateful she couldn't feel any heat in her face presently. She was shown into the house and smiled warmly at the maid who had come to take her things. She quickly removed her bonnet and gloves, then focused her attention to her blue pelisse.

"I'm so sorry," she said to the poor maid, who stood there, still waiting, while she fidgeted with the buttons. "Normally, I can manage without any trouble, but today…"

"Can I help you, Miss Morledge?" the maid offered with a sweet smile.

Grace laughed and shook her head. "You are kind, but I'll only be a moment." She forced her mind to clear, and finally managed the last two buttons, as any sensible woman ought to have done.

Sensible. She used to be considered sensible. Nothing could have been further from the truth today. She was insensible, frantic, and quite clumsy. She'd have to mind all tables and fragile items, or she would be embarrassing herself continuously and would have to explain herself to Prue and Cam, if not the entire group of Spinsters, as well.

Just then, the butler strode by them, smiling politely, and the door behind her opened. "Good morning, my lord. Mr. Vale is expecting you."

"Would there be any point in handing you my card, then?" came the cheeky response.

Grace froze in the act of removing her pelisse, her breath stuttering in her chest.

Aubrey.

"Wait here, sir. Mr. Vale asked to fetch you himself. I hope this doesn't offend."

"Not in the least. It takes a great deal to offend me."

The butler must have nodded, for he passed Grace again with a smile.

Which meant that, for the present, Aubrey was still there. With her.

Her knees shook with the desire to run, to flee the house entirely or to flee into its depths. She wanted to hide, to vanish into thin air, to do anything to avoid the forthcoming awkwardness. She closed her eyes and prayed he would pass by her without taking time to notice her.

"Oh…"

Grace felt her lungs give in despair, and she bit back a whimper. But she could not ignore him, not for politeness and not for her own needs. She opened her eyes and looked over at him as she resumed the removal of her pelisse.

He stared at her with round eyes, frank in his gaze and as stunned to see her as she was him. There was a small comfort in that, she supposed. "Good morning," he belatedly said.

Grace swallowed once and dipped her chin. "My lord."

She saw his face tighten at the formality, but he had no quip to reply with. He simply stared, and so did she. The air between them grew thick and tense, something that made her wary and alert, unsure how it would proceed, or what she ought to do.

The maid took Grace's pelisse from her and bobbed, disappearing quickly down the corridor.

Fortunate girl.

Aubrey cleared his throat. "Are the Spinsters meeting here today?" he asked, his voice as taut as the rest of him. "I thought you normally meet at Charlotte's."

She nodded, determined to maintain the politeness he was pretending at. "We normally do, yes. Mrs. Wright had arranged a gathering of her friends today, unaware that we were to meet, and so Prue kindly offered to host us."

"Ah." He clasped his hands behind his back, still staring.

Oh, but this was painful. "And what brings you here?"

Aubrey gestured to the house faintly, his lips forming an almost-smile that seemed unnatural. "I have a meeting with Mr. Vale."

"About what?"

"Estate management."

"Sounds serious."

"It is."

"Cam's not very serious."

"Neither am I."

"True."

They stared at each other, blinking, barely breathing, Grace felt exposed and awkward, laid bare for him to see. She had the most intense desire to fold her arms, cover herself, and become smaller. Suddenly, she could recall the taste of him on her lips, and to her horror, her cheeks began a slow burn that would soon be visible.

She had to leave, and leave now.

"Well, I'd best not be late," she said in a rush. "The others will talk. Good day, Lord Ingram." She gave him the briefest curtsey known to man, and rushed off, frantically wondering if she remembered the way to the drawing room.

Why hadn't someone come to show her the way? Or had the maid indicated that she should follow, and Grace had been too stupidly engrossed in Aubrey's arrival to pay any attention?

Thankfully, Prue appeared just then, and beamed at her. "Grace! I was afraid you would become lost in the house, so I thought I'd better come in search of you."

Grace could have gone to her knees in gratitude before her friend but settled for smiling with all the relief in the world. "A few moments more, and I might have been, but I trust I have been correct so far."

Prue nodded and came to take her arm. "You have, indeed! I wanted to keep things comfortable for us, I hope you don't mind."

"Not at all," Grace assured her, putting her hand over Prue's. "Am I the last to arrive?"

"You are, but only just." Prue smiled almost mischievously up at her. "Elinor had to beg off. She must have tea with her sister today, and she is most put out about it."

Grace chuckled, feeling more natural the more time she spent in

Prue's company. "It is undoubtedly for the best that we are spared the ordeal of her tirade, then."

"Whose tirade?" Charlotte asked as the two of them entered the room. "Not mine, I hope."

Prue gave her a look as she released Grace's arms. "No, dear, we are used to yours. We were speaking of Elinor."

Charlotte waved a hand and snorted dismissively. "That child will turn into a right termagant if she does not mind herself."

"Oh, be nice," Izzy insisted in her usual way.

Grace exhaled slowly as she took a seat next to Edith. The longer the focus of conversation could avoid her, she would be quite pleased to take part in any way she could. She could not deny that she was still rattled from encountering Aubrey in the foyer, but it needn't live in the front of her mind for the rest of the day.

She would be free to dwell on it extensively after all of this.

"Are you all right, lass?" Edith asked very softly as she sipped her tea. "You look a little flushed."

Grace bit back one of the more colorful curses she had learned from Aubrey and fought a scowl. "I knew it. I just knew it, and he would have seen it, which means he knows…"

Edith nudged her quickly. "Hush now. Don't let them hear." She eyed the others quickly, smiling at something Prue said. "He being… him?"

Grace nodded once, forcing her lips to smile, though they would much have preferred to grimace or scowl. "Him."

"He's here?"

Again, Grace barely nodded. "Meeting with Cam."

Edith sipped her tea again, taking her time to do so and swallowing. "Something's happened, has it?"

Something. Yes, something had indeed. A very great, very magical, very confusing something. Something that had changed her life, changed her perspective, something that had changed… her.

Something she was afraid to consider the ramifications of. Something that utterly terrified and excited her. Something that she greatly feared would not mean as much to him as it had to her. Something that would change everything between them.

Something.

Slowly, Grace dipped her chin once more, a faint tremor beginning a slow trickle across her skin. She inhaled with it, an accompanying shuddering exhale shortly following.

"Oh, Grace," Edith murmured in a sympathetic tone. "It's all over your face."

"I know," she whispered, raising a hand to her suddenly feverish cheek. "I'm going mad, Edith."

Her friend reached over and squeezed her hand tightly. "We're all a little mad at times."

She had to smile a little at that. "I cannot bear questions today. I can't..."

"Then let's take the focus from him and make your blushes about something else," Edith insisted. "Your father, perhaps."

"I haven't seen my father in days."

"Perfect." Edith cleared her throat and set down her teacup. "So, your father isn't supervising these fault-finding sessions?" she asked in a louder tone, drawing the attention of others.

Suddenly, every eye was on Grace, and she felt the weight of it. She shook her head quickly. "No. No, in fact, he hasn't seen a moment of it."

"I hope you've given thanks for that appropriately," Charlotte remarked easily, resting her head in one hand. "The idea of him watching over the pair of you as a second set of eyes like a hawk is a disturbing one."

Grace shuddered and drummed her fingers on the armrest beside her. "It would make things so much worse. I would never manage to be myself if he were there."

Izzy shook her head, sighing with sympathy. "Under the circumstances, you really must be as close to yourself as possible. It would not be a fair evaluation otherwise."

"It's not exactly a fair evaluation now, is it?" Charlotte retorted with a furrowed brow. "The poor thing is on display at any given moment. Any moment Aubrey is around, she could be being evaluated."

His name sent a jolt into Grace's fingers, and she splayed those fingers impulsively, straining to rid them of the sensation, and of him.

Prue looked at Grace with concern. "Surely, Aubrey doesn't look for faults in you all the time. He wouldn't, w-would he?"

What could she say? What *should* she say? How could she know what Aubrey thought while they were together? If he spotted faults when she wasn't exactly being examined?

If he found faults when he kissed her...

"I don't know," she admitted at last, smiling very weakly. "I honestly do not know."

Why was she here? Why was she *here*?

He was here. He was meeting with Camden Vale, and he had expressly wished to do so at the Vale residence because he knew that it would be a Spinster meeting day, and therefore no one would be about to remind him of Grace.

Now she was in the same blasted building, and she had blushed at their distinctly uncomfortable meeting in the foyer. That blush that drove him mad, made her skin glow, made him wild to kiss her, and knowing what an experience kissing her was, made the wanting all the greater. Yet he could barely speak a word to her, let alone step in her direction.

He should have thought of this when he kissed her the other day. How it would change everything between them, how awkward and self-conscious he would feel when seeing her again, never mind what she must have felt. How torn he would feel between grinning at her and apologizing for kissing her, not because he regretted it, but because of how it altered everything.

He couldn't regret kissing her. Would not do so. It had been a glorious thing of beauty and upheaval, so much so that even the thought of it now thrust giddiness into every one of his limbs.

Aubrey had felt shy, even. Of all things he had ever felt in his life, shyness had never been one of them. But he'd also never been in this situation before, having kissed a woman who in return had kissed him senseless, and then having to continue on associating with her repeatedly and feeling at a loss for how to do so. How did he pick up the pieces of the friendship they had formed after that?

Or did he?

The strangest feeling of loss had settled into the pit of his stomach, and he hadn't found a way to rid himself of the painful sensation.

How did any man of sense behave as such under these circumstances?

He blinked and forced himself to pay attention to what Cam was saying, looking over the layout of the Vales' estate in Hertfordshire. Gableshead was, by all accounts, a gorgeous estate, and wouldn't require all that much to improve its productivity. If Aubrey could focus on the task, he could tell Cam exactly what he would suggest.

The trouble was that he couldn't remember what he'd already said, or how Cam had responded.

"And the steward believes the farms will prosper," Cam was saying, "provided we give them half a chance and keep them stocked enough. My wife's aunt spent many years listening to poor advisors who routed money into their own pockets instead of distributing it as they ought. We were quick to dismiss all of them, and as my wife cares nothing for riches, she insists a majority of funds be diverted back into the farms."

Aubrey found himself nodding absently, then earnestly as the words sank in. "It would certainly be a measure of good faith for the tenants, though I would advise against a sum so generous that it cannot be salvaged, should the farms not progress as hoped."

Cam grinned at him, a surprisingly cocky grin, considering their conversation. "I agree, which is why I was careful to never settle on exact sums with my wife."

The strategy made Aubrey laugh and he nodded his approval. "Very wise, very wise. But why not just do as you like with it? Upon your marriage, did the funds not become yours?"

The amusement faded in Cam's face and was replaced by a hard look that confirmed everything that Aubrey had heard about Camden Vale.

"No," he said tersely, "nor would I have wished for it. My wife's fortune was entirely hers, and I could not touch it. She determines every course of it." There was a faint echo of his former smile then. "Except, of course, for when she needs saving from her own good heart. After all, there are lives depending on us, and that fortune keeps us all hale."

It was a rare sort of speech from a man married to an heiress, but all in all, Aubrey approved of it, and he returned the faint smile with one of his own. "Fair enough. Balancing generosity with strategy would be the best course."

Cam nodded, the hard edge all but fading from his features. "Agreed. There are minor renovations still needed on the house itself, but those can be done bit by bit, nothing to rush."

"Probably for the best," Aubrey replied, looking over the layouts. "You'll want to be making some sort of profit before you get too extensive there. You said the east wing was the better of the two?"

They spent the next several minutes going over specific details about the estate itself, the renovations, and suggestions for improvement in general. Aubrey felt his mind grow sharper the more they discussed. He found new points to make and specifics to discuss for that express purpose.

Anything to keep his mind from wandering where it would do no good.

"Sounds as if you learned a lot with your own estate," Cam commented as he turned to lean against the desk they had been poring over. "Was it so poorly off?"

Aubrey nodded, smiling without humor. "My father didn't need corrupt advisors to make poor choices. He accomplished enough on his own. I nearly had to dismantle the entire estate. I think the house was the only thing in decent condition." He snorted and shook his head. "I have done nothing else since completing my education, and the fact that there is nothing to tend to at the present leaves me a bit at odds as to what to do with myself."

Cam made a sound somewhere between scoffing and laughing. "That's not what I've heard."

Aubrey looked over at him, raising a brow. When Cam didn't go on, Aubrey matched his pose, leaning against the desk, folding his arms, and gesturing for the man to get on with it.

"I hear you are fault-finding," Cam said, tone and expression unreadable. "Officially."

Gads, how had he found out about that? Aubrey groaned and

shook his head. "Don't remind me."

"Oh, not having a good time?" Cam made a mocking sympathetic sound. "I won't say I'm not pleased by that. I don't think you should have a good time of it."

Aubrey scowled. "I didn't exactly take this on for my own amusement. I never expected to enjoy it."

"Oh good, so you're not as much of an idiot as I thought."

"Have you ever tried to find fault in perfection?" Aubrey demanded defensively, his folded arms tightening against him.

Cam grunted once. "Yes. It's more fun that way."

Aubrey shook his head very firmly. "Not this."

"Why not?"

He heaved a sigh and looked straight ahead, his gaze finding various spines of books to rest upon. "There are no faults. There's nothing to find. I've assessed topic after topic, anything I or the Spinsters could think of, and there is not one thing wrong with her." He swallowed, suddenly fighting the rising tide of a strange sense of panic. "In fact, the harder I look, the more I..." His voice faded and he shook his head again, almost frantic this time.

"Uh oh," Cam murmured slowly.

Aubrey jerked to look at him. "What?"

"I know that look," Cam said with a wry smile. "I know it all too well."

"What look?" he asked even as his insides began to twitch sporadically.

Cam chuckled and pushed off of his desk. "Oh, Lord Ingram. You need a drink. Or twelve."

Aubrey scoffed easily, nearly sputtering, clearly overdoing his attempt at dismissal. "No, I don't."

That earned him a pitying, sardonic look. "You're in love with Grace Morledge, and you promised to find faults for her father. You need all the drinks in the world for that."

He was... *what?*

Startled laughter erupted from somewhere within him, which did nothing to the state of his internal organs or the set of his shoulders. "You're mad."

"That's a given," Cam replied as he continued to pour drinks, "but it doesn't follow that I am also wrong. You don't have to accept it yet, if you like. These things do take time."

"Stop," Aubrey laughed. "You're growing more insane by the syllable."

Cam ignored him and turned around, glasses in hand. "I myself took weeks to come 'round to the idea, and longer to admit it to Prue. It's extraordinary, after that has been accomplished, you find you want to say it before and after every breath you take. Rather disconcerting for strong, robust men like us, but there it is."

Aubrey gaped, feeling as though he should shake his head again, redundant though it would have been. What was this man going on about? What, exactly, had led him to believe that Aubrey could have been in love with Grace? He'd barely even mentioned her, other than his struggle with finding faults in her.

Anyone would have struggled with that. Even the codgers and crones Trenwick could have brought on would have had a hard time in this task. There wasn't anything at all romantic in anything Aubrey had said.

Anything at all.

So long as he never gave a hint about the kiss he'd shared with her.

He inhaled impulsively, taking the glass from Cam and downing it in one gulp, wincing against the immediate burn he felt.

"That's what I thought," Cam affirmed, now smiling in full.

"What?" Aubrey coughed, wiping his mouth and handing his glass back. "I thought we agreed I needed a drink. I've never been the sort to sip mildly."

Cam nodded, clearly not believing a single word Aubrey said. "Of course, of course. And it had nothing at all to do with you spending an extended amount of time unaccompanied in the presence of Grace Morledge."

Well, when put like that...

He pictured Grace just as he had seen her this morning, only a short time ago. Simply adorned, natural in her beauty and elegance, and watching him with eyes he could have happily drowned in. He could have watched that tantalizingly slow blush creep across her skin with the same adoration one gave the sunrise, and it would strike him just as much.

Lord, what he wouldn't give to have more time with her, not for finding fault or because he was assigned to be around her, but just to be. Knowing what she felt like against him, what she tasted like, how fervently she responded to his kiss, he could easily crave stolen moments for eternity.

"Nothing at all," he retorted a hair too late to be convincing, wondering if *he* would be blushing soon.

Cam held the second drink out of Aubrey's reach, raising a brow. "Say that you aren't in love with Grace. Go on. Say the words."

Aubrey reached for the glass, his mouth working to form the words.

Except they wouldn't come. Couldn't come. Refused to come.

He couldn't say it.

Gads, he was in love with the only goddess on earth he had ever seen, and the one he was supposed to find fault in. He was in love with Grace Morledge.

He wasn't sure if he should laugh or cry out in terror, though he desperately wanted to do both. His eyes met Cam's, and he knew full well that his utter bewilderment was plain to see.

Cam's mouth formed a tight line, and this time his nod was entirely sympathetic. "There it is. Right, drink number two for you, sir, and as many more as you need. I'll send you home passed out in a carriage if I must."

Aubrey took the drink, downed it again, and held the empty glass out once more. "I think you must."

Chapter Sixteen

―――――⸙⸙―――――

When in doubt, one can always dance. Minimal conversation, minimal focus, and a bit of exercise to brighten one's outlook... who could ask for more than that?

-*The Spinster Chronicles, 12 August 1818*

"Why are we doing dancing again? It's already been evaluated."

"Correction, your abilities in certain dances were evaluated. Your Lord Ingram consulted us on various areas of evaluation, with your consent, and we, knowing accomplishments as we do, insisted that multiple dances be considered."

Grace scowled at Charlotte as they walked to the ballroom of the Wrights' house, which had been the designated location for today's ridiculous nature. "Well, that wasn't well done, was it?"

Charlotte's dark eyes flicked to hers, one brow rising. "You disagree with our expert opinion? You think looking at a woman dancing a jig will demonstrate how she can dance the quadrille? All the same, are they?"

No, they were not, and Grace knew it well. What was worse was that only weeks ago, she had written an article for the Chronicles about dancing and had been rather specific about each popular dance, as well. Every rational part of her mind knew that the Spinsters had been absolutely right in their insistence.

The rest of her objected wildly and with great enthusiasm.

She hadn't seen Aubrey since they had awkwardly met in the

Vales' entry hall the week before. It was the longest they had gone without seeing each other since the fault-finding venture had commenced, and Grace had begun to wilt with lost hope and disappointment. She was familiar with the sensation, as all young ladies surely must be at some point in their lives, but this was far worse. This was no childish fancy gone awry, it was a numbing torment that left her irascible and short-tempered.

And, at the moment, she was rather inclined to slap Aubrey across the face with something rather hard. It wouldn't have the same level of satisfaction as her hand burning with the impact, but the increased injury to the man in question would more than make up for it.

What else was one to do when a man kissed her senseless and then abandoned her without any indication of what it meant?

"I don't feel like dancing," Grace grumbled as they entered the room, managing only a weak smile for Izzy, Elinor, and Kitty Morton.

"Perfect," Charlotte retorted. "Then you'll be evaluated under the exact same conditions we endure roughly seventy-three percent of the time at any given ball or assembly. Now, kindly avoid biting anyone's head off today, we've just had the floors cleaned. Especially not a certain gentleman whom we all happen to like very much, as I suspect his blood is still tainted by the copious amounts of alcohol he consumed from Cam's stores, and the smell would take ages to sponge from the room."

Grace gave Charlotte a startled look. "His what was what?"

"Blood," Charlotte repeated on a long-suffering sigh. "Tainted. I stayed a bit later at Prue's the other day, and Aubrey was fully and completely soused. Nigh unconscious, if Cam's efforts in hauling him into the carriage was any indication." She shook her head with some sympathy. "His head must have been positively raging for days. I wonder what could have driven him to it."

Aubrey had been drinking excessively with Cam? Whatever for? What would have brought that about? Aubrey wasn't the sort to turn profligate, no matter how sardonic he could get, and he was never careless about anything.

This made absolutely no sense.

"Had Cam been drinking, as well?" Grace pressed without

hesitation.

Charlotte flicked at something on her bodice, not nearly as invested in this topic as she ought to have been. "Oh, I'm sure he had been, but not nearly to the same extent. I couldn't even smell it on him. He was perfectly coherent and himself. Nothing at all compared to the state in which poor Aubrey got himself into."

Elinor tsked loudly. "I've never approved of excessive inebriation."

"Then may you never have reason to succumb to it."

Grace stiffened at hearing the all too familiar drawl, her curiosity over the new revelation edging out her fury for the moment. She turned to watch as he and Lieutenant Henshaw entered the ballroom, both looking handsome and hale. Aubrey, in particular, seemed to be free of any concerns or constraints.

She forced herself not to glower, as Henshaw might assume the look was for him, and she did not need the misunderstanding.

"Henshaw, have you been roped into a turn as a dancing monkey like the rest of us?" Charlotte asked politely as she folded her arms.

Henshaw grinned and gave a quick bow of acquiescence. "When it comes to this particular gathering of ladies, I am willing to subject myself to a vast majority of things."

"I wouldn't admit that too loudly," Elinor laughed, sharing a look with Kitty, whose amusement did not extend to the same degree, but her smile was sure enough.

Oh, to be a shy girl and not expected to perform in any particular way.

Aubrey surveyed the group with an assessing eye, glancing over Grace with as much interest as he'd done the rest of them. She felt the sting of such a cursory look sharply and inhaled shortly at the pain.

"Right," Aubrey said, completely unaware of her current state, "do we have enough, Charlotte?"

Charlotte counted quickly, then shrugged as she looked back at him. "Enough to be passable, which is as much as we could hope, I expect."

"Charmingly optimistic," Elinor commented wryly, making Kitty and Izzy snicker.

Aubrey paid no mind to Elinor, which was undoubtedly for the best.

"Which of you plays the best?" Aubrey asked.

Izzy's lips quirked. "Grace does."

Grace bit down on her cheek to keep from laughing. While she would never claim to be exceptional in her musical abilities, she could safely attest to being accomplished, and the best player of the Spinsters.

"Not particularly helpful," Aubrey remarked with a fond smile for Izzy. "Perhaps I'll rephrase; who will be playing for the dancers today?"

Grace was stunned, and clearly Aubrey was as well, when Kitty Morton raised her hand without a hint of shyness. "I will," Kitty's voice rang out, the slightest quiver in her declaration.

Aubrey stared just a moment longer than he should have done, then his mouth curved into the gentlest smile Grace had ever seen on his face. "Alas that we are to be deprived of your lovely dancing, Kitty Morton, but your playing will be the magic to spur our feet into their steps."

Grace nearly rolled her eyes, though the words were politely said, and smirked as Kitty's cheeks flamed even as the girl smiled. Aubrey knew Kitty enough to know of her shyness, and he respected that, but surely he knew the flattery would make things worse.

She shook her head and stepped to Kitty, giving her a warm smile as they moved to the piano situated to one side of the room. "Never mind the rest of us, dear. He's assessing my dancing, not your playing, so I don't want you to have a single worry about it."

Kitty nodded, exhaling slowly, quietly. "I might not play very well," she admitted so only Grace could hear.

Grace squeezed her hand. "We'll hardly be listening, Kitty. Do the best you can, whatever it is, and we'll just dance to it. Pretend you're at home practicing, if you like."

The girl's pale eyes raised to Grace's, a hesitant smile on her lips. "I don't even play perfectly at home."

"Well, I know a little about lack of perfection," Grace murmured as she leaned a little closer. "And I'll enjoy your playing all the more for it."

194

Seeming satisfied, and no longer looking like a scared mouse, Kitty sat at the piano and began playing a neat series of scales in preparation.

Grace turned back to the others, returning a grateful smile from Izzy, and ignoring the curiously fixed look from Aubrey. "Shall we get on with this, then?" she asked, glancing in his direction yet avoiding meeting his eyes.

He cleared his throat quickly and nodded. "Yes, of course. I believe we are starting with a quadrille, aren't we, Charlotte?"

"Correct, sir," came the cheeky response. "Come on, everyone, form the square."

Grace folded her arms, a last bit of resistance making itself known. "Who named Charlotte the dance supervisor?"

"I did," Aubrey shot back with a daring look. "It's her house, and I am not fool enough to try to dictate to her while in it."

"Wise man," Charlotte praised with a sage nod for him. She leveled a dark look at Grace. "Come over here, Miss Morledge, and kindly recall no one looks murderous while dancing a quadrille."

Grace offered her friend a patronizing, strained smile that made the others laugh, and trudged over to the forming square with the rest. Elinor stood with Henshaw, Izzy stood across from them, Charlotte stood alone across from Aubrey, and Aubrey...

Aubrey looked at Grace expectantly.

A very naughty French curse she'd once heard her aunt use suddenly flashed into her mind.

Nothing for it, then.

She exhaled shortly and forced her irritation back if for no other reason than to give him nothing to criticize about her dancing or her manner while doing so. She obediently came to stand beside him, smiling across the square at Charlotte, then giving a sidelong look to Izzy, standing diagonally to her. Izzy flashed a tight smile of sympathy, though she could not possibly comprehend exactly what Grace's particular complaint was at this moment. She only knew how Grace felt about being evaluated, and that was enough.

It was not wrong, certainly. It only failed to capture the full extent of her emotional state.

Kitty struck up an appropriate tune and Grace hummed to

herself as Izzy, with her pretend partner, began the first movements with Elinor and Henshaw.

"I had no idea you were so against a quadrille," Aubrey muttered beside her.

"What?" she snapped, not bothering to look at him as the others returned to their sides of the square.

He held out a hand, which she took, and they proceeded to meet Charlotte, and her imagined partner, in their formation. "You're as sour as lemons and have a rind twice as thick. Is it the dancing or is it me?"

She stiffened as they parted, and she prayed her expression would be made bland as she danced with the pretend partner.

Alas, when she returned to Aubrey, he chuckled. "That answers that question. Whatever it is, I apologize profusely, and beg you to take pity on me."

Grace scoffed a laugh as they returned to their first position. "Take pity on you? Why?"

"Well, for one, you've trodden on my toes three times in as many minutes."

She glanced down as they began the next movement, intentionally doing so once more. "Four," she corrected with a bright smile as she returned to look at him.

He chuckled again as he turned her for the dance, and they promenaded for a moment or two. "Or you could take pity on me for the blistering headache that took two days to recover from. No doubt Charlotte told you about it."

Grace smirked as they met Charlotte in the center of the square, Aubrey taking one of her hands as the three of them moved in a circle, careful to leave space for the imagined fourth. "I will not pity you for that. It was your own fault, and your own stupidity that gave it to you."

"True enough," Aubrey said as they danced back to their position. "Though I cannot say I bear the fault of the motivation to behave with such stupidity."

"No?" Grace's heart skipped a beat, even as she skipped in the dance. "Whatever could motivate a man to do something so foolish, knowing where it would lead?"

Aubrey flashed a smile at her that tickled her insides, the look intense and warm, though she noticed a hint of hesitation in it. "A need to be momentarily blind, deaf, and dumb, for the world as he knows it has vanished."

Her throat went dry, and she was grateful for the reprieve of dancing with Izzy's imagined partner to her left while Aubrey danced with Elinor.

Surely, he didn't mean... He couldn't mean...

She looked at him closely as he returned to her, but whatever intensity she had seen, whatever sincerity, had gone, and only Aubrey's cheerful countenance remained.

"And surely," he told her when they took hands once more, "you must pity me for this dance, as I fear Charlotte's imagined partner is clearly the best gentleman among the group."

"Too right he is," Charlotte crowed with a clap of her hand as she turned herself about. "I may marry this one."

"Speak for yourself, Ingram," Henshaw chortled, he and Elinor promenading to the center to meet Izzy. "I, for one, am dancing beautifully."

Aubrey shook his head, squeezing Grace's hand in a way that warmed her heart, even if she did not know the meaning behind it. "Passable at best, man. Elinor must be crying for a partner as capable as myself."

"See how my tears fall," Elinor called out drily, making Grace laugh.

"That's better," Aubrey whispered. "Come on, then, let's enjoy this."

Grace hesitated, remnants of her laughter still echoing through her. Could she give herself up to enjoying a dance with a man she wanted to question at times and kiss at times, and let go of the indignation that had been keeping her company?

"Please?"

She nearly groaned at his faint request; the words were barely audible. She could not resist that. Could not resist him. Could not resist this.

"Oh, all right," she replied, sighing for good measure. "It's for the best anyway. I so dislike being cross."

"You're very good at it, though," Aubrey insisted with the crooked grin she so adored.

She quirked her brows as she passed him in the next movement. "I know. You should see it when I mean it."

The grin wavered, and she laughed merrily at that, her steps lighter for it.

The list of his idiotic ideas was growing longer by the second, it seemed, and he wasn't quite sure what to make of it.

As if dancing with Grace the first time around hadn't ruined everything for him, he'd thought the best way to rejoin the fault-finding festivities would be to do so again.

Because he was somehow a martyr, a glutton for punishment, and a person lacking any real sense of self-preservation. Which was bewildering, as he'd always considered self-preservation to be his greatest motivator in life. Yet here he was, literally sacrificing himself on the altar of Grace Morledge without a single concern in his mind but that of making her smile and laugh.

Well, at least that had been accomplished, though he may have sold his soul several times over in the process. If his current state of nausea, panic, and a bizarre euphoria was anything to go by, he most certainly had. Each part of the quadrille had become more and more enjoyable, and he had a long-standing tradition of hating the quadrille. It was too involved, there was too much to remember, and one was rarely paired with couples who could complete each part with the necessary precision.

None of that had mattered here. He'd actually wished the quadrille had gone on longer so that he could have more time clasping Grace's hand, or turning her about, or skipping in a rough estimation of a circle beside her. He'd wanted more of it all, and his joy had to have been apparent to the rest of them.

By the end of it, they had all been laughing and barely able to get a single word out with any sort of clear translation.

Then Charlotte had recovered and informed the group that they would have a waltz next.

Oh, *hell* no.

If he was beginning to fray in the quadrille, the waltz would incinerate him.

"Not for me, thank you," he announced pleasantly, waving his hand. "I'll never be able to assess properly if I am waltzing myself, being so abysmal a partner. I'll stand over here and observe."

The entire room looked at him with varying degrees of curiosity, the highest of which belonged to Grace and Henshaw.

A flash of hurt crossed Grace's face, and he felt an echo of that same hurt lance him somewhere under his ribs. He would likely earn himself a second round of damnation for putting such an expression on her face, but he was willing to go so far if it gave him a few moments of uninterrupted clarity.

Henshaw merely looked startled by the pronouncement, which was undoubtedly to be expected. They hadn't discussed Aubrey's current state of emotional discord, nor had he revealed to the man anything resembling Camden Vale's outlandish claims, for fear of almost certain death. But Henshaw was a cunning and observant man, and Aubrey had a sneaking suspicion that he already knew.

Aubrey cleared his throat and gestured to the group. "Henshaw, you partner with Grace. Charlotte and the rest can determine who knows the male part of the dance best and go from there."

Henshaw's eyes narrowed, but he smiled. "Of course, I only need a moment to catch my breath. The quadrille, you know. Most laborious."

Grace's eyes continued to linger on Aubrey, confusion mixing with the hurt and curiosity there, then she turned to the others and began to converse in low tones.

Freed from the captivity of her gaze, Aubrey managed to exhale far more roughly than he would have done otherwise.

"Would you mind telling me what you are doing?"

Aubrey looked up into Henshaw's bemused expression, keeping his own perfectly bland. "Preparing to assess the waltz. Are you prepared for that?"

"I could waltz blindfolded on my own in front of every Society matron and you without blinking twice," Henshaw shot back. "I want to know what *you* are doing."

So did Aubrey, but that wasn't exactly clear at the moment. So, he settled for the only thing that was clear.

Habit.

He smiled at his friend. "Preparing to assess the waltz."

Henshaw rolled his eyes. "All right, then." He took one step back, looked over his shoulder, and cleared his throat. "I solemnly swear to you that this waltz is purely because you are forcing me to take your place, as you are too terrified of a close proximity with Grace to do so yourself."

Aubrey coughed in surprise and straightened up. "What? Are you calling me a coward?"

"No, sir, not at all," Henshaw blustered as he puffed out his chest. "Just extraordinarily foolish. Enjoy the show."

"I will kill you," Aubrey vowed as Henshaw slowly backed away.

Henshaw grinned. "Kindly after the waltz. Grace is a marvelous dancer." He tipped an imaginary hat in Aubrey's direction, then turned and swept towards the ladies with all the airs of a carefree gentleman.

The moment the man touched Grace's hand, Aubrey's temper erupted.

Thankfully, he had always been a controlled man in his anger, so it did nothing except make him surly and enraged, burning and seething himself into a towering inferno that couldn't move. Wouldn't move.

Didn't move.

Kitty Morton struck up a waltz on the pianoforte, and the two couples began their dance, swirling and turning with a fluid grace that would have suited any ballroom in London. Henshaw was a tall man, but there was nothing awkward or ungainly about his dancing. He moved Grace about the room easily, turning her effortlessly, his steps crisp and sure, saying something that made her smile as he did so.

Aubrey felt himself snarl as he watched them, the music a twisted accompaniment to the farce he was witnessing.

A ridiculous, moronic, laughable farce about which no one was laughing.

Grace tipped her head back with a musical laugh that constricted

Aubrey's insides, his jaw clenching as the light through a window caught her hair. Every step she made could have touched a cloud, every turn highlighted another stunning angle of her features, every swish of her skirts taunting him from across the room. She danced with all the lightness of a breeze, and she could not have looked more angelic had a halo begun to glow above her.

And he was standing over here.

Watching.

Henshaw glanced at Aubrey, one corner of his mouth twitching suspiciously.

The man would be dead by the end of the day, if only Aubrey could decide on a proper course of assassination.

Then again, this had all been Aubrey's idea. Henshaw had only agreed to it, and then proceeded to take great pleasure in fulfilling that agreement.

A thrashing instead of a murder, then. All the better.

He was obsessed, and he couldn't even bring himself to care. He watched her hungrily, eagerly, tracking every single minute motion she made. Every detail was precious. Anything he could catch, any sign, any flicker...

He ran a hand over his face, working his jaw absently to loosen it.

Ridiculous.

A turn of the waltz and Grace was looking in his direction, and then, suddenly, at him. Directly. Frankly.

He met her gaze without shame. He didn't care if she saw his yearning; he wanted her to know he saw.

She swallowed and wrenched her gaze away, back to Henshaw.

Aubrey felt his mouth curve in dark satisfaction. If she could upend his world so completely, at least he was giving hers a bit of a nudge in return, if nothing else.

He could work with that.

The waltz came to an end, and he applauded politely, as did Izzy, who had chosen to sit beside Kitty for the duration. The dancers smiled amongst themselves, and Charlotte turned to Aubrey, hands on her hips

"Well, Lord Ingram," she called cheerily, "have you seen

enough?"

He grinned at her and bowed. "I have, Miss Wright, and I thank you for your kind hospitality."

"Oh lord," Grace groaned, rubbing at her brow.

She seemed tired, fatigued somehow, and his jaunty air faded at once. He wanted to ask her what was wrong, see if he could mend it, see if he had done this. He knew he had been a bit of a cad of late, and that an apology was due, but how could he...? What could he...?

Not here. Not now.

He bit the inside of his lip very softly, waiting as the others began to leave one by one. He bid them all farewell, as he must, and maintained his usual demeanor as best he could, his eyes always tracking Grace. The moment she left, the very instant she left the room, he would be behind her. He would follow, he would explain, he would...

He paused as he realized there were only two others in the room now. Just two.

Grace and Charlotte.

Somehow, he had missed whatever moment Henshaw had left, which he would undoubtedly hear about later, but he would take it. He would take every single bit of ribbing, teasing, and ridicule that came to him. This would be worth it.

She was worth it.

A wave of warmth and need slowly washed over him, leaving him surprisingly comfortable and at ease. And unnervingly clear.

Grace finally began to move to the door, her eyes darting towards him, but not at him, her cheeks heating. Not with pleasure, but with shame.

Why did he know that? *How* did he know that?

He blinked as she moved away from him, down the corridor, and the stairs.

"Aubrey."

He turned to look at Charlotte quickly. "What?"

She grinned in a manner he had never seen her do before. "I bid you good day, and all that politeness, but I will push you down the stairs myself if you don't run right this moment."

Now, he was the one who grinned. "I adore you, Charlotte

Wright, and I don't care who knows it." He darted out of the room to the sound of her merry laughter, though her response was completely lost on him.

He moved with a speed he'd forgotten he had, racing without any sort of manner through a house that was not his in pursuit of the woman he... The woman...

Well, in pursuit of Grace Morledge, of all people.

"Grace!" he called out in relief as he saw her, standing in the foyer with her hands on her bonnet ribbons.

She paused and looked up at him, eyes wide as he fumbled his way down the stairs. "Aubrey?"

"Wait," he panted as he made his way down to her. "Wait. Just wait."

Her pale brow furrowed. "Waiting..."

His knees shook in relief and delight at her wit, and he exhaled as he reached her. "So I see."

Grace was silent a moment, then gestured with her hand. "What am I waiting for?"

What, indeed.

Insanity consumed him, and he strode to her, hands going to her face. "This," he whispered as his lips descended on hers in a delicious foray that had spent far too long pent up within him.

She stiffened in his hold for only a moment, then blessedly relaxed against him, her hands gripping his wrists tightly. Her mouth softened beneath his, responding with a gentle steadiness that stole his breath.

Gads, how he loved kissing her.

He broke off with a gasp, dropping one hand from her skin and pressing it against the wall behind her. When exactly had there been a wall behind her?

Grace's thumb moved against the exposed skin of his wrist and he shivered, dropping his head to nuzzle against her tenderly. "What was that for?" she asked wryly.

Aubrey pulled back to look at her, his fingers brushing against her cheek. "I didn't want you to think my feelings have changed simply because I wasn't dancing with you. I was... well, I was saving myself."

She tilted her head in his hold. "From what?"

"From you, of course." He shook his head, stroking her cheek once more. "I didn't think I could hide this from them if we waltzed. I doubt I hid it anyway."

Grace lifted her chin, her perfect lips curving rather the way his toes were at the present. "And what is this, exactly? What do you feel?"

He chuckled. "Hell if I know, but I'm not about to complain." He leaned down to kiss her again, taking great care to use restraint this time, only lingering in the very corner of her lips.

She sighed, and he felt the pleasure in it. "Is there a flaw in allowing oneself to be kissed in a private foyer of a friend's home?"

"I hope not. Best slap me for assaulting your virtue, just in case."

Grace seemed to consider that, and he narrowed his eyes, daring her to do it.

One of her hands went to his cheek, patting gently as though in thought. Then she rose up on her toes and pressed her lips to his other cheek instead, the kiss a gentle blossom of feeling he'd never experience in his entire life and now would die without. She nuzzled against the spot, then trailed her fingers across his lips as she moved away.

He turned as she went to the door, watched as her fingers deftly tied the ribbons, and only exhaled when the door closed behind her.

"Guh," he bleated as his legs shook, his hands flying to the decorative ledge of the wall nearest him for support.

He stared at the door in fascinated wonder, blinking as though Grace stood there still.

Curses... He was in for it now.

Chapter Seventeen

There are some things for which there is no explanation.

-*The Spinster Chronicles, 23 June 1815*

"You cannot be serious."

"Oh, but I am. Entirely."

"He wouldn't."

"He would."

"He would subject you to comment in such a way?"

"So it would seem."

"I cannot understand it."

"No, I suppose you couldn't." Grace sputtered a disgruntled sound, shaking her head. "He suggested the thing over dinner, and would you believe that my brother agreed to the idea?"

Edith seemed to consider that. "Would I believe that your brother would agree with your father that paying men to court you was a good idea? Yes, I believe I would. I know your brother better, and that is entirely worthy of him."

Grace laughed in surprise, reaching for her tea. "You have met my brother perhaps three times, all told."

"That was enough to know I don't have much to recommend him," Edith shot back with a mischievous grin. "He reminds me of my brother, actually."

"Does he?" Grace asked, sipping slowly. As a general rule, Edith did not speak of her family. All anybody knew of them was that her father had not been well pleased with her, and that he had been keen to have her married off. She'd never heard of any siblings, except for the brother who'd asked Henshaw to look after her, and that was all she knew. The prospect of further revelation gave her a flutter of excitement.

Edith nodded, her smile still in place, though turning rueful. "Aye."

It was clear that for any sort of deeper response, Grace would to have to do a little prodding, if not outright suggestion. She scoffed softly, settling her tea in her lap. "What? Your brother is also obsessed with finery and the ridiculous, all too superior, desperate for attention and going about earning it in all the wrong ways?"

The Scottish beauty tossed her dark hair back on a laugh. "Sharp tongue, lass, but a well-placed description. No, he's not obsessed with finery, for we never had any to be obsessed with. And I canna say he takes joy in the ridiculous either. He's a bit rougher, you might say. But he is all too superior, desperate for attention, and certainly earning some in the wrong ways." She winked at Grace with a knowing smirk. "Though not in the same wrong ways that your brother employs."

Grace lifted her teacup once more. "To wayward brothers and their various wrongs. May we never fall under their protection."

Edith raised hers with a nod. "Amen."

They giggled as they sipped, and Grace shook her head. "I don't think you're supposed to say amen in a toast! What would you say at home?"

Edith's lips curved a little "*Slàinte*," she murmured softly.

Grace eyed her friend for a moment. "Do you miss Scotland?"

"Terribly," came the whispered reply.

"And your family?"

Edith's reverie broke and she grinned once more, raising a brow. "Not so terribly, if you can believe that."

"But I am absolutely certain that they miss you," boomed a voice from the doorway.

Grace felt her cheeks crack with a beaming grin as she turned to see Aubrey standing there, glorious and charming as he strode in, his fawn-colored breeches perfectly accentuating his legs as they vanished into pristine boots. His dark waistcoat and green coat heightened his complexion, and Grace thought he somehow seemed more tanned and robust today than before, though it had barely been a day since she had seen him last.

"Aubrey!" she cried belatedly, rising from her chair, thankfully setting her tea aside before she upset it.

His grin matched hers, and her heart leapt to her throat at the sight of it. "Grace," he replied, his voice gentling as he said it.

Heavens, she would swoon where she stood.

Aubrey turned to Edith quickly and bowed deeply. "Lady Edith."

Edith shook her head, smiling to herself, and curtseyed. "Aubrey. And I can assure you, my family doesna miss me overly much."

"Nonsense!" he protested, reaching for her hand and kissing it fondly. "I'd miss you daily, were you my family. Perhaps even hourly."

"Och," she scoffed, her cheeks coloring. "Away wi' you, flatterer."

Aubrey chuckled and turned his still-smiling face towards Grace.

She couldn't help it; she kept grinning like a fool. "Why are you here? Were we supposed to meet?"

"No," he said simply, tugging at his coat, "but it's so delightful to surprise you, and you react so splendidly, I thought I might take the opportunity to do so."

Her cheeks flamed on cue, and she saw how his smile deepened at the sight of it. "I'm not normally known for enjoying surprises," she murmured, suddenly feeling terribly shy, pushing a strand of nonexistent hair behind her ear.

"That isn't what I've heard," he replied, his eyes darkening.

A delicious shiver started making its way down her spine, and a sigh began building within her.

"Right," Edith said slowly, turning to pick up her tea and saucer. "I am going to remove myself from this very private conversation and enjoy a spot of sunshine. Over there." She pointed to the exact opposite side of the room, where a large window overlooked the garden. "And where I willna be able to hear anything the pair of you

207

are saying." She nodded and started to move, then thought better of it as she snatched a cake and crumpet from the table before sweeping away.

Grace blushed more furiously, her eyes darting to Edith's retreating figure.

Aubrey did not so much as blink. "I've always liked Edith. She's very astute."

"There's not much to dislike," Grace agreed weakly as her fingers began to twist at each other.

He only hummed in response, still looking at her.

"You're staring," she whispered, biting her lip.

His eyes moved to her mouth as she did so. "Yes. I am."

"Stop."

"No."

"Stop!"

"No."

"Aubrey!"

He heaved an almost dramatic sigh. "Grace, I take great delight in drinking in the very sight of you, and I'll thank you not to revoke such a pleasurable pastime."

She tried to look annoyed, despite the surge of affection currently constricting her throat. "Oh, please…"

"Now, now," Aubrey scolded, his brow furrowing deeply. "I believe it is customary for the mere mortals to beg from the goddesses, not the other way around. Don't confuse our roles here."

Grace stared at the man in outright bewilderment now. "Goddess? Where in the world do you see a goddess?"

He stared, then gestured at her, then stepped back and did so much more grandly. "Exhibit A, my dear."

"I am no goddess," she murmured, shaking her head very firmly. "If anything, Aubrey, you of all people know how very mortal and flawed I am."

He made a thoughtful face, then scrunched it up in disagreement. "No, I can't say that I do, and as the sole individual tasked with actually finding your flaws, I am in a position to know."

The affection she felt was beginning to grow more and more uncomfortable, and she wondered if one could swoon purely from excessive blushing. "Aubrey, please…"

"Too much?" He came back to her, expression apologetic. "I'm sorry. I don't mean to be. I just… Grace, I haven't the faintest idea what I'm doing, so if I'm fumbling around in a buffoonish way, it is only because I am entirely out of my depth."

"I don't believe either of us have actually stated what we're doing," she replied with a sheepish smile. "I wouldn't even know what to call it."

Aubrey laughed once and reached for her hand, stroking it softly. "I'd call it courtship, but I'm afraid several ceilings would begin to crack and fall upon various heads if we said anything so formal. I'd call it exploration, but I hate to think of this as merely an expedition. I'd call it flirtation, but that's a paltry description. I don't know what it is, Grace. I just know I can't help it."

Of all the lovely things he could have said, that might have been the loveliest. She sighed, and he laughed again at the sound.

"You like that, eh?" he murmured, stroking her hand in a way that seemed to burn the bottom of her feet.

She nodded, momentarily without words. Then she swallowed. "Sometimes, Aubrey Flint, you really do say delightful things."

"I know," he replied with a wink. "I practice daily. Sundrey is quite tired of giving critiques."

"Poor Sundrey."

Aubrey snorted once. "Don't say that too loudly, he'll hear you. The man has the ears of a bloodhound."

"Fairly certain bloodhounds are known for their noses, not their ears," Edith announced from her side of the room, her tone that of one musing aloud.

Aubrey scowled, but did not turn. "Thank you for not listening as promised, Edith," he called.

Grace looked beyond him and saw Edith grinning as she sipped her tea. "It's your own fault," she hissed as she returned her attention to him. "Edith and I were having a lovely tea up until you interrupted us."

"You didn't seem to mind," he hissed back, quirking a brow.

"I don't," she insisted, smiling with the truth of things. "But you cannot blame Edith for being here when you were not expected to be. I refuse to send her home simply because you're here now."

Aubrey's smile turned particularly devilish. "I'd wager I could persuade her to go of her own accord, if you'd let me."

Oh... Lord... Grace's eyes widened, and she swallowed hard. "Did you have a flaw to explore today?" she said a little too loudly. "Or exploit, as the case may be?"

Aubrey muffled a laugh, then played along. "As a matter of fact, I did."

He did? She rather thought she'd take him by surprise with that one, but if he'd had a plan... "Oh, really?"

He nodded, sweeping his hands behind his back. "I believe in order to get the full scope of things, I really must examine your penmanship."

The room stilled, which was particularly impressive as neither Edith nor Grace had been making any particular sounds. Yet it went more silent at his ridiculous statement.

"My penmanship," she repeated slowly.

Again, he nodded. "I've found that a great many letters are examined not just for the content but for an appreciation of the hand in which they were written. Or a criticism of said hand, if the form is not quite the thing."

"You saw a letter I wrote," Grace pointed out, folding her arms. "I've even sent you notes. You know what my penmanship looks like."

"Might not want to spread that one around," he quipped, leaning closer. "Especially in this company. Edith might suspect something."

"Yes, I tend to suspect quite a lot," Edith chimed in dryly around a bite of crumpet. "Quite nosy in that regard."

Aubrey gestured as if to emphasize the point.

The pair of them were really quite terrible, but Grace wouldn't be put off. "You think I could be a spinster because of my penmanship?"

"It's not about why I think you could be a spinster," Aubrey explained, only slightly more serious. "It's about exploring every possible avenue, angle, and facet of you to find what doesn't fit."

Grace blinked once. "My *penmanship*, Aubrey?"

"Truth be told," he said sheepishly, "I couldn't think of anything else."

Strangely, that delighted Grace to no end, and she fought the desire to laugh. Instead, she nodded primly and moved to a writing desk in a corner of the room, sitting as perfectly as she could and pulling out a sheet of paper from a drawer.

Aubrey came to stand beside her, perhaps a bit too close for politeness, though for all appearances, he was being quite studious in his observations.

Grace carefully dipped the pen into the ink, wiped the excess off the nib, then put the pen to paper. In her best hand, without a single hint of hesitation, and at a slower, more sedate pace than usual to emphasize her skills, she wrote the thought chiefest in her mind.

Aubrey is an idiot.

She laid the pen down and turned the paper for his better examination.

He snorted and looked at her, smiling crookedly. "Very true, Miss Morledge. And very well done."

"Thank you," she acknowledged with a modest dip of her chin.

Aubrey glanced at Edith, then bent and kissed Grace quickly, almost silently, his lips teasing and pulling just enough to make her follow as he broke off.

"But he's a very charming idiot," he whispered, laughing at her faint moan. "Charming and rather charmed, as well."

"How fortunate for him," Grace replied.

"Quite." Aubrey straightened and turned towards Edith now. "Edith, how are you at drawing? I haven't evaluated Grace's abilities there as yet, and I really think she would be more comfortable and natural with someone else also participating."

As it turned out, Grace was a talented artist.

No surprise there.

Thankfully, she was not exceptional, and the only reason he could tell that was because Edith *was* exceptional. There was no flaw or fault to be found in Grace's drawing, even the stodgiest of art masters would have agreed. But Edith's...

There was something breathtaking about what she could put to paper.

Still, the three of them had a merry time in their drawing session, not that Aubrey had participated in anything actually resembling art. The ladies had tried to convince him, but he had withstood every one of their pleadings, jabs, and arguments. He was not artistic, and he was not about to start pretending otherwise now.

He much preferred watching.

It was strange, but he'd spent almost the whole of the afternoon at Trenwick House in a drawing room with two spinsters, and he was convinced he had never spent a better afternoon in his entire life. He'd laughed, he'd teased, he'd been impressed, and he'd seen real beauty. He had felt his breath stolen, and he had rendered the breath of someone else more difficult.

And he had smiled.

Lord, how he'd smiled. He was more jubilant than a clergyman with a full congregation on Christmas morning, and twice as prone to sing praises. He barely recognized himself, except he was positive that he had never felt more himself. This fervency, this depth of feeling, this unending need to see her, to smile at her, to let himself feel anything and everything he felt in her very presence... This was everything he had ever wanted, and all he had hoped to experience.

He hadn't known that before, of course, or he would have fled in several other directions to avoid the sheer madness of such sensations, but that was neither here nor there. He was stuck in the middle of it now, and he was far too pleasantly engrossed to wish anything different. It was rather enjoyable being tossed about and giddy, particularly when he knew how easy it was to have secluded moments with the object of his giddy madness.

Granted, today Edith had given him a spot of trouble, but she was such an agreeable obstacle that it made the whole thing more entertaining. He could adapt his plans easily enough to accommodate her, as the case need be, and it would not always be so restricted. And yet the restriction made moments between Grace and him more exhilarating for being stolen. The risk of being observed and found out made the rewards all the sweeter.

And oh, how sweet they were.

He'd thought admiring Grace without emotion a pleasing enough experience, as any healthy male in possession of his senses and eyesight would have done. But to look upon her with his heart burning against the bones of his chest, to feel the blood pumping through him as though by thunderstorm, to regard her with a tenderness that shook him… There was no description for the beauty in each glimpse of her when feeling what he did in those moments, nor for the delight they gave.

A sharp jolt raced across his chest as Camden Vale's words flashed in his mind.

You're in love with Grace Morledge.

He gasped and swayed a bit, just as he had then, but without the same panic. He knew he was in love with her. He had known it then, which is why he had drunk himself into oblivion and spent two days sick over it. He'd known it and denied it despite knowing it.

Refused it, if for no other reason than because loving Grace was a terrifying prospect.

It was no less terrifying now, but he was through denying it. Refusing it. Fighting it.

Yes, he was ready to accept the truth. Yes, he was surrendering. Yes, he was well-aware that he would receive teasing, superiority, and outright ridicule from several people of his acquaintance for the rest of his days.

Because undeniably yes, he was in love with Grace Morledge, and he was quite pleased with that.

Now all he needed was for her to come back into this room so he could kiss the blazes out of her with this thrilling new vigor in him.

His mouth spread in frank anticipation of the scene that would unfold then.

"Ingram."

Had he been a man of less control, Aubrey would have yelped with all the guilt of a naughty schoolboy. But he was a man of great control, so he only turned sharply, feeling as though he had swallowed his insides after they'd been tied in knots. All of which were now attempting to strangle him.

How very disconcerting.

"Lord Trenwick," Aubrey greeted with all the mildness of winter in Inverness.

The man in question stood in the second door to this room, smiling with the same sort of thin smile he usually did, which gave no indication as to pleasure or displeasure. "Have you been assessing my daughter today?"

Why, yes, he had, but perhaps not in the way Trenwick would have expected.

"I have, my lord," Aubrey replied, somehow keeping his cheek in check. "We have met several times, as I am sure you have been aware."

Trenwick nodded with the same indeterminate expression. "Yes, I have. And what was the topic today, if I may ask?"

Well, Aubrey had spent a very long time assessing the merits of the turn of Grace's throat, but he doubted that was what her father had in mind.

"She was taking tea with Lady Edith, sir," Aubrey said truthfully. "I called unexpectedly today rather than schedule a meeting."

"Ah," Trenwick unexpectedly replied, nodding as though he understood. "To give my daughter less time to prepare for your arrival. Very strategic, Ingram. I approve."

Aubrey thought it best to ignore that. Grace would never forgive him if she knew her father approved of his surprising her. "Indeed. But due to Lady Edith's presence, sir, my plan for the day had to alter. I could not expect Lady Edith to adjust her plans without seeming rude, and as you are wishing to keep this matter private, I thought it best to continue on as though it were merely a social call."

Trenwick continued to nod, which was strangely unnerving without real expression. Then, he stopped, the stillness twice as unsettling. "And how did my daughter behave with a woman so far below her when in your company?"

So far... Lady Edith was the widow of a knight and daughter of an earl, and that put her squarely in respectable circles. Her husband had been a blackguard, it was true, but that did not negate her position.

Still, now was not the time to argue that particular point of taste. "She behaved with all the manners one could have hoped, sir," he told Trenwick, a hard edge seeping into his tone. "Far better than any other I have seen. She is poised and respectful, and remarkably kind. Lady Edith is good for her, I think. I was impressed, my lord, and I will not deny it."

"Excellent," Trenwick replied, returning to the absent nodding. "Most excellent. A father is always pleased to hear his children behave as he would wish."

At that moment, it was clear that Trenwick heard nothing about James' behavior at any given time, but no matter.

"But it tells me nothing about my daughter's faults," Trenwick went on, his voice rising suddenly. "Come with me, Ingram. We have much to discuss." He turned back out of the doorway, and Aubrey looked longingly towards the other door, but followed nonetheless.

They had reached the study, and Aubrey moved to follow Trenwick when a flash of blue caught his eye and he paused. Grace stood just down the corridor, her eyes wide. He stared, pouring every ounce of longing and regret he could into his expression. He watched her elegant throat move on a swallow, then saw her chin dip in a half nod.

How had they forgotten, in the midst of everything, that her father was controlling this entire spectacle?

He wrenched his gaze away and entered the study, closing the door behind him.

Trenwick situated himself behind his desk and gestured for Aubrey to take the chair opposite. "Do sit, Ingram."

Aubrey sat, feeling rather like a child again.

He stared at the desk before him, waiting for something to begin. A speech, a tirade, a rant... Something to get this whole bloody business over with so he could get back to the more pleasant aspect of the madness.

"Ingram, I know you are uncomfortable with the circumstance in which I have placed you," Trenwick began in a much more temperate tone than Aubrey had expected. "I recall that you objected most strenuously when the idea was first put forth."

"I did, my lord," Aubrey said with a nod, though he said nothing else. He was not about to volunteer information about his dealings with Grace, and he wouldn't have done so before he'd fallen in love with her.

Trenwick did not continue, drawing Aubrey's attention to him. The man stared at him, waiting.

Aubrey exhaled and shifted uncomfortably. "My lord, I apologize if you're expecting me to give you a report on my progress with assessing your daughter for faults or misdeeds. I fear I would disappoint you in that regard."

"Would you?" Trenwick asked mildly, not seeming particularly concerned, though he did not look pleased.

Strange for a man so involved to be so unaffected.

Aubrey had the sudden feeling that he was being toyed with, and he did not care for it one bit. He was no man's pawn, and he refused to be treated as such. "It would be impolite to your daughter to reveal to you all that goes on in our meetings. She is feeling vulnerable enough as it is, knowing she's being evaluated, and I have pledged to make this as painless as possible for her. It's the least I can do out of respect for her with regards to her position and her person. I will not give you notes on our progress, sir, as I have not done thus far. I have promised to report what I find when I have completed my study, as Miss Morledge knows well. If you wish me to accomplish the task you've set before me, you must trust me to do so in the manner I best see fit. And that includes respecting the privacy of myself, your daughter, and our meetings."

There was no sound in the room, and while Aubrey was prepared for a booming rant of outrage at such a speech, he was pleased that one had not occurred.

In fact, Trenwick did not look in the least perturbed.

"Good," the man said, upending everything Aubrey had expected. "I was hoping you were truly as trustworthy and discreet about the whole affair as you had claimed you would be. I am pleased to have you be so involved and invested. You see now how important it is for us to protect Grace and see to it that she comes to no harm in all this."

Of course Aubrey saw that. He had always seen that, which was why he had even agreed in the first place. It was Trenwick who had not understood that previously, or so he had thought. Why was he now so very concerned for his daughter's feelings?

216

"Indeed," Aubrey responded without much conviction, suspicions rising.

"I may now put another task to you," Trenwick said, leaning forward on his desk and looking far more earnest than he had been in some time. "One that I was hesitant to apply before, but you have proven yourself worthy of it."

Blast, this was how Aubrey proved worthy of his trust? He should have kissed Grace passionately in full view of Almack's and the king's privy council, if not directly before her father's face.

"I must ask you," Trenwick went on, unaware he had effectively ruined Aubrey's appetite for an entire month with his statement, "to also evaluate my daughter's reputation."

Her what?

Aubrey blinked. "Her reputation, sir? Is it in question?" He nearly snarled the question, his fingers digging into the wood of the chair in which he sat.

"No, of course not," Trenwick snapped. "I have not raised a hoyden of questionable morality. I only need to know what it is. One can never trust what one says to a parent of a young lady of Society. I need to know what is truly being said about her, for good or for ill. I trust London gossip to carry the truth of Grace's impediment, and I need you to uncover it. Why my daughter is unmarried. Why her education and upbringing have failed her. Why a young woman of station, breeding, fortune, and beauty is spurned by all respectable options. Why she is failing us all. Why she is a disgrace. You must find out, Ingram. You must listen to every word of it."

"Sir…" Aubrey protested weakly, feeling more and more ill the longer he sat here.

"I do consider this part of our contract," Trenwick overrode, his eyes fully blazing now. "The most important part, if not the whole reason for it. And you gave your word, sir. As a gentleman."

Aubrey stared at the man, the bland image of Trenwick from his youth shattering in his mind. This was the man who would find fault in a faultless daughter, who would have her evaluated for imperfections, and then burn those imperfections into dust in his own cruel refiner's fire, if only he had bellows enough to heat it.

The blinders of childhood were gone. The reality of disdain

sprang free.

"Indeed, sir," Aubrey replied in the same tone one might have damned another to hell. "My word." A vile taste rose in his throat, and he nodded. "And now, if you'll excuse me, I have a meeting with my solicitor. Breyerly needs my attention."

Trenwick blustered some response to that, something simpering, pompous, and ridiculous, but Aubrey could only hear the buzzing of an irritating insect. He pried himself free from the handshake and left the room, his hand cramping in objection at his side.

Reputation. Imperfection. Failing. Disgrace. He burned with indignation at every slanderous word, his head swimming among it all. How was a man so deluded in his own importance as to only see his offspring for their ability to advance his influence?

And this was what Grace had grown up with?

"Aubrey?"

He looked around wildly, her sweet voice breaking through his heated fog. Grace stood near the stairs, waiting for him, her expression worried. He moved towards her at once, seeking her solace and her influence to cleanse him of what he had just witnessed.

"What was that about?" she asked, her eyes searching his.

Aubrey swallowed and cupped her face, surprising her. He touched his brow to hers and exhaled roughly.

"Aubrey?" Her hands came to his chest, pressing against his heart.

He tilted his head and kissed her very softly. "I will not break you," he vowed in a harsh whisper, his hands nearly clenching against her.

Her fingers gripped his coat tightly. "I know," she replied in the same tone. She went up on tiptoe and kissed him hard, then pulled one of his hands from her face and kissed it, as well. "You won't."

The certainty in her voice bolstered him, and he nodded, stroking a finger against her cheek. "We will find a way, won't we?"

Grace nodded, smiling with the brilliance of the dawn. "Of course, we will. And if we get lost, we'll just wander a bit."

Aubrey felt himself soften the longer he looked into her eyes, and he tilted his head towards the door, letting her escort him towards it. "Well, I am particularly good at wandering."

Chapter Eighteen

———— ❦ ————

A woman is a strong, powerful, beautiful creation capable of a great many things. But all should take care with her, for a woman is also more fragile than her strength may suggest.

-The Spinster Chronicles, 1 November 1816

As it happened, wandering about from day to day with Aubrey as he paid her particular attention was a rather enjoyable experience for Grace. The man was even more charming when he was sincere than he was when he was playful, and for all his composure in public settings, he seemed to have an impossible time hiding his feelings when they were together.

She could tell that it drove him mad that he was so exposed, and that she could read him so easily.

She, on the other hand, adored it.

It was refreshing to have someone be so open with her, even if it was somewhat against his will. So much of her world in Society was for appearances only, and it was difficult to know what was truth and what was fiction. But with Aubrey, there was no pretense. Everything was natural, easy, and real, sometimes breathtakingly so.

She had always known that Aubrey was a dedicated, driven individual, and one with a capacity for great feeling, but never had she imagined what an effect such passion would have on the object of his attention. He was constantly taking her hand, staring too long, smiling too warmly, or making her laugh until her sides ached. And the man could not seem to stop kissing her at any opportunity.

She had no objections there.

Under the guise of their usual fault-finding meetings, they had managed to attempt to find faults in several areas. First on Aubrey's list had been her billiard playing, which had been difficult enough to manage with him flirting with all the skill of a rake and attempting to teach her the proper manner of it. She hadn't thought that billiards involved quite so much distraction, but she'd never been particularly skilled at the game during the best of times. Under his "helpful" tutelage, she was not likely to improve any time soon.

Card playing was his next suggestion, and thanks to a small gathering with several of their friends, he was able to assess her abilities in loo, whist, and vingt et un. Grace had taken great pride in being able to cheat successfully in all of them, thanks to a very educational visit to the estate of a great uncle when she was ten. No one suspected her, nor had they ever, and Aubrey, much to his bewilderment, had not managed to take more than two hands in any single game.

She had to let him win once or twice, or else he would have begun to accuse her.

They'd walked Hyde Park with her mother, taking great care that Aubrey should happen upon them rather than attend on them, and while they had not been able to enjoy real privacy there, it had been time together. He'd been so attentive to her mother, had taken care that she should not feel as though she grew tiresome, and had been so engaging that her mother had not stopped talking of it since. And Aubrey had insisted that assessing Grace's manner of walking a park was of vital importance to his evaluation, so the excursion had been beneficial from any aspect.

Grace would have to have him explain that one to her at some later time.

He was always finding excuses for doing one thing or another, something that would relate to his attempts to find fault in her. It had become the most entertaining sort of game between them, his suggestions growing more and more absurd and her attempts to engage in the proposed topic growing more and more eager. At this rate, they would be assessing her ability to climb a tree or slide a bannister in the next few days, followed by his evaluation of her ability to navigate the shops in Bond Street.

Throughout each and every session, never once did she feel as though Aubrey were really searching for a fault. He participated in whatever it was he'd thought up for the day with the same energy he might have done had this been a real courtship.

Had it been a courtship.

It felt rather like a courtship, if she understood courtships at all. With only an outside perspective on the thing, it was difficult to say. But he was finding excuses to spend time with her, showing her real and genuine affection, making her feel things that she did not understand.

Making her want...

She shivered in the warm daylight of the parlor, looking out over the street in front of the house. He had promised to come today, and she was wild to see him. She was always wild to see him these days, and she quite liked such a thrilling feeling racing up and down her limbs.

But where would it lead? Where would it end?

What if he found a flaw?

She was no fool; she knew full well she had flaws, and many in her character, if nothing else. She was not actually perfect and had spent ages telling people so.

Yet Aubrey liked perfect. Aubrey loved perfect; he'd said so himself.

What if she wasn't perfect?

What if this venture of her father's not only worked, but in the process distanced Aubrey from her due to something unspeakable he might uncover?

It was silly; she was being ridiculous. Aubrey was a flawed human, as any other person in the world was, and he could not expect Grace to be perfect, despite apparent difficulties in identifying the glaring faults that rendered her a spinster.

But what if Aubrey wanted perfect?

What would she do then?

Her more independent side balked at such maudlin thoughts, scolded her for caring so much what one man thought, berated her for simpering about whether or not she was what he would want. The softer, secret, more vulnerable side of her curled up into a ball and shook with the fear that she would not be enough for him. Just as she was not, and had never been, enough for any other gentleman in this world.

Including her father.

"Grace."

Speak of the very devil…

She turned to see him enter the drawing room and curtseyed in an automatic response. "Father."

To her surprise, her mother followed her father into the room, and while she knew her mother's expressions and unspoken emotions well, this time she had no hint of what would follow.

Except that her mother would not meet her eyes, and that was certainly not a good sign.

"Mama," Grace murmured with all the trepidation she had ever known in childhood.

Her father's face tightened, and Grace winced, belatedly recollecting her father's distaste for such names. "I wondered, Grace, if you might spare a moment for a word with your mother and me."

As if she would have been permitted to refuse.

She nodded and moved to a nearby chair, knowing whatever this turned out to be, it would require her apparent attention, and would likely take some time.

Grace watched as her mother sat on the sofa near her, but took care to stay close to her father. As united a front as they could be, she supposed.

Her throat went dry as a wave of uneasiness filled her. "Have I done something wrong?" she heard herself ask, cursing herself for the childish tone.

"Not that we know of," her father replied in what he undoubtedly thought was a consoling manner.

A jolt of panic hit Grace squarely in the stomach. Had he found out about the Spinsters? Was she about to be castigated for aligning herself with a group of unmarried women? Her father had the power to forbid her anything and everything, and if he forced her to give them up…

"I have spoken with Lord Ingram," her father went on formally. "He has informed me of his progress in your evaluation."

He had? What could he have said?

The look on his face the other day as he had left her father's study suddenly rose in her mind, and she heard his harsh words as he'd cupped her face in his hands.

I will not break you.

Her body went cold, and swallowing was suddenly impossible.

"He says you have been very poised and respectful." Something that was almost a smile crossed her father's lips and he nodded once. "I was most pleased to hear it, as you might imagine."

Grace slowly released the breath she'd been holding. She couldn't find the words to respond, so she only dipped her chin in a nod.

Her father began to slowly pace before her. "It pleases me that you are taking this matter so seriously. No doubt, you must wish to have your faults identified, as well, so that you might remedy the situation and marry well."

Grace flicked her gaze to her mother, who very slightly shook her head. "Yes, Father," she murmured through dry lips.

"While Lord Ingram continues his investigation," her father intoned as he continued to move before her, "I have charged him with another. That of your reputation."

"My... my reputation?"

He gave her a brusque nod. "It must be done. In order to get the full measure of this unfortunate circumstance, we must discover what is being said. I have taken the liberty of sending him several suggestions for how to properly go about it, including some individuals that might provide him some useful information. I would have done this myself, but I feared being your father would limit the scope of things. I would not wish for you to be painted in a more favorable light than the reality."

No, of course not. Why would her father want to hear good things about her? She bit her tongue softly, pressing her teeth deep into the flesh to stop herself from snapping defensively at him.

"I have no reason to doubt that Ingram will be as thorough in this matter as he has been others," her father continued. "His care with restoring his family's estate alone proves he will leave no stone unturned on something he has set his mind to. We will get the truth with him; of that, I have no doubt."

Because the care of restoring a man's estate directly correlated to the care a man placed in unearthing gossip and finding faults. Everybody knew that.

Grace swallowed slowly, willing her willful thoughts to stop their frantic pounding. She pressed her teeth further into her tongue, a sharp sting of pain rising.

Her father's pacing suddenly stopped. "But what I want to know, Grace, is what we are missing."

She hadn't expected that. The room was silent, and slowly, the beating of her heart filled that silence in her ears as she looked up at her father in confusion.

"What we are missing, sir?"

The faint lines on his face seemed to stand out as his features hardened. "We are putting in all this effort for you, pulling a respectable man from his own interests in London to examine you, seeking out comments and gossip from Society, potentially exposing the entire family to ridicule, all in an attempt to root out your failings. To discover the areas in which you are lacking. Seeking out your deficiencies." He exhaled shortly through his nose and clasped his hands behind his back, his eyes narrowing on her. "A great deal of effort and risk, Grace, when it could very easily be settled by taking our questions directly to the source of the problem."

Her heart stopped it's not quite steady pounding as she stared up at him.

"You, Grace. You."

She felt her jaw drop, though she managed somehow, to keep it from being obvious. Her eyes burned, not with tears, but with the sudden widening that seemed to strain them beyond their abilities. "Me? Why me?"

That was not what her father wanted to hear, and he broke his cold, formal character to scoff loudly, his hands flying to his hips. "Can you really be so ignorant as to recognize that you are at the center of this problem, Grace? In case it has escaped your notice, you are the one who is unmarried, and you are the one who cannot provide a reasonable explanation as to why that is. Did you even read the missives I sent you before my coming? I don't remember receiving any sort of favorable reply. I did not think it possible that a daughter I had raised would think so little of the responsibilities and expectations that lay before a young woman of birth and situation. Is it really so very hard to get a husband, Grace?"

Her mouth worked, but she had absolutely no voice for it.

"Your sister managed it well enough," he said, flinging an arm out as though Anne were there in the room. "She had not your looks nor your good temper, but she managed to secure a husband. One of impeccable lineage, even if his title is less than one might hope. And she did so without ever reaching an age that would raise comment."

Had she not been torn between wounded and furious, Grace might have pointed out that Anne's husband was terrified of his wife and worshipped the ground she walked on in the most god-fearing manner. He was a good sort, and she was fond of him, but her sister was tyrannical, and there was no denying it.

But she didn't mention that. She couldn't. She stared at her father with all the wide-eyed vacancy of a mute.

Which he took to be attentiveness.

"Why do you think we invested so much into seeing you so well accomplished?" her father raged, his dark eyes widening now. "Your mother and I knew from very early on that you would far outstrip Anne in looks, and a handsome woman must have accomplishments that would be worthy of admiration and respect. We sought out the best tutors and instructors, spared no expense in shaping you into a woman that would be a diamond of the first water. We created the perfect young lady of Society. One without blemish and without excesses." He sniffed in disdain, shaking his head. "I thought I might need to curb your accomplishments so you would not be thought to outstrip anyone else, for one does not wish to appear so very mercenary. But how could I have known that instead I was creating a daughter who would be so very unremarkable, who would blend in so completely that she would be mistaken for the curtains?"

Grace saw her mother shift in her seat, but she said nothing. Her color was high, her eyes were lowered, and Grace had the impression that this discussion had been rehearsed before now. And without a

225

hope of preventing it.

"I am sorry to be a disappointment," Grace managed to reply, surprised at the emotional tremor she heard. She was not near to tears, and she felt no telltale choking sensation. Yet her words had no power, and her body had no strength.

"A disappointment?" Her father laughed without humor. "A disappointment would have been a daughter that is too thin or too plain to be considered handsome, but at least that sort of daughter would have been all the more appreciated for what she *did* possess! This is beyond a disappointment, Grace. I have been patient, and I have tried to be understanding."

He had? When exactly had that been?

He turned and pointed at her mother. "I have even taken counsel from your mother, who assured me that you were all I should be proud of. When I returned to London, I was convinced that she was right. Yet now, I am left to wonder if she was wrong."

A sudden weight descended upon Grace's shoulders, and she felt as though she were being pressed into the chair she sat upon, sinking with it into the floor beneath her. Her chest began to squeeze, the pressure slowly increasing by degrees the more she breathed.

"I am not ready to give up yet," her father insisted, seeming to regain some of his senses and returning to a more restrained tone. "As I have said, I trust Ingram to be able to discern the extent of damage here."

The word cut across her with a swift burn that singed a number of her ribs, and her eyes welled with newfound moisture. She looked down at her father's shoes, shining with all the perfection he expected from her.

Perfect. Without spot or smudge.

Not damaged.

"So, tell me, Grace, if you can: what am I missing?"

A thousand and twelve responses swirled in her mind, each of them falling pitifully by the wayside. Nothing was worthy of voicing, and none of them would be acceptable to the great Lord Trenwick.

So, she said the one thing that could honestly be believed.

"I don't know, sir."

The perfectly shined shoes moved towards her, stopping in

perfect alignment with each other.

She waited, head lowered, hands tight in her lap, shoulders quaking.

"Then I trust you will make that question a significant subject for your daily consideration," he told her in the same tone she had known as a child. "You must put in the same effort as the rest of us to solve this quandary."

Grace bobbed her chin obediently. "Yes, sir."

The shoes moved away, clipped in their step, cracking against the floor with authority. Then they stopped. "It is not pleasant for me to be harsh with you, my child. I only mean to stress upon you the severity of your situation."

Again, she bobbed her chin.

This apparently satisfied him, and his footsteps resumed, vanishing down the corridor.

The room was silent once more, and this time not even her heart could be heard.

"I am so sorry, my love," her mother whispered tearfully.

Grace could not respond, not without dissolving into tears, and she would not do so here, and not now. She only nodded, knowing her mother was as powerless as she, if not more so, and there would be nothing gained by raging at her.

After a moment, her mother left her with her solitude, closing the door behind her. Only then could Grace breathe freely, and she was surprised that her tears fell slowly, without any sort of energy or haste. There was no upset to her breathing, no powerful release of pent up emotion or distress.

The tears simply fell, and with them, a part of herself.

Damaged. Failing. Disappointment. Unremarkable.

How had she forgotten that this was at the heart of the matter? That she was the shame of her family and the despair of her father? That Aubrey was not meant to encourage, romance, or entertain her, but to evaluate her? He was to examine her. Assess her.

Fix her.

Aubrey had spoken with her father, had updated him on their progress. Had he been reporting regularly? Had he been telling her father more than he was telling her?

Could he be flirting with her to expose her? Could every one of his kisses be used against her in all of this?

Did her father know about that?

Everything she thought she knew and felt suddenly seemed fleeting and foreign, uncertainty shrouding anything familiar and warm. She was cold and abandoned, shivering in the darkness of her father's shadow. She knew no joy, only doubt.

Only fear.

She sat in the chair, staring at nothing, unable to move for the terrifying vulnerability she suddenly felt. Was the whole of the household aware of this maddening search for her deficiencies? What would the investigation of her reputation turn up? Did all of London see her with the same degree of blemish as her father?

What did they say and think?

What would Aubrey hear?

Would he tell her?

Or would her father be the one to reveal the whole miserable report to her in one crushing dialogue of defamation?

"Lord Ingram, Miss Morledge."

Grace blinked faintly, another fall of tears setting free on their wandering course.

Wandering. Like she was. Like she'd thought they were. Like she longed to do at Withrow. To just wander and stray wherever one fancied without any concern for destination or distance, just wandering for the sheer pleasure of existing.

"I've had a letter from Sterling, which means it's from Georgie, and apparently someone has been reporting... Egads, are you ill?"

Grace blinked again, and this time, her eyes moved to look at him, noting his wide-eyed concern mingled with a hint of terror.

"No," she said simply, her tone firm, if soft.

His brow furrowed, and his fingers rubbed against each other absently. "You sure? You're pale as death, and it's quite scared me out of my wits."

Her throat worked twice on a swallow. "Good."

"Good?" he repeated, his brow clearing. "Grace, what's wrong?"

"Have you been investigating my reputation for my father?" she inquired in the calmest tone she had ever heard from her own mouth.

Aubrey's eyes widened further still. "He told you that?"

She felt the first crack in her composure, even as another tear trickled from her eye. "So you are."

He took two steps towards her. "He told me I had to, but it's not as though I'm dredging up gossip from the gorgons. And I don't know what he's said, but I'm not telling him anything. Whatever he's told you…"

"What are they saying?" Grace asked, choosing, for the moment, not to pursue the possibility of his betrayal. "Tell me."

"You know what they say," he responded at once, his fingers shifting again. "You've heard it all before."

"I haven't. All I've heard is that I am perfect, which we both know isn't true. You've been looking into it. What have you heard?"

Aubrey folded his arms, his expression disbelieving and irritable. "What is this? Why do I feel as though I am on trial for something of which I am ignorant?"

Something inside her snapped and she shot to her feet, tears starting to flow with the fury she'd forgotten all about. "Tell me what they say, dammit!" she screamed, her voice cracking. "I am entitled to know what my own reputation is, and if I am to be found wanting by the world, surely I have the right to bloody know why!"

He fell back a step, irritation gone, and stared at her for the space of several heartbeats. Then he straightened and cleared his throat. "You're right. I won't pretend that I haven't begun to make discreet inquiries, but I also will not pretend that I have done so extensively. I like this no more than you, and I told your father I refused to violate your privacy by revealing what our sessions here entail. I told him I respected you too much to do so, and that you deserve the dignity of such. Kindly stop considering me as though I am in league with your father in my intentions."

Suitably chastened without any vehemence, Grace felt tension begin to ebb from her shoulders, though her spine had lost none of its stiffness. "Very well. Tell me, then. Please."

Aubrey nodded, seemingly content with that. "I will not insult you by sharing what you already know about what people say, which truly is most of what I have heard from people I have spoken with, and you know how I feel about people as a general rule."

A fleeting impulse to smile lit her lips, but then it was gone.

"Thus far," Aubrey went on, giving her an earnest look, "the only thing less than exemplary I have heard from anyone is that one or two gentlemen have refrained from any sort of pursuit of courtship of your person on account of your father. They have found, or have heard, that he is a man of some intimidation, and they did not feel it would be worth the risk." He shook his head in disgust. "I could have said so many things to such a statement of idiocy, but I refrained for your sake."

Grace stared for a long moment as the words sunk in. "So, I am to be neglected and ignored as a prospect for matrimony because my father is intimidating? How is that my fault?"

"It isn't," Aubrey insisted, taking another step towards her. "Such cowardly reasoning isn't indicative of you in any way. That only reflects poorly on them. And it is but one, possibly two, Grace."

She tried for a weak smile even as her eyes welled further. "But it adds another layer to the matter of my lacking whatever is required to make a woman appealing, don't you see?" She hiccupped softly and sank back down into her chair. "I have been picked apart and trod upon, interrogated and accused, observed and dismissed, and I have no answers for it. I had no answers today. Nothing to say for myself, nothing to answer him with."

"Him?" Aubrey said sharply, moving to stand before her. "Your father?"

She nodded, a weak sob escaping. "I've been getting missives from my father for months and months, each one chipping away at my self-respect and my contentment, and now I have my father here in my home as a constant reminder."

"Of what?"

"How I have disappointed him," she whispered, closing her eyes on fresh tears. "How I fail him. Shame him. Every time he looks at me, I wonder what he sees or does not see. I cannot please him, no matter what I do or how I try."

Her hand was suddenly seized and gripped tightly, and she felt Aubrey suddenly before her. A hand brushed at her tears. "You cannot live your life to please him, Grace."

She sniffed and nodded. "I know. Because even living my life doesn't seem to please him."

Again, Aubrey wiped at her tears, and with a faint stroke of his thumb, her eyes fluttered open. His eyes sought hers with a raw pain that echoed the keening sounds of her heart. "Grace…"

"I have lived the last several months of my life in two extremes," she murmured, turning her hands to clutch at his. "Perfect in the eyes of the world, and a failure in the eyes of my father. Which of the two extremes do you think I am more prone to believe?"

"You are not a failure," Aubrey told her firmly, his hand cupping her cheek.

She nodded against the pressure of his palm. "I know. But I'm not perfect, either. So, what am I, Aubrey? What am I?"

His thumb stoked absently against her cheek again, and his throat worked, but he said nothing. How could he? What could he say? Even Grace had no answers here, and the question hung between them without answer.

She didn't want an answer.

Not yet.

"I cannot endure fault-finding today," she whispered apologetically. "I've been scrubbed raw, and I cannot bear being more exposed, not even to you."

Aubrey blinked and his lips curved in a tender smile. "All right. No session today. If you like, I'll leave the room and come back in just as myself, as your friend, and start this whole thing over."

Grace smiled back, feeling a surge of affection towards this sweet man before her. "I don't want you to go, but what will we do instead?"

He dropped his hand from her face and returned it to the other in her lap. "Whatever you like. I am completely at your disposal."

"Would you teach me to fence?" she asked, tilting her head with the question. "I feel like stabbing something."

He laughed warmly and gripped her hands. "Not a chance in hell, goddess. Next option."

Grace grinned and let her fingers brush against his in his hold. "Chess. I know very little, and I want you to teach me."

Within minutes, a chess board was brought in, the rules explained, and a game begun. Aubrey advised her every move, matching hers with too-kind moves of his own, clearly taking pity on her inexperience. He chatted aimlessly, never venturing back onto the topic of her outburst or even that of finding fault. He never even referred back to his announcement about a letter from Tony and Georgie, nor anything that might remind her of any faults or the finding of them.

She nearly cried again as she considered him across the board from her, eying his own chess pieces with some intensity. "Thank you, Aubrey."

He grunted. "For swiping your pawn? My pleasure, I'm about to do it again."

"Aubrey," she said again, letting the tenderness she felt for him seep into her tone.

His eyes were on hers at once.

She smiled with real emotion. "I mean it. Thank you."

Aubrey stared, as Aubrey usually did, and just when she thought he might say nothing, he reached out and took her hand, drawing it to his lips softly, tenderly caressing the skin of her fingers.

"I am at your service, Grace," he murmured, kissing her hand once more. "Whatever it is. I hope you know that, if nothing else."

Her heart soared, and at that moment, she loved him. Then and there, she gave her heart over to him and to none other. Come what may of this whole dismal affair, she loved Aubrey, and nothing had ever felt more perfect.

"I know," she whispered happily, extending a finger to brush against his chin. "And I don't deserve you."

Aubrey smiled at her, kissing the tip of her finger, then resting her hand back on the table, though he held it still. "Actually, I think the sentiment is reversed. Goddesses being what they are, mere mortals really haven't any hope…"

Chapter Nineteen

The wise individual finds allies wherever she can, and the wiser individual takes every advantage such allies will allow.

-The Spinster Chronicles, 7 May 1819

Your presence is requested at an evening soirée at the home of Mr. and Mrs. Robert Johnston, at the behest of Mrs. Miranda Sterling, to begin at seven in the evening on the 23rd day of this month.

If you could arrive at two in the afternoon, it would very much be appreciated.

Grace stared at the scribbled addition to the formal invitation as the carriage rolled along the London streets, smiling to herself. Her parents had not received any sort of additional invitation for an afternoon with Miranda, although they had been invited to the soirée. Her father had been surprisingly vague about his attendance, which made Grace wonder what it was Miranda knew about him.

But it seemed that Miranda Sterling was a woman worthy of her father's approval, for he had very nearly ushered Grace out of the door himself. Whatever it was Miranda wanted Grace there for hours before other guests, he was determined she would be present.

It was the first kind thing he had done for her in weeks.

She shook her head to herself as she neared the Johnstons' address. She refused to spend any more time thinking about her father or worrying about his opinions when she had an afternoon and evening of enjoyment ahead of her. Miranda was one of the most refreshing individuals she had ever met, and she would savor every moment in her company today.

Grace was shown into the house without much ceremony, and then brought into a comfortable parlor, smiling as she entered.

"I am so sorry to be late," she apologized as Miranda came towards her, hands outstretched. "James had taken the carriage, and he was delayed in returning…" She shrugged as she trailed off.

"No matter," Miranda gushed, kissing her cheeks fondly. "We did not mind in the slightest, did we?"

"Not at all," came the warm tones of Francis, Lord Sterling, standing behind a settee where his wife sat.

Grace curtseyed to them both, grinning. "That, my lord, is because the pair of you are remarkably good-hearted and patient. How else could one be related to Tony and still enjoy his company?"

Francis laughed and bowed in acknowledgement. "Well, someone had to save the family name, Miss Morledge. It was down to Alice or me, and time will tell which of us is victor."

"How is Alice?" Grace asked at once, moving to the pair of them. "She looked so well the other evening, but I had no chance to speak with her."

"Fully recovered," Janet assured her as she took her hand. "Anxious to make up for lost time."

Grace laughed once, smiling at the energy of such a young woman. Then she sobered. "And Hugh?"

Francis shook his head. "Somewhere in the north, we've not heard from him in some time. One can only hope he is well."

"Enough talk of sad things," Miranda scolded with a clap of her hands. "Everyone can agree that Francis and Janet possess excellent characters, though I am far more partial to she than to he."

"Excuse me?" Francis protested hotly.

Miranda ignored him. "I'm curious how Lord Ingram feels about waiting for Miss Morledge to arrive."

Grace stilled as Miranda turned to indicate the other person in the room, whose presence Grace had entirely missed. Aubrey stood near a tall window, the afternoon light shining through on him as though from heaven itself, and his smile bore all the benevolence of an angel from such realms.

"Well, Aubrey?" Miranda demanded, a knowing sparkle in her eyes.

Aubrey shrugged his shoulders, his eyes trained on Grace. "One would never complain about being kept waiting by a goddess. I am quite sure there are several myths involving such."

On cue, Grace's cheeks flamed, and she shook her head at him. "For shame, Lord Ingram. Do you suggest that all myths are truths we must abide by?"

"Not all," he replied, sliding his hands into the pockets of his dark trousers. "One should never intentionally venture into the underworld, and I would advise against spending a great length of time staring at one's reflection." His smiled deepened just enough to make her toes curl. "Though some of us would have a great deal more to admire there than others."

Francis made a loud sound of dismay and waved Aubrey away. "Such hot air will surely poison the rest of us! Down, Ingram, down."

Aubrey looked at Francis in mild amusement. "It's only hot air if untrue." He returned his gaze to Grace. "And this is not."

Grace would have sighed had she not been in the company of others, but she bit her lip all the same. This was a bold change in him, to be so blatantly flirtatious before others, and she found the experience an exhilarating one. There was great fun in being secretive, but this?

This was delightful.

Still, there was decorum to maintain. Grace turned to Miranda with an embarrassed smile. "May I ask why you invited us so early, Miranda? I don't object in the slightest, only perishing with curiosity."

Miranda linked her arm through Grace's and walked with her a bit. "No particular reason, I only like the company. Mr. Johnston is providing a fine supper for us, and I thought it would be a shame to have such a grand meal wasted on only the three of us. And with Georgie and Tony away for her confinement, I may invite whomever I please without bowing to family niceties. You did bring a change of clothes, did you not?"

At Grace's nod, she clapped almost merrily. "Wonderful. I have a maid who is dying to get her hands on your hair, and I have promised the task to her. She is a marvel, I tell you, and you shall indeed be the goddess Aubrey proclaimed you to be." Miranda stopped then and gave Grace an assessing look. "Which reminds me. Dear Rufus needs a bit of exercise before the excitement of the evening, and I really haven't the desire to wander about in the gardens. Aubrey, would you be a dear and take him out there for me? A bit of running about might do you both some good. And Miss Morledge, perhaps you could keep him from misbehaving?"

Grace's cheeks heated, but she raised a brow in Aubrey's direction. "Aubrey or Rufus?"

Francis applauded her reply while Aubrey only grinned in response. "Likely both, Miss Morledge. If you have the stamina."

She lowered her chin a touch to meet his gaze squarely. "I have. Shall we?"

"Are we to be without adult supervision?" Aubrey asked drily as he moved towards the door, arm extended towards Grace.

Miranda waved a dismissive hand. "Foolish boy, we can see the garden from the windows! How much trouble could you get into there?"

"That would all depend on whether anyone is looking," he replied with a respectful nod, winking at Grace, who immediately thwacked him on the arm.

He hurried them away before Miranda could call her response after them.

Grace felt her chest fill to the brim with giggles and clapped a hand over her mouth to restrain them. Aubrey collected Rufus from a waiting footman, who did not look at either of them as they took the lead and headed for the garden.

"Oh," Grace exhaled, laughing now out in the afternoon air, "is *everyone* trying to throw us together?"

Aubrey nudged her side with his arm. "Consider me thrown."

She looked up at him, beaming without shame and rubbing his arm. "Me, too."

He glanced up at the window briefly, then leaned down to give her a quick kiss, which only made her smile more.

"How long do you think Miranda has known?" Grace murmured with a tilt of her head towards the window.

Aubrey pursed his lips in thought. "Likely since the day she wrote to your father. Don't you remember what she said when we approached her at the ball?"

Grace did remember, and she looked away, focusing her gaze on the flowers of the garden. "Should it have been so obvious?"

"I don't know. I didn't think so then, but now..." Aubrey trailed off, and Grace held her breath, willing him to finish the thought.

"Now?" she prodded, reaching out to touch the flowers of a nearby bush, though hardly paying attention to it.

He stopped, and so did she, keeping her attention on the white petals of the flower. Then Aubrey's hand was at her chin, turning her face towards him with all the gentleness she had used for the petals.

One finger stroked the underside of her chin, and she shivered. "Now," he murmured, his eyes dark, "I'm beginning to wonder what took me so long."

Grace exhaled in a faint pant, her lips parting as though he had drawn them apart. Her legs shook with the desire to arch up and kiss him, to pour out her love and her passion, her need and her hunger, but she stiffened them, willing the impulse to pass. The windows were tall and wide, and there was no telling how closely anyone was looking.

"We should let Rufus off the lead," she whispered weakly, a stroke of his finger raising bumps on her skin. "Perhaps... let him run?"

Aubrey chuckled at the feeble attempt at a distraction, but he dropped his hand from her chin anyway.

"I suppose you're right." He crouched before Rufus and took his face in his hands, turning his voice into a sad sort of cooing. "The poor man has been inside that stuffy house all day with nothing to do and no one to amuse him."

Grace snorted a laugh. "It's not stuffy!"

Aubrey turned his and Rufus's face towards her with matching dour looks. "You have no idea what feels stuffy to a canine, madam. It is practically suffocating." He made Rufus look at him again, pouting. "You want to run free and wild, don't you, boy?"

Rufus licked his jowls with a groan.

"Indeed." Aubrey unhooked the lead, then grinned at the dog. "Hah!" he shouted suddenly, startling Grace as he bolted, Rufus charging after him in a sudden burst of speed.

She watched as Aubrey ran, Rufus galloping after him, cutting and turning as the small garden required. Aubrey dodged the dog here and there, practically dancing out of his reach, spinning and darting off in the opposite direction. Rufus came alive, barking and howling, his great tongue dangling out of his mouth in the imitation of a grin of delight.

Aubrey was taunting the dog now, his words lost on Grace, but he pretended to start running once, twice, three times, then took off again, Rufus racing alongside him. Grace laughed as they headed in her direction, and, not to be outdone, she turned and began to run with them. Rufus looked up at her as he reached her, and she laughed louder, increasing her speed.

He barked and chased after her as she rounded a bush, pausing only when Grace picked up a large stick from the ground, holding it out with one hand, inviting him to take it. "Come on," she panted, still laughing. "Come on, boy. You want it? Do you want the stick?"

Rufus hesitated, started towards it a few times, testing her.

Grace tossed her head back and held it out one more time. "Come on, boy. Come on."

This time Rufus listened, biting the stick and tugging it, but Grace held firm, both hands gripping it. "Ah ha!" she crowed, pulling against him. "Come on. Come on. Oh, you're a strong one, eh?"

Rufus growled against the stick, tugging harder.

"Careful," Aubrey warned as he watched, leaning against a nearby tree, still breathing heavily from his run.

Grace threw him a disbelieving look. "Seriously?" She looked down at Rufus with wide eyes. "He thinks I'm a dainty flower you might crush, Rufus. How insulting is that?"

Rufus dropped the stick and barked three times.

Grace held the stick before her like a baton. "Shall we show the idiot how fragile we are? I think we shall!" She threw the stick across the garden, and Rufus darted after it, Grace chasing right behind him, egging him on.

Then Aubrey was running beside her, following the same path around the bushes and flowers, laughing as much as she was, shifting suddenly as Rufus turned back towards them. He grabbed Grace's arm with a sudden bark of laughter, and they stumbled as Rufus turned back to find his stick, Grace's slippers unable to find a grip on the soft grass.

Down they went in a tumble, and Grace landed on her side with a grunt of surprise, echoed by Aubrey as he fell beside her. She rolled to her back and laughed again, hilarity rising within her at the antics she'd engaged in, something she hadn't done since she was a child. Her sides ached with the laughter, and she grabbed at them, her arms crossing over her midsection.

Aubrey raised up on his elbow beside her, grinning wildly, his hair in disarray. "I take it from your current state of delirium that you are unhurt from your fall?"

Grace nodded, still giggling breathlessly. "It was your fault!" she insisted through tears of mirth. "You grabbed me, and I lost my footing!"

"I was saving you," he corrected magnanimously. "Clearly you would have fallen harder without me."

She shook her head, panting laugh after laugh, unable to stop. "You are such an idiot."

He reached out and brushed her hair back from her face, his fingers tracing against her brow as he moved various strands of her no doubt mangled hair. "I believe we've established that once or twice before."

Her laughter began to evaporate under his touch, her skin tingling where he touched it. She watched him as the lingering traces of laughter still tickled her breath, wondering what his eyes saw as they followed his fingers, now combing through the tendrils she had shaken loose with her exertion.

"It bears repeating," she murmured as one of her hands slid over to begin fiddling with the buttons of his coat. "You are constantly needing reminders."

Aubrey smiled as he looked down at her, his fingers moving down to brush against her cheek. "I am, aren't I? Damned fortunate thing, reminders. I love reminders. I love…"

Grace felt her heart skip as his thumb brushed her bottom lip, and suddenly she couldn't breathe.

Slowly, almost hesitantly, Aubrey leaned down and brushed his lips across hers, tentative as though it was for the first time. They passed over again, and she lifted her chin to bring her lips closer to his, catching them before the contact ended. There was a moment of stillness, lips touching, waiting.

Then he leaned down further and sealed his mouth over hers, and she sighed as her lips parted beneath his, softening under the swirling onslaught. Her hand slid up his chest, fastening itself behind his neck, keeping him close to her. He tilted his head, changing his angle for a kiss that seemed to reach for her very soul, and she gave it, willingly and with enthusiasm, arching up for more of the same. More of this feeling. More of this bliss.

More of him.

More.

Her fingers shifted on his neck, reaching for his hair and digging in against his scalp. Aubrey growled his response against her lips, and she curled closer to him, her free hand fisting in the material of his shirt and waistcoat. His arm slid beneath her, pulling her up against him as the kiss intensified, drawing her closer still, closer than she thought possible, closer…

A very different sort of growl followed by a snuffle of sorts came from beside them, and a cold, wet, insistent nose nuzzled at Grace's arm. Then a snout and head worked its way under that arm, and a lolling tongue swept up the side of Aubrey's face.

Grace shook with laughter even as the rest of her body shook with something else entirely. Aubrey dropped his head, muttered something that sounded like a series of very dark curses, then looked at Grace with a rueful grin.

She shrugged where she lay on the ground and sighed heavily.

Aubrey looked at Rufus, still tucked under Grace's arm, his tail wagging eagerly. "You really are Miranda's dog, aren't you?"

Rufus swallowed, then opened his mouth, tongue lolling once more.

Aubrey exhaled, returned his attention to Grace, then kissed her very briefly. "Come along, goddess. We have a desperate need for adult supervision, you and I."

He pushed off of the ground, then pulled Grace to her feet. She brushed at her skirts and peered up at him. "Would that be considered a flaw, my lord?"

He paused, giving her a singularly heated look. "No. No, it would not."

Grace grinned outright. "But quite inconvenient, I'd expect."

"Now that I can concede."

The fire that Grace had stoked within him that afternoon in the grass did not diminish in the slightest when they returned to the house, when Grace had changed for dinner and come down looking like a masterpiece painted by the hand of God himself, when the other guests had come for the official events of the evening, or when he had been surrounded by several people who knew Grace very well, and had come to know him, as well.

He burned with the very flames of hellfire, yet he stood at the gate of heaven itself.

Well, across the room from heaven, at any rate.

What was this madness, anyway?

To see her and not be permitted to touch her, to exist in her sphere and be forced to remain aloof by someone else's edicts of proposed politeness, to have tasted the sweetness of her lips and act for all the world as though he had not known nectar…

By Jove, he was turning into a raving poet lost in the throes of his own muse.

He downed whatever it was he was drinking and hissed, not at the burn, for there was no burn. Therein lay his disappointment. He needed that burn and craved the oblivion it promised.

"I thought we'd already done this bit," muttered a low voice near him.

Aubrey glowered at the looming form of Camden Vale, his lip curling in a sneer. "Shove off."

Cam chuckled and leaned against the wall next to him. "I'd offer to take you to my club, but I doubt I could pry you from your spot without the inducement of a certain someone to convince you."

"Go to hell."

"Been there. Not impressed."

"Why does he look so murderous?"

Aubrey groaned as Henshaw's voice broke through and shook his head. "Now I know I'm in hell."

"Really?" Henshaw looked about the room in assessment. "I'd expected more brimstone, but there's no accounting for taste."

"If this is hell, who, precisely, is the devil?" Sebastian Morton wondered as he reached them, following Henshaw.

Aubrey glared at Morton darkly. "You, sir, are reputed to be a man of sense and reserve."

Morton smiled with ease. "So I am, by comparison. You may blame or thank my wife for the improvement, if you are so inclined."

"Oh, we do, Morton. We very much do," drawled yet another voice.

Aubrey thumped his head against the wall behind him twice. "Oh, good. Everyone is here with the arrival of Lord Sterling. And I was so concerned I would be left out." He looked at Francis sharply. "So help me, if you produce Tony out of thin air…"

Francis chuckled and sipped his drink. "At ease, the man is ensconced in the country, though he did ask after you in his last letter."

"And you came over here to check on me?"

Francis shrugged. "I just happened to see a crowd. What's the fuss?"

Cam nudged his head towards Aubrey. "Ingram's upset."

"Shut up, Vale," Aubrey warned. He liked each of these men individually, but if anyone decided to reveal certain suspicions, which had *not* been confirmed to any of them, he would tear each of them apart. He started rehearsing an apology to Miranda in his mind, just in case.

"Perhaps he's trying to find fault in Miss Morledge again," Morton suggested as though it were a brilliant notion. "That would make anyone sour."

Henshaw nodded in thought, his brow furrowed slightly. "True, but how could anyone find fault from this distance? In the evening light, and given the relaxed environment, what fault is there in anyone?" He gestured to the room, and each pair of eyes followed.

The Johnston's had arranged several tables in the spacious drawing rooms and various card games were being played, the hum of participant voices a constant amid the various locations. A pianoforte in the corner was being played by Edith, seemingly content to avoid conversation, and Kitty Morton sat beside her to assist with pages. There was space enough that dancing could commence if any were so inclined, though none had ventured yet. Other guests milled about, chatting with each other or examining the card games.

Aubrey noted Mr. Andrews speaking with Lord Trenwick, and wished, most fervently, that Andrews would punch the man across the face. Not that Andrews would have cause, and not that fisticuffs in the Johnstons' home would be a very great thing, but Andrews seemed an athletic enough man to do the job properly. And his reputation was sound enough that most would think he had his reasons and forget the whole matter.

No one would suspect Andrews of carrying secret affection for Grace or speculate as to his intentions. No one would stir gossip regarding him, or Grace, and no one would see his reputation tarnished for doing anything so rash.

Perhaps if he sent a note to Andrews just now…

Grace laughed then, and he somehow caught the sound over the other conversations, music, and aimless tittle-tattle of the men around him. He glanced over at her, his chest seizing as her eyes crinkled adorably with her still-laughing lips curved perfectly. Her skin glowed with a healthy flush of color that bore witness to her enjoyment and pleasure, and her golden hair danced in the candlelight with every motion, the jewels within the tresses winking here and there as the light caught them.

Blast, it was hard to breathe when she looked like this. Or when he felt like this, which was seeming to become his constant of late. Even thinking of her could render him markedly breathless, and his lungs had not learned how to cope as yet.

A new glass was thrust into his hand, and he drank it without thinking. Still no burn, but his throat no longer scratched with the attempt to breathe.

"No flaws, no faults," Henshaw murmured. "How does a man survive that?"

The whimsical note in Henshaw's tone sent Aubrey's ire through the roof, and he half turned to skewer the man with a combination of vitriolic words and venomous gaze, only to find that the man was not looking at Grace at all.

Curious...

"Well, we should ask," Cam suggested, clearly missing Henshaw's meaning. "Ingram?"

Aubrey jerked to look at him. "What?"

Cam raised a dark brow, his smile smug. "What are you going to do?"

The rest all looked at Aubrey expectantly.

What was he going to do?

He turned back to survey Grace for a moment, smirking to himself when she laid down a winning hand for herself and her partner. Had she cheated then, as well, or did she play honestly with her friends?

He wasn't particularly inclined to give her more opportunities either way. It was his turn to monopolize her for a while, and he intended to.

"I think, gentlemen, that I am going to play chess," he announced, handing his glass to one of them as he strode forward.

"Is that a metaphor?" he heard Francis ask, and the question made him smile.

Yes, he supposed it was, though it was also particularly true.

He approached the table before another round of cards could begin. "I wonder, Miss Morledge," he said to the group, "if I might trouble you to indulge me in a game of chess? I have recently learned that you play the game, and I would dearly love to have a worthy opponent."

Grace lowered her chin in a show of modesty, but he caught the flash of mischief in her eyes. "I would be happy to play the game, my lord, but I cannot say how worthy an opponent I would be."

"I'm sure you are too modest," he insisted, offering a hand.

She placed her hand in his, nodding to the others, and let him lead her to a free table where the game was being set.

Clearly, someone had either listened to him or anticipated the need.

Ah, the blessings of allies in the world.

"What are you doing?" Grace whispered with a smile as he helped her to her seat.

"Playing chess," he whispered back, his mouth near her ear in a show of adjusting her chair.

She shivered, and he bit back a grin at the sight, moving to his own seat.

"I did not know you played chess, Grace," her father said, suddenly appearing beside them.

Grace stiffened at the formal tone, and Aubrey pressed his ankle against hers beneath the table to steady her. She immediately returned the pressure. "I've only recently learned, Father."

"What a fine accomplishment!" Miranda crowed at once, flanking Lord Trenwick. "Would that all young ladies in Society engage in such a strategic, intelligent game so well thought of in high circles."

"I'd thought only bluestockings played such," Trenwick muttered with a sidelong look at Miranda. "Not fashionable ladies."

Miranda scoffed loudly. "Not so! Why, I've had it from no less than three sources that the wife of the ambassador from Italy plays brilliantly, and I don't believe anyone would accuse *her* of being anything less than fashionable. Mr. Andrews, were you not recently in Prague? I am sure the ladies there play."

Andrews was a genius and agreed wholeheartedly, citing several examples of the game being played by fine women in various settings.

Seeing he was clearly mistaken, Trenwick voiced no further comment, and watched the game in silence, venturing away when there was nothing of real interest to see or critique. Miranda winked at Aubrey when Trenwick disappeared, and Aubrey did not bother hiding his gratitude before returning his whole attention to the game.

Or, more truthfully, to the pressure of a certain ankle against his.

Which moved slightly, tilting away and sliding up. The arch of a slippered foot now pressed just at his ankle, the toes moving gently against the back of his foot.

His throat dried at once, parched in an instant. He glanced up to find Grace perusing the board before her, one hand at her jaw, impervious to all else in the room.

The little minx...

Aubrey adjusted his position in his seat, dislodging her foot from his, and slid his foot forward against the floor until it came beneath her skirts to touch hers. Frowning over his next move, he dipped his foot beneath hers and arched his toes up until they dug into the sole of her foot, biting the inside of his lip when her foot tensed at it.

He took a kingside pawn of hers. She pressed her foot down hard against his.

She captured his queenside castle. He ran the tip of his toe along the inside of her foot.

He checked her king. She rubbed her toes beneath the bone of his ankle.

She took his aggressing pawn. He turned his foot to press against the full length of hers.

He moved to take her queenside knight when she slid her foot back just far enough for her toes to dip against his, and his hand faltered in his motion.

"Who's winning?" Francis asked, suddenly appearing beside their game.

Aubrey cleared his throat, blinking his hazy vision. "It's difficult to say," he managed, his voice tight.

Grace smirked up at Francis proudly. "He's not having his own way, unfortunately."

Aubrey swallowed, fighting a smile as he pointedly ran the tip of his foot along the entire length of the sole of her foot. "No, sadly, I am not."

Grace's left hand splayed spasmodically on the table, her attention returning to the game, eyes wide. He caught one faint, rough pant, and dragged his foot gently across hers again.

"I see you truly have found a worthy opponent, Ingram," Francis praised as he eyed the board, nodding as though impressed.

Aubrey stared at Grace, stroking her foot over and over until she met his eyes, cheeks flushed, eyes dark. "Oh, yes," Aubrey murmured, his lips curving. "It seems that I have."

Chapter Twenty

———— ⌘ ————

One should always take great care when choosing a partner for the waltz. A dance of such intimacy, once regarded as wholly scandalous, should only be engaged in with a partner with whom one can truly dance. To say nothing of those who can turn the waltz into something intimate while not offending those still clinging to the opinions of the past. A true waltz, dear friends, may be something of a confession.

-The Spinster Chronicles, 3 September 1818

The night was already magical, and she hadn't danced a single step yet.

She couldn't have said why; it was not as though there was anything particularly special about the evening. The ballroom of Sterling House had been elegantly lit and filled with tasteful decor that enhanced its beauty, but it could have been any other lovely ballroom in London. Her gown was the pale pink one Aubrey had kissed her in, which made her blush when she put it on, but it was not her most flattering gown, nor her finest. Her father hadn't been any more approving or warmer than he had at any other time in her life and had actually decided on accepting the invitation this evening.

That had not pleased her, but her mother had vowed to do her best to keep him occupied. Charlotte had instructed her father to accommodate him in all social matters as well, so his interference in her evening should have been kept to a minimum, which was all she could have hoped for.

Her hair had been perfectly plaited and curled, pale pink ribbon and small, white flowers interwoven in the locks, and her mother had loaned her a string of pearls and matching earbobs. Her gloves were pristine, her complexion fresh, and her smile fixed.

All was as it should have been, and as it always was for any ball she had ever attended.

But tonight, she could not breathe. Her heart raced in her chest, and her palms felt clammy against the fabric of her gloves. Her knees shook and her feet felt markedly unsteady, and all she had done so far was to greet the host and hostess, accept their charming compliments, and proceed towards her friends while her mother and father made the rounds of the room to let her father feel himself mingling with advantageous connections.

She was utterly terrified, and every swallow burned in her throat.

"Grace, you are shaking like a leaf, whatever is the matter?"

Grace looked over at Lady Hetty, sitting in her usual chair, giving her a more sympathetic look than Grace could ever remember seeing. She tried for a smile. "I'm only excitable, my lady."

"At your age?" Lady Hetty gave her a doubting look. "Not likely."

"Lady Hetty," Izzy protested kindly, looking between the older woman and Grace hesitantly.

"I mean no offense to the girl," Lady Hetty insisted with a wave of her hand. "She is as petrified as Miss Morton was at her first ball, if not dear Prudence, yet she has been to many a soirée with nary a tremor."

"This is true," Elinor mused as she eyed Grace almost critically. "What's there to fear? Is it your father?"

"Don't talk about that man," Charlotte spat as she drew close, shaking her head firmly. "I refuse to spend my evening worrying about Grace worrying about him. He will be sufficiently distracted, and all will be well." Charlotte gave Grace a scolding look. "You aren't thinking about him, are you?"

Grace shook her head at once, because she truly was not thinking of him.

She was thinking of someone else entirely.

"I'm fine," she assured her friends. "I mean, I am of course concerned that my father should hear about the Chronicles, but I trust Mama and Mr. Wright to keep him sufficiently occupied." She sighed and looked around the ballroom, fidgeting with her gloves. "I cannot deny that having him here makes me self-conscious, as though I must be on my very best behavior."

"When are you not?" Prue asked as she approached on Cam's arm. "I've never seen you make a false step."

Grace smiled weakly at her shy friend. "Would you have told me if I had?"

"I would have," Charlotte pointed out. "And so would Elinor."

Elinor nodded fervently, eyes wide. "I would. I never fail to point out missteps."

"You do seem to have your favorite subjects for such things," Izzy pointed out with a laugh.

"Can I help it if Hugh Sterling and the like do nothing but take missteps?" Elinor asked. "Someone has to notice these things."

"Just as someone must notice the good," Cam reminded her. "One should not be so distracted by faults that they are blinded to all else."

"Hear, hear," Lady Hetty said with an approving thump of her walking stick against the floor.

Charlotte looked at Cam in speculation. "That was a rather sweet sentiment from a man like you. Clearly, your wife is a reforming influence."

Cam looked down at Prue in such adoration that Grace felt her own cheeks heat. "Well, that's no surprise, is it?"

Prue returned his look with one of her own, and this time Grace had to look away. She had seen so much change in both Cam and Prue since their marriage, and even the more recent marriage of Izzy and Sebastian had provided change to their natures. Not in extremes, but there was such happiness to be found in each couple. Georgie and Tony were practically blissful, and their impending parenthood was only further proof of that.

She was not naïve enough to think that marriage had done that for them, for she had seen far too many marriages that had not improved either party. But she also knew enough to know that the love of another person, deep, abiding, true love, could move one's soul, could transform a heart, could draw two separate individuals together until they became one.

How did anyone seeing such a glorious thing, such a wondrous transformation, find contentment in a life without it?

Grace Morledge had not given much thought to things of an especially romantic nature since childhood, but ever since Aubrey had reappeared in her life and flipped it on its end, she found she could think of very little else.

And at this moment, she only wanted to be with him, whether in this very ballroom or somewhere in the countryside wandering aimlessly. Or sitting in a quiet room playing chess.

A slow burn of heat began at the back of her neck and began to work its way up into her hair, behind her ears, across her shoulders, and cascading down her front until it disappeared into the neckline of her gown. Her skin tingled with it, and a slow, warm shiver coursed across her frame.

Lord, but she wanted to have this with Aubrey. Moments and heartbeats and endless days of laughing until she cried. Kisses to weaken knees and arms to hold her close. Games to play and looks to give, banter to toss out and teasing to receive, anything and everything, more of the same and the discovery of new...

He was the one she would always yearn for, the man whose heart she would crave, and she could fairly burst with so much emotion if given but half a chance.

"Now that was a beautiful sight," a low voice murmured behind her. "Like the glory of sunrise without a single cloud to diminish such beauty."

An almost guttural sound started in her throat, but she swallowed it back as she turned to face Aubrey, eyes burning with the promise of tears, her lips wavering as she smiled with too much emotion. "Aubrey..."

His eyes were dark and full of appreciation, and she had the sense that he saw everything she felt, everything she couldn't say, and every ounce of love her heart beat with. Those eyes raked over her quickly, and she bit back a gasp as though they touched each part they saw. He smiled more deeply when he met her gaze once more.

"Such a lovely gown," he praised, his tone saying so much more.

"It suits you well."

"Doesn't it, though?" Elinor agreed, completely missing the private conversation occurring. "I was only saying to Mama when we arrived that no one else could have made it look so exquisite."

Aubrey shook his head, somehow listening even though his eyes never left Grace's. "No, indeed. I quite agree."

Grace widened her eyes at him, mouthed the word 'stop', but Aubrey only grinned further still.

She would burst into flames where she stood if he did not look somewhere else soon.

Mercifully, he seemed to know that, and turned to very warmly greet the rest gathered about them, leaving Grace to discreetly gulp in as much air as she could while appearing composed.

One did not pant in ballrooms.

She wasn't sure who created that rule, but she was quite sure it was listed somewhere.

"Has anyone heard from Tony or Georgie of late?" he asked the group without any hint of distress himself. "I wonder how the rustication in preparation for the next Sterling offspring commences."

There was a round of general good-natured chuckling and Izzy grinned. "Georgie sends her love to us all, reminded me to be sure Edith gets out, insists that Elinor send her the latest gossip, and advised that you, sir, remember to whom you owe your current situation."

Aubrey scowled, though Grace could see the faintest hint of color appear in his own face. "I'm not likely to forget who twisted my own words against me, am I? I think we ought to have tested Georgie out on the battlefield and see if she might not have been a better soldier than her husband."

"Oh, she'd be a far cry better," Henshaw boasted as he approached with Sebastian. "Though she'd have been better suited to covert operations, wouldn't you say, Morton?"

Sebastian only shuddered, which brought more laughter from the group.

"Mind yourselves," Lady Hetty muttered, thumping her stick once. "Trenwick spies us, and he seems particularly watchful."

Grace peered over her shoulder, saw his calculating look, then turned back to the group with a wince. "Blast!" she hissed, her voice catching.

"Not to worry," Charlotte said at once, tossing her hair. "I'll have this sorted in no time. Married couples must dance together for the first, then rearranged for the second. Grace, you come with me and dance with my brother. For our sins, we are a family of your father's approval, and I will scrub my tongue with soap this evening for admitting such. Henshaw, dance with Elinor first, then either Kitty or Amelia, and Andrews will take Elinor for the second. After which, you will claim a dance from Grace, who, I hope, will have managed a dance with Lord Elsmere, as he is rather keen to do as I request." She turned to Cam with an authoritative look. "See if Francis can be spared for the third, and you dance with Janet, while he may have his pick of the lot. He must dance with Grace for the fourth. That is imperative. By that point, Trenwick should get over himself and allow himself to be carried off to the card room by my father for talk of business or some such. You're on your own after that."

She turned to Aubrey then, looking quite severe. "You may not dance with her while her father is present. He knows you well, and it will not have any effect at all if you do. I will partner you first, then go with Henshaw and take whichever girl he does not for the second. Mingle for the third, do not dance, and then the fourth go back for either Kitty or Amelia, whichever you did not dance with before. Better yet, Alice Sterling, she has better connections. Understood?"

Aubrey stared at Charlotte with wide eyes, stunned and entirely adrift.

"Where did I lose you?" she asked with some impatience.

"Nowhere," he said at once. "I follow. I'm just wondering where in the world you came from."

Charlotte grinned outright. "From the cradle of London Society, my dear Lord Ingram. No one navigates her as I do, and if this does not work, I will come to the next assembly dressed as a court jester and sing a bawdy tavern song of your choosing for the gathering."

Aubrey looked at Cam hopefully. "Can we see that it fails on that promise alone?"

Cam shrugged, nodding his agreement.

Charlotte whacked Cam across the chest, giving Aubrey the sort of look an overbearing sister would. "If you follow instructions, Ingram, I will prove to be a very, very capable ally." She raised a daring brow, waiting.

Aubrey straightened, sobering at once. "Aye, aye, ma'am. Right you are."

"As I thought," she muttered. She cleared her throat and looked around. "Everyone ready?"

They all murmured their assent, some of them sounding as surprised as Aubrey.

The Spinsters, however, had no such emotion.

This was Charlotte Wright in her element, and they knew their orders.

Charlotte nodded, and moved to Grace, looping her arm through hers. "We'll go to Charles and see that he takes Grace for the first. Ingram, wait five minutes, then come to me. Part the group, for they will gather. Be charming, please, I do have a reputation to uphold."

Without waiting for a response, she turned and led Grace away. "Charlotte," Grace hissed, "there is no need for all this. I am not..."

"Of course, there is," Charlotte overrode briskly. "It will satisfy your father, which should make him leave, and make Aubrey have to wait for any dance with you, which will drive him mad. I approve of both things, so why not be efficient in the task?"

"Why would you want to drive Aubrey mad?" Grace asked with a laugh.

Charlotte smiled up at her slyly. "Why would you *not* want to?"

Grace blanched, then peered back at Aubrey, who had clearly watched her every step, his stance still relaxed, though his eyes were hooded, and his fists clenched.

There was no mistaking where his attention lay, if anyone had cared to notice.

"Oh lord," she breathed, the words catching in her throat, returning her attention forward.

Charlotte hummed a delighted laugh to herself. "You should hear what Miranda has planned. It will be utterly delicious."

"You're all quite mad," Grace giggled, tossing the tendrils of hair from her shoulder.

"Not as mad as he will be!" Charlotte crowed. "Now, do smile, dear. My brother is quite sensitive about that sort of thing."

Whatever he had thought about Charlotte Wright before, he could have worshipped her now. Her scheming navigation of the situation with Trenwick had worked out flawlessly, and he hadn't been in the ballroom for over an hour. Grace had been relaxed and radiant once they had become aware of their success, and he was not the only one to have noticed it.

Which is where the end of worship and the beginning of cursing began.

Once they had secured victory, a new game had commenced. One that Aubrey had not been aware of, and one in which he was clearly the loser.

They were intentionally keeping Grace from him.

Worse than that, they were laughing at him.

They, of course, being the Spinsters, their husbands, their hosts for the evening, and the maddening duo of Henshaw and Miranda, all of whom were now very much in danger of his wrath.

Politely, of course.

This was a Society gathering, after all.

But for the love of everything sacred, holy, and pure, would he never have half a moment with her?

He'd looked for her the moment he'd entered Sterling House, before he'd ever reached the ballroom. Despite his affection and respect for Francis and Janet, he had no purpose in coming here tonight but Grace. Seeing her again, though they had just been at Miranda's three nights ago. Admiring her in the splendor of a grand room in all her finery, though nothing could ever be lovelier than the sight of her racing across a garden behind the heels of a blundering bloodhound, hair falling recklessly from its hold.

Dancing with her after weeks of avoiding doing so in any manner that would be considered close, knowing now that he would damn himself to hell twelve times over if he withheld from doing so one more time.

He was through resisting her, avoiding this, ignoring what could not be denied. Just seeing her at this moment, across the room, engaged in conversation with Amelia and Kitty, he could have proclaimed his love and adoration. Shouted it until the words shook the chandeliers and flickered every one of the candles. He could have dropped to his knees and begged her to take him, poor excuse for a partner and lover he would be, but willing to be anything and everything she wanted.

This was madness.

This was love.

"You do know that we all know about this, yes?"

Aubrey nodded as Francis came to stand beside him. "You've all made that perfectly clear, yes."

"And you don't care." There was no question in the words, purely a statement, an observation of the facts as they stood.

"Not particularly, no."

"Good."

He glanced at Francis, smirking slightly at the grunted reply. "Is it?"

Francis nodded, watching Grace as well, or perhaps Janet, as she had now sidled up to Grace and the others. "I remember, you see, when Tony first suggested that you could fall in love with Grace. I remember the look on your face, and the quite respectful defense you gave for her, all things considered. You would have sold your soul to avoid anyone even suspecting you had any attachment to anyone, let alone her."

"It wasn't personal," Aubrey murmured, fascinated suddenly by the turn of Grace's throat. "I barely remembered her. And yet…"

Francis sipped whatever he was drinking, then prodded, "Yet…?"

Aubrey shook his head. "It wasn't as terrible a thought as I'd made it out to be. And I knew that then. The moment he'd said her name, the thought was in my head, and I couldn't recoil as much as I thought. I didn't recoil at all. And then I came to know her, and…"

"And you were off like a shot," Francis finished with a low laugh.

"Right in her direction, ready to fall."

"Hardly so eager," Aubrey protested, smiling to himself, "but more or less, yes."

Francis shifted beside him and gestured towards the group they watched. "It's always more or less, and we're never quite sure. But you seem fairly set on a course, which is more than I can say for Henshaw."

Aubrey jerked and looked at the other man in surprise. "Henshaw?"

"Of course." Francis glanced at him, then snorted to himself. "You haven't noticed, have you? Never mind, then. Settle your own matters, Ingram, and then, when you can see the rest of the world once more, I'll let you in on that little secret." He nudged Aubrey forward with surprising force. "It's a waltz, man. Go to it."

The musicians began the strains of the next song, and Aubrey found his feet carrying him to Grace without any direction from him. His heart pattered to the cadence of the song's introduction, and the strangest heat began to pound with it from the center of his chest and out to his fingertips.

He reached Grace in moments, and she turned towards him only a breath later, eyes bright.

"Will you share this waltz with me, Miss Morledge?" he heard himself ask, though he hardly sounded like himself. The man doing the asking did so softly, tenderly, and with far too much fervor.

He was far more collected and aloof than that, wasn't he?

Surely, he knew what he was doing, didn't he?

Grace's lips parted, then curved. "Aubrey," she whispered, his name sending a jolt of pleasure into the sole of one foot, "we've already assessed my dancing. Thoroughly."

She thought he was assessing her still? Blessed goddess, could she not see that he had not had a mind for flaws or tasks of any sort for weeks now?

There were no flaws. There were no faults.

There was only Grace.

He shook his head slowly and reached for her hand. "This isn't about that," he told her gently. "This is for no other reason than that I want to dance with you. For the sheer pleasure of the experience of being with you."

She exhaled roughly, her hand sliding into his, the friction of their gloves together creating sparks that crackled somewhere within his chest. Her eyes stayed on his as he led her to the floor, and he realized one particularly startling thought.

He hadn't a bloody clue what he was doing.

Except that he wanted this, wanted her.

More than anything.

He put his hand at her waist, curving it around to her back, swallowing hard as she drew closer to him, placing her hand the same on his. She would feel the tremor in his hand upon her, feel the pounding of the blood in his veins, knowing just how affected by her he was. She would know everything if he went through with this. If they truly waltzed...

He exhaled once, then swept her into the dance, giving himself up to it completely, wholly, and irreversibly. Around and around they turned, following the same pattern as the other couples in the room, though he couldn't see any of them. He couldn't hear the other steps or swishing of skirts and could barely hear the music they danced by.

Hearing was not nearly as important as seeing at this moment. As feeling. As being.

Grace exhaled audibly, an almost emotional sound. "I didn't think you would dance with me," she admitted, her tone higher than he was used to.

"Why not?" he asked as he turned her. "Why would I not?"

"Didn't you once say that in dancing with me, they would know how you felt?" She dropped her gaze to his chin, her cheeks beginning to brighten with a blush. "Whatever it was you felt?"

Aubrey found himself smiling, and his fingers drummed slowly against her waist. "I did say that."

Grace stilled as much as was possible while still waltzing like an angel. "And?"

"They will know."

Her eyes raised to his at once, almost alarmed.

He smiled at her expression, shaking his head. "They will see," he whispered, turning her in a particularly swelling motion, his fingers latching onto hers overhead. "And I don't care that they do."

Her jaw dropped, then slowly spread into the most beautiful, beaming, dazzling grin ever known to man. "You don't?"

Dazed by what he had witnessed, he could only formulate the shape of words, not give voice to them, for the space of several frantic heartbeats. "No," he eventually managed, his voice resembling the sound of a wave dashed on the sea. "In fact, I may even be glad for it."

Grace's eyes crinkled in delight, the dark depths drawing him in until he was lost. "Glad to have them see how you feel about waltzing with me?" she teased.

Could she not know? Could she not see and feel, and practically taste this need he had for her?

Then he felt it. The throbbing pulse at her back, right where his hand sat, pounding furiously against his palm. Through the fabric of gloves and gown, he could feel the beating of her heart over that of his own, and he became entirely attuned to it, fixated on it, encouraged by it. This madness he felt and was consumed by was gripping her, too.

He was not alone in this.

She was with him.

"Glad," he told her, dropping his voice lower still, "to have them see the way I look at you. To have them know what you make me feel. To let them bear witness to the incomparable joy that being with you gives me." He swallowed as emotion began to fill him, grounding himself by the joined pounding of their hearts. "To be seen in the depths of complete adoration, Grace Morledge, for no one else but you."

Grace's breath caught on a faint sob, and he squeezed the hand he held tightly, wishing with the desperation of the damned that they were alone in this room, in this place. In any place at all.

Holding her in this form of the dance was not enough. He needed her closer, needed to cradle her against him, to draw her in until he could not remember how to exist without the feel of her. To kiss her in a thousand different ways and a thousand different places, to bear his heart and soul to her in whatever long-winded attempts at sonnets and pathetic declarations of love and devotion his unworthy lips could form. To sit beside her with their fingers entwined, letting the silence speak for itself.

To make vows, plans, and dreams together.

To be with her.

Simply to be.

Anywhere, anytime, anything would be enough so long as he had her.

Whatever he had wanted, whatever he had planned, it all faded into nothingness. The woman in his arms was more than anything he could have had, created, or brought about, and he would be fortunate beyond his wildest imaginations if only he had half as much love from her as he felt burning through him.

Round and around they danced, slowly pulling each other closer, drawing together helplessly, legs brushing against each other as they moved, eyes steady on each other. He could count every one of her breaths, and she would know how his heart thumped. He memorized the shape of her lips down to the smallest detail, and she might have drawn the exact shade of his eyes from memory.

Lord, to be so lost in another person as to be unaware of anything or anyone else!

Perfection. That was it, that was the feeling between them, the notion swirling about his head and his lips and filling his lungs. Perfection in its most ideal form.

Remarkably, not in her. Obviously not in him.

But in them.

In this.

This was perfection, and how he loved perfection.

The sound of applause accompanied his epiphany, and he found that blissfully apt, until it dawned on him that the waltz had finished, and the music was no more. His ears resumed their usual abilities, and his head swam with the motion his body no longer engaged in. He was still breathless, Grace was still incomparable, and he was still in love with her.

Aubrey stared at her, lost as to how to proceed. Racing off with her into the night was surely frowned upon, and yet…

He slowly drew his hand from her waist, pulling back and dying a slow death as her hand slid against his side. He let his hand move to her arm, fingers trailing along the length of her glove until they captured her own. He held her gaze, her eyes black as the night, then bowed deeply over her hand, and kissed the back, wishing he had the power to reach the skin beneath.

He lingered, whispering a benediction against her hand, then drew up and sighed as her fingers curled tightly against his in a grip that would have shaken a saint to his core.

"Aubrey," Grace whispered through her full, unmoving lips.

He swallowed, shaking his head, beyond words. Even her name was too much to manage at this moment, but he smiled. Smiled with all the tenderness a man is capable of, with the warmth of summer, the bliss of spring, and the passion of a kiss.

With all the love in existence.

He led her from the floor, and reluctantly returned her to Janet's side. No one said a word, but their eyes said volumes.

They knew.

And so did he.

Chapter Twenty-One

If all good things must come to an end, why do we engage in them at all? Perhaps we should refrain and save ourselves the trouble.

-The Spinster Chronicles, 11 July 1815

Had there ever been a morning as glorious as this one?

Had he ever paid any particular attention to them?

Aubrey grinned as he moved from the breakfast room to the front of the house, exhaling with satisfaction, confidence, and some excitement, he could easily admit. He glanced at himself in the looking glass in the hall, nodding at himself, though he could have been the proverbial Society puppy with his boyish grin.

Clipped footsteps approached, and Aubrey turned to greet them. "I'm going to make an offer, Locke."

"To me, sir?"

Aubrey looked at his butler wryly, then sobered at once. "Well, no, Locke. I cannot say I had any idea you were so inclined, and I do feel that I would receive many askew glances for offering for my butler."

Locke stiffened, his face turning red. "Sir…"

"You're the one who said it, Locke," Aubrey pointed out with a shrug. "I was only correcting you."

The butler heaved the long-suffering sigh of those cursed with insolent dependents. "Yes, sir."

"But no, you will be happy to hear that I am going to offer for

Miss Morledge." Aubrey grinned with the delight he could barely contain. "And I think she might accept."

Locke did not look remotely convinced, and Aubrey wondered if he had finally pushed the man past his limits.

Aubrey raised a brow. "You think not?"

"I cannot speak to the lady's tastes and preferences, my lord," Locke replied with a slight bow as Aubrey slid his arms into his greatcoat. "I fear I have no way of knowing how likely she is to accept such an offer."

That was rather a lot of speaking for his butler in response to anything Aubrey said, and he narrowed his eyes at the older man. "But?" he prodded.

Locke's mouth quirked, and Aubrey gaped at the sight. "But it would be most fortuitous for all of us to have Miss Morledge as our mistress, sir."

"Did you just smile at the thought, Locke?" Aubrey accused, not bothering to hide his excitement.

The butler maintained a steady, placid expression. "I might have done, sir."

Good heavens, he'd finally done it. He'd cracked the façade of his butler at last.

Breaking generations of tradition and protocol, Aubrey clapped his butler's arms in both hands. "By Jove, Locke, I do believe the future is looking quite bright for us."

"If you say so, my lord," came the doubtful reply.

This day was destined to be one for glory, he was sure of it now. Grinning, Aubrey nodded to his butler and turned to go. "Tell Sundrey to set out my best clothing, Locke. We will feast tonight!"

"He'll be delighted to hear it, my lord."

Aubrey chuckled to himself as he strode from the house, climbing into the carriage, and setting off at once. He'd been of the same mind for the past two days but hadn't been able to take it up without making inquiries with his solicitor and the like. The details had to be seen to, and he needed to be prepared in all things before taking himself off to Trenwick on such an errand.

There was no telling how the buzzard would react to hearing such news, which was why Aubrey had set into motion several contingency plans and additional measures.

And now he would be able to proceed.

He'd have asked Grace first, but with Trenwick as her father, he'd have to do this according to his tastes, and those would not involve Grace at all.

Surely, she'd forgive him for that, given the end result would be the same.

From the moment he'd let her out of his arms after the waltz at Sterling House, he'd known his life as he had known it was over, and that he was at the start of a new one. He had to have her, and he would not stop until he did. He had to give her himself, and he had never been more willing to do anything so self-sacrificing. It did not even feel like a sacrifice, but an offering wherein he would come out the more fortunate party.

Aubrey Flint was diving headfirst into the ocean of love, marriage, and Grace Morledge.

May he drown in such depths and never come up for air.

He was shown into the house at once, Bennett never revealing a word or giving him the slightest sign of encouragement. Clearly, he would need to double his efforts to win over this butler as he had his own.

"His lordship will see you, sir," Bennett informed him before Aubrey could request a meeting and escorted him to the study.

"How did he...?" Aubrey asked in a low tone.

Bennett silenced him with a look. "He's in a right state, my lord," came the almost whispered reply. "None can say why."

Aubrey stiffened, his jaw tightening. "Grace?"

Bennett shook his head. "None can say, sir," he said again.

"Marvelous," Aubrey muttered, straightening his waistcoat and adjusting his cravat. "Thank you for the warning."

The butler knocked at the door, then showed Aubrey in.

Trenwick rose behind his desk, expression set as though in stone. "Fortuitous arrival, Ingram. I was in the process of sending for you. Sit, please."

The hair at the back of Aubrey's neck and along his arms stood on end, the clipped, cool tone warning him off of his course. He sat without response and folded his hands in his lap, waiting for his host to enlighten him.

"I will not engage in politeness, my lord," Trenwick began as the door closed. "I pray you will forgive me for it, but there is far too much to discuss and I am eager to get on with it."

Aubrey nodded once, hands tightening in anticipation.

Trenwick pressed his fists into his desk, leaning on them, eyes hard on Aubrey. "Something has come to my attention, Ingram, and it could not wait. I could not believe my ears when I heard it, and I thought it must be slanderous falsehood. So, you can imagine my surprise when my own investigation into the matter revealed it to be true."

Good heavens, what was this? How could he have known when there had been nothing at all to tell? Aubrey swallowed and made no reply, did not move his head or any other part of him. He could not risk revealing anything of his own, not yet.

Trenwick needed no reply, and his eyes hardened. "Were you aware, sir, of my daughter's involvement in a particular circulation known as the Spinster Chronicles?"

The first emotion was that of profound relief, followed very quickly by equally profound panic.

"I had discovered that recently, my lord, yes," Aubrey admitted evasively, taking to express truth without elaborating on it.

Trenwick tilted his head in inquiry, saying nothing.

Aubrey cleared his throat, adjusting his position in his seat. "I believe we had agreed, my lord, that I would express my findings to you when my examination was complete. And with the recent addition of your daughter's reputation, I was still in process of compiling information."

An abrupt nod met this response. "And in the compiling of this information, Ingram, have you been informed of her association with this group known as the Spinsters? I believe with a capital S."

"I have, my lord." His heart sank with lightning speed into the region of his bowels and seemed to tighten his throat in the process.

"This group," Trenwick went on, straightening from his position and beginning to pace behind the desk, "involving women who are supposedly of a high enough station to be better behaved, yet who are determined to flaunt their inability to find husbands as though it were a mark of some great honor."

Aubrey bit back a retort about a few of them having been lately married, knowing it would not do any good.

His lack of response seemed to trigger something in Trenwick, and the man snorted softly. "Yes, I know some of them have surrendered to the pressures of Society and married against whatever edicts they had set for themselves, but the sentiment of the thing remains the same. A band of women collecting dust on the shelves of London together rather than apart, whilst also recruiting other young ladies to join in their cause."

Oh, this would end badly, wherever it led. He could not consider offering for Grace now, not when Trenwick was in high dudgeon, and not when the discovery of the Spinsters was upon them. The fallout would hinder everything, and he needed to tread carefully.

Trenwick stopped and looked at Aubrey, hands sweeping behind his back. "Apologies, my personal feelings are clouding my good sense. Ingram, I must ask you now, and I beg you to be frank. Have you found significant faults in my daughter?"

Aubrey swallowed, all hope for the day's plans vanishing into thin air. "No, sir."

"As I suspected." Trenwick lifted his chin, straightening further still. "Is it possible, my lord, that my daughter's unmarried condition could be due to her involvement with this particular circulation and this particular group? Is she a spinster, my lord, because she is, to use the phrase, one of the Spinsters?"

Aubrey stared at the older man, dread, horror, and every other foul emotion settling into various parts of him.

He should lie. He should lie outright and inform Trenwick that people were mistaken. That no one could properly see Grace. That Society was full to the brim with imbeciles. That the Spinsters were some of the most fascinating, intelligent, entertaining, and remarkably good women he had ever encountered.

He should insist on satisfaction for the woman he loved.

He should...

Forgive me, Grace.

"I believe it is possible, my lord," Aubrey admitted, the words tasting of bile. "If nothing else. The opinions of the Spinsters are varied, and… It is possible."

Trenwick nodded once, then again. "I suspected no less. Thank you for confirming it. Had I known about this sooner, there would have been no need to bring you in for this ridiculous farce at all. One simple explanation for the whole thing, and no one could give it to me before this. Not even my own daughter."

Aubrey winced. "Sir…"

"No apology needed, Ingram," Trenwick overrode, raising a hand. "I know you could not have known." He turned to look towards the fire, eyeing the flames in thought, and Aubrey could see the man's teeth grinding together. "This will be dealt with; I can assure you."

That was what Aubrey was afraid of. "My lord…"

Trenwick looked at him then, seeming decided. "Come with me, Ingram. I will need your support, and my daughter will need to understand." He moved to the door and opened it, gesturing for him to exit.

Aubrey would have given his entire fortune to not proceed, to remain where he was, to avoid the disaster that was looming before him.

Forgive me, Grace, he prayed again as he rose and exited, his legs somehow no longer in existence, yet carrying him anyway. *Forgive me.*

Heaven did not reply, and he feared he was walking to his doom.

"Your father wants to speak with you."

Grace did not bother to look up from her book. "Why should today be any different?"

"Grace…"

Her mother's tone brought her head up slowly and Grace stared warily. "Mama?"

"Now," her mother whispered, eyes wide and worried. "Right this minute. He is most displeased."

Grace rose quickly, setting her book aside. "I cannot bear another routing, Mama. I haven't done anything."

"I know," her mother soothed, taking her arm and rubbing it as they made their way out of the parlor. "Just bear it as best you can. Perhaps Aubrey will soften him."

"Aubrey?" Grace looked at her mother, her heart somehow leaping and falling at the same time. "Aubrey is here?"

Her mother nodded, gripping Grace's arm tightly for a moment. "I've never seen either look so somber."

Grace bit her lip, turning her gaze to the art on the walls. Why would they look so severe? Why would her father be displeased if Aubrey was here?

What had Aubrey said?

After the Sterlings' ball, she had been so certain that something significant would occur, that he would approach her father and officially court her, that he would declare himself, or that she would. Nothing had happened yet, and she had been on edge ever since. Waiting. Wanting. Hoping.

But this...

The drawing room had never been so silent, and the clouds outside had given way to the rain within them, yet there was no sound of the drops against the glass. Only the gloom and dreariness from such a day to add gravity to the moment.

Grace curtseyed upon entering, and nearly whimpered as her mother's arm slid from hers and vanished. She locked her knees and swallowed, staring at her father. "Father."

He kept his eyes on her, his mouth a thin line.

Grace could see Aubrey just behind her father, but she didn't dare look at him.

"It has come to my attention," her father began in cool, clipped tones, "that my daughter has been engaging with a group that has directly contributed to her failure to attain a husband."

Her eyes widened, and her heart skipped. *No...*

"It has further come to my attention that the opinion of Society is that this is, in fact, the prime reason for her not obtaining a husband."

The air vanished from her lungs, and her locked knees began to shake.

Her father's eyes narrowed, his upper lip twitching in a hint of a sneer. "And were it not for the studious work of individuals truly dedicated to my expectations of my family, I might never have known that my daughter takes such pleasure and pride in her shameful situation that she regularly boasts about it in a cheap gossip sheet that is circulated about London for the entertainment of the masses." His look became one of absolute disgust. "Have you no shame, daughter?"

Grace opened her mouth, but without air or concise thought, nothing came forth, her lips moving soundlessly.

"After all I have done for you," her father spat, abhorrence seeping from every line on his face, "this is how you repay me? This is how you would honor your family? By making us a laughingstock and a disgrace in Society? You were not raised to act with independent thought and a disregard for the standards set for a respectable young woman. You were not brought up to make yourself a spectacle to be mocked by every class in London, to do anything that would detract from the one task you had to accomplish in life. All you had to do was make a good match, Grace. One simple task that girls of fewer accomplishments, less education, less taste, and less breeding accomplish every single day. And you have wasted it all on some frivolous, printed rags while associating with the world's future harlots and shrews."

"Father," Grace protested feebly, her voice squeaking in distress.

He turned thunderous in a moment. "Not a word, daughter. You will never see those women again. You will never write another word for that drivel of a column. And you will conduct yourself as I see fit for the remainder of the Season. If you cannot act wisely without supervision, you can be certain you will submit yourself with it." He nodded once, ending the conversation as he brushed passed her, dismissing any response she might have given.

His footsteps echoed down the corridor, and when they had faded, she exhaled slowly.

So, she could breathe after all.

What a waste.

"Grace…"

Her eyes lifted to Aubrey with a sharpness she could only have inherited from her father, and whatever they held made Aubrey take a step back.

Good.

She said nothing, staring at him as her jaw tightened, hardened, her spine stiffening, and a wrought iron cage closing around her heart.

He returned her look, seeming younger, weaker, and more uncertain than she would ever have thought him capable of. Which was fitting, as she suddenly felt older, harsher, and absolutely resolute.

"You told him."

Aubrey shook his head once. "He knew. He found out."

"You confirmed it."

He hesitated, which was answer enough. "I had to."

"Did you?" she asked in the same sort of formal tone she had heard throughout her life, letting coldness enter it. "Did you really?"

"Grace, listen to me…"

"Why?" she interrupted, the word clipped. "Because you have a feasible explanation for informing my father that the reason for nobody wanting me is that I made friends with other women that nobody wanted, and we tried to make the best of our situation?"

Aubrey grimaced as though she had slapped him, and she wished at that moment she had, her palm burning with the desire to.

"That was your answer, was it?" She sniffed in derision, the gnawing sting of betrayal creeping across her skin. "That was your grand solution to my father, who only needed an excuse to prove that I was lacking? My friends, Aubrey?"

"It's not what you think," he insisted.

Grace raised a brow. "And how would you know what I think? You haven't known that yet, or you would not have dared to suggest such a heartless thing. My friends, Aubrey? They are the reason you believe I am a spinster?"

He shook his head. "This isn't about me."

"Isn't it, then?" she shot back. "This whole affair has been about you. Making me trust you so that you can twist me to your will, expose my inadequacies with ease and with very little inconvenience to yourself at all. Did you write the list of other candidates yourself to ensure that I would accept you? Or was that my father's idea?"

Aubrey's expression darkened at once. "Surely, you don't believe…"

Grace nodded before he could finish. "Oh, I most certainly do believe it. I should have believed it from the start, but it seems one of my failings is that I am far more naïve and simple than I dreamed. But let me tell you one thing, Lord Ingram. I have found more strength and renewal in my friends than many individuals have found in their entire life. I have found more acceptance and loyalty in their ranks than anything I felt from my own father, let alone my siblings. I have found a voice with those women that had been stripped from me while still in my childhood, because a young woman does not possess a voice that was not put there for her. And I would rather be a spinster for the rest of my days and be a Spinster with a capital S than to be miserable, married off, and made into my father's creation."

Her voice carried in the room, though she had not raged. There had been no shouting, no roaring, and nothing at all to indicate that she possessed any sort of temper, though she burned with a deep fury that would eat away at her for days.

She was a woman of quality and class, and they did not raise their voices.

But oh, could they inflict venom all the same.

And the icy tone of her voice proved a most perfect pairing.

Perfection at last.

Oh, what irony.

"I will not deny," Aubrey began in his own even tone, "that I confirmed your father's findings. I will not deny that he has acted as he has based on my answers. And I will also not deny that I stand by what I said, much as it pains you."

Grace lifted her chin, daring him to go on.

Never one to back down, Aubrey did so, but without the retaliatory air she had expected. "I do believe that your association with the Spinsters contributes to your being unmarried. Participation in such a divisive group could not help but to sway public opinion, no matter how respectable those opinions might have been before."

Her mouth curved in a cold, satisfied smile. "So, the truth comes out. What a relief."

Aubrey tilted his head, expression unreadable. "If you could not see that, Grace, you are not nearly as observant as I took you for."

"Clearly, we were both mistaken in each other, then."

He stared for a long moment. "I wasn't."

She folded her arms and raised a brow. "No?"

"No." He shook his head. "I was not mistaken in you then, and I am not now."

"How pleasant for you."

Grace waited for him to snap, to take her sneered response and toss it back at her. To stir her indignation into something louder, fiercer, and far more explosive. To drive her to tears of fury cascading with the destruction of a waterfall upon rocks.

But he didn't roar, he didn't rage, and there were no tears to be found, burning, welling, or falling.

Not a single one.

His chest moved on an exhale, and he slid his hands into his trousers pockets in the same easy, relaxed stance that she had always loved about him.

The sight of it tugged at her heart, slamming it against the cage now holding it, and she tightened her arms against each other. Would he not go and leave her to her impending heartbreak?

"Strawberries," he said at last.

Grace blinked, certain she'd heard him wrong. "What?"

One side of his mouth curved. "You prefer your porridge with strawberries. Fresh ones, straight from the garden, though you will accept ones from the market if they are the freshest to be had. And cinnamon with a little sugar. If you're feeling particularly sour, you add additional milk, if not cream. On rainy days, you also take toast with jam. And God help the servant who puts a single blueberry in."

She stared at him in wonder, couldn't breathe, couldn't move, could not feel her fingers tucked against her body.

How could he have known? *How* could he...?

He shrugged one shoulder. "I thought you ought to know." His hands went to his side and he bowed perfectly before her. "Good day, Miss Morledge. I apologize for disrupting your morning."

Then he was gone, striding out the door before she could do more than blink and watch him go.

No vitriol. No recrimination. No heated defense of his own actions or defamation of her direct attack on him.

No temper.

Yet he had one. She had seen it flare at times, yet today he had not had one.

There hadn't even been anger.

But there had been pain. She had seen that, had felt that, and even he would not have denied it.

Why, at this moment, would she have preferred his anger to his pain?

She blinked once more, and with an exhale, her knees lost their rigidity, shaking in their release. She fumbled for a chair and sank into it, her lungs working in agitation to inhale and exhale in a somewhat effective manner. Her eyes never burned, and her throat never closed.

Yet she felt such an ache, such a cruel, twisting ache deep within her chest. As though her heart would burst with any particular twinge and send her crumbling to pieces.

She could not crumble. She could not break.

"He will not break me," she hissed to herself.

A faint hiccup followed the words, and she shook her head, swallowing hard.

She would not be broken.

But maybe, just maybe, she would let herself bend a little once she could lock herself in her room and hide a tear or two from any watchful eyes.

And perhaps one tear more for the dreams now lost.

Chapter Twenty-Two

Every now and again, the heart may need a little help.

-The Spinster Chronicles, 25 October 1816

She could freely admit to a breaking heart now.

Not broken, but breaking.

Cracked, but still whole.

Aching, but whole.

And yet, a whole heart does not work as well with the injuries placed upon it, as her low spirits and reduced energy would attest.

Bit of an inconvenience, that.

Still, some time with her friends should help to dull the ache.

It had been a week since she had seen any of the Spinsters, what with her father's edict against seeing any of them. Even the prospect of Charlotte Wright couldn't persuade him, and she'd been forced into playing the obedient and biddable daughter for a time. It hadn't helped that he'd been hovering over her every action since that horrible day.

Today, there had been a reprieve, however. He had gone to see to some business out in the country, and her mother had insisted that Grace accompany her to pay calls only to then deliver her to Charlotte's home for the regular Spinster gathering.

Grace had never been hugged so fiercely in her entire life, and it had nearly brought the tears she cried at night to the surface.

Now, they had settled her into a chair, plied her with cakes and tea, and finally calmed their reactions to seeing her.

Edith held her hand on her left while Prue hovered protectively close on her right.

Their closeness warmed her heart as much as her mother's delivery had.

"I am telling you the truth," Elinor insisted to whoever had questioned her. "Mr. Andrews *was* seen calling upon Amelia Perry! The man has never called upon any single woman, and he just so happens to do so with the only woman in London fascinated with him?"

Izzy rolled her eyes with a sigh. "She is not the *only* one fascinated by him. Alice Sterling asked about him just the other day."

"Lord, save the man from the Sterling machinations," Elinor prayed aloud.

"You like Alice," Prue reminded her.

Elinor nodded once. "I do. Just not for Andrews."

"Oh, now we're more particular, are we?" Edith asked with a laugh, squeezing Grace's hand. "Or do you just object to anything Sterling?"

Elinor scrunched up her face. "I like Lord Sterling. And Tony and Georgie, of course."

"They send their love, by the way," Izzy broke in, looking to Grace with a warm smile. "They've heard everything."

Grace nodded, her cheeks oddly feeling chilled rather than warm. "And, how are they?"

"Large," Charlotte replied with all her usual frankness. "Well, Georgie is, anyway. I imagine Tony is the same size as before. But the doctor says she's a month away from delivery at least. So much for an accurate confinement."

"I'm sure she'll not mind it," Prue murmured, smiling to herself. "Time in the country with her husband will be a precious thing."

Charlotte eyed Prue suspiciously. "Something to say there, Mrs. Vale?"

Prue's cheeks flamed brightly. "N-no," she stammered, lowering her eyes. "I only love being in the country with my own husband."

"As do I," Izzy sighed. She tossed her copper curls and grinned at the lot. "Husbands. Wonderful for the constitution."

"Sometimes," Edith muttered to Grace. "The loss of mine did my constitution a world of good."

Grace bit back a laugh and nodded.

"Grace," Elinor said suddenly, her voice surprisingly gentle, "may I ask you something rather impertinent?"

Having anticipated something of the sort being brought up during this visit, Grace nodded, her throat drying as her hands curved more tightly against each other.

"Careful," Charlotte murmured, watching Grace.

Elinor nodded once. "I know that something happened with your father, and that something passed between you and Aubrey, but there's been no word of the details. I don't want to pry into your personal matters, but…"

"That's what you're doing now," Charlotte pointed out with a laugh.

An embarrassed smile spread across Elinor's face, and she turned apologetic as she took in Grace once more. "If you can bear to, will you tell us what it is?"

It was astonishing to see and hear Elinor behave more like one of their group than like the zealous admirer she had once been. She'd recently discovered a new level of maturity, though it was not always present, and the promise of a wiser, more sensible version of her in the future was encouraging.

Had it been Elinor alone that had asked, Grace might have put her off. But in the presence of the others, and with their influence to temper the less mature aspects of Elinor's nature, she was willing to open herself to the vulnerabilities of the past few days.

She nodded, and quickly related the experience with her father's discovery of her involvement with the Spinsters, the Chronicles, and her fault-finding in general, as well as Aubrey's confession of his opinion there. She'd been avoiding thinking too much about the topic, fearing her lingering resentment would outweigh her good sense, and that the feelings of betrayal would spring up once more.

Worse than that, she feared she would miss Aubrey more fiercely than she already did, even with the betrayal, resentment, and dismay over the whole thing. She ached to see his face, to touch his hand, to share a smile, and her lips burned to murmur apologies over and over,

275

though she wasn't entirely sure what she would be apologizing for. He had betrayed her, there was no doubt, and she had been right to confront him.

But she was sorry for all of it and wanted him near her.

The others were quiet, strangely without any sort of indignation themselves.

"Well, he's not wrong," Charlotte finally said, nodding thoughtfully.

Grace stared at her, stunned by the admission from her, of all people. More bewildering, she saw the others in the room nodding, as well.

"What?" she cried, looking from one to the other in quick succession.

Charlotte smiled at her confusion. "Do I shock you? I should be raging in a towering fury and rising to our defense, should I not?"

Well, not to be so predictable in expectation, but she had rather expected something of that sort, and nodded in exasperation.

"Were the comment from your father alone," Charlotte explained, seeming to choose her words with great care, "and combined with the insults he felt necessary, I would do so. I'd spit at him, if I thought I'd be able to control myself. I'm not at all agreeing with his ignorant assessment."

That was a relief, to be sure.

"But where Aubrey is concerned," she went on, her eyes seeming to lose focus as she spoke, "I cannot wholly disagree. There is no proof, to be sure, that your association with us is limiting your prospects for matrimony, as we cannot say what would have happened had we not adopted you into the ranks. But anyone can see that it does not help matters."

Again with the nods around the room, and Grace's confusion began to ebb.

Izzy turned towards Grace in her chair, her sweet smile more motherly than ever. "We were not a popular set before you joined us, you know. That was why we banded together. Charlotte is the exception, as she could likely commit murder and still have courtiers."

They all laughed, and Charlotte dipped her chin in an attempt at demure acknowledgement.

"But," Izzy said, sobering, "you were different. We wanted you as our friend, but we never expected you to remain with us for this long. Surely, someone would have snatched you up, even Georgie suspected that. Yet here you are, as unmarried as we ever were. And the only thing that changed in your situation, dear, was your friendship with us."

Grace shook her head, swallowing hard. "I wouldn't give it up," she confessed thickly. "Not for a single day or a single moment. This friendship has meant more to me than I can ever say."

"Amen," Edith murmured, rubbing her hand and seeming to be fighting her own emotions, as well.

Prue scooted closer and laid her head against Grace's shoulder. "And we would never give you up. I am sorry it has caused you pain, but I cannot regret having you with us."

"Stop!" Elinor cried, wiping at her eyes. "I didn't mean for us all to confess undying friendship as though we were parting ways!"

Charlotte laughed and made a shooing motion as though to send the emotions on their way. "You are absolutely correct; we must stop this sentimental nonsense this very moment! Away with our more feminine tendencies!"

Grace sighed and looked up at the decorative ceiling, not a single hint of age or decay upon it. "So, what you're saying," she asked of the room as a whole, "is that I was wrong to be so cruel to Aubrey and to have mislaid all good sense and judgment in feeling betrayed by him?"

"I'm not sure I would go that far," Charlotte told her with a slight squint. "Surely, he could have lied to your father or come up with some great heroic defense."

"Oh, please," Edith scoffed as she sat forward and poured herself another cup of tea. "The man has a moral conscience, and he was pressed into this whole mess by her father and by Georgie, if not us. He can hardly be blamed for being honest, especially when we all know good and well that his heart is no' in the same place as her father's."

Grace winced with a faint hiss and looked down at her feet, her toes rubbing anxiously together in her slippers.

"Grace…" Charlotte said very slowly.

She looked up at her friend in hesitation.

Charlotte's dark eyes were all too knowing as they looked at her. "Did you make the mistake of thinking Aubrey had been a puppet of Terrible Trenwick all along and hadn't been truthful in his behavior with you?"

Grace bit her lip, feeling the tears beginning to rise.

"Oh, Grace," Prue murmured beside her, rubbing her arm. "That's not Aubrey."

"No indeed," Izzy agreed, looking as though she might leap from her seat and hug Grace again. "Aubrey adores you; anyone could see that. He would never have treated you so ill. Have you forgotten how he fought against finding fault with you?"

"I don't know what to believe," Grace whispered, her jaw quivering. "Everything has grown so twisted and confusing, so distorted with my father's manipulations that I cannot see clearly anymore. I want to think... I want to hope..."

She couldn't finish the thought, couldn't dare to voice the cries of her heart.

What if she was mistaken there? What if he would break her after all?

What if she was too late?

"Don't tell me," Charlotte murmured in a voice filled with mischief, "that the man did not leave you with some idea as to how he truly feels. I saw the waltz between the two of you, and as someone who was keeping a weather eye open, I can promise you that your father was nowhere to be seen during that whole dramatic venture. No one is that talented an actor, Grace Morledge. Especially not someone as without social graces and ambitions as Aubrey, Lord Ingram."

"Oh, Charlotte," Izzy groaned as she sat back against the settee, shaking her head in despair. "Must everybody's motivations be driven by societal ambitions?"

"Of course!" came the scandalized reply. "What other motivation could there possibly be?"

A banter-filled discussion commenced on the topic, leaving Grace to puzzle over her thoughts.

To be seen in the depths of complete adoration, Grace Morledge...

I could never marry a man who does not know how I prefer my porridge...

A thousand memories flooded her mind, a thousand looks and smiles, and moment after moment when her heart had soared. When their wits had battled, when they had laughed, when they had raced on foot or on horseback. When they had talked of the country, played each other in various games, when he had held her in his arms and kissed her with a tenderness that at once broke her heart and made it whole...

Oh, how she loved him! With a depth and a pain that seemed to wrack her frame with a delirious sense of joy.

And how she prayed she might have the chance to tell him.

"Let's try this again, shall we?"

Aubrey shook his head as he held his breath, entering Trenwick House for the first time in almost two weeks. He'd have returned sooner, though business had kept him out of London when word had reached him that he ought to do so.

Allies were a blessed thing indeed.

No matter, he was even more prepared this time than he had been before, and there was no chance of being waylaid by Trenwick this time.

The man wasn't even at home, if his ally had been accurate, which he presumed to be the case.

She would never have been mistaken about this.

Bennett nodded his welcome, smiling in a manner that surely betrayed all butlers everywhere. "My lord. Will the blue room do?"

"Whatever you think best, Bennett," Aubrey demurred in an attempt to hide his pleasure at the change in the man.

The blue room it was to be, and within Aubrey waited, shaking his head as his heart skipped every other beat.

"Steady on, Ingram," he muttered to a potted plant. "She might ask for your head on a pike."

Not particularly likely, he supposed, but Grace was always surprising him.

Soft footsteps met his ears and he turned, exhaling very briefly.

Grace entered, looking more demure than he had seen her in some time, her gown a silky shade of grey that would have commanded his attention had her eyes, lips, and blush not done so.

"Aubrey," she greeted, curtseying to a depth he did not deserve, and he bowed in response.

"Grace." He nearly choked on her name, but smiled instead. "I'd hoped you would receive me."

She nodded, lowering her eyes. "I'd have received you sooner, had you come."

His heart leapt to his throat, and his gaze turned adoring, though she would not see it.

Now they were getting somewhere.

"Well, I would have come sooner, certainly," he told her, keeping his tone as casual as it had been in days past. "Only I've just recently returned from the country and wouldn't have been near enough to do so."

One corner of her mouth lifted in a faint smile. "It seems everyone was in the country lately. My father was visiting also. What took you there?"

"Meeting with your father, as it happens."

Grace's head shot up and her eyes searched his. "What?"

Aubrey nodded in confirmation. "Your father and I met in Derbyshire."

Her high brow furrowed, somehow sending a ringlet near her ear dancing. "But you were both in London, why would you meet in Derbyshire?"

"Well, he insisted I had to physically inspect a place before I made purchase of it," Aubrey exhaled noisily, shaking his head in some annoyance, "so there was an entire drive out to Derbyshire, and then I had to meet my estate manager at Breyerly to make him aware of the situation, and *then* came the drawn out process of walking through Withrow, which was wholly useless, as I remembered every detail…"

"Withrow?" she cried, her eyes wide, her breathing less than steady.

He pretended not to hear her. "I don't know where your father found that estate manager of his, but the man is utterly worthless. It's no wonder the estate is failing and left to rot. Gads, once we get our hands on it in truth, we'll show the neighborhood what a fine place it is, mark my words. Thank God the papers have all been signed, I wouldn't trust the pair of them with it for another day at most."

Grace swayed where she stood, then cleared her throat and took one step towards him. "Aubrey. Stop."

He swept his hands behind his back and tilted his head in inquiry. "Yes?"

She blinked twice, then laced her fingers together, trying to hide the fact that they were tight and clenching. "You purchased Withrow."

"I did," he replied simply.

"From my father."

"He did own the place, so yes."

There was brief flash of irritation, which made him grin. "Why?"

He let the grin spread. "Why what?"

Grace stepped forward again, still too far away from him. "Why would you purchase a failing estate left to rot that neighbors your own? It has nothing to recommend it and offers no benefit to you whatsoever. Why would you throw your money away?"

Aubrey waited just one moment, collecting himself. "Because I love you, Grace Morledge. Because Withrow is your home, failing or not, and I could not let someone take that from you."

"You... you what?" she breathed, color vanishing from her cheeks.

"Love you," he repeated, taking a step closer to her. "Quite desperately, as it happens. You can imagine my distress as I realized I had to find faults in the woman I love. I thought the Lord would smite me for it."

Grace exhaled roughly, almost gasping as she stared at him. "Aubrey..."

He stepped closer, sobering just enough to be as sincere as possible. "I came here today to report my findings. On your examination, that is. I have completed my assessment, and believe the results are conclusive."

He heard her sharp inhale, and the pain behind it. Then she

suddenly was as composed as an actress of the stage. "I see. And you've told my father?"

"Not at all," Aubrey replied at once. "I promised to tell you first, and so I shall. Then we may decide together what to tell your father."

Grace frowned, the cool composure cracking in her confusion.

Aubrey smiled again, shaking his head at the goddess before him. "Grace Morledge, I did find flaws in you that it seems the world has missed. I know better than anyone that you are not the embodiment of perfection, and I can tell you why. For starters, you can't dance the quadrille without stepping on toes."

Grace's brows shot up. "I beg your pardon?"

"You are an abysmal lawn bowler," he went on, "and even worse at billiards. You cheat at cards, and you do it better than I do."

She was beginning to smile now, and it warmed him to his core.

"The hair at your right temple does not match your left, but one has to brush your hair back to notice," he confessed. "And I may be the only person on earth to know that. You laugh far too much, and look far too attractive when you do, which renders the observer inconveniently breathless. You are too witty for convention, too intelligent for discretion, and too beautiful for all decency."

Her eyes began to shine with a light he'd missed the last two weeks, and one he'd spent every day of those two weeks yearning for.

"But I can't tell your father or Georgie or Miranda any of this," he confessed, spreading his hands out, "because I don't see these as faults. Not a single one. Each and every one of these things made me fall even more in love with you."

"Aubrey," Grace whispered shakily.

He shook his head, giving up his teasing pretense entirely now. "And if the Spinsters truly are what kept you from getting married, then I will thank God every day for Georgie Sterling." He stepped forward, nearly to her now, hiding nothing at all from his gaze. "Without her, someone else would have married you, and I would never have known how perfect my life could have been."

She bit down on her trembling lower lip, those dark eyes welling with unshed tears that undid him.

"The greatest flaw in you, Grace Morledge, is that, for better or worse, my heart lies in your possession. It is a lifetime with me that I am offering. And that is a damn shame."

"No, it isn't," she whispered, smiling at him fully. "And it's not a flaw."

"I'm the fault finder. I would know."

She shook her head, closing the distance between them and reaching for his face. "No. You're an idiot, Aubrey Flint. And I love you, too."

He kissed her then, deeply and tenderly, cradling her in his arms and drawing her body to his. She was soft and pliable, insistent in her attentions, and fervent in her response. Perfection in a kiss the first time his lips had touched hers, and perfection as they did so now.

And he had no doubt perfection each and every time.

"I love you," she murmured against his lips, the feel of them somehow better than the sound of them.

He groaned and kissed her once more, heady and exhilarated as her lips danced with his again and again. He would never get enough, could never get enough, and the realization humbled him to the depths of his soul.

Grace pulled back, looking dazed and pleased, which might have been his new favorite combination for her. She sighed and ran her hand along his jaw. "You didn't have to buy up Withrow to persuade me. I was already in love with you."

Aubrey chuckled. "Oh, I didn't. That was almost purely selfish. I love the place almost as much as you do, and if my buying it will keep your father out of England for the foreseeable future, I would beggar myself to do so."

She eyed him with concern, worry lines forming at her eyes. "You didn't, did you? How can you afford to…?"

He cupped her face, silencing her with both thumbs gently pressing at her lips. "Grace… I don't know what we'll make of Withrow and Breyerly. I don't know if we'll tear both down and build a ruddy palace of our dreams and combine the lands into one, or if we'll restore Withrow so you'll have somewhere to go when you tire of me."

"Never!" she whispered against his thumbs.

He smiled and shifted his hands, stroking her cheeks. "I don't care what we do with them, we can parse that all out later. All I care about is that we are the ones deciding it. We. You and me, together. I'd sell both our houses and twenty other people's houses just to have that."

"I do know how you feel about people in general."

He grinned swiftly, then turned serious once more, searching her eyes. "But do you know how I feel about you in particular?"

She dipped her chin in a faint nod. "I'm beginning to."

Aubrey fell silent, gazing at the face between his hands, his heart soaring into breathlessness as it sank in that this beloved, blessed, near-perfect goddess loved him. Wanted him.

Hell, that she even *liked* him was a miracle.

One for which he was eternally grateful.

"I love you," he said again, his voice raw as he emphasized every word. "Will you marry me?"

Grace beamed with the glories of heaven and nodded in his hold. "Yes. Yes, please."

He laughed once, then swallowed a lump in his throat. "Well," he managed around it, "you did say please."

"Poor manners would be a fault," she pointed out. "I couldn't have that."

"I should say not. What would we tell your father?"

"I have a couple of things we could tell him."

Aubrey's eyes darkened, and her favorite furrow appeared between his brows. "I would rage at him for you, you know. Defend you with blinding vitriolic and turn the man out on his pompous hide for his defamation of you. Say the word, love, and it will be done."

Affection welled within her, and she shook her head, laying a hand along his cheek. "It won't do any good, Aubrey. I thought to confront him, stand up against the injustice and injury, but it wouldn't have helped matters. My father is who he is, and I could have lost my family over such an action. I would not put it past him to cut me off if I did one more thing to earn his disapproval."

"I'd marry you anyway," Aubrey vowed. "I don't care."

"And I love you for that. But I am decided on it; we won't sharpen any barbs for him. We cannot."

"Perhaps you're right," he said with a sigh. "Best to leave those to Miranda. She's the only safe one."

Grace smiled and leaned in for a kiss, then pulled back suddenly. "How did you know I would receive you, anyway? Did Miranda think it was safe?"

"Undoubtedly," he replied. "But in this case, I had a most insistent letter from Charlotte. Seems she was of the opinion long ago that we simply had to be together."

She made a soft tsking noise. "We couldn't possibly disappoint her *and* Georgie *and* Miranda."

"My thoughts exactly. Best marry me and make them happy."

Grace nodded, brushing her nose against his. "Sounds like perfection."

Aubrey kissed her nose, then her smiling lips. "Well, I do love perfection."

"You would."

"And I do."

Epilogue

———— ‹✸ ❀ ✸› ————

The trouble with secrets is that, one way or another, they always seem to come to light. One must guard one's secrets and take care not to ignore them. A secret ignored may grow until there is no hope of minimizing its effects when made known to the world. And a secret told may do more harm than good.

-The Spinster Chronicles, 12 July 1819

"A boy, eh? Tony must be pleased."

"Undoubtedly, though I think a daughter would have pleased him just as well."

"And they named him after his father?"

"Tony's father, yes. Thomas."

"Does anyone in this room believe that Izzy will *not* be named godmother?"

The room snickered, and Izzy rolled her eyes as she folded the letter once more. "You don't know that."

"Yes, we do," Charlotte insisted dryly. "You are Georgie's favorite cousin, and the only logical choice."

Izzy raised a brow as she handed a teacup and saucer to Kitty. "What about Janet? Or Miranda? Or any of you?"

Elinor snorted softly as she perused the book in her lap. "Why would they want to choose any of us? Can you imagine Charlotte being a godmother? Edith would suit, as would Prue, but the rest of us…"

"The rest of you," Edith replied as she worked at needlepoint in her lap, "amounts to yourself, Kitty, and Grace."

Elinor threw her a look. "Kitty isn't well enough known by Tony or Georgie to be considered, and you know it. And Grace is not here yet."

"Nor should she be," Prue murmured with a smile. "With the welcome they had last night? I'd still be abed recovering."

"Particularly if your husband were with you," Charlotte drawled, examining her nails.

Prue turned scarlet, averting her eyes. "Well, there is that, yes."

"Prudence Vale!" Izzy squealed, clapping her hands in delight.

"Come, come, Mrs. Morton," Charlotte said, turning to her. "Your tardiness has increased these last few months, as well."

"Someone speak of something else," Kitty pleaded, covering her ears. "She's married to my brother…"

Elinor made a face, shaking her head. "I cannot imagine what that must be like. My brother will never manage a wife, I am sure of it. But siblings are a trial no matter their situation."

Charlotte made a dubious noise. "Child, your brother is awkward, of course you don't think he'll get a wife." She looked at the rest with exasperation. "So snappish, isn't she?"

"When your older sister has twin girls and doesn't name you godmother," Elinor retorted, "you are entitled to be snappish!"

Edith looked heavenward with a sigh. They'd been hearing about the indignity for weeks now, and they were all tired of the subject. Elinor had been doing so well of late, and then this setback had brought out her more surly, spoiled sensibilities. Their reprieve was at an end, it seemed.

"I am sure you'll get over it by Christmas," Izzy said, attempting to soothe Elinor.

It didn't work. "Not likely. Christmas with my family at the estate in the Lake District? We're far away from anyone and everyone every year, and I grow so tired of every single…"

"Ignore her," Prue whispered, leaning closer to Edith. "She always dreads her family Christmas, but she would be distraught to miss a single moment."

Edith nodded, returning her focus to the needlepoint. "Families can be a complicated business."

"Particularly when one marries," Prue agreed with a nod. "My mother wants us to come to her, but neither of us are so inclined, as I'm sure you can imagine. We want to have Chadwick and Lydia come to us, and I believe it would be better for me." She shrugged and sighed. "Did you have dilemmas such as these with your husband?"

Edith shook her head very firmly, her jaw setting. "No. I was not married long enough to deal with such things."

But there had been plenty of other problems. Plenty of dilemmas still in her life.

Some, she feared would never leave.

"Surely, Tony's brother will be godfather, yes?" Kitty asked, bringing them all back to the topic of the newest Sterling addition. "He's a physician?"

"In Dorset," Elinor confirmed, sitting up and suddenly scheming. "I've heard he's fearfully handsome, Kitty Morton, and of a more reserved nature than his brother."

Kitty sat back, instantly wary. "Why is she saying it like that?"

"Because she wants to marry you off, dear girl, and she's not bothering to hide it."

Edith looked up to see Grace in the doorway of the parlor, stunning as usual, in a yellow sprigged muslin gown that seemed designed for her. She looked so happy and at peace that Edith couldn't help but smile at her. "The Spinsters do seem to be falling victim one by one, don't they?"

Grace curtseyed playfully. "Consider me delightfully victimized. I've sent Georgie a gift with my gratitude, and I suspect she's already plotting for another one of you."

"I'm not a Spinster officially," Kitty offered with a raise of her hand. "Do not plot for me."

"Too late," Elinor chimed in, rubbing her hands together. "It's been an age since I have been excited about matrimonial prospects, do not diminish my enthusiasm."

"Oh lord," Grace said, shaking her head as she swept into the room. She sank down next to Kitty and took her hand, patting it gently. "I will look after you, dear. You still have plenty of time." She gave Elinor a severe look, smiling with the same sort of mischief her husband usually did. "As do you, Elinor."

Elinor blanched at once. "How is Aubrey? I barely got a word in with him last evening, but he looks well."

Grace beamed, and Edith had to blink at the brilliance, as did some of the others. "He is," she murmured, her voice softening. "He's wonderful."

"Ugh," Charlotte groaned as she slumped in her chair. "Do not go on, I beg you. I cannot bear another lovesick, swooning, practically pining friend. I swear, the lot of you cannot be away from those men for more than two hours without missing them."

"Aren't you the one determined to have a sweeping romance?" Grace shot back. "One that brings you, and he, to your knees, both of you burning, yearning, and perishing for love of the other?"

Incredibly, Charlotte seemed to blush, which had only happened perhaps once in all the time that Edith had known the lass.

"Originally, yes," Charlotte answered with some reluctance. "But after seeing the trouble you lot have been through to achieve it, I begin to wonder if the whole mess is even worth the effort."

"It is," Prue, Grace, and Izzy said at the same time, laughing when they heard the others do so.

Kitty saw that Edith did not reply, but the girl said nothing about it.

She was a perfect companion in such situations. Wise enough to remain silent, shy enough to hesitate, and sweet enough not to pry, all of which were incredibly valuable traits.

There would be too much to discover, if anyone did pry. Too much to see, too much to explain.

None of it could be disclosed, not until she had found a resolution.

She hadn't had luck so far, but most of her letters had not been answered as yet.

Her cheeks colored as talk of love, marriage, and husbands continued. She could only weave her needle in and out of the pattern, no longer cognizant of what she was attempting to stitch. The repeated pattern would give her occupation, and distraction, which was all she needed.

She had nothing to add to this conversation. Nothing worthy of repeating. The line had always been that she was married for five minutes, that her husband had not been worth mourning, that her experience as a married woman had been quick and therefore lacking, all of which were true. She teased herself about it, laughed about it, allowed others to laugh about it.

But there were horrors that had come with her short marriage and her inexperience. There were trials that lay behind her and before her, and around her, making every step more treacherous.

It was harder to laugh now, and harder to even speak of.

If a resolution could not be found through means she had already attempted, she would have to resort to another, more terrifying, option.

Society would never accept her return to their ranks, but it might be the only path left to save her.

Coming Soon

God Rest Ye Merry Spinster

The Spinster Chronicles

Book Five

"Have a holly, jolly Spinster."

by

REBECCA CONNOLLY

CPSIA information can be obtained
at www.ICGtesting.com
Printed in the USA
BVHW041027241019
561882BV00007BA/188/P